I0785691

B. M. Bower

Her Prairie Knight, Lonesome Land & The Uphill Climb: Complete Western Trilogy

OK Publishing 2021

*B. M. Bower*

# Her Prairie Knight, Lonesome Land & The Uphill Climb: Complete Western Trilogy

Published by

## MUSAICUM

Books

- Advanced Digital Solutions & High-Quality book Formatting -

musaicumbooks@okpublishing.info

2021 OK Publishing

ISBN 978-80-272-7566-3

# Contents

# Her Prairie Knight

# Chapter 1. Stranded on the Prairie

"By George, look behind us! I fancy we are going to have a storm." Four heads turned as if governed by one brain; four pairs of eyes, of varied color and character, swept the wind-blown wilderness of tender green, and gazed questioningly at the high-piled thunderheads above. A small boy, with an abundance of yellow curls and white collar, almost precipitated himself into the prim lap of a lady on the rear seat.

"Auntie, will God have fireworks? Say, auntie, will He? Can I say prayers widout kneelin' down'? Uncle Redmon' crowds so. I want to pray for fireworks, auntie. Can I?"

"Do sit down, Dorman. You'll fall under the wheel, and then auntie would not have any dear little boy. Dorman, do you hear me? Redmond, do take that child down! How I wish Parks were here. I shall have nervous prostration within a fortnight."

Sir Redmond Hayes plucked at the white collar, and the small boy retired between two masculine forms of no mean proportions. His voice, however, rose higher.

"You'll get all the fireworks you want, young man, without all that hullabaloo," remarked the driver, whom Dorman had been told, at the depot twenty miles back, he must call his Uncle Richard.

"I love storms," came cheerfully from the rear seat-but the voice was not the prim voice of "auntie." "Do you have thunder and lightning out here, Dick?"

"We do," assented Dick. "We don't ship it from the East in refrigerator cars, either. It grows wild."

The cheerful voice was heard to giggle.

"Richard," came in tired, reproachful accents from a third voice behind him, "you were reared in the East. I trust you have not formed the pernicious habit of speaking slightingly of your birthplace."

That, Dick knew, was his mother. She had not changed appreciably since she had nagged him through his teens. Not having seen her since, he was certainly in a position to judge.

"Trix asked about the lightning," he said placatingly, just as he was accustomed to do, during the nagging period. "I was telling her."

"Beatrice has a naturally inquiring mind," said the tired voice, laying reproving stress upon the name.

"Are you afraid of lightning, Sir Redmond?" asked the cheerful girl-voice.

Sir Redmond twisted his neck to smile back at her. "No, so long as it doesn't actually chuck me over."

After that there was silence, so far as human voices went, for a time.

"How much farther is it, Dick?" came presently from the girl.

"Not more than ten-well, maybe twelve-miles. You'll think it's twenty, though, if the rain strikes 'Dobe Flat before we do. That's just what it's going to do, or I'm badly mistaken. Hawk! Get along, there!"

"We haven't an umbrella with us," complained the tired one. "Beatrice, where did you put my raglan?"

"In the big wagon, mama, along with the trunks and guns and saddles, and Martha and Katherine and James."

"Dear me! I certainly told you, Peatrice —"

"But, mama, you gave it to me the last thing, after the maids were in the wagon, and said you wouldn't wear it. There isn't room here for another thing. I feel like a slice of pressed chicken."

"Auntie, I want some p'essed chicken. I'm hungry, auntie! I want some chicken and a cookie-and I want some ice-cream."

"You won't get any," said the young woman, with the tone of finality. "You can't eat me, Dorman, and I'm the only thing that looks good enough to eat."

"Beatrice!" This, of course, from her mother, whose life seemed principally made up of a succession of mental shocks, brought on by her youngest, dearest, and most irrepressible.

"I have Dick's word for it, mama; he said so, at the depot."

"I want some chicken, auntie."

"There is no chicken, dear," said the prim one. "You must be a patient little man."

"I won't. I'm hungry. Mens aren't patient when dey're hungry." A small, red face rose, like a tiny harvest moon, between the broad, masculine backs on the front seat.

"Dorman, sit down! Redmond!"

A large, gloved hand appeared against the small moon and it set ignominiously and prematurely, in the place where it had risen. Sir Redmond further extinguished it with the lap robe, for the storm, whooping malicious joy, was upon them.

First a blinding glare and a deafening crash. Then rain-sheets of it, that drenched where it struck. The women huddled together under the doubtful protection of the light robe and shivered. After that, wind that threatened to overturn the light spring wagon; then hail that bounced and hopped like tiny, white rubber balls upon the ground.

The storm passed as suddenly as it came, but the effect remained. The road was sodden with the water which had fallen, and as they went down the hill to 'Dobe Flat the horses strained at the collar and plodded like a plow team. The wheels collected masses of adobe, which stuck like glue and packed the spaces between the spokes. Twice Dick got out and poked the heavy mess from the wheels with Sir Redmond's stick-which was not good for the stick, but which eased the drag upon the horses wonderfully-until the wheels accumulated another load.

"Sorry to dirty your cane," Dick apologized, after the second halt. "You can rinse it off, though, in the creek a few miles ahead."

"Don't mention it!" said Sir Redmond, somewhat dubiously. It was his favorite stick, and he had taken excellent care of it. It was finely polished, and it had his name and regiment engraved upon the silver knob-and a date which the Boers will not soon forget, nor the English, for that matter.

"We'll soon be over the worst," Dick told them, after a time. "When we climb that hill we'll have a hard, gravelly trail straight to the ranch. I'm sorry it had to storm; I wanted you to enjoy this trip."

"I am enjoying it," Beatrice assured him. "It's something new, at any rate, and anything is better than the deadly monotony of Newport."

"Beatrice!" cried her mother "I'm ashamed of you!"

"You needn't be, mama. Why won't you just be sorry for yourself, and let it end there? I know you hated to come, poor dear; but you wouldn't think of letting me come alone, though I'm sure I shouldn't have minded. This is going to be a delicious summer —I feel it in my bones."

"Be-atrice!"

"Why, mama? Aren't young ladies supposed to have bones?"

"Young ladies are not supposed to make use of unrefined expressions. Your poor sister."

"There, mama. Dear Dolly didn't live upon stilts, I'm sure. Even when she married."

"Be-atrice!"

"Dear me, mama! I hope you are not growing peevish. Peevish elderly people —"

"Auntie! I want to go home!" the small boy wailed.

"You cannot go home now, dear," sighed his guardian angel. "Look at the pretty —" She hesitated, groping vaguely for some object to which she might conscientiously apply the adjective.

"Mud," suggested Beatrice promptly "Look at the wheels, Dorman; they're playing patty-cake. See, now they say, 'Roll 'em, and roll 'em,' and now, 'Toss in the oven to bake!' And now —"

"Auntie, I want to get out an' play patty-cake, like de wheels. I want to awf'lly!"

"Beatrice, why did you put that into his head?" her mother demanded, fretfully.

"Never mind, honey," called Beatrice cheeringly. "You and I will make hundreds of mud pies when we get to Uncle Dick's ranch. Just think, hon, oodles of beautiful, yellow mud just beside the door!"

"Look here, Trix! Seems to me you're promising a whole lot you can't make good. I don't live in a 'dobe patch."

"Hush, Dick; don't spoil everything. You don't know Dorman.'

"Beatrice! What must Miss Hayes and Sir Redmond think of you? I'm sure Dorman is a sweet child, the image of poor, dear Dorothea, at his age."

"We all think Dorman bears a strong resemblance to his father," said his Aunt Mary.

Beatrice, scenting trouble, hurried to change the subject. "What's this, Dick-the Missouri River?"

"Hardly. This is the water that didn't fall in the buggy. It isn't deep; it makes bad going worse, that's all."

Thinking to expedite matters, he struck Hawk sharply across the flank. It was a foolish thing to do, and Dick knew it when he did it; ten seconds later he knew it better.

Hawk reared, tired as he was, and lunged viciously.

The double-trees snapped and splintered; there was a brief interval of plunging, a shower of muddy water in that vicinity, and then two draggled, disgusted brown horses splashed indignantly to shore and took to the hills with straps flying.

"By George!" ejaculated Sir Redmond, gazing helplessly after them. "But this is a beastly bit of luck, don't you know!"

"Oh, you Hawk—" Dick, in consideration of his companions, finished the remark in the recesses of his troubled soul, where the ladies could not overhear.

"What comes next, Dick?" The voice of Beatrice was frankly curious.

"Next, I'll have to wade out and take after those—" This sentence, also, was rounded out mentally.

"In the meantime, what shall we do?"

"You'll stay where you are-and thank the good Lord you were not upset. I'm sorry,"—turning so that he could look deprecatingly at Miss Hayes—"your welcome to the West has been so-er-strenuous. I'll try and make it up to you, once you get to the ranch. I hope you won't let this give you a dislike of the country."

"Oh, no," said the spinster politely. "I'm sure it is a—a very nice country, Mr. Lansell."

"Well, there's nothing to be done sitting here." Dick climbed down over the dashboard into the mud and water.

Sir Redmond was not the man to shirk duty because it happened to be disagreeable, as the regiment whose name was engraved upon his cane could testify. He glanced regretfully at his immaculate leggings and followed.

"I fancy you ladies won't need any bodyguard," he said. Looking back, he caught the light of approval shining in the eyes of Beatrice, and after that he did not mind the mud, but waded to shore and joined in the chase quite contentedly. The light of approval, shining in the eyes of Beatrice, meant much to Sir Redmond.

## Chapter 2. A Handsome Cowboy to the Rescue

Beatrice took immediate possession of the front seat, that she might comfort her heartbroken young nephew.

"Never mind, honey. They'll bring the horses back in a minute, and we'll make them run every step. And when you get to Uncle Dick's ranch you'll see the nicest things-bossy calves, and chickens, and, maybe, some little pigs with curly tails."

All this, though alluring, failed of its purpose; the small boy continued to weep, and his weeping was ear-splitting.

"Be still, Dorman, or you'll certainly scare all the coyotes to death."

"Where are dey?"

"Oh, all around. You keep watch, hon, and maybe you'll see one put the tip of his nose over a hill."

"What hill?" Dorman skipped a sob, and scoured his eyes industriously with both fists.

"M-m —that hill. That little one over there. Watch close, or you'll miss him."

The dove of peace hovered over them, and seemed actually about to alight. Beatrice leaned back with a relieved breath.

"It is good of you, my dear, to take so much trouble," sighed his Aunt Mary. "How I am to manage without Parks I'm sure I cannot tell."

"You are tired, and you miss your tea." soothed Beatrice, optimistic as to tone. "When we all have a good rest we will be all right. Dorman will find plenty to amuse him. We are none of us exactly comfortable now."

"Comfortable!" sniffed her mother. "I am half dead. Richard wrote such glowing letters home that I was misled. If I had dreamed of the true conditions, Miss Hayes, I should never have sanctioned this wild idea of Beatrice's to come out and spend the summer with Richard."

"It's coming, Be'trice! There it is! Will it bite, auntie? Say, will it bite?"

Beatrice looked. A horseman came over the hill and was galloping down the long slope toward them. His elbows were lifted contrary to the mandates of the riding-school, his long legs were encased in something brown and fringed down the sides. His gray hat was tilted rakishly up at the back and down in front, and a handkerchief was knotted loosely around his throat. Even at that distance he struck her as different from any one she had ever seen.

"It's a highwayman!" whispered Mrs. Lansell "Hide your purse, my dear!"

"I —I —where?" Miss Hayes was all a-flutter with fear.

"Drop it down beside the wheel, into the water. Quick! I shall drop my watch."

"He-he is coming on this side! He can see!" Her whisper was full of entreaty and despair.

"Give them here. He can't see on both sides of the buggy at once." Mrs. Lansell, being an American —a Yankee at that-was a woman of resource.

"Beatrice, hand me your watch quick!"

Beatrice paid no attention, and there was no time to insist upon obedience. The horseman had slowed at the water's edge, and was regarding them with some curiosity. Possibly he was not accustomed to such a sight as the one that met his eyes. He came splashing toward them, however, as though he intended to investigate the cause of their presence, alone upon the prairie, in a vehicle which had no horses attached in the place obviously intended for such attachment. When he was close upon them he stopped and lifted the rakishly tilted gray hat.

"You seem to be in trouble. Is there anything I can do for you?" His manner was grave and respectful, but his eyes, Beatrice observed, were having a quiet laugh of their own.

"You can't get auntie's watch, nor gran'mama's. Gran'mama frowed 'em all down in the mud. She frowed her money down in the mud, too," announced Dorman, with much complacency. "Be'trice says you is a coyote. Is you?"

There was a stunned interval, during which nothing was heard but the wind whispering things to the grass. The man's eyes stopped laughing; his jaw set squarely; also, his brows drew perceptibly closer together. It was Mrs. Lansell's opinion that he looked murderous.

Then Beatrice put her head down upon the little, blue velvet cap of Dorman and laughed. There was a rollicking note in her laughter that was irresistible, and the eyes of the man relented and joined in her mirth. His lips forgot they were angry and insulted, and uncovered some very nice teeth.

"We aren't really crazy," Beatrice told him, sitting up straight and drying her eyes daintily with her handkerchief. "We were on our way to Mr. Lansell's ranch, and the horses broke something and ran away, and Dick-Mr. Lansell-has gone to catch them. We're waiting until he does."

"I see." From the look in his eyes one might guess that what he saw pleased him. "Which direction did they take?"

Beatrice waved a gloved hand vaguely to the left, and, without another word, the fellow touched his hat, turned and waded to shore and galloped over the ridge she indicated; and the clucketycluck of his horse's hoofs came sharply across to them until he dipped out of sight.

"You see, he wasn't a robber," Beatrice remarked, staring after him speculatively. "How well he rides! One can see at a glance that he almost lives in the saddle. I wonder who he is."

"For all you know, Beatrice, he may be going now to murder Richard and Sir Redmond in cold blood. He looks perfectly hardened."

"Oh, do you think it possible?" cried Miss Hayes, much alarmed.

"No!" cried Beatrice hotly. "One who did not know your horror of novels, mama, might suspect you of feeding your imagination upon 'penny dreadfuls.' I'm sure he is only a cowboy, and won't harm anybody."

"Cowboys are as bad as highwaymen," contended her mother, "or worse. I have read how they shoot men for a pastime, and without even the excuse of robbery."

"Is it possible?" quavered Miss Hayes faintly.

"No, it isn't!" Beatrice assured her indignantly.

"He has the look of a criminal," declared Mrs. Lansell, in the positive tone of one who speaks from intimate knowledge of the subject under discussion. "I only hope he isn't going to murder —"

"They're coming back, mama," interrupted Beatrice, who had been watching closely the hill-top. "No, it's that man, and he is driving the horses."

"He's chasing them," corrected her mother testily. "A horse thief, no doubt. He's going to catch them with his snare —"

"Lasso, mama."

"Well, lasso. Where can Richard be? To think the fellow should be so bold! But out here, with miles upon miles of open, and no police protection anything is possible. We might all be murdered, and no one be the wiser for days-perhaps weeks. There, he has caught them." She leaned back and clasped her hands, ready to meet with fortitude whatever fate might have in store.

"He's bringing them out to us, mama. Can't you see the man is only trying to help us?"

Mrs. Lansell, beginning herself to suspect him of honest intentions, sniffed dissentingly and let it go at that. The fellow was certainly leading the horses toward them, and Sir Redmond and Dick, appearing over the hill just then, proved beyond doubt that neither had been murdered in cold blood, or in any other unpleasant manner.

"We're all right now, mother," Dick called, the minute he was near enough.

His mother remarked skeptically that she hoped possibly she had been in too great haste to conceal her valuables-that Miss Hayes might not feel grateful for her presence of mind, and was probably wondering if mud baths were not injurious to fine, jeweled time-pieces. Mrs. Lansell was uncomfortable, mentally and physically, and her manner was frankly chilly when her son presented the stranger as his good friend and neighbor, Keith Cameron. She was still privately convinced that he looked a criminal-though, if pressed, she must surely have admitted that he was an uncommonly good-looking young outlaw. It would seem almost as if she regarded his being a decent, law-abiding citizen as pure effrontery.

Miss Hayes greeted him with a smile of apprehension which plainly amused him. Beatrice was frankly impersonal in her attitude; he represented a new species of the genus man, and she, too, evidently regarded him in the light of a strange animal, viewed unexpectedly at close range.

While he was helping Dick mend the double-tree with a piece of rope, she studied him curiously. He was tall-taller even than Sir Redmond, and more slender. Sir Redmond had the straight, sturdy look of the soldier who had borne the brunt of hard marches and desperate fighting; Mr. Cameron, the lithe, unconscious grace and alertness of the man whose work demands quick movement and quicker eye and brain. His face was tanned to a clear bronze which showed the blood darkly beneath; Sir Redmond's year of peace had gone far toward lightening his complexion. Beatrice glanced briefly at him and admired his healthy color, and was glad he did not have the look of an Indian. At the same time, she caught herself wishing that Sir Redmond's eyes were hazel, fringed with very long, dark lashes and topped with very straight, dark brows-eyes which seemed always to have some secret cause for mirth, and to laugh quite independent of the rest of the face. Still, Sir Redmond had very nice eyes-blue, and kind, and steadfast, and altogether dependable-and his lashes were quite nice enough for any one. In just four seconds Beatrice decided that, after all, she did not like hazel eyes that twinkle continually; they make one feel that one is being laughed at, which is not comfortable. In six seconds she was quite sure that this Mr. Cameron thought himself handsome, and Beatrice detested a man who was proud of his face or his figure; such a man always tempted her to "make faces," as she used to do over the back fence when she was little.

She mentally accused him of trying to show off his skill with his rope when he leaned and fastened it to the rig, rode out ahead and helped drag the vehicle to shore; and it was with some resentment that she observed the ease with which he did it, and how horse and rope seemed to know instinctively their master's will, and to obey of their own accord.

In all that he had done-and it really seemed as if he did everything that needed to be done, while Dick pottered around in the way-he had not found it necessary to descend into the mud and water, to the ruin of his picturesque, fringed chaps and high-heeled boots. He had worked at ease, carelessly leaning from his leathern throne upon the big, roan horse he addressed occasionally as Redcloud. Beatrice wondered where he got the outlandish name. But, with all his imperfections, she was glad she had met him. He really was handsome, whether he knew it or not; and if he had a good opinion of himself, and overrated his actions-all the more fun for herself! Beatrice, I regret to say, was not above amusing herself with handsome young men who overrate their own charms; in fact, she had the reputation among her women acquaintances of being a most outrageous flirt.

In the very middle of these trouble-breeding meditations, Mr. Cameron looked up unexpectedly and met keenly her eyes; and for some reason-let us hope because of a guilty conscience-Beatrice grew hot and confused; an unusual experience, surely, for a girl who had been out three seasons, and has met calmly the eyes of many young men. Until now it had been the young men who grew hot and confused; it had never been herself.

Beatrice turned her shoulder toward him, and looked at Sir Redmond, who was surreptitiously fishing for certain articles beside the rear wheel, at the whispered behest of Mrs. Lansell, and was certainly a sight to behold. He was mud to his knees and to his elbows, and he had managed to plaster his hat against the wheel and to dirty his face. Altogether, he looked an abnormally large child who has been having a beautiful day of it in somebody's duck-pond; but Beatrice was nearer, at that moment, to loving him than she had been at any time during her six weeks' acquaintance with him-and that is saying much, for she had liked him from the start.

Mr. Cameron followed her glance, and his eyes did not have the laugh all to themselves; his voice joined them, and Beatrice turned upon him and frowned. It was not kind of him to laugh at a man who is proving his heart to be much larger than his vanity; Beatrice was aware of Sir Redmond's immaculateness of attire on most occasions.

"Well," said Dick, gathering up the reins, "you've helped us out of a bad scrape, Keith. Come over and take dinner with us to-morrow night. I expect we'll be kept riding the rim-rocks, over at the Pool, this summer. Unless this sister of mine has changed a lot, she won't rest till she's been over every foot of country for forty miles around. It will just about keep our strings rode down to a whisper keeping her in sight."

"Dear me, Richard!" said his mother. "What Jargon is this you speak?"

"That's good old Montana English, mother. You'll learn it yourself before you leave here. I've clean forgot how they used the English language at Yale, haven't you, Keith?"

"Just about," Keith agreed. "I'm afraid we'll shock the ladies terribly, Dick. We ought to get out on a pinnacle with a good grammar and practice."

"Well, maybe. We'll look for you to-morrow, sure. I want you to help map out a circle or two for Trix. About next week she'll want to get out and scour the range."

"Dear me, Richard! Beatrice is not a charwoman!" This, you will understand, was from his mother; perhaps you will also understand that she spoke with the rising inflection which conveys a reproof.

When Keith Cameron left them he was laughing quietly to himself, and Beatrice's chin was set rather more than usual.

# Chapter 3. A Tilt With Sir Redmond

Beatrice, standing on the top of a steep, grassy slope, was engaged in the conventional pastime of enjoying the view. It was a fine view, but it was not half as good to look upon as was Beatrice herself, in her fresh white waist and brown skirt, with her brown hair fluffing softly in the breeze which would grow to a respectable wind later in the day, and with her cheeks pink from climbing.

She was up where she could see the river, a broad band of blue in the surrounding green, winding away for miles through the hills. The far bank stood a straight two hundred feet of gay-colored rock, chiseled, by time and stress of changeful weather, into fanciful turrets and towers. Above and beyond, where the green began, hundreds of moving dots told where the cattle were feeding quietly. Far away to the south, heaps of hazy blue and purple slept in the sunshine; Dick had told her those were the Highwoods. And away to the west, a jagged line of blue-white glimmered and stood upon tip-toes to touch the swimming clouds-touched them and pushed above proudly; those were the Rockies. The Bear Paws stood behind her; nearer they were-so near they lost the glamour of mysterious blue shadows, and became merely a sprawling group of huge, pine-covered hills, with ranches dotted here and there in sheltered places, with squares of fresh, dark green that spoke of growing crops.

Ten days, and the metropolitan East had faded and become as hazy and vague as the Highwoods. Ten days, and the witchery of the West leaped in her blood and held her fast in its thralldom.

A sound of scrambling behind her was immediately followed by a smothered epithet. Beatrice turned in time to see Sir Redmond pick himself up.

"These grass slopes are confounded slippery, don't you know," he explained apologetically. "How did you manage that climb?"

"I didn't." Beatrice smiled. "I came around the end, where the ascent is gradual; there's a good path."

"Oh!" Sir Redmond sat down upon a rock and puffed. "I saw you up here-and a fellow doesn't think about taking a roundabout course to reach his heart's —"

"Isn't it lovely?" Beatrice made haste to inquire.

"Lovely isn't half expressive enough," he told her. "You look —"

"The river is so very blue and dignified. I've been wondering if it has forgotten how it must have danced through those hills, away off there. When it gets down to the cities-this blue water-it will be muddy and nasty looking. The 'muddy Missouri' certainly doesn't apply here. And that farther shore is simply magnificent. I wish I might stay here forever."

"The Lord forbid!" cried he, with considerable fervor. "There's a dear nook in old England where I hope —"

"You did get that mud off your leggings, I see," Beatrice remarked inconsequentially. "James must have worked half the time we've been here. They certainly were in a mess the last time I saw them."

"Bother the leggings! But I take it that's a good sign, Miss Lansell-your taking notice of such things."

Beatrice returned to the landscape. "I wonder who originated that phrase, 'The cattle grazing on a thousand hills'? He must have stood just here when he said it."

"Wasn't it one of your American poets? Longfellow, or-er —"

Beatrice simply looked at him a minute and said "Pshaw!"

"Well," he retorted, "you don't know yourself who it was."

"And to think," Beatrice went on, ignoring the subject, "some of those grazing cows and bossy calves are mine-my very own. I never cared before, or thought much about it, till I came out and saw where they live, and Dick pointed to a cow and the sweetest little red and white calf, and said: 'That's your cow and calf, Trix.' They were dreadfully afraid of me, though —I'm afraid they didn't recognize me as their mistress. I wanted to get down and pet the calf-it had the dearest little snub nose but they bolted, and wouldn't let me near them."

"I fancy they were not accustomed to meeting angels unawares."

"Sir Redmond, I wish you wouldn't. You are so much nicer when you're not trying to be nice."

"I'll act a perfect brute," he offered eagerly, "if that will make you love me."

"It's hardly worth trying. I think you would make a very poor sort of villain, Sir Redmond. You wouldn't even be picturesque."

Sir Redmond looked rather floored. He was a good fighter, was Sir Redmond, but he was clumsy at repartee-or, perhaps, he was too much in earnest to fence gracefully. Just now he looked particularly foolish.

"Don't you think my brand is pretty? You know what it is, don't you?"

"I'm afraid not," he owned. "I fancy I need a good bit of coaching in the matter of brands."

"Yes," agreed Beatrice, "I fancy you do. My brand is a Triangle Bar-like this." With a sharp pointed bit of rock she drew a more or less exact diagram in the yellow soil. "There are ever so many different brands belonging to the Northern Pool; Dick pointed them out to me, but I can't remember them. But whenever you see a Triangle Bar you'll be looking at my individual property. I think it was nice of Dick to give me a brand all my own. Mr. Cameron has a pretty brand, too —a Maltese Cross. The Maltese Cross was owned at one time by President Roosevelt. Mr. Cameron bought it when he left college and went into the cattle business. He 'plays a lone hand,' as he calls it; but his cattle range with the Northern Pool, and he and Dick work together a great deal. I think he has lovely eyes, don't you?" The eyes of Beatrice were intent upon the Bear Paws when she said it-which brought her shoulder toward Sir Redmond and hid her face from him.

"I can't say I ever observed Mr. Cameron's eyes," said Sir Redmond stiffly.

Beatrice turned back to him, and smiled demurely. When Beatrice smiled that very demure smile, of which she was capable, the weather-wise generally edged toward their cyclone-cellars. Sir Redmond was not weather-wise —he was too much in love with her-and he did not possess a cyclone cellar; he therefore suffered much at the hands of Beatrice.

"But surely you must have noticed that deep, deep dimple in his chin?" she questioned innocently. Keith Cameron, I may say, did not have a dimple in his chin at all; there was, however, a deep crease in it.

"I did not." Sir Redmond rubbed his own chin, which was so far from dimpling that is was rounded like half an apricot.

"Dear me! And you sat opposite to him at dinner yesterday, too! I suppose, then, you did not observe that his teeth are the whitest, evenest."

"They make them cheaply over here, I'm told," he retorted, setting his heel emphatically down and annihilating a red and black caterpillar.

"Now, why did you do that? I must say you English are rather brutal?"

"I can't abide worms."

"Well, neither can I. And I think it would be foolish to quarrel about a man's good looks," Beatrice said, with surprising sweetness.

Sir Redmond hunched his shoulders and retreated to the comfort of his pipe. "A bally lot of good looks!" he sneered. "A woman is never convinced, though."

"I am." Beatrice sat down upon a rock and rested her elbows on her knees and her chin in her hands-and an adorable picture she made, I assure you. "I'm thoroughly convinced of several things. One is Mr. Cameron's good looks; another is that you're cross."

"Oh, come, now!" protested Sir Redmond feebly, and sucked furiously at his pipe.

"Yes," reiterated Beatrice, examining his perturbed face judicially; "you are downright ugly."

The face of Sir Redmond grew redder and more perturbed; just as Beatrice meant that it should; she seemed to derive a keen pleasure from goading this big, good-looking Englishman to the verge of apoplexy.

"I'm sure I never meant to be rude; but a fellow can't fall down and worship every young farmer, don't you know-not even to please you!"

Beatrice smiled and threw a pebble down the slope, watching it bound and skip to the bottom, where it rolled away and hid in the grass.

"I love this wide country," she observed, abandoning her torture with a suddenness that was a characteristic of her nature. When Beatrice had made a man look and act the fool she was ready to stop; one cannot say that of every woman. "One can draw long, deep breaths without robbing one's neighbor of oxygen. Everything is so big, and broad, and generous, out here. One can ride for miles and miles through the grandest, wildest places,—and-there aren't any cigar and baking-powder and liver-pill signs plastered over the rocks, thank goodness! If man has traveled that way before, you do not have the evidence of his passing staring you in the face. You can make believe it is all your own-by right of discovery. I'm afraid your England would seem rather little and crowded after a month or two of this." She swept her hand toward the river, and the grass-land beyond, and the mountains rimming the world.

"You should see the moors!" cried Sir Redmond, brightening under this peaceful mood of hers. "I fancy you would not find trouble in drawing long breaths there. Moor Cottage, where your sister and Wiltmar lived, is surrounded by wide stretches of open-not like this, to be sure, but not half-bad in its way, either."

"Dolly grew to love that place, though she did write homesick letters at first. I was going over, after my coming out-and then came that awful accident, when she and Wiltmar were both drowned-and, of course, there was nothing to go for. I should have hated the place then, I think. But I should like —" Her voice trailed off dreamily, her eyes on the hazy Highwoods.

Sir Redmond watched her, his eyes a-shine; Beatrice in this mood was something to worship. He was almost afraid to speak, for fear she would snuff out the tiny flame of hope which her half-finished sentence had kindled. He leaned forward, his face eager.

"Beatrice, only say you will go-with me, dear!"

Beatrice started; for the moment she had forgotten him. Her eyes kept to the hills. "Go-to England? One trip at a time, Sir Redmond. I have been here only ten days, and we came for three months. Three months of freedom in this big, glorious place."

"And then?" His voice was husky.

"And then-freckle lotions by the quart, I expect."

Sir Redmond got upon his feet, and he was rather white around the mouth.

"We Englishmen are a stubborn lot, Miss Beatrice. We won't stop fighting until we win."

"We Yankees," retorted she airily, "value our freedom above everything else. We won't surrender it without fighting for it first."

He caught eagerly at the lack of finality in her tones. "I don't want to take your freedom, Beatrice. I only want the right to love you."

"Oh, as for that, I suppose you may love me as much as you please-only so you don't torment me to death talking about it."

Beatrice, not looking particularly tormented, waved answer to Dick, who was shouting something up at her, and went blithely down the hill, with Sir Redmond following gloomily, several paces behind.

"D'you want to see the boys work a bunch of cattle, Trix?" Dick said to her, when she came down to where he was leaning against a high board fence, waiting for her.

"'Deed I do, Dicky-only I've no idea what you mean."

"The boys are going to cut out some cattle we've contracted to the government-for the Indians, you know. They're holding the bunch over in Dry Coulee; it's only three or four miles. I've got to go over and see the foreman, and I thought maybe you'd like to go along."

"There's nothing I can think of that I would like better. Won't it be fine, Sir Redmond?"

Sir Redmond did not say whether he thought it would be fine or not. He still had the white streak around his mouth, and he went through the gate and on to the house without a word-which was undoubtedly a rude thing to do. Sir Redmond was not often rude. Dick watched him speculatively until he was beyond hearing them. Then, "What have you done to milord, Trix?" he wanted to know.

"Nothing," said Beatrice.

"Well," Dick said, with decision, "he looks to me like a man that has been turned down-hard. I can tell by the back of his neck."

This struck Beatrice, and she began to study the retreating neck of her suitor. "I can't see any difference," she announced, after a brief scrutiny.

"It's rather sunburned and thick."

"I'll gamble his mind is a jumble of good English oaths-with maybe a sprinkling of Boer maledictions. What did you do?"

"Nothing-unless, perhaps, he objects to being disciplined a bit. But I also object to being badgered into matrimony-even with Sir Redmond."

"Even with Sir Redmond!" Dick whistled. "He's 'It,' then, is he?"

Beatrice had nothing to say. She walked beside Dick and looked at the ground before her.

"He doesn't seem a bad sort, sis, and the title will be nice to have in the family, if one cares for such things. Mother does. She was disappointed, I take it, that Wiltmar was a younger son."

"Yes, she was. She used to think that Sir Redmond might get killed down there fighting the Boers, and then Wiltmar would be next in line. But he didn't, and it was Wiltmar who went first. And now oh, it's humiliating, Dick! To be thrown at a man's head —" Tears were not far from her voice just then.

"I can see she wants you to nab the title. Well, sis, if you don't care for the man —"

"I never said I didn't care for him. But I just can't treat him decently, with mama dinning that title in my ears day and night. I wish there wasn't any title. Oh, it's abominable! Things have come to that point where an American girl with money is not supposed to care for an Englishman, no matter how nice he may be, if he has a title, or the prospect of one. Every one laughs and thinks it's the title she wants; they'd think it of me, and they'd say it. They would say Beatrice Lansell took her half-million and bought her a lord. And, after a while, perhaps Sir Redmond himself would half-believe it-and I couldn't bear that! And so I am-unbearably flippant and —I should think he'd hate me!"

"So you reversed the natural order of things, and refused him on account of the title?" Dick grinned surreptitiously.

"No, I didn't —not quite. I'm afraid he's dreadfully angry with me, though. I do wish he wasn't such a dear."

"You're the same old Trix. You've got to be held back from the trail you're supposed to take, or you won't travel it; you'll bolt the other way. If everybody got together and fought the notion, you would probably elope with milord inside a week. Mother means well, but she isn't on to her job a little bit. She ought to turn up her nose at the title."

"No fear of that! I've had it before my eyes till I hate the very thought of it. I —I wish I could hate him." Beatrice sighed deeply, and gave her hand to Dorman, who scurried up to her.

"I'll have the horses saddled right away," said Dick, and left them.

"Where you going, Be'trice? You going to ride a horse? I want to, awf'lly."

"I'm afraid you can't, honey; it's too far." Beatrice pushed a yellow curl away from his eyes with tender, womanly solicitude.

"Auntie won't care, 'cause I'm a bother. Auntie says she's goin' to send for Parks. I don't want Parks; 'sides, Parks is sick. I want a pony, and some ledder towsers wis fringes down 'em, and I want some little wheels on my feet. Mr. Cam'ron says I do need some little wheels, Be'trice."

"Did he, honey?"

"Yes, he did. I like Mr. Cam'ron, Be'trice; he let me ride his big, high pony. He's a berry good pony. He shaked hands wis me, Be'trice-he truly did."

"Did he, hon?" Beatrice, I am sorry to say, was not listening. She was wondering if Sir Redmond was really angry with her-too angry, for instance, to go over where the cattle were. He really ought to go, for he had come West in the interest of the Eastern stockholders in the Northern Pool, to investigate the actual details of the work. He surely would not miss this opportunity, Beatrice thought. And she hoped he was not angry.

"Yes, he truly did. Mr. Cam'ron interduced us, Be'trice. He said, 'Redcloud, dis is Master Dorman Hayes. Shake hands wis my frien' Dorman.' And he put up his front hand, Be'trice, and nod his head, and I shaked his hand. I dess love that big, high pony, Be'trice. Can I buy him, Be'trice?"

"Maybe, kiddie."

"Can I buy him wis my six shiny pennies, Be'trice?"

"Maybe."

"Mr. Cam'ron lives right over that hill, Be'trice. He told me."

"Did he, hon?"

"Yes, he did. He 'vited me over, Be'trice. He's my friend, and I've got to buy my big, high pony. I'll let you shake hands wis him, Be'trice. I'll interduce him to you. And I'll let you ride on his back, Be'trice. Do you want to ride on his back?"

"Yes, honey."

Before Beatrice had time to commit herself they reached the house, and she let go Dorman's hand and hurried away to get into her riding-habit.

Dorman straightway went to find his six precious, shiny pennies, which Beatrice had painstakingly scoured with silver polish one day to please the little tyrant, and which increased their value many times-so many times, in fact, that he hid them every night in fear of burglars. Since he concealed them each time in a different place, he was obliged to ransack his auntie's room every morning, to the great disturbance of Martha, the maid, who was an order-loving person.

Martha appeared just when he had triumphantly pounced upon his treasure rolled up in the strings of his aunt's chiffon opera-bonnet.

"Mercy upon us, Master Dorman! Whatever have you been doing?"

"I want my shiny pennies," said the young gentleman, composedly unwinding the roll, "to buy my big, high pony."

"Naughty, naughty boy, to muss my lady's fine bonnet like that! Look at things scattered over the floor, and my lady's fine handkerchiefs and gloves —" Martha stopped and meditated whether she might dare to shake him.

Dorman was laboriously counting his wealth, with much wrinkling of stubby nose and lifting of eyebrows. Having satisfied himself that they were really all there, he deigned to look around, with a fine masculine disdain of woman's finery.

"Oh, dose old things!" he sniffed. "I always fordet where I put my shiny pennies. Robbers might find them if I put them easy places. I'm going to buy my big, high pony, and you can't shake his hand a bit, Martha."

"Well, I'm sure I don't want to!" Martha snapped back at him, and went down on all fours to gather up the things he had thrown down. "Whatever Parks was thinking of, to go and get fever, when she was the only one that could manage you, I don't know! And me picking up after you till I'm fair sick!"

"I'm glad you is sick," he retorted unfeelingly, and backed to the door. "I hopes you get sicker so your stummit makes you hurt. You can't ride on my big, high pony."

"Get along with you and your high pony!" cried the exasperated Martha, threatening with a hairbrush. Dorman, his six shiny pennies held fast in his damp little fist, fled down the stairs and out into the sunlight.

Dick and Beatrice were just ready to ride away from the porch. "I want to go wis you, Uncle Dick." Dorman had followed the lead of Beatrice, his divinity; he refused to say Richard, though grandmama did object to nicknames.

"Up you go, son. You'll be a cow-puncher yourself one of these days. I'll not let him fall, and this horse is gentle." This last to satisfy Dorman's aunt, who wavered between anxiety and relief.

"You may ride to the gate, Dorman, and then you'll have to hop down and run back to your auntie and grandma. We're going too far for you to-day." Dick gave him the reins to hold, and let the horse walk to prolong the joy of it.

Dorman held to the horn with one hand, to the reins with the other, and let his small body swing forward and back with the motion of the horse, in exaggerated imitation of his friend, Mr. Cameron. At the gate he allowed himself to be set down without protest, smiled importantly through the bars, and thrust his arm through as far as it would reach, that he might wave good-by. And his divinity smiled back at him, and threw him a kiss, which pleased him mightily.

"You must have hurt milord's feelings pretty bad," Dick remarked. "I couldn't get him to come. He had to write a letter first, he said."

"I wish, Dick," Beatrice answered, a bit petulantly, "you would stop calling him milord."

"Milord's a good name," Dick contended. "It's bad enough to 'Sir' him to his face; I can't do it behind his back, Trix. We're not used to fancy titles out here, and they don't fit the country, anyhow. I'm like you—I'd think a lot more of him if he was just a plain, everyday American, so I could get acquainted enough to call him 'Red Hayes.' I'd like him a whole lot better."

Beatrice was in no mood for an argument-on that subject, at least. She let Rex out and raced over the prairie at a gait which would have greatly shocked her mother, who could not understand why Beatrice was not content to drive sedately about in the carriage with the rest of them.

When they reached the round-up Keith Cameron left the bunch and rode out to meet them, and Dick promptly shuffled responsibility for his sister's entertainment to the square shoulders of his neighbor.

"Trix wants to wise up on the cattle business, Keith. I'll just turn her over to you for a-while, and let you answer her questions; I can't, half the time. I want to look through the bunch a little."

Keith's face spoke gratitude, and spoke it plainly. The face of Beatrice was frankly inattentive. She was watching the restless, moving mass of red backs and glistening horns, with horsemen weaving in and out among them in what looked to her a perfectly aimless fashion-until one would wheel and dart out into the open, always with a fleeing animal lumbering before. Other horsemen would meet him and take up the chase, and he would turn and ride leisurely back into the haze and confusion. It was like a kaleidoscope, for the scene shifted constantly and was never quite the same.

Keith, secure in her absorption, slid sidewise in the saddle and studied her face, knowing all the while that he was simply storing up trouble for himself. But it is not given a man to flee human nature, and the fellow who could sit calmly beside Beatrice and not stare at her if the opportunity offered must certainly have the blood of a fish in his veins. I will tell you why.

Beatrice was tall, and she was slim, and round, and tempting, with the most tantalizing curves ever built to torment a man. Her hair was soft and brown, and it waved up from the nape of her neck without those short, straggling locks and thin growth at the edge which mar so many feminine heads; and the sharp contrast of shimmery brown against ivory white was simply irresistible. Had her face been less full of charm, Keith might have been content to gaze and gaze at that lovely hair line. As it was, his eyes wandered to her brows, also distinctly marked, as though outlined first with a pencil in the fingers of an artist who understood. And there were her lashes, dark and long, and curled up at the ends; and her cheek, with its changing, come-and-go coloring; her mouth, with its upper lip creased deeply in the middle-so deeply that a bit more would have been a defect-and with an odd little dimple at one corner; luckily, it was on the side toward him, so that he might look at it all he wanted to for once; for it was always there, only growing deeper and wickeder when she spoke or laughed. He could not see her eyes, for they were turned away, but he knew quite well the color; he had settled that point when he looked up from coiling his rope the day she came. They were big, baffling, blue-brown eyes, the like of which he had never seen before in his life-and he had thought he had seen every color and every shade under the sun. Thinking of them and their wonderful deeps and shadows, he got hungry for a sight of them. And suddenly she turned to ask a question, and found him staring at her, and surprised a look in his eyes he did not know was there.

For ten pulse-beats they stared, and the cheeks of Beatrice grew red as healthy young blood could paint them; Keith's were the same, only that his blood showed darkly through the tan. What question had been on her tongue she forgot to ask. Indeed, for the time, I think she forgot the whole English language, and every other-but the strange, wordless language of Keith's clear eyes.

And then it was gone, and Keith was looking away, and chewing a corner of his lip till it hurt. His horse backed restlessly from the tight-gripped rein, and Keith was guilty of kicking him with his spur, which did not better matters. Redcloud snorted and shook his outraged head, and Keith came to himself and eased the rein, and spoke remorseful, soothing words that somehow clung long in the memory of Beatrice.

Just after that Dick galloped up, his elbows flapping like the wings of a frightened hen.

"Well, I suppose you could run a cow outfit all by yourself, with the knowledge you've got from Keith," he greeted, and two people became even more embarrassed than before. If Dick noticed anything, he must have been a wise young man, for he gave no sign.

But Beatrice had not queened it in her set, three seasons, for nothing, even if she was capable of being confused by a sweet, new language in a man's eyes. She answered Dick quietly.

"I've been so busy watching it all that I haven't had time to ask many questions, as Mr. Cameron can testify. It's like a game, and it's very fascinating-and dusty. I wonder if I might ride in among them, Dick?"

"Better not, sis. It isn't as much fun as it looks, and you can see more out here. There comes milord; he must have changed his mind about the letter."

Beatrice did not look around. To see her, you would swear she had set herself the task of making an accurate count of noses in that seething mass of raw beef below her. After a minute she ventured to glance furtively at Keith, and, finding his eyes turned her way, blushed again and called herself an idiot. After that, she straightened in the saddle, and became the self-poised Miss Lansell, of New York.

Keith rode away to the far side of the herd, out of temptation; queer a man never runs from a woman until it is too late to be a particle of use. Keith simply changed his point of view, and watched his Heart's Desire from afar.

# Chapter 5. The Search for Dorman

"Oh, I say," began Sir Redmond, an hour after, when he happened to stand close to Beatrice for a few minutes, "where is Dorman? I fancied you brought him along."

"We didn't," Beatrice told him. "He only rode as far as the gate, where Dick left him, and started him back to the house."

"Mary told me he came along. She and your mother were congratulating each other upon a quiet half-day, with you and Dorman off the place together. I'll wager their felicitations fell rather flat."

Beatrice laughed. "Very likely. I know they were mourning because their lace-making had been neglected lately. What with that trip to Lost Canyon to-morrow, and to the mountains Friday, I'm afraid the lace will continue to suffer. What do you think of a round-up, Sir Redmond?"

"It's deuced nasty," said he. "Such a lot of dust and noise. I fancy the workmen don't find it pleasant."

"Yes, they do; they like it," she declared. "Dick says a cowboy is never satisfied off the range. And you mustn't call them workmen, Sir Redmond. They'd resent it, if they knew. They're cowboys, and proud of it. They seem rather a pleasant lot of fellows, on the whole. I have been talking to one or two."

"Well, we're all through here," Dick announced, riding up. "I'm going to ride around by Keith's place, to see a horse I'm thinking of buying. Want to go along, Trix? Or are you tired?"

"I'm never tired," averred his sister, readjusting a hat-pin and gathering up her reins. "I always want to go everywhere that you'll take me, Dick. Consider that point settled for the summer. Are you coming, Sir Redmond?"

"I think not, thank you," he said, not quite risen above his rebuff of the morning. "I told Mary I would be back for lunch."

"I was wiser; I refused even to venture an opinion as to when I should be back. Well, 'so-long'!"

"You're learning the lingo pretty fast, Trix," Dick chuckled, when they were well away from Sir Redmond. "Milord almost fell out of the saddle when you fired that at him. Where did you pick it up?"

"I've heard you say it a dozen times since I came. And I don't care if he is shocked —I wanted him to be. He needn't be such a perfect bear; and I know mama and Miss Hayes don't expect him to lunch, without us. He just did it to be spiteful."

"Jerusalem, Trix! A little while ago you said he was a dear! You shouldn't snub him, if you want him to be nice to you."

"I don't want him to be nice," flared Beatrice. "I don't care how he acts. Only, I must say, ill humor doesn't become him. Not that it matters, however."

"Well, I guess we can get along without him, if he won't honor us with his company. Here comes Keith. Brace up, sis, and be pleasant."

Beatrice glanced casually at the galloping figure of Dick's neighbor, and frowned.

"You mustn't flirt with Keith," Dick admonished gravely. "He's a good fellow, and as square a man as I know; but you ought to know he's got the reputation of being a hard man to know. Lots of girls have tried to flirt and make a fool of him, and wound up with their feelings hurt worse than his were."

"Is that a dare?" Beatrice threw up her chin with a motion Dick knew of old.

"Not on your life! You better leave him alone; one or the other of you would get the worst of it, and I'd hate to see either of you feeling bad. As I said before, he's a bad man to fool with."

"I don't consider him particularly dangerous-or interesting. He's not half as nice as Sir Redmond." Beatrice spoke as though she meant what she said, and Dick had no chance to argue the point, for Keith pulled up beside them at that moment.

Beatrice seemed inclined to silence, and paid more attention to the landscape than she did to the conversation, which was mostly about range conditions, and the scanty water supply, and the drought.

She was politely interested in Keith's ranch, and if she clung persistently to her society manner, why, her society manner was very pleasing, if somewhat unsatisfying to a fellow fairly drunk with her winsomeness. Keith showed her where she might look straight up the coulee to her brother's ranch, two miles away, and when she wished she might see what they were doing up there, he went in and got his field-glass. She thanked him prettily, and impersonally, and focused the glass upon Dick's house-which gave Keith another chance to look at her without being caught in the act.

"How plain everything is! I can see mama, out on the porch, and Miss Hayes." She could also see Sir Redmond, who had just ridden up, and was talking to the ladies, but she did not think it necessary to mention him, for some reason; she kept her eyes to the glass, however, and appeared much absorbed. Dick rolled himself a cigarette and watched the two, and there was a twinkle in his eyes.

"I wonder-Dick, I do think —I'm afraid —" Beatrice hadn't her society manner now; she was her unaffected, girlish self; and she was growing excited.

"What's the matter?" Dick got up, and came and stood at her elbow.

"They're acting queerly. The maids are running about, and the cook is out, waving a large spoon, and mama has her arm around Miss Hayes, and Sir Redmond."

"Let's see." Dick took the glass and raised it to his eyes for a minute. "That's right," he said. "They're making medicine over something. See what you make of it, Keith."

Keith took the glass and looked through it. It was like a moving picture; one could see, but one wanted the interpretation of sound.

"We'd better ride over," he said quietly. "Don't worry, Miss Lansell; it probably isn't anything serious. We can take the short cut up the coulee, and find out." He put the glass into its leathern case and started to the gate, where the horses were standing. He did not tell Beatrice that Miss Hayes had just been carried into the house in a faint, or that her mother was behaving in an undignified fashion strongly suggesting hysterics. But Dick knew, from the look on his face, that it was serious. He hurried before them with long strides, leaving Beatrice, for the second time that morning, to the care of his neighbor.

So it was Keith who held his hand down for the delicious pressure of her foot, and arranged her habit with painstaking care, considering the hurry they were in. Dick was in the saddle, and gone, before Keith had finished, and Keith was not a slow young man, as a rule. They ran the two miles without a break, except twice, where there were gates to close. Dick, speeding a furlong before, had obligingly left them open; and a stockman is hard pressed indeed-or very drunk-when he fails to close his gates behind him. It is an unwritten law which becomes second nature.

Almost within sound of the place, Dick raced back and met them, and his face was white.

"It's Dorman!" he cried. "He's lost. They haven't seen him since we left. You know, Trix, he was standing at the gate."

Beatrice went white as Dick; whiter, for she was untanned. An overwhelming sense of blame squeezed her heart tight. Keith, seeing her shoulders droop limply, reined close, to catch her in his arms if there was the slightest excuse. However, Beatrice was a healthy young woman, with splendid command of her nerves, and she had no intention of fainting. The sickening weakness passed in a moment.

"It's my fault," she said, speaking rapidly, her eyes seeking Dick's for comfort. "I said 'yes' to everything he asked me, because I was thinking of something else, and not paying attention. He was going to buy your horse, Mr. Cameron, and now he's lost!"

This, though effective, was not particularly illuminating. Dick wanted details, and he got them-for Beatrice, having remorse to stir the dregs of memory, repeated nearly everything

Dorman had said, even telling how the big, high pony put up his front hand, and he shaked it, and how Dorman truly needed some little wheels on his feet.

"Poor little devil," Keith muttered, with wet eyes.

"He-he said you lived over there," Beatrice finished, pointing, as Dorman had pointed-which was not toward the "Cross" ranch at all, but straight toward the river.

Keith wheeled Redcloud; there was no need to hear more. He took the hill at a pace which would have killed any horse but one bred to race over this rough country. Near the top, the forced breathing of another horse at his heels made him look behind. It was Beatrice follow-ing, her eyes like black stars. I do not know if Keith was astonished, but I do know that he was pleased.

"Where's Dick?" was all he said then.

"Dick's going to meet the men-the cowboys. Sir Redmond went after them, when they found Dorman wasn't anywhere about the place."

Keith nodded understandingly, and slowed to let her come alongside.

"It's no use riding in bunches," he remarked, after a little. "On circle we always go in pairs. We'll find him, all right."

"We must," said Beatrice, simply, and shaded her eyes with her hand. For they had reached the top, and the prairie land lay all about them and below, lazily asleep in the sunshine.

Keith halted and reached for his glass. "It's lucky I brought it along," he said. "I wasn't thinking, at the time; I just slung it over my shoulder from habit."

"It's a good habit, I think," she answered, trying to smile; but her lips would only quiver, for the thought of her blame tortured her. "Can you see-anything?" she ventured wistfully.

Keith shook his head, and continued his search. "There are so many little washouts and coulees, down there, you know. That's the trouble with a glass-it looks only on a level. But we'll find him. Don't you worry about that. He couldn't go far."

"There isn't any real danger, is there?"

"Oh, no," Keith said. "Except —" He bit his lip angrily.

"Except what?" she demanded. "I'm not silly, Mr. Cameron-tell me."

Keith took the glass from his eyes, looked at her, and paid her the compliment of deciding to tell her, just as if she were a man.

"Nothing, only-he might run across a snake," he said. "Rattlers."

Beatrice drew her breath hard, but she was plucky. Keith thought he had never seen a pluck-ier girl, and the West can rightfully boast brave women.

She touched Rex with the whip. "Come," she commanded. "We must not stand here. It has been more than three hours."

Keith put away the glass, and shot ahead to guide her.

"We must have missed him, somewhere." The eyes of Beatrice were heavy with the weariness born of anxiety and suspense. They stood at the very edge of the steep bluff which rimmed the river. "You don't think he could have —" Her eyes, shuddering down at the mocking, blue-gray ripples, finished the thought.

"He couldn't have got this far," said Keith. "His legs would give out, climbing up and down. We'll go back by a little different way, and look."

"There's something moving, off there." Beatrice pointed with her whip.

"That's a coyote," Keith told her; and then, seeing the look on her face: "They won't hurt any one. They're the rankest cowards on the range."

"But the snakes —"

"Oh, well, he might wander around for a week, and not run across one. We won't borrow trouble, anyway."

"No," she agreed languidly. The sun was hot, and she had not had anything to eat since early breakfast, and the river mocked her parched throat with its cool glimmer below. She looked down at it wistfully, and Keith, watchful of every passing change in her face, led her back to where a cold, little spring crept from beneath a rock; there, lifting her down, he taught her how to drink from her hand.

For himself, he threw himself down, pushed back his hat, and drank long and leisurely. A brown lock of hair, clinging softly together with moisture, fell from his forehead and trailed in the clear water, and Beatrice felt oddly tempted to push it back where it belonged. Standing quietly watching his picturesque figure, she forgot, for the moment, that a little boy was lost among these peaceful, sunbathed hills; she remembered only the man at her feet, drinking long, satisfying drafts, while the lock of hair floated in the spring.

"Now we'll go on." He stood up and pushed back the wet lock, which trickled a tiny stream down his cheek, and settled his gray hat in place.

Again that day he felt her foot in his palm, and the touch went over him in thrills. She was tired, he knew; her foot pressed heavier than it had before. He would have liked to take her in his arms and lift her bodily into the saddle, but he hardly dared think of such a blissful proceeding.

He set the pace slower, however, and avoided the steepest places, and he halted often on the higher ground, to scan sharply the coulees. And so they searched, these two, together, and grew to know each other better than in a month of casual meetings. And the grass nodded, and the winds laughed, and the stern hills looked on, quizzically silent. If they knew aught of a small boy with a wealth of yellow curls and white collar, they gave no sign, and the two rode on, always seeking hopefully.

A snake buzzed sharply on a gravelly slope, and Keith, sending Beatrice back a safe distance, took down his rope and gave battle, beating the sinister, gray-spotted coil with the loop until it straightened and was still. He dismounted then, and pinched off the rattles-nine, there were, and a "button" —and gave them to Beatrice, who handled them gingerly, and begged Keith to carry them for her. He slipped them into his pocket, and they went on, saying little.

Back near the ranch they met Dick and Sir Redmond. They exchanged sharp looks, and Dick shook his head.

"We haven't found him-yet. The boys are riding circle around the ranch; they're bound to find him, some of them, if we don't."

"You had better go home," Sir Redmond told her, with a note of authority in his voice which set Keith's teeth on edge. "You look done to death; this is men's work."

Beatrice bit her lip, and barely glanced at him. "I'll go-when Dorman is found. What shall we do now, Dick?"

"Go down to the house and get some hot coffee, you two. We all snatched a bite to eat, and you need it. After that, you can look along the south side of the coulee, if you like."

Beatrice obediently turned Rex toward home, and Keith followed. The ranch seemed very still and lonesome. Some chickens were rolling in the dust by the gate, and scattered, cackling indignantly, when they rode up. Off to the left a colt whinnied wistfully in a corral. Beatrice, riding listlessly to the house, stopped her horse with a jerk.

"I heard-where is he?"

Keith stopped Redcloud, and listened. Came a thumping noise, and a wail, not loud, but unmistakable.

"Aunt-ie!"

Beatrice was on the ground as soon as Keith, and together they ran to the place-the bunkhouse. The thumping continued vigorously; evidently a small boy was kicking, with all his might, upon a closed door; it was not a new sound to the ears of Beatrice, since the arrival in America of her young nephew. Keith flung the door wide open, upsetting the small boy, who howled.

Beatrice swooped down upon him and gathered him so close she came near choking him. "You darling. Oh, Dorman!"

Dorman squirmed away from her. "I los' one shiny penny, Be'trice-and I couldn't open de door. Help me find my shiny penny."

Keith picked him up and set him upon one square shoulder. "We'll take you up to your auntie, first thing, young man."

"I want my one shiny penny. I want it!" Dorman showed symptoms of howling again.

"We'll come back and find it. Your auntie wants you now, and grandmama."

Beatrice, following after, was treated to a rather unusual spectacle; that of a tall, sun-browned fellow, with fringed chaps and brightly gleaming spurs, racing down the path; upon his shoulder, the wriggling form of an extremely disreputable small boy, with cobwebs in his curls, and his once white collar a dirty rag streaming out behind.

# Chapter 6. Mrs. Lansell's Lecture

When the excitement had somewhat abated, and Miss Hayes was convinced that her idol was really there, safe, and with his usual healthy appetite, and when a messenger had been started out to recall the searchers, Dorman was placed upon a chair before a select and attentive audience, and invited to explain, which he did.

He had decided to borrow some little wheels from the bunkhouse, so he could ride his big, high pony home. Mr. Cameron had little wheels on his feet, and so did Uncle Dick, and all the mens. (The audience gravely nodded assent.) Well, and the knob wasn't too high when he went in, but when he tried to open the door to go out, it was away up there! (Dorman measured with his arm.) And he fell down, and all his shiny pennies rolled and rolled. And he looked and looked where they rolled, and when he counted, one was gone. So he looked and looked for the one shiny penny till he was tired to death. And so he climbed up high, into a funny bed on a shelf, and rested. And when he was rested he couldn't open the door, and he kicked and kicked, and then Be'trice came, and Mr. Cam'ron.

"And you said you'd help me find my one penny," he reminded Keith, blinking solemnly at him from the chair. "And I want to shake hands wis your big, high pony. I'm going to buy him wis my six pennies. Be'trice said I could."

Beatrice blushed, and Keith forgot where he was, for a minute, looking at her.

"Come and find my one shiny penny," Dorman commanded, climbing down. "And I want Be'trice to come. Be'trice can always find things."

"Beatrice cannot go," said his grandmother, who didn't much like the way Keith hovered near Beatrice, nor the look in his eyes. "Beatrice is tired."

"I want Be'trice!" Dorman set up his everyday howl, which started the dogs barking outside. His guardian angel attempted to soothe him, but he would have none of her; he only howled the louder, and kicked.

"There, there, honey, I'll go. Where's your hat?"

"Beatrice, you had better stay in the house; you have done quite enough for one day." The tone of the mother suggested things.

"It is imperative," said Beatrice, "for the peace and the well-being of this household, that Dorman find his penny without delay." When Beatrice adopted that lofty tone her mother was in the habit of saying nothing-and biding her time. Beatrice was so apt, if mere loftiness did not carry the day, to go a step further and flatly refuse to obey. Mrs. Lansell preferred to yield, rather than be openly defied.

So the three went off to find the shiny penny-and in exactly thirty-five minutes they found it. I will not say that they could not have found it sooner, but, at any rate, they didn't, and they reached the house about two minutes behind Dick and Sir Redmond, which did not improve Sir Redmond's temper to speak of.

After that, Keith did not need much urging from Dick to spend the rest of the afternoon at the "Pool" ranch. When he wanted to, Keith could be very nice indeed to people; he went a long way, that afternoon, toward making a friend of Miss Hayes; but Mrs. Lansell, who was one of those women who adhere to the theory of First Impressions, in capitals, continued to regard him as an incipient outlaw, who would, in time and under favorable conditions, reveal his true character, and vindicate her keen insight into human nature. There was one thing which Mrs. Lansell never forgave Keith Cameron, and that was the ruin of her watch, which refused to run while she was in Montana.

That night, when Beatrice was just snuggling down into the delicious coolness of her pillow, she heard someone rap softly, but none the less imperatively, on her door. She opened one eye stealthily, to see her mother's pudgy form outlined in the feeble moonlight.

"Beatrice, are you asleep?"

Beatrice did not say yes, but she let her breath out carefully in a slumbrous sigh. It certainly sounded as if she were asleep.

"Be-atrice!" The tone, though guarded, was insistent.

The head of Beatrice moved slightly, and settled back into its little nest, for all the world like a dreaming, innocent baby.

If she had not been the mother of Beatrice, Mrs. Lansell would probably have gone back to her room, and continued to bide her time; but the mother of Beatrice had learned a few things about the ways of a wilful girl. She went in, and closed the door carefully behind her. She did not wish to keep the whole house awake. Then she went straight to the bed, laid hand upon a white shoulder that gleamed in the moonlight, and gave a shake.

"Beatrice, I want you to answer me when I speak."

"M-m —did you —m-m —speak, mama?" Beatrice opened her eyes and closed them, opened them again for a minute longer, yawned daintily, and by these signs and tokens wandered back from dreamland obediently.

Her mother sat down upon the edge of the bed, and the bed creaked. Also, Beatrice groaned inwardly; the time of reckoning was verily drawing near. She promptly closed her eyes again, and gave a sleepy sigh.

"Beatrice, did you refuse Sir Redmond again?"

"M-m —were you speaking-mama?"

Mrs. Lansell, endeavoring to keep her temper, repeated the question.

Beatrice began to feel that she was an abused girl. She lifted herself to her elbow, and thumped the pillow spitefully.

"Again? Dear me, mama! I've never refused him once!"

"You haven't accepted him once, either," her mother retorted; and Beatrice lay down again.

"I do wish, Beatrice, you would look at the matter in a sensible light I'm sure I never would ask you to marry a man you could not care for. But Sir Redmond is young, and good-looking, and has birth and breeding, and money-no one can accuse him of being a fortune-hunter, I'm sure. I was asking Richard to-day, and he says Sir Redmond holds a large interest in the Northern Pool, and other English investors pay him a salary, besides, to look after their interests. I wouldn't be surprised if the holdings of both of you would be sufficient to control the business."

Beatrice, not caring anything for business anyway, said nothing.

"Any one can see the man's crazy for you. His sister says he never cared for a woman before in his life."

"Of course," put in Beatrice sarcastically. "His sister followed him down to South Africa, and all around, and is in a position to know."

"Any one can see he isn't a lady's man."

"No —" Beatrice smiled reminiscently; "he certainly isn't."

"And so he's in deadly earnest. And I'm positive he will make you a model husband."

"Only think of having to live, all one's life, with a model husband!" shuddered Beatrice hypocritically.

"Be-atrice! And then, it's something to marry a title."

"That's the worst of it," remarked Beatrice.

"Any other girl in America would jump at the chance. I do believe, Beatrice, you are hanging back just to be aggravating. And there's another thing, Beatrice. I don't approve of the way this Keith Cameron hangs around you."

"He doesn't!" denied Beatrice, in an altogether different tone. "Why, mama!"

"I don't approve of flirting, Beatrice, and you know it. The way you gadded around over the hills with him —a perfect stranger-was disgraceful; perfectly disgraceful. You don't know any thing about the fellow, whether he's a fit companion or not —a wild, uncouth cowboy —"

"He graduated from Yale, a year after Dick. And he was halfback, too."

"That doesn't signify," said her mother, "a particle. I know Miss Hayes was dreadfully shocked to see you come riding up with him, and Sir Redmond forced to go with Richard, or ride alone."

"Dick is good company," said Beatrice. "And it was his own fault. I asked him to go with us, when Dick and I left the cattle, and he wouldn't. Dick will tell you the same. And after that I did not see him until just before we —I came home, Really, mama, I can't have a leading-string on Sir Redmond. If he refuses to come with me, I can hardly insist."

"Well, you must have done something. You said something, or did something, to make him very angry. He has not been himself all day. What did you say?"

"Dear me, mama, I am not responsible for all Sir Redmond's ill-humor."

"I did not ask you that, Beatrice."

Beatrice thumped her pillow again. "I don't remember anything very dreadful, mama. I —I think he has indigestion."

"Be-atrice! I do wish you would try to conquer that habit of flippancy. It is not ladylike. And I warn you, Sir Redmond is not the man to dangle after you forever. He will lose patience, and go back to England without you-and serve you right! I am only talking for your own good, Beatrice. I am not at all sure that you want him to leave you alone."

Beatrice was not at all sure, either. She lay still, and wished her mother would stop talking for her good. Talking for her good had meant, as far back as Beatrice could remember, saying disagreeable things in a disagreeable manner.

"And remember, Beatrice, I want this flirting stopped."

"Flirting, mama?" To hear the girl, you would think she had never heard the word before.

"That's what I said, Beatrice. I shall speak to Richard in the morning about this fellow Cameron. He must put a stop to his being here two-thirds of the time. It is unendurable."

"He and Dick are chums, mama, and have been for years. And to-morrow we are going to Lost Canyon, you know, and Mr. Cameron is to go along. And there are several other trips, mama, to which he is already invited. Dick cannot recall those invitations."

"Well, it must end there. Richard must do something. I cannot see what he finds about the fellow to like-or you, either, Beatrice. Just because he rides like a —a wild Indian, and has a certain daredevil way —"

"I never said I liked him, mama," Beatrice protested, somewhat hastily. "I —of course, I try to treat him well —"

"I should say you did!" exploded her mother angrily. "You would be much better employed in trying to treat Sir Redmond half as well. It is positively disgraceful, the way you behave toward him-as fine a man as I ever met in my life. I warn you, Beatrice, you must have more regard for propriety, or I shall take you back to New York at once. I certainly shall."

With that threat, which she shrewdly guessed would go far toward bringing this wayward girl to time, Mrs. Lansell got up off the bed, which creaked its relief, and groped her way to her own room.

The pillow of Beatrice received considerable thumping during the next hour —a great deal more, in fact, than it needed. Two thoughts troubled her more than she liked. What if her mother was right, and Sir Redmond lost patience with her and went home? That possibility was unpleasant, to say the least. Again, would he give her up altogether if she showed Dick she was not afraid of Keith Cameron, for all his good looks, and at the same time taught that young man a much-needed lesson? The way he had stared at her was nothing less than a challenge and Beatrice was sorely tempted.

# Chapter 7. Beatrice's Wild Ride

"Well, are we all ready?" Dick gathered up his reins, and took critical inventory of the load. His mother peered under the front seat to be doubly sure that there were at least four umbrellas and her waterproof raglan in the rig; Mrs. Lansell did not propose to be caught unawares in a storm another time. Miss Hayes straightened Dorman's cap, and told him to sit down, dear, and then called upon Sir Redmond to enforce the command. Sir Redmond repeated her command, minus the dear, and then rode on ahead to overtake Beatrice and Keith, who had started. Dick climbed up over the front wheel, released the brake, chirped at the horses, and they were off for Lost Canyon.

Beatrice was behaving beautifully, and her mother only hoped to heaven it would last the day out; perhaps Sir Redmond would be able to extract some sort of a promise from her in that mood, Mrs. Lansell reflected, as she watched Beatrice chatting to her two cavaliers, with the most decorous impartiality. Sir Redmond seemed in high spirits, which argued well; Mrs. Lansell gave herself up to the pleasure of the drive with a heart free from anxiety. Not only was Beatrice at her best; Dorman's mood was nothing short of angelic, and as the weather was simply perfect, the day surely promised well.

For a mile Keith had showed signs of a mind not at ease, and at last he made bold to speak.

"I thought Rex was to be your saddle-horse?" he said abruptly to Beatrice.

"He was; but when Dick brought Goldie home, last night, I fell in love with him on sight, and just teased Dick till he told me I might have him to ride."

"I thought Dick had some sense," Keith said gloomily.

"He has. He knew there would be no peace till he surrendered."

"I didn't know you were going to ride him, when I sold him to Dick. He's not safe for a woman."

"Does he buck, Mr. Cameron? Dick said he was gentle." Beatrice had seen a horse buck, one day, and had a wholesome fear of that form of equine amusement.

"Oh, no. I never knew him to."

"Then I don't mind anything else. I'm accustomed to horses," said Beatrice, and smiled welcome to Sir Redmond, who came up with them at that moment.

"You want to ride him with a light rein," Keith cautioned, clinging to the subject. "He's tenderbitted, and nervous. He won't stand for any jerking, you see."

"I never jerk, Mr. Cameron." Keith discovered that big, baffling, blue-brown eyes can, if they wish, rival liquid air for coldness. "I rode horses before I came to Montana."

Of course, when a man gets frozen with a girl's eyes, and scorched with a girl's sarcasm, the thing for him to do is to retreat until the atmosphere becomes normal. Keith fell behind just as soon as he could do so with some show of dignity, and for several miles tried to convince himself that he would rather talk to Dick and "the old maid" than not.

"Don't you know," Sir Redmond remarked sympathetically, "some of these Western fellows are inclined to be deuced officious and impertinent."

Sir Redmond got a taste of the freezing process that made him change the subject abruptly.

The way was rough and lonely; the trail wound over sharp-nosed hills and through deep, narrow coulees, with occasional, tantalizing glimpses of the river and the open land beyond, that kept Beatrice in a fever of enthusiasm. From riding blithely ahead, she took to lagging far behind with her kodak, getting snap-shots of the choicest bits of scenery.

"Another cartridge, please, Sir Redmond," she said, and wound industriously on the finished roll.

"It's a jolly good thing I brought my pockets full." Sir Redmond fished one out for her. "Was that a dozen?"

"No; that had only six films. I want a larger one this time. It is a perfect nuisance to stop and change. Be still, Goldie!"

"We're getting rather a long way behind-but I fancy the road is plain."

"We'll hurry and overtake them. I won't take any more pictures."

"Until you chance upon something you can't resist. I understand all that, you know." Sir Redmond, while he teased, was pondering whether this was an auspicious time and place to ask Beatrice to marry him. He had tried so many times and places that seemed auspicious, that the man was growing fearful. It is not pleasant to have a girl smile indulgently upon you and deftly turn your avowals aside, so that they fall flat.

"I'm ready," she announced, blind to what his eyes were saying.

"Shall we trek?" Sir Redmond sighed a bit. He was not anxious to overtake the others.

"We will. Only, out here people never 'trek,' Sir Redmond. They 'hit the trail'."

"So they do. And the way these cowboys do it, one would think they were couriers, by Jove! with the lives of a whole army at stake. So I fancy we had better hit the trail, eh?"

"You're learning," Beatrice assured him, as they started on. "A year out here, and you would be a real American, Sir Redmond."

Sir Redmond came near saying, "The Lord forbid!" but he thought better of it. Beatrice was intensely loyal to her countrymen, unfortunately, and would certainly resent such a remark; but, for all that, he thought it.

For a mile or two she held to her resolve, and then, at the top of a long hill overlooking the canyon where they were to eat their lunch, out came her kodak again.

"This must be Lost Canyon, for Dick has stopped by those trees. I want to get just one view from here. Steady, Goldie! Dear me, this horse does detest standing still!"

"I fancy he is anxious to get down with the others. Let me hold him for you. Whoa, there!" He put a hand upon the bridle, a familiarity Goldie resented. He snorted and dodged backward, to the ruin of the picture Beatrice was endeavoring to get.

"Now you've frightened him. Whoa, pet! It's of no use to try; he won't stand."

"Let me have your camera. He's getting rather an ugly temper, I think." Sir Redmond put out his hand again, and again Goldie dodged backward.

"I can do better alone, Sir Redmond." The cheeks of Beatrice were red. She managed to hold the horse in until her kodak was put safely in its case, but her temper, as well as Goldie's, was roughened. She hated spoiling a film, which she was perfectly sure she had done.

Goldie felt the sting of her whip when she brought him back into the road, and, from merely fretting, he took to plunging angrily. Then, when Beatrice pulled him up sharply, he thrust out his nose, grabbed the bit in his teeth, and bolted down the hill, past all control.

"Good God, hold him!" shouted Sir Redmond, putting his horse to a run.

The advice was good, and Beatrice heard it plainly enough, but she neither answered nor looked back. How, she thought, resentfully, was one to hold a yellow streak of rage, with legs like wire springs and a neck of iron? Besides, she was angrily alive to the fact that Keith Cameron, watching down below, was having his revenge. She wondered if he was enjoying it.

He was not. Goldie, when he ran, ran blindly in a straight line, and Keith knew it. He also knew that the Englishman couldn't keep within gunshot of Goldie, with the mount he had, and half a mile away-Keith shut his teeth hard together, and went out to meet her. Redcloud lay along the ground in great leaps, but Keith, bending low over his neck, urged him faster and faster, until the horse, his ears laid close against his neck, did the best there was in him. From the tail of his eye, Keith saw Sir Redmond's horse go down upon his knees, and get up limping-and the sight filled him with ungenerous gladness; Sir Redmond was out of the race. It was Keith and Redcloud-they two; and Keith could smile over it.

He saw Beatrice's hat loosen and lift in front, flop uncertainly, and then go sailing away into the sage-brush, and he noted where it fell, that he might find it, later. Then he was close enough to see her face, and wondered that there was so little fear written there. Beatrice was plucky, and she rode well, her weight upon the bit; but her weight was nothing to the clinched teeth of the horse; and, though she had known it from the start, she was scarcely frightened. There was a good deal of the daredevil in Beatrice; she trusted a great deal to blind luck.

Just there the land was level, and she hoped to check him on the slope of the hill before them. She did not know it was moated like a castle, with a washout ten feet deep and twice that in width, and that what looked to her quite easy was utterly impossible.

Keith gained, every leap. In a moment he was close behind.

"Take your foot out of the stirrup," he commanded, harshly, and though Beatrice wondered why, something in his voice made her obey.

Now Redcloud's nose was even with her elbow; the breath from his wide-flaring nostrils rose hotly in her face. Another bound, and he had forged ahead, neck and neck with Goldie, and it was Keith by her side, keen-eyed and calm.

"Let go all hold," he said. Reaching suddenly, he caught her around the waist and pulled her from the saddle, just as Redcloud, scenting danger, plowed his front feet deeply into the loose soil and stopped dead still.

It was neatly done, and quickly; so quickly that before Beatrice had more than gasped her surprise, Keith lowered her to the ground and slid out of the saddle. Beatrice looked at him, and wondered at his face, and at the way he was shaking. He leaned weakly against the horse and hid his face on his arm, and trembled at what had come so close to the girl-the girl, who stood there panting a little, with her wonderful, waving hair cloaking her almost to her knees, and her blue-brown eyes wide and bright, and full of a deep amazement. She forgot Goldie, and did not even look to see what had become of him; she forgot nearly everything, just then, in wonder at this tall, clean-built young fellow, who never had seemed to care what happened, leaning there with his face hidden, his hat far hack on his head and little drops standing thickly upon his forehead. She waited a moment, and when he did not move, her thoughts drifted to other things.

"I wonder," she said abstractedly, "if I broke my kodak."

Keith lifted his head and looked at her. "Your kodak-good Lord!" He looked hard into her eyes, and she returned the stare.

"Come here," he commanded, hoarsely, catching her arm. "Your kodak! Look down there!" He led her to the brink, which was close enough to set him shuddering anew. "Look! There's Goldie, damn him! It's a wonder he's on his feet; I thought he'd be dead-and serve him right. And you-you wonder if you broke your kodak!"

Beatrice drew back from him, and from the sight below, and if she were frightened, she tried not to let him see. "Should I have fainted?" She was proud of the steadiness of her voice. "Really, I am very much obliged to you, Mr. Cameron, for saving me from an ugly fall. You did it very neatly, I imagine, and I am grateful. Still, I really hope I didn't break my kodak. Are you very disappointed because I can't faint away? There doesn't seem to be any brook close by, you see-and I haven't my er-lover's arms to fall into. Those are the regulation stage settings, I believe, and —"

"Don't worry, Miss Lansell. I didn't expect you to faint, or to show any human feelings whatever. I do pity your horse, though."

"You didn't a minute ago," she reminded him. "You indulged in a bit of profanity, if I remember."

"For which I beg Goldie's pardon," he retorted, his eyes unsmiling.

"And mine, I hope."

"Certainly."

"I think it's rather absurd to stand here sparring, Mr. Cameron. You'll begin to accuse me of ingratitude, and I'm as grateful as possible for what you did. Sir Redmond's horse was too slow to keep up, or he would have been at hand, no doubt."

"And could have supplied part of the stage setting. Too bad he was behind." Keith turned and readjusted the cinch on his saddle, though it was not loose enough to matter, and before he had finished Sir Redmond rode up.

"Are you hurt, Beatrice?" His face was pale, and his eyes anxious.

"Not at all. Mr. Cameron kindly helped me from the saddle in time to prevent an accident. I wish you'd thank him, Sir Redmond. I haven't the words."

"You needn't trouble," said Keith hastily, getting into the saddle. "I'll go down after Goldie. You can easily find the camp, I guess, without a pilot." Then he galloped away and left them, and would not look back; if he had done so, he would have seen Beatrice's eyes following him remorsefully. Also, he would have seen Sir Redmond glare after him jealously; for Sir Redmond was not in a position to know that their tete-a-tete had not been a pleasant one, and no man likes to have another fellow save the life of a woman he loves, while he himself is limping painfully up from the rear.

However, the woman he loved was very gracious to him that day, and for many days, and Keith Cameron held himself aloof during the rest of the trip, which should have contented Sir Redmond.

# Chapter 8. Dorman Plays Cupid

Dorman toiled up the steps, his straw hat perilously near to slipping down his back, his face like a large, red beet, and his hands vainly trying to reach around a baking-powder can which the Chinaman cook had given him.

He marched straight to where Beatrice was lying in the hammock. If she had been older, or younger, or a plain young woman, one might say that Beatrice was sulking in the hammock, for she had not spoken anything but "yes" and "no" to her mother for an hour, and she had only spoken those two words occasionally, when duty demanded it. For one thing, Sir Redmond was absent, and had been for two weeks, and Beatrice was beginning to miss him dreadfully. To beguile the time, she had ridden, every day, long miles into the hills. Three times she had met Keith Cameron, also riding alone in the hills, and she had endeavored to amuse herself with him, after her own inimitable fashion, and with more or less success. The trouble was, that sometimes Keith seemed to be amusing himself with her, which was not pleasing to a girl like Beatrice. At any rate, he proved himself quite able to play the game of Give and Take, so that the conscience of Beatrice was at ease; no one could call her pastime a slaughter of the innocents, surely, when the fellow stood his ground like that. It was more a fencing-bout, and Beatrice enjoyed it very much; she told herself that the reason she enjoyed talking with Keith was because he was not always getting hurt, like Sir Redmond-or, if he did, he kept his feelings to himself, and went boldly on with the game. Item: Beatrice had reversed her decision that Keith was vain, though she still felt tempted, at times, to resort to "making faces" —when she was worsted, that was.

To return to this particular day of sulking; Rex had cast a shoe, and lamed himself just enough to prevent her riding, and so Beatrice was having a dull day of it in the house. Besides, her mother had just finished talking to her for her good, which was enough to send an angel into the sulks-and Beatrice lacked a good deal of being an angel.

Dorman laid his baking-powder can confidingly in his divinity's lap. "Be'trice, I did get some grasshoppers; you said I couldn't. And you wouldn't go fishin', 'cause you didn't like to take Uncle Dick's make-m'lieve flies, so I got some really ones, Be'trice, that'll wiggle dere own self."

"Oh, dear me! It's too hot, Dorman."

"'Tisn't, Be'trice It's dest as cool-and by de brook it's awf-lly cold. Come, Be'trice!" He pulled at the smart little pink ruffles on her skirt.

"I'm too sleepy, hon."

"You can sleep by de brook, Be'trice. I'll let you," he promised generously, "'cept when I need anudder grasshopper; nen I'll wake you up."

"Wait till to-morrow. I don't believe the fish are hungry to-day. Don't tear my skirt to pieces, Dorman!"

Dorman began to whine. He had never found his divinity in so unlovely a mood. "I want to go now! Dey are too hungry, Be'trice! Looey Sam is goin' to fry my fishes for dinner, to s'prise auntie. Come, Be'trice!"

"Why don't you go with the child, Beatrice? You grow more selfish every day." Mrs. Lansell could not endure selfishness-in others. "You know he will not give us any peace until you do."

Dorman instantly proceeded to make good his grandmother's prophecy, and wept so that one could hear him a mile.

"Oh, dear me! Be still, Dorman-your auntie has a headache. Well, get your rod, if you know where it is-which I doubt." Beatrice flounced out of the hammock and got her hat, one of those floppy white things, fluffed with thin, white stuff, till they look like nothing so much as a wisp of cloud, with ribbons to moor it to her head and keep it from sailing off to join its brothers in the sky.

Down by the creek, where the willows nodded to their own reflections in the still places, it was cool and sweet scented, and Beatrice forgot her grievances, and was not sorry she had come.

(It was at about this time that a tall young fellow, two miles down the coulee, put away his field glass and went off to saddle his horse.)

"Don't run ahead so, Dorman," Beatrice cautioned. To her had been given the doubtful honor of carrying the baking-powder can of grasshoppers. Even divinities must make themselves useful to man.

"Why, Be'trice?" Dorman swished his rod in unpleasant proximity to his divinity's head.

"Because, honey"—Beatrice dodged—"you might step on a snake, a rattlesnake, that would bite you."

"How would it bite, Be'trice?"

"With its teeth, of course; long, wicked teeth, with poison on them."

"I saw one when I was ridin' on a horse wis Uncle Dick. It kept windin' up till it was round, and it growled wis its tail, Be'trice. And Uncle Dick chased it, and nen it unwinded itself and creeped under a big rock. It didn't bite once-and I didn't see any teeth to it."

"Carry your rod still, Dorman. Are you trying to knock my hat off my head? Rattlesnakes have teeth, hon, whether you saw them or not. I saw a great, long one that day we thought you were lost. Mr. Cameron killed it with his rope. I'm sure it had teeth."

"Did it growl, Be'trice? Tell me how it went."

"Like this, hon." Beatrice parted her lips ever so little, and a snake buzzed at Dorman's feet. He gave a yell of terror, and backed ingloriously.

"You see, honey, if that had been really a snake, it would have bitten you. Never mind, dear-it was only I."

Dorman was some time believing this astonishing statement. "How did you growl by my feet, Be'trice? Show me again."

Beatrice, who had learned some things at school which were not included in the curriculum, repeated the performance, while Dorman watched her with eyes and mouth at their widest. Like some older members of his sex, he was discovering new witcheries about his divinity every day.

"Well, Be'trice!" He gave a long gasp of ecstasy. "I don't see how can you do it? Can't I do it, Be'trice?"

"I'm afraid not, honey-you'd have to learn. There was a queer French girl at school, who could do the strangest things, Dorman-like fairy tales, almost. And she taught me to throw my voice different places, and mimic sounds, when we should have been at our lessons. Listen, hon. This is how a little lamb cries, when he is lost.... And this is what a hungry kittie says, when she is away up in a tree, and is afraid to come down."

Dorman danced all around his divinity, and forgot about the fish-until Beatrice found it in her heart to regret her rash revelation of hitherto undreamed-of powers of entertainment.

"Not another sound, Dorman," she declared at length, with the firmness of despair. "No, I will not be a lost lamb another once. No, nor a hungry kittie, either-nor a snake, or anything. If you are not going to fish, I shall go straight back to the house."

Dorman sighed heavily, and permitted his divinity to fasten a small grasshopper to his hook.

"We'll go a bit farther, dear, down under those great trees. And you must not speak a word, remember, or the fish will all run away."

When she had settled him in a likely place, and the rapt patience of the born angler had folded him close, she disposed herself comfortably in the thick grass, her back against a tree, and took up the shuttle of fancy to weave a wonderful daydream, as beautiful, intangible as the lacy, summer clouds over her head.

A man rode quietly over the grass and stopped two rods away, that he might fill his hungry eyes with the delicious loveliness of his Heart's Desire.

"Got a bite yet?"

Dorman turned and wrinkled his nose, by way of welcome, and shook his head vaguely, as though he might tell of several unimportant nibbles, if it were worth the effort.

Beatrice sat a bit straighter, and dexterously whisked some pink ruffles down over two distracting ankles, and hoped Keith had not taken notice of them. He had, though; trust a man for that!

Keith dismounted, dropped the reins to the ground, and came and laid himself down in the grass beside his Heart's Desire, and Beatrice noticed how tall he was, and slim and strong.

"How did you know we were here?" she wanted to know, with lifted eyebrows.

Keith wondered if there was a welcome behind that sweet, indifferent face. He never could be sure of anything in Beatrice's face, because it never was alike twice, it seemed to him-and if it spoke welcome for a second, the next there was only raillery, or something equally unsatisfying.

"I saw you from the trail," he answered promptly, evidently not thinking it wise to mention the fieldglass. And then: "Is Dick at home?" Not that he wanted Dick-but a fellow, even when he is in the last stages of love, feels need of an excuse sometimes.

"No-we women are alone to-day. There isn't a man on the place, except Looey Sam, and he doesn't count."

Dorman squirmed around till he could look at the two, and his eyebrows were tied in a knot. "I wish, Be'trice, you wouldn't talk, 'less you whisper. De fishes won't bite a bit."

"All right, honey-we won't."

Dorman turned back to his fishing with a long breath of relief. His divinity never broke a promise, if she could help it.

If Dorman Hayes had been Cupid himself, he could not have hit upon a more impish arrangement than that. To place a girl like Beatrice beside a fellow like Keith —a fellow who is tall, and browned, and extremely good-looking, and who has hazel eyes with a laugh in them always —a fellow, moreover, who is very much in love and very much in earnest about it-and condemn him to silence, or to whispers!

Keith took advantage of the edict, and moved closer, so that he could whisper in comfort-and be nearer his Heart's Desire. He lay with his head propped upon his hand, and his elbow digging into the sod and getting grass-stains on his shirt sleeve, for the day was too warm for a coat. Beatrice, looking down at him, observed that his forearm, between his glove and wrist-band, was as white and smooth as her own. It is characteristic of a cowboy to have a face brown as an Indian, and hands girlishly white and soft.

"I haven't had a glimpse of you for a week-not since I met you down by the river. Where have you been?" he whispered.

"Here. Rex went lame, and Dick wouldn't let me ride any other horse, since that day Goldie bolted-and so the hills have called in vain. I've stayed at home and made quantities of Duchesse lace —I almost finished a love of a center piece-and mama thinks I have reformed. But Rex is better, and tomorrow I'm going somewhere."

"Better help me hunt some horses that have been running down Lost Canyon way. I'm going to look for them to-morrow," Keith suggested, as calmly as was compatible with his eagerness and his method of speech. I doubt if any man can whisper things to a girl he loves, and do it calmly. I know Keith's heart was pounding.

"I shall probably ride in the opposite direction," Beatrice told him wickedly. She wondered if he thought she would run at his beck.

"I never saw you in this dress before," Keith murmured, his eyes caressing.

"No? You may never again," she said. "I have so many things to wear out, you know."

"I like it," he declared, as emphatically as he could, and whisper. "It is just the color of your cheeks, after the wind has been kissing them a while."

"Fancy a cowboy saying pretty things like that!"

Beatrice's cheeks did not wait for the wind to kiss them pink.

"Ya-as, only fawncy, ye knaw." His eyes were daringly mocking.

"For shame, Mr. Cameron! Sir Redmond would not mimic your speech."

"Good reason why; he couldn't, not if he tried a thousand years."

Beatrice knew this was the truth, so she fell back upon dignity.

"We will not discuss that subject, I think."

"I don't want to, anyway. I know another subject a million times more interesting than Sir Redmond."

"Indeed!" Beatrice's eyebrows were at their highest. "And what is it, then?"

"You!" Keith caught her hand; his eyes compelled her.

"I think," said Beatrice, drawing her hand away, "we will not discuss that subject, either."

"Why?" Keith's eyes continued to woo.

"Because."

It occurred to Beatrice that an unsophisticated girl might easily think Keith in earnest, with that look in his eyes.

Dorman, scowling at them over his shoulder, unconsciously did his divinity a service. Beatrice pursed her lips in a way that drove Keith nearly wild, and took up the weapon of silence.

"You said you women are alone-where is milord?" Keith began again, after two minutes of lying there watching her.

"Sir Redmond is in Helena, on business. He's been making arrangements to lease a lot of land."

"Ah-h!" Keith snapped a twig off a dead willow.

"We look for him home to-day, and Dick drove in to meet the train."

"So the Pool has gone to leasing land?" The laugh had gone out of Keith's eyes; they were clear and keen.

"Yes-the plan is to lease the Pine Ridge country, and fence it. I suppose you know where that is."

"I ought to," Keith said quietly. "It's funny Dick never mentioned it."

"It isn't Dick's idea," Beatrice told him. "It was Sir Redmond's. Dick is rather angry, I think, and came near quarreling with Sir Redmond about it. But English capital controls the Pool, you know, and Sir Redmond controls the English capital, so he can adopt whatever policy he chooses. The way he explained the thing to me, it seems a splendid plan-don't you think so?"

"Yes." Keith's tone was not quite what he meant it to be; he did not intend it to be ironical, as it was. "It's a snap for the Pool, all right. It gives them a cinch on the best of the range, and all the water. I didn't give milord credit for such business sagacity."

Beatrice leaned over that she might read his eyes, but Keith turned his face away. In the shock of what he had just learned, he was, at the moment, not the lover; he was the small cattleman who is being forced out of the business by the octopus of combined capital. It was not less bitter that the woman he loved was one of the tentacles reaching out to crush him. And they could do it; they-the whole affair resolved itself into a very simple scheme, to Keith. The gauntlet had been thrown down-because of this girl beside him. It was not so much business acumen as it was the antagonism of a rival that had prompted the move. Keith squared his shoulders, and mentally took up the gauntlet. He might lose in the range fight, but he would win the girl, if it were in the power of love to do it.

"Why that tone? I hope it isn't —will it inconvenience you?"

"Oh, no. No, not at all. No —" Keith seemed to forget that a superabundance of negatives breeds suspicion of sincerity.

"I'm afraid that means that it will. And I'm sure Sir Redmond never meant —"

"I believe that kid has got a bite at last," Keith interrupted, getting up. "Let me take hold, there, Dorman; you'll be in the creek yourself in a second." He landed a four-inch fish, carefully rebaited the hook, cast the line into a promising eddy, gave the rod over to Dorman, and went back to Beatrice, who had been watching him with troubled eyes.

"Mr. Cameron, if I had known —" Beatrice was good-hearted, if she was fond of playing with a man's heart.

"I hope you're not letting that business worry you, Miss Lansell. You remind me of a painting I saw once in Boston. It was called June."

"But this is August, so I don't apply. Isn't there some way you —"

"Did you hear about that train-robbery up the line last week?" Keith settled himself luxuriously upon his back, with his hands clasped under his head, and his hat tipped down over his eyes-but not enough to prevent him from watching his Heart's Desire. And in his eyes laughter-and something sweeter-lurked. If Sir Redmond had wealth to fight with, Keith's weapon was far and away more dangerous, for it was the irresistible love of a masterful man-the love that sweeps obstacles away like straws.

"I am not interested in train-robberies," Beatrice told him, her eyes still clouded with trouble. "I want to talk about this lease."

"They got one fellow the next day, and another got rattled and gave himself up; but the leader of the gang, one of Montana's pet outlaws, is still ranging somewhere in the hills. You want to be careful about riding off alone; you ought to let some one-me, for instance-go along to look after you."

"Pshaw!" said his Heart's Desire, smiling reluctantly. "I'm not afraid. Do you suppose, if Sir Redmond had known —"

"Those fellows made quite a haul-almost enough to lease the whole country, if they wanted to. Something over fifty thousand dollars-and a strong box full of sand, that the messenger was going to fool them with. He did, all right; but they weren't so slow. They hustled around and got the money, and he lost his sand into the bargain."

"Was that meant for a pun?" Beatrice blinked her big eyes at him. "If you're quite through with the train-robbers, perhaps you will tell me how —"

"I'm glad old Mother Nature didn't give every woman an odd dimple beside the mouth," Keith observed, reaching for her hat, and running a ribbon caressingly through his fingers.

"Why?" Beatrice smoothed the dimple complacently with her finger-tips.

"Why? Oh, it would get kind of monotonous, wouldn't it?"

"This from a man known chiefly for his pretty speeches!" Beatrice's laugh had a faint tinge of chagrin.

"Wouldn't pretty speeches get monotonous, too?" Keith's eyes were laughing at her.

"Yours wouldn't," she retorted, spitefully, and immediately bit her lip and hoped he would not consider that a bid for more pretty speeches.

"Be'trice, dis hopper is awf-lly wilted!" came a sepulchral whisper from Dorman.

Keith sighed, and went and baited the hook again. When he returned to Beatrice, his mood had changed.

"I want you to promise —"

"I never make promises of any sort, Mr. Cameron." Beatrice had fallen back upon her airy tone, which was her strongest weapon of defense-unless one except her liquid-air smile.

"I wasn't thinking of asking much," Keith went on coolly. "I only wanted to ask you not to worry about that leasing business."

"Are you worrying about it, Mr. Cameron?"

"That isn't the point. No, I can't say I expect to lose sleep over it. I hope you will dismiss anything I may have said from your mind."

"But I don't understand. I feel that you blame Sir Redmond, when I'm sure he —"

"I did not say I blamed anybody. I think we'll not discuss it."

"Yes, I think we shall. You'll tell me all about it, if I want to know." Beatrice adopted her coaxing tone, which never had failed her.

"Oh, no!" Keith laughed a little. "A girl can't always have her own way just because she wants it, even if she —"

"I've got a fish, Mr. Cam'ron!" Dorman squealed, and Keith was obliged to devote another five minutes to diplomacy.

"I think you have fished long enough, honey," Beatrice told Dorman decidedly. "It's nearly dinner time, and Looey Sam won't have time to fry your fish if you don't hurry home. Shall I tell Dick you wished to see him, Mr. Cameron?"

"It's nothing important, so I won't trouble you," Keith replied, in a tone that matched hers for cool courtesy. "I'll see him to-morrow, probably." He helped Dorman reel in his line, cut a willow-wand and strung the three fish upon it by the gills, washed his hands leisurely in the creek, and dried them on his handkerchief, just as if nothing bothered him in the slightest degree. Then he went over and smoothed Redcloud's mane and pulled a wisp of forelock from under the brow-band, and commanded him to shake hands, which the horse did promptly.

"I want to shake hands wis your pony, too," Dorman cried, and dropped pole and fish heedlessly into the grass.

"All right, kid."

Dorman went up gravely and clasped Redcloud's raised fetlock solemnly, while the tall cowpuncher smiled down at him.

"Kiss him, Redcloud," he said softly; and then, when the horse's nose was thrust in his face: "No, not me-kiss the kid." He lifted the child up in his arms, and when Redcloud touched his soft nose to Dorman's cheek and lifted his lip for a dainty, toothless nibble, Dorman was speechless with fright and rapture thrillingly combined.

"Now run home with your fish; it lacks only two hours and forty minutes to dinner time, and it will take at least twenty minutes for the fish to fry-so you see you'll have to hike."

Beatrice flushed and looked at him sharply, but Keith was getting into the saddle and did not appear to remember she was there. The fingers that were tying her hat-ribbons under her chin fumbled awkwardly and trembled. Beatrice would have given a good deal at that moment to know just what Keith Cameron was thinking; and she was in a blind rage with herself to think that it mattered to her what he thought.

When he lifted his hat she only nodded curtly. She mimicked every beast and bird she could think of on the way home, to wipe him and his horse from the memory of Dorman, whose capacity for telling things best left untold was simply marvelous.

It is saying much for Beatrice's powers of entertainment that Dorman quite forgot to say anything about Mr. Cameron and his pony, and chattered to his auntie and grandmama about kitties up in a tree, and lost lambs and sleepy birds, until he was tucked into bed that night. It was not until then that Beatrice felt justified in drawing a long breath. Not that she cared whether any one knew of her meeting Keith Cameron, only that her mother would instantly take alarm and preach to her about the wickedness of flirting; and Beatrice was not in the mood for sermons.

# Chapter 9. What it Meant to Keith

"Dick, I wish you'd tell me about this leasing business. There are points which I don't understand." Beatrice leaned over and smoothed Rex's sleek shoulder with her hand.

"What do you want to understand it for? The thing is done now. We've got the fence-posts strung, and a crew hired to set them."

"You needn't snap your words like that, Dick. It doesn't matter-only I was wondering why Mr. Cameron acted so queer yesterday when I told him about it."

"You told Keith? What did he say?"

"He didn't say anything. He just looked things."

"Where did you see him?" Dick wanted to know.

"Well, dear me! I don't see that it matters where I saw him. You're getting as inquisitive as mama. If you think it concerns you, why, I met him accidentally when I was fishing with Dorman. He was coming to see you, but you were gone, so he stopped and talked for a few minutes. Was there anything so strange about that? And I told him you were leasing the Pine Ridge country, and he looked-well, peculiar. But he wouldn't say anything."

"Well, he had good reason for looking peculiar. But you needn't have told him I did it, Trix. Lay that at milord's door, where it belongs. I don't want Keith to blame me."

"But why should he blame anybody? It isn't his land, is it?"

"No, it isn't. But-you see, Trix, it's this way: A man goes somewhere and buys a ranch-or locates on a claim-and starts into the cattle business. He may not own more than a few hundred acres of land, but if he has much stock he needs miles of prairie country, with water, for them to range on. It's an absolute necessity, you see. He takes care to locate where there is plenty of public land that is free to anybody's cattle.

"Take the Pool outfit, for instance. We don't own land enough to feed one-third of our cattle. We depend on government land for range for them. The Cross outfit is the same, only Keith's is on a smaller scale. He's got to have range outside his own land, which is mostly hay land. This part of the State is getting pretty well settled up with small ranchers, and then the sheep men keep crowding in wherever they can get a show-and sheep will starve cattle to death; they leave a range as bare as a prairie-dog town. So there's only one good bit of range left around here, and that's the Pine Ridge country, as it's called. That's our main dependence for winter range; and now when this drought has struck us, and everything is drying up, we've had to turn all our cattle down there on account of water.

"Ever since I took charge of the Pool, Keith and I threw in together and used the same range, worked our crews together, and fought the sheepmen together. There was a time when they tried to gobble the Pine Ridge range, but it didn't go. Keith and I made up our minds that we needed it worse than they did-and we got it. Our punchers had every sheep herder bluffed out till there wasn't a mutton-chewer could keep a bunch of sheep on that range over-night.

"Now, this lease law was made by stockmen, for stockmen. They can lease land from the government, fence it-and they've got a cinch on it as long as the lease lasts. A cow outfit can corral a heap of range that way. There's the trick of leasing every other section or so, and then running a fence around the whole chunk; and that's what the Pool has done to the Pine Ridge. But you mustn't repeat that, Trix.

"Milord wasn't long getting on to the leasing graft; in fact, it turns out the company got wind of it over in England, and sent him over here to see what could be done in that line. He's done it, all right enough!

"And there's the Cross outfit, frozen out completely. The Lord only knows what Keith will do with his cattle now, for we'll have every drop of water under fence inside of a month. He's in a hole, for sure. I expect he feels pretty sore with me, too, but I couldn't help it. I explained how it was to milord, but-you can't persuade an Englishman, any more than you can a —"

"I think," put in Beatrice firmly, "Sir Redmond did quite right. It isn't his fault that Mr. Cameron owns more cattle than he can feed. If he was sent over here to lease the land, it was his duty to do so. Still, I really am sorry for Mr. Cameron."

"Keith won't sit down and take his medicine if he can help it," Dick said moodily. "He could sell out, but I don't believe he will. He's more apt to fight."

"I can't see how fighting will help him," Beatrice returned spiritedly.

"Well, there's one thing," retorted Dick. "If milord wants that fence to stand he'd better stay and watch it. I'll bet money he won't more than strike Liverpool till about forty miles, more or less, of Pool fence will need repairs mighty bad-which it won't get, so far as I'm concerned."

"Do you mean that Keith Cameron would destroy our fencing?"

Dick grinned. "He'll be a fool if he don't, Trix. You can tell milord he'd better send for all his traps, and camp right here till that lease runs out. My punchers will have something to do beside ride fence."

"I shall certainly tell Sir Redmond," Beatrice threatened. "You and Mr. Cameron hate him just because he's English. You won't see what a splendid fellow he is. It's your duty to stand by him in this business, instead of taking sides with Keith Cameron. Why didn't he lease that land himself, if he wanted to?"

"Because he plays fair."

"Meaning, I suppose, that Sir Redmond doesn't. I didn't think you would be so unjust. Sir Redmond is a perfect gentleman."

"Well, you've got a chance to marry your 'perfect gentleman,'" Dick retorted, savagely. "It's a wonder you don't take him if you think so highly of him."

"I probably shall. At any rate, he isn't a male flirt."

"You don't seem to fancy a fellow that can give you as good as you send," Dick rejoined. "I thought you wouldn't find Keith such easy game, even if he does live on a cattle ranch. You can't rope him into making a fool of himself for your amusement, and I'm glad of it."

"Don't do your shouting too soon. If you could overhear some of the things he says you wouldn't be so sure —"

"I suppose you take them all for their face value," grinned Dick ironically.

"No, I don't! I'm not a simple country girl, let me remind you. Since you are so sure of him, I'll have the pleasure of saying, 'No, thank you, sir,' to your Keith Cameron-just to convince you I can."

"Oh, you will! Well, you just tell me when you do, Trix, and I'll give you your pick of all the saddle horses on the ranch."

"I'll take Rex, and you may as well consider him mine. Oh, you men! A few smiles, judiciously dispensed, and —" Beatrice smiled most exasperatingly at her brother, and Dick went moody and was very poor company the rest of the way home.

# Chapter 10. Pine Ridge Range Ablaze

At dusk that night a glow was in the southern sky, and the wind carried the pungent odor of burning grass. Dick went out on the porch after dinner, and sniffed the air uneasily.

"I don't much like the look of it," he admitted to Sir Redmond. "It smells pretty strong, to be across the river. I sent a couple of the boys out to look a while ago. If it's this side of the river we'll have to get a move on."

"It will be the range land, I take it, if it's on this side," Sir Redmond remarked.

Just then a man thundered through the lane and up to the very steps of the porch, and when he stopped the horse he was riding leaned forward and his legs shook with exhaustion.

"The Pine Ridge Range is afire, Mr. Lansell," the man announced quietly.

Dick took a long pull at his cigar and threw it away. "Have the boys throw some barrels and sacks into a wagon-and git!" He went inside and grabbed his hat, and when he turned Sir Redmond was at his elbow.

"I'm going, too, Dick," cried Beatrice, who always seemed to hear anything that promised excitement. "I never saw a prairie-fire in my life."

"It's ten miles off," said Dick shortly, taking the steps at a jump.

"I don't care if it's twenty —I'm going. Sir Redmond, wait for me!"

"Be-atrice!" cried her mother detainingly; but Beatrice was gone to get ready. A quick job she made of it; she threw a dark skirt over her thin, white one, slipped into the nearest jacket, snatched her riding-gauntlets off a chair where she had thrown them, and then couldn't find her hat. That, however, did not trouble her. Down in the hall she appropriated one of Dick's, off the hall tree, and announced herself ready. Sir Redmond laughed, caught her hand, and they raced together down to the stables before her mother had fully grasped the situation.

"Isn't Rex saddled, Dick?"

Dick, his foot in the stirrup, stopped long enough to glance over his shoulder at her. "You ready so soon? Jim, saddle Rex for Miss Lansell." He swung up into the saddle.

"Aren't you going to wait, Dick?"

"Can't. Milord can bring you." And Dick was away on the run.

Men were hurrying here and there, every move counting something done. While she stood there a wagon rattled out from the shadow of a haystack, with empty water-barrels dancing a mad jig behind the high seat, where the driver perched with feet braced and a whip in his hand. After him dashed four or five riders, silent and businesslike. In a moment they were mere fantastic shadows galloping up the hill through the smothery gloom.

Then came Jim, leading Rex and a horse for himself; Sir Redmond had saddled his gray and was waiting. Beatrice sprang into the saddle and took the lead, with nerves a-tingle. The wind that rushed against her face was hot and reeking with smoke. Her nostrils drank greedily the tang it carried.

"You gipsy!" cried Sir Redmond, peering at her through the murky gloom.

"This-is living!" she laughed, and urged Rex faster.

So they raced recklessly over the hills, toward where the night was aglow. Before them the wagon pounded over untrailed prairie sod, with shadowy figures fleeing always before.

Here, wild cattle rushed off at either side, to stop and eye them curiously as they whirled past. There, a coyote, squatting unseen upon a distant pinnacle, howled, long-drawn and quavering, his weird protest against the solitudes in which he wandered.

The dusk deepened to dark, and they could no longer see the racing shadows. The rattle of the wagon came mysteriously back to them through the black.

Once Rex stumbled over a rock and came near falling, but Beatrice only laughed and urged him on, unheeding Sir Redmond's call to ride slower.

They splashed through a shallow creek, and came upon the wagon, halted that the cowboys might fill the barrels with water. Then they passed by, and when they heard them following the wagon no longer rattled glibly along, but chuckled heavily under its load.

The dull, red glow brightened to orange. Then, breasting at last a long hill, they came to the top, and Beatrice caught her breath at what lay below.

A jagged line of leaping flame cut clean through the dark of the coulee. The smoke piled rosily above and before, and the sullen roar of it clutched the senses-challenging, sinister. Creeping stealthily, relentlessly, here a thin gash of yellow hugging close to the earth, there a bold, bright wall of fire, it swept the coulee from rim to rim.

"The wind is carrying it from us," Sir Redmond was saying in her ear. "Are you afraid to stop here alone? I ought to go down and lend a hand."

Beatrice drew a long gasp. "Oh, no, I'm not afraid. Go; there is Dick, down there."

"You're sure you won't mind?" He hesitated, dreading to leave her.

"No, no! Go on-they need you."

Sir Redmond turned and rode down the ridge toward the flames. His straight figure was silhouetted sharply against the glow.

Beatrice slipped off her horse and sat down upon a rock, dead to everything but the fiendish beauty of the scene spread out below her. Millions of sparks danced in and out among the smoke wreaths which curled upward-now black, now red, now a dainty rose. Off to the left a coyote yapped shrilly, ending with his mournful howl.

Beatrice shivered from sheer ecstasy. This was a world she had never before seen —a world of hot, smoke-sodden wind, of dead-black shadows and flame-bright light; of roar and hoarse bellowing and sharp crackles; of calm, star-sprinkled sky above-and in the distance the uncanny howling of a coyote.

Time had no reckoning there. She saw men running to and fro in the glare, disappearing in a downward swirl of smoke, coming to view again in the open beyond. Always their arms waved rhythmically downward, beating the ragged line of yellow with water-soaked sacks. The trail they left was a wavering, smoke-traced rim of sullen black, where before had been gay, dancing, orange light. In places the smolder fanned to new life behind them and licked greedily at the ripe grass like hungry, red tongues. One of these Beatrice watched curiously. It crept slyly into an unburned hollow, and the wind, veering suddenly, pushed it out of sight from the fighters and sent it racing merrily to the south. The main line of fire beat doggedly up against the wind that a minute before had been friendly, and fought bravely two foes instead of one. It dodged, ducked, and leaped high, and the men beat upon it mercilessly.

But the little, new flame broadened and stood on tiptoes defiantly, proud of the wide, black trail that kept stretching away behind it; and Beatrice watched it, fascinated by its miraculous growth. It began to crackle and send up smoke wreaths of its own, with sparks dancing through; then its voice deepened and coarsened, till it roared quite like its mother around the hill.

The smoke from the larger fire rolled back with the wind, and Beatrice felt her eyes sting. Flakes of blackened grass and ashes rained upon the hilltop, and Rex moved uneasily and pawed at the dry sod. To him a prairie-fire was not beautiful-it was an enemy to run from. He twitched his reins from Beatrice's heedless fingers and decamped toward home, paying no attention whatever to the command of his mistress to stop.

Still Beatrice sat and watched the new fire, and was glad she chanced to be upon the south end of a sharp-nosed hill, so that she could see both ways. The blaze dove into a deep hollow, climbed the slope beyond, leaped exultantly and bellowed its challenge. And, of a sudden, dark forms sprang upon it and beat it cruelly, and it went black where they struck, and only thin streamers of smoke told where it had been. Still they beat, and struck, and struck again, till the fire died ingloriously and the hillside to the south lay dark and still, as it had been at the beginning.

Beatrice wondered who had done it. Then she came back to her surroundings and realized that Rex had left her, and she was alone. She shivered-this time not in ecstasy, but partly from loneliness-and went down the hill toward where Dick and Sir Redmond and the others were fighting steadily the larger fire, unconscious of the younger, new one that had stolen away from them and was beaten to death around the hill.

Once in the coulee, she was compelled to take to the burnt ground, which crisped hotly under her feet and sent up a rank, suffocating smell of burned grass into her nostrils. The whole country was alight, and down there the world seemed on fire. At times the smoke swooped blindingly, and half strangled her. Her skirts, in passing, swept the black ashes from grass roots which showed red in the night.

Picking her way carefully around the spots that glowed warningly, shielding her face as well as she could from the smoke, she kept on until she was close upon the fighters. Dick and Sir Redmond were working side by side, the sacks they held rising and falling with the regularity of a machine for minutes at a time. A group of strange horsemen galloped up from the way she had come, followed by a wagon of water-barrels, careering recklessly over the uneven ground. The horsemen stopped just inside the burned rim, the horses sidestepping gingerly upon the hot turf.

"I guess you want some help here. Where shall we start in?" Beatrice recognized the voice. It was Keith Cameron.

"Sure, we do!" Dick answered, gratefully. "Start in any old place."

"I'm not sure we want your help," spoke the angry voice of Sir Redmond. "I take it you've already done a devilish sight too much."

"What do you mean by that?" Keith demanded; and then, by the silence, it seemed that every one knew. Beatrice caught her breath. Was this one of the ways Dick meant that Keith could fight?

"Climb down, boys, and get busy," Keith called to his men, after a few breaths. "This is for Dick. Wait a minute! Pete, drive the wagon ahead, there. I guess we'd better begin on the other end and work this way. Come on-there's too much hot air here." They clattered on across the coulee, kicking hot ashes up for the wind to seize upon. Beatrice went slowly up to Dick, feeling all at once very tired and out of heart with it all.

"Dick," she called, in an anxious little voice, "Rex has run away from me. What shall I do?"

Dick straightened stiffly, his hands upon his aching loins, and peered through the smoke at her.

"I guess the only thing to do, then, is to get into the wagon over there. You can drive, Trix, if you want to, and that will give us another man here. I was just going to have some one take you home; now-the Lord only knows! —you're liable to have to stay till morning. Rex will go home, all right; you needn't worry about him."

He bent to the work again, and she could hear the wet sack thud, thud upon the ground. Other sacks and blankets went thud, thud, and down here at close range the fire was not so beautiful as it had been from the hilltop. Down here the glamour was gone. She climbed up to the high wagon seat and took the reins from the man, who immediately seized upon a sack and went off to the fight. She felt that she was out of touch. She was out on the prairie at night, miles away from any house, driving a water-wagon for the men to put out a prairie fire. She had driven a coaching-party once on a wager; but she had never driven a lumber-wagon with barrels of water before. She could not think of any girl she knew who had.

It was a new experience, certainly, but she found no pleasure in it; she was tired and sleepy, and her eyes and throat smarted cruelly with the smoke. She looked back to the hill she had just left, and it seemed a long, long time since she sat upon a rock up there and watched the little, new fire grow and grow, and the strange shadows spring up from nowhere and beat it vindictively till it died.

Again she wondered vaguely who had done it; not Keith Cameron, surely, for Sir Redmond had all but accused him openly of setting the range afire. Would he stamp out a blaze that was just reaching a size to do mischief, if left a little longer? No one would have seen it for hours, probably. He would undoubtedly have let it run, unless-But who else could have set the fire? Who else would want to see the Pine Ridge country black and barren? Dick said Keith Cameron would not sit down and take his medicine-perhaps Dick knew he would do this thing.

As the fighters moved on across the coulee she drove the wagon to keep pace with them. Often a man would run up to the wagon, climb upon a wheel and dip a frayed gunny sack into a barrel, lift it out and run with it, all dripping, to the nearest point of the fire. Her part was to keep the wagon at the most convenient place. She began to feel the importance of her position, and to take pride in being always at the right spot. From the calm appreciation of the picturesque side, she drifted to the keen interest of the one who battles against heavy odds. The wind had veered again, and the flames rushed up the long coulee like an express train. But the path it left was growing narrower every moment. Keith Cameron was doing grand work with his crew upon the other side, and the space between them was shortening perceptibly.

Beatrice found herself watching the work of the Cross men. If they were doing it for effect, they certainly were acting well their part. She wondered what would happen when the two crews met, and the danger was over. Would Sir Redmond call Keith Cameron to account for what he had done? If he did, what would Keith say? And which side would Dick take? Very likely, she thought, he would defend Keith Cameron, and shield him if he could.

Beatrice found herself crying quietly, and shivering, though the air was sultry with the fire. For the life of her, she could not tell why she cried, but she tried to believe it was the smoke in her eyes. Perhaps it was.

The sky was growing gray when the two crews met. The orange lights were gone, and Dick, with a spiteful flop of the black rag which had been a good, new sack, stamped out the last tiny red tongue of the fire. The men stood about in awkward silence, panting with heat and weariness. Sir Redmond was ostentatiously filling his pipe. Beatrice knew him by his straight, soldierly pose. In the drab half-light they were all mere black outlines of men, and, for the most part, she could not distinguish one from another. Keith Cameron she knew; instinctively by his slim height, and by the way he carried his head. Unconsciously, she leaned down from the high seat and listened for what would come next.

Keith seemed to be making a cigarette. A match flared and lighted his face for an instant, then was pinched out, and he was again only a black shape in the half-darkness.

"Well, I'm waiting for what you've got to say, Sir Redmond." His voice cut sharply through the silence. If he had known Beatrice was out there in the wagon he would have spoken lower, perhaps.

"I fancy I said all that is necessary just now," Sir Redmond answered calmly. "You know what I think. From now on I shall act."

"And what are you going to do, then?" Keith's voice was clear and unperturbed, as though he asked for the sake of being polite.

"That," retorted Sir Redmond, "is my own affair. However, since the matter concerns you rather closely, I will say that when I have the evidence I am confident I shall find, I shall seek the proper channels for retribution. There are laws in this country, aimed to protect a man's property, I take it. I warn you that I shall not spare-the guilty."

"Dick, it's up to you next. I want to know where you stand."

"At your back, Keith, right up to the finish. I know you; you fight fair."

"All right, then. I didn't think you'd go back on a fellow. And I tell you straight up, Sir Redmond Hayes, I'm not out touching matches to range land-not if it belonged to the devil himself. I've got some feeling for the dumb brutes that would have to suffer. You can get right to work hunting evidence, and be damned! You're dead welcome to all you can find; and in this part of the country you won't be able to buy much! You know very well you deserve to get your rope crossed, or you wouldn't be on the lookout for trouble. Come, boys; let's hit the trail. So long, Dick!"

Beatrice watched them troop off to their horses, heard them mount and go tearing off across the burned coulee bottom toward home. Dick came slowly over to her.

"I expect you're good and tired, sis. You've made a hand, all right, and helped us a whole lot, I can tell you. I'll drive now, and we'll hit the high places."

Beatrice smiled wanly. Not one of her Eastern acquaintances would have recognized Beatrice Lansell, the society beauty, in this remarkable-looking young woman, attired in a most haphazard fashion, with a face grimed like a chimney sweep, red eyelids drooping over tired, smarting eyes, and disheveled, ash-filled hair topped by a man's gray felt hat. When she smiled her teeth shone dead white, like a negro's.

Dick regarded her critically, one foot on the wheel hub. "Where did you get hold of Keith Cameron's hat?" he inquired.

Beatrice snatched the hat from her head with childish petulance, and looked as if she were going to throw it viciously upon the ground. If her face had been clean Dick might have seen how the blood had rushed into her cheeks; as it was, she was safe behind a mask of soot. She placed the hat back upon her head, feeling, privately, a bit foolish.

"I supposed it was yours. I took it off the halltree." The dignity of her tone was superb, but, unfortunately, it did not match her appearance of rakish vagabondage.

Dick grinned through a deep layer of soot "Well, it happens to be Keith's. He lost it in the wind the other day, and I found it and took it home. It's too bad you've worn his hat all night and didn't know it. You ought to see yourself. Your own mother won't know you, Trix."

"I can't look any worse than you do. A negro would be white by comparison. Do get in, so we can start! I'm tired to death, and half-starved." After these unamiable remarks, she refused to open her lips.

They drove silently in the gray of early morning, and the empty barrels danced monotonously their fantastic jig in the back of the wagon. Sootyfaced cowboys galloped wearily over the prairie before them, and Sir Redmond rode moodily alongside.

Of a truth, the glamour was gone.

# Chapter 11. Sir Redmond Waits His Answer

Beatrice felt distinctly out of sorts the next day, and chose an hour for her ride when she felt reasonably secure from unwelcome company. But when she went out into the sunshine there was Sir Redmond waiting with Rex and his big gray. Beatrice was not exactly elated at the sight, but she saw nothing to do but smile and make the best of it. She wanted to be alone, so that she could dream along through the hills she had learned to love, and think out some things which troubled her, and decide just how she had best go about winning Rex for herself; it had become quite necessary to her peace of mind that she should teach Dick and Keith Cameron a much-needed lesson.

"It has been so long since we rode together," he apologized. "I hope you don't mind my coming along."

"Oh, no! Why should I mind?" Beatrice smiled upon him in friendly fashion. She liked Sir Redmond very much-only she hoped he was not going to make love. Somehow, she did not feel in the mood for love-making just then.

"I don't know why, I'm sure. But you seem rather fond of riding about these hills by yourself. One should never ask why women do things, I fancy. It seems always to invite disaster."

"Does it?" Beatrice was not half-listening. They were passing, just then, the suburbs of a "dog town," and she was never tired of watching the prairie-dogs stand upon their burrows, chip-chip defiance until fear overtook their impertinence, and then dive headlong deep into the earth. "I do think a prairie-dog is the most impudent creature alive and the most shrewish. I never pass but I am scolded by these little scoundrels till my ears burn. What do you think they say?"

"They're probably inviting you to stop with them and be their queen, and are scolding because your heart is hard and you only laugh and ride on."

"Queen of a prairie-dog town! Dear me! Why this plaintive mood?"

"Am I plaintive? I do not mean to be, I'm sure."

"You don't appear exactly hilarious," she told him. "I can't see what is getting the matter with us all. Mama and your sister are poor company, even for each other, and Dick is like a bear. One can't get a civil word out of him. I'm not exactly amiable, myself, either; but I relied upon you to keep the mental temperature up to normal, Sir Redmond."

"Perhaps it's a good thing we shall not stop here much longer. I must confess I don't fancy the country-and Mary is downright homesick. She wants to get back to her parish affairs; she's afraid some rheumatic old woman needs coddling with jelly and wine, and that sort of thing. I've promised to hurry through the business here, and take her home. But I mean to see that Pine Ridge fence in place before I go; or, at least, see it well under way."

"I'm sure Dick will attend to it properly," Beatrice remarked, with pink cheeks. If she remembered what she had threatened to tell Sir Redmond, she certainly could not have asked for a better opportunity. She was reminding herself at that moment that she always detested a tale bearer.

"Your brother Dick is a fine fellow, and I have every confidence in him; but you must see yourself that he is swayed, more or less, by his friendship for-his neighbors. It is only a kindness to take the responsibility off his shoulders till the thing is done. I'm sure he will feel better to have it so."

"Yes," she agreed; "I think you're right. Dick always was very soft-hearted, and, right or wrong, he clings to his friends." Then, rather hastily, as though anxious to change the trend of the conversation: "Of course, your sister will insist on keeping Dorman with her. I shall miss that little scamp dreadfully, I'm afraid." The next minute she saw that she had only opened a subject she dreaded even more.

"It is something to know that there is even one of us that you will miss," Sir Redmond observed. Something in his tone hurt.

"I shall miss you all," she said hastily. "It has been a delightful summer."

"I wish I might know just what element made it delightful. I wish —"

"I scarcely think it has been any particular element," she broke in, trying desperately to stave off what she felt in his tone. "I love the wild, where I can ride, and ride, and never meet a human being-where I can dream and dally and feast my eyes on a landscape man has not touched. I have lived most of my life in New York, and I love nature so well that I'm inclined to be jealous of her. I want her left free to work out all her whims in her own way. She has a keen sense of humor, I think. The way she modeled some of these hills proves that she loves her little jokes. I have seen where she cut deep, fearsome gashes, with sides precipitous, as though she had some priceless treasure hidden away in the deep, where man cannot despoil it. And if you plot and plan, and try very hard, you may reach the bottom at last and find the treasure-nothing. Or, perhaps, a tiny little stream, as jealously guarded as though each drop were priceless."

Sir Richmond rode for a few minutes in silence. When he spoke, it was abruptly.

"And is that all? Is there nothing to this delightful summer, after all, but your hills?"

"Oh, of course, I—it has all been delightful. I shall hate to go back home, I think." Beatrice was a bit startled to find just how much she would hate to go back and wrap herself once more in the conventions of society life. For the first time since she could remember, she wanted her world to stand still.

Sir Redmond went doggedly to the point he had in mind and heart.

"I hoped, Beatrice, you would count me, too. I've tried to be patient. You know, don't you, that I love you?"

"You've certainly told me often enough," she retorted, in a miserable attempt at her old manner.

"And you've put me off, and laughed at me, and did everything under heaven but answer me fairly. And I've acted the fool, no doubt. I know it. I've no courage before a woman. A curl of your lip, and I was ready to cut and run. But I can't go on this way forever —I've got to know. I wish I could talk as easy as I can fight; I'd have settled the thing long ago. Where other men can plead their cause, I can say just the one thing —I love you, Beatrice. When I saw you first, in the carriage I loved you then. You had some fur-brown fur-snuggled under your chin, and the pink of your cheeks, and your dear, brown eyes shining and smiling above-Good God! I've always loved you! From the beginning of the world, I think! I'd be good to you, Beatrice, and I believe I could make you happy-if you give me the chance."

Something in Beatrice's throat ached cruelly. It was the truth, and she knew it. He did love her, and the love of a brave man is not a thing to be thrust lightly aside. But it demanded such a lot in return! More, perhaps, than she could give. A love like that —a love that gives everything-demands everything in return. Anything less insults it.

She stole a glance at him. Sir Redmond was looking straight before him, with the fixed gaze that sees nothing. There was the white line around his mouth which Beatrice had seen once before. Again that griping ache was in her throat, till she could have cried out with the pain of it. She wanted to speak, to say something-anything-which would drive that look from his face.

While her mind groped among the jumble of words that danced upon her tongue, and that seemed, all of them, so pitifully weak and inadequate, she heard the galloping hoofs of a horse pounding close behind. A choking cloud of dust swept down upon them, and Keith, riding in the midst, reined out to pass. He lifted his hat. His eyes challenged Beatrice, swept coldly the face of her companion, and turned again to the trail. He swung his heels backward, and Redcloud broke again into the tireless lope that carried him far ahead, until there was only a brown dot speeding over the prairie.

Sir Redmond waited until Keith was far beyond hearing, then he filled his lungs deeply and looked at Beatrice. "Don't you feel you could trust me-and love me a little?"

Beatrice was deadly afraid she was going to cry, and she hated weeping women above all things. "A little wouldn't do," she said, with what firmness she could muster. "I should want to love you as much-quite as much as you deserve, Sir Redmond, or not at all. I'm afraid I can't. I wish I could, though. I —I think I should like to love you; but perhaps I haven't much heart. I like you very much-better than I ever liked any one before; but oh, I wish you wouldn't insist on an answer! I don't know, myself, how I feel. I wish you had not asked me-yet. I tried not to let you."

"A man can keep his heart still for a certain time, Beatrice, but not for always. Some time he will say what his heart commands, if the chance is given him; the woman can't hold him back. I did wait and wait, because I thought you weren't ready for me to speak. And-you don't care for anybody else?"

"Of course I don't. But I hate to give up my freedom to any one, Sir Redmond. I want to be free-free as the wind that blows here always, and changes and changes, and blows from any point that suits its whim, without being bound to any rule."

"Do you think I'm an ogre, that will lock you in a dungeon, Beatrice? Can't you see that I am not threatening your freedom? I only want the right to love you, and make you happy. I should not ask you to go or stay where you did not please, and I'd be good to you, Beatrice!"

"I don't think it would matter," cried Beatrice, "if you weren't. I should love you because I couldn't help myself. I hate doing things by rule, I tell you. I couldn't care for you because you were good to me, and I ought to care; it must be because I can't help myself. And I —" She stopped and shut her teeth hard together; she felt sure she should cry in another minute if this went on.

"I believe you do love me, Beatrice, and your rebellious young American nature dreads sur- render." He tried to look into her eyes and smile, but she kept her eyes looking straight ahead. Then Sir Redmond made the biggest blunder of his life, out of the goodness of his heart, and because he hated to tease her into promising anything.

"I won't ask you to tell me now, Beatrice," he said gently. "I want you to be sure; I never could forgive myself if you ever felt you had made a mistake. A week from to-night I shall ask you once more-and it will be for the last time. After that-But I won't think —I daren't think what it would be like if you say no. Will you tell me then, Beatrice?"

The heart of Beatrice jumped into her throat. At that minute she was very near to saying yes, and having done with it. She was quite sure she knew, then, what her answer would be in a week. The smile she gave him started Sir Redmond's blood to racing exultantly. Her lips parted a little, as if a word were there, ready to be spoken; but she caught herself back from the decision. Sir Redmond had voluntarily given her a week; well, then, she would take it, to the last minute.

"Yes, I'll tell you a week from to-night, after dinner. I'll race you home, Sir Redmond-the first one through the big gate by the stable wins!" She struck Rex a blow that made him jump, and darted off down the trail that led home, and her teasing laugh was the last Sir Redmond heard of her that day; for she whipped into a narrow gulch when the first turn hid her from him, and waited until he had thundered by. After that she rode complacently, deep into the hills, wickedly pleased at the trick she had played him.

Every day during the week that followed she slipped away from him and rode away by herself, resolved to enjoy her freedom to the full while she had it; for after that, she felt, things would never be quite the same.

Every day, when Dick had chance for a quiet word with her, he wanted to know who owned Rex-till at last she lost her temper and told him plainly that, in her opinion, Keith Cameron had left the country for two reasons, instead of one. (For Keith, be it known, had not been seen since the day he passed her and Sir Redmond on the trail.) Beatrice averred that she had a poor opinion of a man who would not stay and face whatever was coming.

There was just one day left in her week of freedom, and Dick still owned Rex, with the chances all in his favor for continuing to do so. Still, Beatrice was vindictively determined upon one point. Let Keith Cameron cross her path, and she would do something she had never done before; she would deliberately lead him on to propose-if the fellow had nerve enough to do so, which, she told Dick, she doubted.

"'Traveler, what lies over the hill?'" questioned a mischievous voice.

Keith, dreaming along a winding, rock-strewn trail in the canyon, looked up quickly and beheld his Heart's Desire sitting calmly upon her horse, ten feet before Redcloud's nose, watching him amusedly. Redcloud must have been dreaming also, or he would have whinnied warning and welcome, with the same breath.

"'Traveler, tell to me,'" she went on, seeing Keith only stared.

Keith, not to be outdone, searched his memory hurriedly for the reply which should rightly follow; secretly he was amazed at her sudden friendliness.

"'Child, there's a valley over there'—but it isn't 'pretty and wooded and shy'—not what you can notice. And there isn't any 'little town,' either, unless you go a long way. Why?" Keith rested his gloved hands, one above the other, on the saddle horn, and let his eyes riot with the love that was in him. He had not seen his Heart's Desire for a week. A week? It seemed a thousand years! And here she was before him, unusually gracious.

"Why? I discovered that hill two hours ago, it seems to me, and it wasn't more than a mile off. I want to see what lies on the other side. I feel sure no man ever stood upon the top and looked down. It is my hill-mine by the right of discovery. But I've been going, and going, and I think it's rather farther away, if anything, than it was before."

"Good thing I met you'" Keith declared, and he looked as if he meant it. "You're probably lost, right now, and don't know it. Which way is home?"

Beatrice smiled a superior smile, and pointed.

"I thought so," grinned Keith joyously. "You're pointing straight toward Claggett."

"It doesn't matter," said Beatrice, "since you know, and you're here. The important thing is to get to the top of that hill."

"What for?" Keith questioned.

"Why, to be there!" Beatrice opened her big eyes at him. "That," she declared whimsically, "is the top of the world, and it is mine. I found it. I want to go up there and look down."

"It's an unmerciful climb," Keith demurred hypocritically, to strengthen her resolution.

"All the better. I don't value what comes easily."

"You won't see anything, except more hills."

"I love hills-and more hills."

"You're a long way from home, and it's after one o'clock."

"I have a lunch with me, and I often stay out until dinner time."

Keith gave a sigh that shook the saddle, making up, in volume, what it lacked in sincerity. The blood in him was a-jump at the prospect of leading his Heart's Desire up next the clouds-up where the world was yet young. A man in love is fond of self-torture.

"I have not said you must go." Beatrice answered with the sigh.

"You don't have to," he retorted. "It is a self evident fact. Who wants to go prowling around these hills by night, with a lantern that smokes an' has an evil smell, losing sleep and yowling like a bunch of coyotes, hunting a misguided young woman who thinks north is south, and can't point straight up?"

"You draw a flattering picture, Mr. Cameron."

"It's realistic. Do you still insist upon getting up there, for the doubtful pleasure of looking down?" Secretly, he hoped so.

"Certainly."

"Then I shall go with you."

"You need not. I can go very well by myself, Mr. Cameron."

Beatrice was something of a hypocrite herself.

"I shall go where duty points the way."

"I hope it points toward home, then."

"It doesn't, though. It takes the trail you take."

"I never yet allowed my wishes to masquerade as Disagreeable Duty, with two big D's," she told him tartly, and started off.

"Say! If you're going up that hill, this is the trail. You'll bump up against a straight cliff if you follow that path."

Beatrice turned with seeming reluctance and allowed him to guide her, just as she had intended he should do.

"Dick tells me you have been away," she began suavely.

"Yes. I've just got back from Fort Belknap," he explained quietly, though he must have known his absence had been construed differently. "I've rented pasturage on the reservation for every hoof I own. Great grass over there-the whole prairie like a hay meadow, almost, and little streams everywhere."

"You are very fortunate," Beatrice remarked politely.

"Luck ought to come my way once in a while. I don't seem to get more than my share, though."

"Dick will be glad to know you have a good range for your cattle, Mr. Cameron."

"I expect he will. You may tell him, for me, that Jim Worthington-he's the agent over there, and was in college with us-says I can have my cattle there as long as he's running the place."

"Why not tell him yourself?" Beatrice asked.

"I don't expect to be over to the Pool ranch for a while." Keith's tone was significant, and Beatrice dropped the subject.

"Been fishing lately?" he asked easily, as though he had not left her that day in a miff. "No. Dorman is fickle, like all male creatures. Dick brought him two little brown puppies the other day, and now he can hardly be dragged from the woodshed to his meals. I believe he would eat and sleep with them if his auntie would allow him to."

The trail narrowed there, and they were obliged to ride single file, which was not favorable to conversation. Thus far, Beatrice thought, she was a long way from winning her wager; but she did not worry-she looked up to where the hill towered above them, and smiled.

"We'll have to get off and lead our horses over this spur," he told her, at last. "Once on the other side, we can begin to climb. Still in the humor to tackle it?"

"To be sure I am. After all this trouble I shall not turn back."

"All right," said Keith, inwardly shouting. If his Heart's Desire wished to take a climb that would last a good two hours, he was not there to object. He led her up a steep, rock-strewn ridge and into a hollow. From there the hill sloped smoothly upward.

"I'll just anchor these cayuses to a rock, to make dead-sure of them," Keith remarked. "It wouldn't be fun to be set afoot out here; now, would it? How would you like the job of walking home, eh?"

"I don't think I'd enjoy it much," Beatrice said, showing her one dimple conspicuously. "I'd rather ride."

"Throw up your hands!" growled a voice from somewhere.

Keith wheeled toward the sound, and a bullet spatted into the yellow clay, two inches from the toe of his boot. Also, a rifle cracked sharply. He took the hint, and put his hands immediately on a level with his hat crown.

"No use," he called out ruefully. "I haven't anything to return the compliment with."

"Well, I've got t' have the papers fur that, mister," retorted the voice, and a man appeared from the shelter of a rock and came slowly down to them —a man, long-legged and lank, with haggard, unshaven face and eyes that had hunger and dogged endurance looking out. He picked his way carefully with his feet, his eyes and the rifle fixed unswervingly at the two. Beatrice was too astonished to make a sound.

"What sort of a hold-up do you call this?" demanded Keith hotly, his hands itching to be down and busy. "We don't carry rolls of money around in the hills, you fool!"

"Oh, damn your money!" the man said roughly. "I've got money t' burn. I want t' trade horses with yuh. That roan, there, looks like a stayer. I'll take him."

"Well, seeing you seem to be head push here, I guess it's a trade," Keith answered. "But I'll thank you for my own saddle."

Beatrice, whose hands were up beside her ears, and not an inch higher, changed from amazed curiosity to concern. "Oh, you mustn't take Redcloud away from Mr. Cameron!" she protested. "You don't know-he's so fond of that horse! You may take mine; he's a good horse-he's a perfectly splendid horse, but I —I'm not so attached to him."

The fellow stopped and looked at her-not, however, forgetting Keith, who was growing restive. Beatrice's cheeks were very pink, and her eyes were bright and big and earnest. He could not look into them without letting some of the sternness drop out of his own.

"I wish you'd please take Rex —I'd rather trade than not," she coaxed. When Beatrice coaxed, mere man must yield or run. The fellow was but human, and he was not in a position to run, so he grinned and wavered.

"It's fair to say you'll get done," he remarked, his eyes upon the odd little dimple at the corner of her mouth, as if he had never seen anything quite so fetching.

"Your horse won't cr-buck, will he?" she ventured doubtfully. This was her first horse trade, and it behooved her to be cautious, even at the point of a rifle.

"Well, no," said the man laconically; "he won't. He's dead."

"Oh!" Beatrice gasped and blushed. She might have known, she thought, that the fellow would not take all this trouble if his horse was in a condition to buck. Then: "My elbows hurt. I —I think I should like to sit down."

"Sure," said the man politely. "Make yourself comfortable. I ain't used t' dealin' with ladies. But you got t' set still, yuh know, and not try any tricks. I can put up a mighty swift gun play when I need to-and your bein' a lady wouldn't cut no ice in a case uh that kind."

"Thank you." Beatrice sat down upon the nearest rock, folded her hands meekly and looked from him to Keith, who seethed to claim a good deal of the man's attention. She observed that, at a long breath from Keith, his captor was instantly alert.

"Maybe your elbows ache, too," he remarked dryly. "They'll git over it, though; I've knowed a man t' grab at the clouds upwards of an hour, an' no harm done."

"That's encouraging, I'm sure." Keith shifted to the other foot.

"How's that sorrel?" demanded the man. "Can he go?"

Keith hesitated a second.

"Indeed he can go!" put in Beatrice eagerly. "He's every bit as good as Redcloud."

"Is that sorrel yours?" The man's eyes shifted briefly to her face.

"No-o." Beatrice, thinking how she had meant to own him, blushed.

"That accounts for it." He laughed unpleasantly. "I wondered why you was so dead anxious t' have me take him."

The eyes of Beatrice snapped sparks at him, but her manner was demure, not to say meek. "He belongs to my brother," she explained, "and my brother has dozens of good saddle-horses. Mr. Cameron's horse is a pet. It's different when a horse follows you all over the place and fairly talks to you. He'll shake hands, and —"

"Uh-huh, I see the point, I guess. What d'yuh say, kid?"

Keith might seem boyish, but he did not enjoy being addressed as "kid." He was twenty-eight years old, whether he looked it or not.

"I say this: If you take my horse, I'll kill you. I'll have twenty-five cow-punchers camping on your trail before sundown. If you take this girl's horse, I'll do the same."

The man shut his lips in a thin line.

"No, he won't!" cried Beatrice, leaning forward. "Don't mind a thing he says! You can't expect a man to keep his temper with his hands up in the air like that. You take Rex, and I'll promise for Mr. Cameron."

"Trix-Miss Lansell!" —sternly.

"I promise you he won't do a thing," she went on firmly. "He-he isn't half as fierce, really, as-as he looks."

Keith's face got red.

The man laughed a little. Evidently the situation amused him, whether the others could see the humor of it or not. "So I'm to have your cayuse, eh?"

Keith saw two big tears tipping over her lower lids, and gritted his teeth.

"Well, it ain't often I git a chance t' please a lady," the fellow decided. "I guess Rex'll do, all right. Go over and change saddles, youngster-and don't git gay. I've got the drop, and yuh notice I'm keeping it."

"Are you going to take his saddle?" Beatrice stood up and clenched her hands, looking very much as if she would like to pull his hair. Keith in trouble appealed to her strangely.

"Sure thing. It's a peach, from the look of it. Mine's over the hill a piece. Step along there, kid! I want t' be movin'."

"You'll need to go some!" flared Keith, over his shoulder.

"I expect t' go some," retorted the man. "A fellow with three sheriff's posses campin' on his trail ain't apt t' loiter none."

"Oh!" Beatrice sat down and stared. "Then you must be —"

"Yep," the fellow laughed recklessly. "You ca, tell your maw yuh met up with Kelly, the darin' train-robber. I wouldn't be s'prised if she close herded yuh fer a spell till her scare wears off. Bu I've hung around these parts long enough. I fooled them sheriffs a-plenty, stayin' here. Gee! you'r' swift —I don't think!" This last sentence was directed at Keith, who was putting a snail to shame, and making it appear he was in a hurry.

"Git a move on!" commanded Kelly, threatening with his eyes.

Keith wisely made no reply-nor did he show any symptoms of haste, despite the menacing tone Slowly he pulled his saddle off Redcloud, and carefully he placed it upon the ground. When a fellow lives in his saddle, almost, he comes to think a great deal of it, and he is reluctant under any circumstances, to surrender it to another; to have a man deliberately confiscate it with the authority which lies in a lump of lead the size of a child thumb is not pleasant.

Through Keith's brain flashed a dozen impracticable plans, and one that offered a slender-very slender-chance of success. If he could get a little closer! He moved over beside Rex an unbuckling the cinch of Beatrice's saddle, pulled it sullenly off.

"Now, put your saddle on that there Rex horse, and cinch it tight!"

Keith picked up the saddle-his saddle, and threw it across Rex's back, raging inwardly at his helplessness. To lose his saddle worse, to let Beatrice lose her horse. Lord! a pretty figure he must cut in her eyes!

"Dry weather we're havin'," Kelly remarked politely to Beatrice; without, however, looking in her direction. "Prairie fires are gittin' t' be the regular thing, I notice."

Beatrice studied his face, and found no ulterior purpose for the words.

"Yes," she agreed, as pleasantly as she could, in view of the disquieting circumstances. "I helped fight a prairie-fire last week over this way. We were out all night."

"Prairie-fires is mean things t' handle, oncet they git started. I always hate t' see 'em git hold of the grass. What fire was that you mention?"

Beatrice glanced toward Keith, and was thankful his back was turned to her. But a quick suspicion had come to her, and she went steadily on with the subject.

"It was the Pine Ridge country. It started very mysteriously."

"It wasn't no mystery t' me." Kelly laughed grimly. "I started that there blaze myself acciden-tally. I throwed a cigarette down, thinkin' it had gone out. After a while I seen a blaze where I'd jest left, but I didn't have no license t' go back an' put it out-my orders was to git out uh that. I seen the sky all lit up that night. Kid, are yuh goin' t' sleep?"

Keith started. He had been listening, and thanking his lucky star that Beatrice was listening also. If she had suspected him of setting the range afire, she knew better now. A weight lifted off Keith's shoulders, and he stood a bit straighter; those chance words meant a great deal to him, and he felt that he would not grudge his saddle in payment. But Rex-that was another matter. Beatrice should not lose him if he could prevent it; still, what could he do?

He might turn and spring upon Kelly, but in the meantime Kelly would not be idle; he would probably be pumping bullets out of the rifle into Keith's body-and he would still have the horse. He stole a glance at Beatrice, and went hot all over at what he thought he read in her eyes. For once he was not glad to be near his Heart's Desire; he wished her elsewhere-anywhere but sitting on that rock, over there, with her little, gloved hands folded quietly in her lap, and that adorable, demure look on her face-the look which would have put her mother instantly upon the defensive-and a gleam in her eyes Keith read for scorn.

Surely he might do something! Barely six feet now separated him from Kelly. If one of those lumps of rock that strewed the ground was in his hand-he stooped to reach under Rex's body for the cinch, and could almost feel Kelly's eyes boring into his back. A false move-well, Keith had heard of Kelly a good many times; if this fellow was really the man he claimed to be, Keith did not need to guess what would follow a suspicious move; he knew. He looked stealthily toward him, and Kelly's eyes met his with a gleam sinister.

Kelly grinned. "I wouldn't, kid," he said softly.

Keith swore in a whisper, and his fingers closed upon the cinch. It was no use to fight the devil with cunning, he thought, bitterly.

Just then Beatrice gave an unearthly screech, that made the horses' knees bend under them. When Keith whirled to see what it was, she was standing upon the rock, with her skirts held tightly around her, like the pictures of women when a mouse gets into the room.

"Oh, Mr. Cameron! A sn-a-a-ke!"

Came a metallic br-r-r, the unmistakable war cry of the rattler. Into Kelly's eyes came a look of fear, and he sidled gingerly. The buzz had sounded unpleasantly close to his heels. For one brief instant the cold eye of his rifle regarded harmlessly the hillside. During that instant a goodly piece of sandstone whinged under his jaw, and he went down, with Keith upon him like a mountain lion. The latter snatched the rifle and got up hurriedly, for he had not forgotten the rattler. Kelly lay looking up at him in a dazed way that might have been funny at any other time.

"I wondered if you were good at grasping opportunities," said Beatrice. When he looked, there she was, sitting down on the rock, with her little, gloved hands folded in her lap, and that adorable demure look on her face; and a gleam in her eyes he knew was not scorn, though he could not rightly tell what it really did mean.

Keith wondered at her vaguely, but a man can't have his mind on a dozen things at once. It was important that he keep a sharp watch on Kelly, and his eyes were searching for a gleaming, gray spotted coil which he felt to be near.

"You needn't look, Mr. Cameron. There isn't any snake. It-it was I."

"You!" Keith's jaw dropped.

"Look out, Mr. Cameron. It wouldn't work a second time, I'm afraid."

Keith turned back before Kelly had more than got to his elbow; plainly Kelly was not feeling well just then. He looked unhappy, and rather sick.

"If you'll hand me the gun, Mr. Cameron, I think I can hold it steady while you fix the saddles. And then we'll go home. I —I don't think I really care to climb the hill."

What Keith wanted to do was to take her in his arms and kiss her till he was tired. What he did do was back toward her, and let her take the rifle quickly and deftly from his hands. She rested the gun upon her knee, and brought it to bear upon Mr. Kelly with a composure not assuring to that gentleman, and she tried to look as if she really and truly would shoot a man-and managed to look only the more kissable.

"Don't squirm, Mr. Kelly. I won't bite, if I do buzz sometimes."

Kelly stared at her meditatively a minute, and said: "Well, I'll be damned!"

Keith looked at her also, but he did not say anything.

The way he slapped his saddle back upon Redcloud and cinched it, and saddled Rex, was a pretty exhibition of precision and speed, learned in roundup camps. Kelly watched him grimly.

"I knowed you wasn't as swift as yuh knew how 't be, a while back," he commented. "I've got this t' say fur you two: You're a little the toughest proposition I ever run up ag'inst-and I've been up ag'inst it good and plenty."

"Thanks," Keith said cheerfully. "You'd better take Rex now and go ahead, Miss Lansell. I'll take that gun and look after this fellow. Get up, Kelly."

"What are you going to do with him?"

Kelly got unsteadily upon his feet. Beatrice looked at him, and then at Keith. She asked a question.

"March him home, and send him in to the nearest sheriff." Keith was businesslike, and his tone was crisp.

Beatrice's eyes turned again to Kelly. He did not whine, or beg, or even curse. He stood looking straight before him, at something only his memory could see, and in his face was weariness, and a deep loneliness, and a certain, grim despair. There was an ugly bruise where the rock had struck, but the rest of his face was drawn and white.

"If you do that," cried Beatrice, in a voice hardly more than a fierce whisper, "I shall hate you always. You are not a man-hunter. Let him stay here, and take his chance in the hills."

Keith was not a hard man to persuade into being merciful. "It's easy enough to say yes, Miss Lansell. I always was chicken-hearted when a fellow seemed down on his luck. You can stay here, Kelly—I don't want you, anyway." He laughed boyishly and irresponsibly, for he felt that Kelly had done him a service that day.

Beatrice flashed him a smile that went to his head and made him dizzy, and took up Rex's bridle rein. She hesitated, looked doubtfully at Kelly, who stood waiting stoically, and turned to her saddle. She untied a bundle and went quickly over to him.

"You—I don't want my lunch, after all. I'm going home now. I—I want you to take it, please. There are some sandwiches-with veal loaf, that Looey Sam makes deliciously-and some cake. I—I wish it was more. I know you'll like the veal loaf."

Kelly looked down at her, and God knows what thoughts were in his mind. He did not answer her with words; he just swallowed hard.

"Poor devil!" was what Keith said to himself, and the gun he was holding threatened, for a minute, to wing a cloud.

Beatrice laid the package in Kelly's unresisting hand, looked up into his averted face and said simply: "Good-by, Mr. Kelly."

After that she hurried Rex up the steep ridge much faster than she had gone down it, endangering his bones and putting herself very empty lunged.

At the top of the ridge Keith stopped and looked down.

"Hi, Kelly!"

Kelly showed that he heard.

"Here's your gun, on this rock. You can come up and get it, if you want to. And-say! I've got a few broke horses ranging down here somewhere. VN brand, on left shoulder. I won't scour the hills, very bad, if I should happen to miss a cayuse. So long!"

Kelly waved his hand for farewell.

# Chapter 13. Keith's Masterful Wooing

Keith faced toward home, with Redcloud following at his heels like a pet dog. For some reason, which he did not try to analyze, he was feeling light of heart-as though something very nice had happened to him. It might have been the unexpected clearing up of the mystery of the prairie-fire, though he was not dwelling particularly upon that. He was thinking a great deal more of Beatrice's blue-brown eyes, which had never been more baffling, so far as he knew. And his blood was still dancing with the smile she had given him; it hardly seemed possible that a girl could smile just like that and not mean anything.

When he reached the level, where she was waiting for him, he saw that she had her arms around the neck of her horse, and that she was crying dismally, heart-brokenly, with an abandon that took no thought of his presence. Keith had never seen a girl cry like that before. He had seen them dab at their eyes with their handkerchief, and smile the next breath-but this was different. For a minute he didn't quite know what to do; he could hear the blood hammering against his temples while he stood dumbly watching her. He went hesitatingly up, and laid a gloved hand deprecatingly upon her shoulder.

"Don't do that, Miss Lansell! The fellow isn't worth it. He's only living the life he chose for himself, and he doesn't mind, not half as much as you imagine. I know how you feel —I felt sorry for him myself-but he doesn't deserve it, you know." He stopped; not being able, just at the moment, to think of anything more to say about Kelly. Beatrice, who had not been thinking of Kelly at all, but remorsefully of a fellow she had persisted in misjudging, only cried the harder.

"Don't —don't cry like that! I —Miss Lansell-Trix-darling!" Keith's self-control snapped suddenly, like a rope when the strain becomes too great. He caught her fiercely in his arms, and crushed her close against him.

Beatrice stopped crying, and gasped.

"Trixie, if you must cry, I wish you'd cry for me. I'm about as miserable a man —I want you so! God made you for me, and I'm starving for the feel of your lips on mine." Then Keith, who was nothing if not daring, once he was roused, bent and kissed her without waiting to see if he might-and not only once, but several times.

Beatrice made a half-hearted attempt to get free of his arms, but Keith was not a fool-he held her closer, and laughed from pure, primitive joy.

"Mr. Cameron!" It was Beatrice's voice, but it had never been like that before.

"I think you might call me Keith," he cut in. "You've got to begin some time, and now is as good a time as any."

"You-you're taking a good deal for granted," she said, wriggling unavailingly in his arms.

"A man's got to, with a girl like you. You're so used to turning a fellow down I believe you'd do it just from habit."

"Indeed?" She was trying to be sarcastic and got kissed for her pains.

"Yes, 'indeed.'" He mimicked her tone. "I want you. I want you! I wanted you long before I ever saw you. And so I'm not taking any chances —I didn't dare, you see. I just had to take you first, and ask you afterward."

Beatrice laughed a little, with tears very close to her lashes, and gave up. What was the use of trying to resist this masterful fellow, who would not even give her a chance to refuse him? She did not know quite how to say no to a man who did not ask her to say yes. But the queer part, to her, was the feeling that she would have hated to say no, anyway. It never occurred to her, till afterward, that she might have stood upon a pedestal of offended dignity and cried, "Unhand me, villain!" —and that, if she had, Keith would undoubtedly have complied instantly. As it was, she just laughed softly, and blushed a good deal.

"I believe mama is right about you, after all," she said wickedly. "At heart, you're a bold highwayman."

"Maybe. I know I'd not stand and see some other fellow walk off with my Heart's Desire, without putting up a fight. It did look pretty blue for me, though, and I was afraid-but it's all right now, isn't it? Possession is nine points in law, they say, and I've got you now! I'm going to keep you, too. When are you going to come over and take charge of the Cross ranch?"

"Dear me!" said Beatrice, snuggling against his shoulder, and finding it the best place in the world to be. "I never said I was going to take charge at all!" Then the impulse of confession seized her. "Will you hate me, if I tell you something?"

"I expect I will," Keith assented, his eyes positively idolatrous. "What is it, girlie?"

"Well, I —it was Dick's fault; I never would have thought of such a thing if he hadn't goaded me into it-but-well, I was going to make you propose, on a wager —" The brown head of Beatrice went down out of sight, on his arm. "I was going to refuse you-and get Rex —"

"I know." Keith held her closer than ever. "Dick rode over and told me that day. And I wasn't going to give you a chance, missy. If you hadn't started to cry, here — Oh! what's the use? You didn't refuse me-and you're not going to, either, are you, girlie?"

Beatrice intimated that there was no immediate danger of such a thing happening.

"You see, Dick and I felt that you belonged to me, by rights. I fell in love with a picture of you, that you sent him-that one taken in your graduation gown-and I told Dick I was going to take the next train East, and carry you off by force, if I couldn't get you any other way. But Dick thought I'd stand a better show to wait till he'd coaxed you out here. We had it all fixed, that you'd come and find a prairie knight that was ready to fight for you, and he'd make you like him, whether you wanted to or not; and then he'd keep you here, and we'd all be happy ever after. And Dick would pull out of the Northern Pool-and of course you would-and we'd have a company of our own. Oh! we had some great castles built out here on the prairie, let me tell you! And then, when you finally came here, you had milord tagging along-and you thinking you were in love with him! Maybe you think I wasn't shaky, girlie! The air castles got awfully wobbly, and it looked like they were going to cave in on us. But I was bound to stay in the game if I could, and Dick did all he could to get you to looking my way-and it's all right, isn't it, Trixie?" Keith kept recurring to the ecstatic realization that it was all right.

Beatrice meditated for a minute.

"I never dreamed-Dick never even mentioned you in any of his letters," she said, in a rather dazed tone. "And when I came he made me believe you were a horrible flirt, and I never can resist the temptation to measure lances."

"And take a fall out of a male flirt," Keith supplemented. "Dick," he went on sententiously and slangily, "was dead onto his job." After that he helped her into the saddle, and they rode blissfully homeward.

Near the ranch they met Dick, who pulled up and eyed them anxiously at first, and then with a broad smile.

"Say, Trix," he queried slyly, "who does Rex belong to?"

Keith came to the rescue promptly, just as a brave knight should. "You," he retorted. "But I tell you right now, he won't very long. You're going to do the decent thing and give him to Trixie-for a wedding present."

Dick looked as though Trix was welcome to any thing he possessed.

"Before long, dear, we shall get on the great ship, and ride across the large, large ocean, and be at home. You will be delighted to see Peggy, and Rupert, and the dogs, won't you, dear?" Miss Hayes, her cheeks actually getting some color into them at the thought of going home, buttered a fluffy biscuit for her idol.

Dorman took two bites while he considered. "Rupert'll want my little wheels, for my feet, what Mr. Cam'ron gave me-but he can't have 'em, dough. I 'spect he'll be mad. I wonder what'll Peggy say bout my two puppies. I've got to take my two puppies wis me. Will dey get sick riding on de water, auntie? Say, will dey?"

"I —I think not, dear," ventured his auntie cautiously. His auntie was a conscientious woman, and she knew very little about puppies.

"Be'trice will help me take care of dem if dey're sick," he remarked comfortably.

Then something in his divinity's face startled his assurance. "You's going wis us, isn't you, Be'trice? I want you to help take care of my two puppies. Martha can't, 'cause she slaps dere ears. Is you going wis us, Be'trice?"

This, at the dinner table, was, to say the least, embarrassing-especially on this especial evening, when Beatrice was trying to muster courage to give Sir Redmond the only answer it was possible to give him now. It was an open secret that, in case she had accepted him, the home-going of Miss Hayes would be delayed a bit, when they would all go together. Beatrice had overheard her mother and Miss Hayes discussing this possibility only the day before. She undertook the impossible, and attempted to head Dorman off.

"Perhaps you'll see a whale, honey. The puppies never saw a whale, I'm sure. What do you suppose they'd think?"

"Is you going?"

"You'd have to hold them up high, you know, so they could see, and show them just where to look, and —"

"Is you going, Be'trice?"

Beatrice sent a quick, despairing glance around the table. Four pairs of eyes were fixed upon her with varying degrees of interest and anxiety. The fifth pair-Dick's —were trying to hide their unrighteous glee by glaring down at the chicken wing on his plate. Beatrice felt a strong impulse to throw something at him. She gulped and faced the inevitable. It must come some time, she thought, and it might as well be now-though it did seem a pity to spoil a good dinner for every one but Dick, who was eating his with relish.

"No, honey" —her voice was clear and had the note of finality —"I'm not going-ever."

Sir Redmond's teeth went together with a click, and he picked up the pepper shaker mechanically and peppered his salad until it was perfectly black, and Beatrice wondered how he ever expected to eat it. Mrs. Lansell dropped her fork on the floor, and had to have a clean one brought. Miss Hayes sent a frightened glance at her brother. Dick sat and ate fried chicken.

"Why, Be'trice? I wants you to-and de puppies'll need you-and auntie, and —" Dorman gathered himself for the last, crushing argument —"and Uncle Redmon' wants you awf'lly!"

Beatrice took a sip of ice water, for she needed it.

"Why, Be'trice? Gran-mama'll let you go, guess. Can't she go, gran'mama?"

It was Mrs. Lansell's turn to test the exquisite torture of that prickly chill along the spine. Like Beatrice, she dodged.

"Little boys," she announced weakly, "should not speak until they're spoken to."

Dick came near strangling on a shred of chicken.

"Can't she go, gran'mama? Say, can't she? Tell Be'trice to go home wis us, gran'mama!"

"Beatrice" —Mrs. Lansell swallowed —"is not a little child any longer, Dorman. She is a woman and can do as she likes. I" —she was speaking to the whole group —"I can only advise her."

Dorman gave a squeal of triumph. "See? You can go, Be'trice! Gran'mama says you can go. You will go, won't you, Be'trice? Say yes!"

"No!" said Beatrice, with desperate emphasis. "I won't."

"I want-Be'trice-to go-o!" Dorman slid down upon his shoulder blades, gave a squeal which was not triumph, but temper, and kicked the table till every dish on it danced.

"Dorman sit up!" commanded his auntie. "Dorman, stop, this instant! I'm ashamed of you; where is my good little man? Redmond."

Sir Redmond seemed glad of the chance to do something besides sit quietly in his place and look calm. He got up deliberately, and in two minutes, or less, Dorman was in the woodshed with him, making sounds that frightened his puppies dreadfully and put the coyotes to shame.

Beatrice left the table hurriedly to escape the angry eyes of her mother. The sounds in the woodshed had died to a subdued sniffling, and she retreated to the front porch, hoping to escape observation. There she nearly ran against Sir Redmond, who was staring off into the dusk to where the moon was peering redly over a black pinnacle of the Bear Paws.

She would have slipped back into the house, but he did not give her the chance. He turned and faced her steadily, as he had more than once faced the Boers, when he knew that before him was nothing but defeat.

"So you're not going to England ever?"

Pride had squeezed every shade of emotion from his voice.

"No." Beatrice gripped her fingers together tightly.

"Are you sure you won't be sorry-afterward?"

"Yes, I'm sure." Beatrice had never done anything she hated more.

Sir Redmond, looking into her eyes, wondered why those much-vaunted sharpshooters, the Boers, had blundered and passed him by.

"I don't suppose it matters much now-but will you tell me why? I believed you would decide differently." He was holding his voice down to a dead level, and it was not easy.

"Because —" Beatrice faced the moon, which threw a soft glow upon her face, and into her wonderful, deep eyes a golden light. "Oh, I'm sorry, Sir Redmond! But you see, I didn't know. I —I just learned to-day what it means to-to love. I —I am going to stay here. A new company- is about to be formed, Sir Redmond. The Maltese Cross and the-Triangle Bar-are going to cast their lot together." The golden glow deepened and darkened, and blended with the red blood which flushed cheek and brow and throat.

It took Sir Redmond a full minute to comprehend. When he did, he breathed deep, shut his lips upon words that would have frightened her, and went down the steps into the gloom.

Beatrice watched him stride away into the dusky silence, and her heart ached with sympathy for him. Then she looked beyond, to where the lights of the Cross ranch twinkled joyously, far down the coulee, and the sweet egotism of happiness enfolded her, shutting him out. After that she forgot him utterly. She looked up at the moon, sailing off to meet the stars, smiled good-fellowship and then went in to face her mother.

# Lonesome Land

## Chapter I. The Arrival of Val

In northern Montana there lies a great, lonely stretch of prairie land, gashed deep where flows the Missouri. Indeed, there are many such-big, impassive, impressive in their very loneliness, in summer given over to the winds and the meadow larks and to the shadows fleeing always over the hilltops. Wild range cattle feed there and grow sleek and fat for the fall shipping of beef. At night the coyotes yap quaveringly and prowl abroad after the long-eared jack rabbits, which bounce away at their hunger-driven approach. In winter it is not good to be there; even the beasts shrink then from the bleak, level reaches, and shun the still bleaker heights.

But men will live anywhere if by so doing there is money to be gained, and so a town snuggled up against the northern rim of the bench land, where the bleakness was softened a bit by the sheltering hills, and a willow-fringed creek with wild rosebushes and chokecherries made a vivid green background for the meager huddle of little, unpainted buildings.

To the passengers on the through trains which watered at the red tank near the creek, the place looked crudely picturesque-interesting, so long as one was not compelled to live there and could retain a perfectly impersonal viewpoint. After five or ten minutes spent hi watching curiously the one little street, with the long hitching poles planted firmly and frequently down both sides-usually within a very few steps of a saloon door-and the horses nodding and stamping at the flies, and the loitering figures that appeared now and then in desultory fashion, many of them imagined that they understood the West and sympathized with it, and appreciated its bigness and its freedom from conventions.

One slim young woman had just told the thin-faced school teacher on a vacation, with whom she had formed one of those evanescent traveling acquaintances, that she already knew the West, from instinct and from Manley's letters. She loved it, she said, because Manley loved it, and because it was to be her home, and because it was so big and so free. Out here one could think and grow and really live, she declared, with enthusiasm. Manley had lived here for three years, and his letters, she told the thin-faced teacher, were an education in themselves.

The teacher had already learned that the slim young woman, with the yellow-brown hair and yellow-brown eyes to match, was going to marry Manley-she had forgotten his other name, though the young woman had mentioned it-and would live on a ranch, a cattle ranch. She smiled with somewhat wistful sympathy, and hoped the young woman would be happy; and the young woman waved her hand, with the glove only half pulled on, toward the shadow-dappled prairie and the willow-fringed creek, and the hills beyond.

"Happy!" she echoed joyously. "Could one be anything else, in such a country? And then-you don't know Manley, you see. It's horribly bad form, and undignified and all that, to prate of one's private affairs, but I just can't help bubbling over. I'm not looking for heaven, and I expect to have plenty of bumpy places in the trail-trail is anything that you travel over, out here; Manley has coached me faithfully-but I'm going to be happy. My mind is quite made up. Well, good-by —I'm so glad you happened to be on this train, and I wish I might meet you again. Isn't it a funny little depot? Oh, yes-thank you! I almost forgot that umbrella, and I might need it. Yes, I'll write to you —I should hate to drop out of your mind completely. Address me Mrs. Manley Fleetwood, Hope, Montana. Good-by —I wish —"

She trailed off down the aisle with eyes shining, in the wake of the grinning porter. She hurried down the steps, glanced hastily along the platform, up at the car window where the faded little school teacher was smiling wearily down at her, waved her hand, threw a dainty little kiss, nodded a gay farewell, smiled vaguely at the conductor, who had been respectfully pleasant to her-and then she was looking at the rear platform of the receding train mechanically, not yet quite realizing why it was that her heart went heavy so suddenly. She turned then and looked about her in a surprised, inquiring fashion. Manley, it would seem, was not at hand to welcome her. She had expected his face to be the first she looked upon in that town, but she tried not to be greatly perturbed at his absence; so many things may detain one.

At that moment a young fellow, whose clothes emphatically proclaimed him a cowboy, came diffidently up to her, tilted his hat backward an inch or so, and left it that way, thereby unconsciously giving himself an air of candor which should have been reassuring.

"Fleetwood was detained. You were expecting to-you're the lady he was expecting, aren't you?"

She had been looking questioningly at her violin box and two trunks standing on their ends farther down the platform, and she smiled vaguely without glancing at him.

"Yes. I hope he isn't sick, or —"

"I'll take you over to the hotel, and go tell him you're here," he volunteered, somewhat curtly, and picked up her bag.

"Oh, thank you." This time her eyes grazed his face inattentively. She followed him down the rough steps of planking and up an extremely dusty road-one could scarcely call it a street-to an uninviting building with crooked windows and a high, false front of unpainted boards.

The young fellow opened a sagging door, let her pass into a narrow hallway, and from there into a stuffy, hopelessly conventional fifth-rate parlor, handed her the bag, and departed with another tilt of the hat which placed it at a different angle. The sentence meant for farewell she did not catch, for she was staring at a wooden-faced portrait upon an easel, the portrait of a man with a drooping mustache, and porky cheeks, and dead-looking eyes.

"And I expected bearskin rugs, and antlers on the walls, and big fireplaces!" she remarked aloud, and sighed. Then she turned and pulled aside a coarse curtain of dusty, machine-made lace, and looked after her guide. He was just disappearing into a saloon across the street, and she dropped the curtain precipitately, as if she were ashamed of spying. "Oh, well—I've heard all cowboys are more or less intemperate," she excused, again aloud.

She sat down upon an atrocious red plush chair, and wrinkled her nose spitefully at the porky-cheeked portrait. "I suppose you're the proprietor," she accused, "or else the proprietor's son. I wish you wouldn't squint like that. If I have to stop here longer than ten minutes, I shall certainly turn you face to the wall." Whereupon, with another grimace, she turned her back upon it and looked out of the window. Then she stood up impatiently, looked at her watch, and sat down again upon the red plush chair.

"He didn't tell me whether Manley is sick," she said suddenly, with some resentment. "He was awfully abrupt in his manner. Oh, you—" She rose, picked up an old newspaper from the marble-topped table with uncertain legs, and spread it ungently over the portrait upon the easel. Then she went to the window and looked out again. "I feel perfectly sure that cowboy went and got drunk immediately," she complained, drumming pettishly upon the glass. "And I don't suppose he told Manley at all."

The cowboy was innocent of the charge, however, and he was doing his energetic best to tell Manley. He had gone straight through the saloon and into the small room behind, where a man lay sprawled upon a bed in one corner. He was asleep, and his clothes were wrinkled as if he had lain there long. His head rested upon his folded arms, and he was snoring loudly. The young fellow went up and took him roughly by the shoulder.

"Here! I thought I told you to straighten up," he cried disgustedly. "Come alive! The train's come and gone, and your girl's waiting for you over to the hotel. D' you hear?"

"Uh-huh!" The man opened one eye, grunted, and closed it again.

The other yanked him half off the bed, and swore. This brought both eyes open, glassy with whisky and sleep. He sat wobbling upon the edge of the bed, staring stupidly.

"Can't you get anything through you?" his tormentor exclaimed. "You want your girl to find out you're drunk? You got the license in your pocket. You're supposed to get spliced this evening-and look at you!" He turned and went out to the bartender.

"Why didn't you pour that coffee into him, like I told you?" he demanded. "We've got to get him steady on his pins *somehow!*"

The bartender was sprawled half over the bar, apathetically reading the sporting news of a torn Sunday edition of an Eastern paper. He looked up from under his eyebrows and grunted.

"How you going to pour coffee down a man that lays flat on his belly and won't open his mouth?" he inquired, in an injured tone. "Sleep's all he needs, anyway. He'll be all right by morning."

The other snorted dissent. "He'll be all right by dark-or he'll feel a whole lot worse," he promised grimly. "Dig up some ice. And a good jolt of bromo, if you've got it-and a towel or two."

The bartender wearily pushed the paper to one side, reached languidly under the bar, and laid hold of a round blue bottle. Yawning uninterestedly, he poured a double portion of the white crystals into a glass, half filled another under the faucet of the water cooler, and held them out.

"Dump that into him, then," he advised. "It'll help some, if you get it down. What's the sweat to get him married off to-day? Won't the girl wait?"

"I never asked her. You pound up some ice and bring it in, will you?" The volunteer nurse kicked open the door into the little room and went in, hastily pouring the bromo seltzer from one glass to the other to keep it from foaming out of all bounds. His patient was still sitting upon the edge of the bed where he had left him, slumped forward with his head in his hands. He looked up stupidly, his eyes bloodshot and swollen of lid.

"'S the train come in yet?" he asked thickly. "'S you, is it, Kent?"

"The train's come, and your girl is waiting for you at the hotel. Here, throw this into you-and for God's sake, brace up! You make me tired. Drink her down quick-the foam's good for you. Here, you take the stuff in the bottom, too. Got it? Take off your coat, so I can get at you. You don't look much like getting married, and that's no josh."

Fleetwood shook his head with drunken gravity, and groaned. "I ought to be killed. Drunk to-day!" He sagged forward again, and seemed disposed to shed tears. "She'll never forgive me; she —"

Kent jerked him to his feet peremptorily. "Aw, look here! I'm trying to sober you up. You've got to do your part-see? Here's some ice in a towel-you get it on your head. Open up your shirt, so I can bathe your chest. Don't do any good to blubber around about it. Your girl can't hear you, and Jim and I ain't sympathetic. Set down in this chair, where we can get at you." He enforced his command with some vigor, and Fleetwood groaned again. But he shed no more tears, and he grew momentarily more lucid, as the treatment took effect.

The tears were being shed in the stuffy little hotel parlor. The young woman looked often at her watch, went into the hallway, and opened the outer door several times, meditating a search of the town, and drew back always with a timid fluttering of heart because it was all so crude and strange, and the saloons so numerous and terrifying in their very bald simplicity.

She was worried about Manley, and she wished that cowboy would come out of the saloon and bring her lover to her. She had never dreamed of being treated in this way. No one came near her-and she had secretly expected to cause something of a flutter in this little town they called Hope.

Surely, young girls from the East, come out to get married to their sweethearts, weren't so numerous that they should be ignored. If there were other people in the hotel, they did not manifest their presence, save by disquieting noises muffled by intervening partitions.

She grew thirsty, but she hesitated to explore the depths of this dreary abode, in fear of worse horrors than the parlor furniture, and all the places of refreshment which she could see from the window or the door looked terribly masculine and unmoral, and as if they did not know there existed such things as ice cream, or soda, or sherbet.

It was after an hour of this that the tears came, which is saying a good deal for her courage. It seemed to her then that Manley must be dead. What else could keep him so long away from her, after three years of impassioned longing written twice a week with punctilious regularity?

He knew that she was coming. She had telegraphed from St. Paul, and had received a joyful reply, lavishly expressed in seventeen words instead of the ten-word limit. And they were to have been married immediately upon her arrival.

That cowboy had known she was coming; he must also have known why Manley did not meet her, and she wished futilely that she had questioned him, instead of walking beside him without a word. He should have explained. He would have explained if he had not been so very anxious to get inside that saloon and get drunk.

She had always heard that cowboys were chivalrous, and brave, and fascinating in their picturesque dare-deviltry, but from the lone specimen which she had met she could not see that they possessed any of those qualities. If all cowboys were like that, she hoped that she would not be compelled to meet any of them. And *why* didn't Manley come?

It was then that an inner door—a door which she had wanted to open, but had lacked courage-squeaked upon its hinges, and an ill-kept bundle of hair was thrust in, topping a weather-beaten face and a scrawny little body. Two faded, inquisitive eyes looked her over, and the woman sidled in, somewhat abashed, but too curious to remain outside.

"Oh yes!" She seemed to be answering some inner question. "I didn't know you was here." She went over and removed the newspaper from the portrait. "That breed girl of mine ain't got the least idea of how to straighten up a room," she observed complainingly. "I guess she thinks this picture was made to hang things on. I'll have to round her up again and tell her a few things. This is my first husband. He was in politics and got beat, and so he killed himself. He couldn't stand to have folks give him the laugh." She spoke with pride. "He was a real handsome man, don't you think? You mighta took off the paper; it didn't belong there, and he does brighten up the room. A good picture is real company, seems to me. When my old man gets on the rampage till I can't stand it no longer, I come in here and set, and look at Walt. 'T ain't every man that's got nerve to kill himself-with a shotgun. It was turrible! He took and tied a string to the trigger —"

"Oh, please!"

The landlady stopped short and stared at her. "What? Oh, I won't go into details-it was awful messy, and that's a fact. I didn't git over it for a couple of months. He coulda killed himself with a six-shooter; it's always been a mystery why he dug up that old shotgun, but he did. I always thought he wanted to show his nerve." She sighed, and drew her fingers across her eyes. "I don't s'pose I ever will git over it," she added complacently. "It was a turrible shock."

"Do you know," the girl began desperately, "if Mr. Manley Fleetwood is in town? I expected him to meet me at the train."

"Oh! I kinda *thought* you was Man Fleetwood's girl. My name's Hawley. You going to be married to-night, ain't you?"

"I —I haven't seen Mr. Fleetwood yet," hesitated the girl, and her eyes filled again with tears. "I'm afraid something may have happened to him. He —"

Mrs. Hawley glimpsed the tears, and instantly became motherly in her manner. She even went up and patted the girl on the shoulder.

"There, now, don't you worry none. Man's all right; I seen him at dinner time. He was —" She stopped short, looked keenly at the delicate face, and at the yellow-brown eyes which gazed back at her, innocent of evil, trusting, wistful. "He spoke about your coming, and said he'd want the use of the parlor this evening, for the wedding. I had an idea you was coming on the six-twenty train. Maybe he thought so, too. I never heard you come in —I was busy frying doughnuts in the kitchen-and I just happened to come in here after something. You'd oughta rapped on that door. Then I'd 'a' known you was here. I'll go and have my old man hunt him up. He must be around town somewheres. Like as not he'll meet the six-twenty, expecting you to be on it."

She smiled reassuringly as she turned to the inner door.

"You take off your hat and jacket, and pretty soon I'll show you up to a room. I'll have to round up my old man first-and that's liable to take time." She turned her eyes quizzically to the porky-cheeked portrait. "You jest let Walt keep you company till I get back. He was real good company when he was livin'."

She smiled again and went out briskly, came back, and stood with her hand upon the cracked doorknob.

"I clean forgot your name," she hinted. "Man told me, at dinner time, but I'm no good on earth at remembering names till after I've seen the person it belongs to."

"Valeria Peyson-Val, they call me usually, at home." The homesickness of the girl shone in her misty eyes, haunted her voice. Mrs. Hawley read it, and spoke more briskly than she would otherwise have done.

"Well, we're plumb strangers, but we ain't going to stay that way, because every time you come to town you'll have to stop here; there ain't any other place to stop. And I'm going to start right in calling you Val. We don't use no ceremony with folk's names, out here. Val's a real nice name, short and easy to say. Mine's Arline. You can call me by it if you want to. I don't let everybody-so many wants to cut it down to Leen, and I won't stand for that; I'm *lean* enough, without havin' it throwed up to me. We might jest as well start in the way we're likely to keep it up, and you won't feel so much like a stranger.

"I'm awful glad you're going to settle here-there ain't so awful many women in the country; we have to rake and scrape to git enough for three sets when we have a dance-and more likely we can't make out more 'n two. D' you dance? Somebody said they seen a fiddle box down to the depot, with a couple of big trunks; d' you play the fiddle?"

"A little," Valeria smiled faintly.

"Well, that'll come in awful handy at dances. We'd have 'em real often in the winter if it wasn't such a job to git music. Well, I got too much to do to be standin' here talkin'. I have to keep right after that breed girl all the time, or she won't do nothing. I'll git my old man after your fellow right away. Jest make yourself to home, and anything you want ask for it in the kitchen." She smiled in friendly fashion and closed the door with a little slam to make sure that it latched.

Valeria stood for a moment with her hands hanging straight at her sides, staring absently at the door. Then she glanced at Walt, staring wooden-faced from his gilt frame upon his gilt easel, and shivered. She pushed the red plush chair as far away from him as possible, sat down with her back to the picture, and immediately felt his dull, black eyes boring into her back.

"What a fool I must be!" she said aloud, glancing reluctantly over her shoulder at the portrait. She got up resolutely, placed the chair where it had stood before, and stared deliberately at Walt, as if she would prove how little she cared. But in a moment more she was crying dismally.

## Chapter II. Well-Meant Advice

Kent Burnett, bearing over his arm a coat newly pressed in the Delmonico restaurant, dodged in at the back door of the saloon, threw the coat down upon the tousled bed, and pushed back his hat with a gesture of relief at an onerous duty well performed.

"I had one hell of a time," he announced plaintively, "and that Chink will likely try to poison me if I eat over there, after this-but I got her ironed, all right. Get into it, Man, and chase yourself over there to the hotel. Got a clean collar? That one's all-over coffee."

Fleetwood stifled a groan, reached into a trousers pocket, and brought up a dollar. "Get me one at the store, will you, Kent? Fifteen and a half-and a tie, if they've got any that's decent. And hurry! Such a triple-three-star fool as I am ought to be taken out and shot."

He went on cursing himself audibly and bitterly, even after Kent had hurried out. He was sober now-was Manley Fleetwood-sober and self-condemnatory and penitent. His head ached splittingly; his eyes were heavy-lidded and bloodshot, and his hands trembled so that he could scarcely button his coat. But he was sober. He did not even carry the odor of whisky upon his breath or his person; for Kent had been very thoughtful and very thorough. He had compelled his patient to crunch and swallow many nauseous tablets of "whisky killer," and he had sprinkled his clothes liberally with Jockey Club; Fleetwood, therefore, while he emanated odors in plenty, carried about him none of the aroma properly belonging to intoxication.

In ten minutes Kent was back, with a celluloid collar and two ties of questionable taste. Manley just glanced at them, waved them away with gloomy finality, and swore.

"They're just about the limit, and that's no dream," sympathized Kent, "but they're clean, and they don't look like they'd been slept in for a month. You've got to put 'em on-by George, I sized up the layout in both those imitation stores, and I drew the highest in the deck. And for the Lord's sake, get a move on. Here, I'll button it for you."

Behind Fleetwood's back, when collar and tie were in place, Kent grinned and lowered an eyelid at Jim, who put his head in from the saloon to see how far the sobering had progressed.

"You look fine!" he encouraged heartily. "That green-and-blue tie's just what you need to set you off. And the collar sure is shiny and nice-your girl will be plumb dazzled. She won't see anything wrong-believe *me*. Now, run along and get married. Here, you better sneak out the back way; if she happened to be looking out, she'd likely wonder what you were doing, coming out of a saloon. Duck out past the coal shed and cut into the street by Brinberg's. Tell her you're sick-got a sick headache. Your looks'll swear it's the truth. Hike!" He opened the door and pushed Fleetwood out, watched him out of sight around the corner of Brinberg's store, and turned back into the close-smelling little room.

"Do you know," he remarked to Jim, "I never thought of it before, but I've been playing a low-down trick on that poor girl. I kinda wish now I'd put her next, and given her a chance to draw outa the game if she wanted to. It's stacking the deck on her, if you ask *me*!" He pushed his hat back upon his head, gave his shoulders a twist of dissatisfaction, and told Jim to dig up some Eastern beer; drank it meditatively, and set down the glass with some force.

"Yes, sir," he said disgustedly, "darn my fool soul, I stacked the deck on that girl-and she looked to be real nice. Kinda innocent and trusting, like she hasn't found out yet how rotten mean men critters can be." He took the bottle and poured himself another glass. "She's sure due to wise up a lot," he added grimly.

"You bet your sweet life!" Jim agreed, and then he reconsidered. "Still, I dunno; Man ain't so worse. He ain't what you can call a real booze fighter. This here's what I'd call an accidental jag; got it in the exuberance of the joyful moment when he knew his girl was coming. He'll likely straighten up and be all right. He —" Jim broke off there and looked to see who had opened the door.

"Hello, Polly," he greeted carelessly.

The man came forward, grinning skinnily. Polycarp Jenks was the outrageous name of him. He was under the average height, and he was lean to the point of emaciation. His mouth was absolutely curveless —a straight gash across his face; a gash which simply stopped short without any tapering or any turn at the corners, when it had reached as far as was decent. His nose was also straight and high, and owned no perceptible slope; indeed, it seemed merely a pendant attached to his forehead, and its upper termination was indefinite, except that somewhere between his eyebrows one felt impelled to consider it forehead rather than nose. His eyes also were rather long and narrow, like buttonholes cut to match the mouth. When he grinned his face appeared to break up into splinters.

He was intensely proud of his name, and his pleasure was almost pathetic when one pronounced it without curtailment in his presence. His skinniness was also a matter of pride. And when you realize that he was an indefatigable gossip, and seemed always to be riding at large, gathering or imparting trivial news, you should know fairly well Polycarp Jenks.

"I see Man Fleetwood's might' near sober enough to git married," Polycarp began, coming up to the two and leaning a sharp elbow upon the bar beside Kent. "By granny, gitting married'd sober anybody! Dinner time he was so drunk he couldn't find his mouth. I met him up here a little ways just now, and he was so sober he remembered to pay me that ten I lent him t' other day —*he-he!* Open up a bottle of pop, James.

"His girl's been might' near crying her eyes out, 'cause he didn't show up. Mis' Hawley says she looked like she was due at a funeral 'stid of a weddin'. 'Clined to be stuck up, accordin' to Mis' Hawley-shied at hearin' about Walt —*he-he!* I'll bet there ain't been a transient to that hotel in the last five year, man or woman, that ain't had to hear about Walt and the shotgun-Pop's all right on a hot day, you bet!

"She's got two trunks and a fiddle over to the depot-don't see how 'n the world Man's going to git 'em out to the ranch; they're might' near as big as claim shacks, both of 'em. Time she gits 'em into Man's shack she'll have to go outside every time she wants to turn around —*he-he!* By granny-two trunks, to one woman! Have some pop, Kenneth, on me.

"The boys are talkin' about a shivaree t'-night. On the quiet, y' know. Some of 'em's workin' on a horse fiddle now, over in the lumber yard. Wanted me to play a coal-oil can, but I dunno. I'm gittin' a leetle old for sech doings. Keeps you up nights too much. Man had any sense, he'd marry and pull outa town. 'Bout fifteen or twenty in the bunch, and a string of cans and irons to reach clean across the street. By granny, I'm going to plug m' ears good with cotton when it comes off —*he-he!* 'Nother bottle of pop, James."

"Who's running the show, Polycarp?" Kent asked, accepting the glass of soda because he disliked to offend. "Funny I didn't hear about it."

Polycarp twisted his slit of a mouth knowingly, and closed one slit of an eye to assist the facial elucidation.

"Ain't funny-not when I tell you Fred De Garmo's handing out the *in*vites, and he sure aims to have plenty of excitement —*he-he!* Betcher Manley won't be able to set on the wagon seat an' hold the lines t'-morrow-not if he comes out when he's called and does the thing proper — *he-he!* An' if he don't show up, they aim to jest about pull the old shebang down over his ears. Hope'll think it's the day of judgment, sure —*he-he!* Reckon I might's well git in on the fun-they won't be no sleepin' within ten mile of the place, nohow, and a feller always sees the joke better when he's lendin' a hand. Too bad you an' Fred's on the outs, Kenneth."

"Oh, I don't know-it suits me fine," Kent declared easily, setting down his glass with a sigh of relief; he hated "pop."

"What's it all about, anyway?" quizzed Polycarp, hungering for the details which had thus far been denied him. "De Garmo sees red whenever anybody mentions your name, Kenneth-but I never did hear no particulars."

"No?" Kent was turning toward the door. "Well, you see, Fred claims he can holler louder than I can, and I say he can't." He opened the door and calmly departed, leaving Polycarp looking exceedingly foolish and a bit angry.

Straight to the hotel, without any pretense at disguising his destination, marched Kent. He went into the office-which was really a saloon-invited Hawley to drink with him, and then wondered audibly if he could beg some pie from Mrs. Hawley.

"Supper'll be ready in a few minutes," Hawley informed him, glancing up at the round, dust-covered clock screwed to the wall.

"I don't want supper—I want pie," Kent retorted, and opened a door which led into the hallway. He went down the narrow passage to another door, opened it without ceremony, and was assailed by the odor of many things-the odor which spoke plainly of supper, or some other assortment of food. No one was in sight, so he entered the dining room boldly, stepped to another door, tapped very lightly upon it, and went in. By this somewhat roundabout method he invaded the parlor.

Manley Fleetwood was lying upon an extremely uncomfortable couch, of the kind which is called a sofa. He had a lace-edged handkerchief folded upon his brow, and upon his face was an expression of conscious unworthiness which struck Kent as being extremely humorous. He grinned understandingly and Manley flushed-also understandingly. Valeria hastily released Manley's hand and looked very prim and a bit haughty, as she regarded the intruder from the red plush chair, pulled close to the couch.

"Mr. Fleetwood's head is very bad yet," she informed Kent coldly. "I really do not think he ought to see-anybody."

Kent tapped his hat gently against his leg and faced her unflinchingly, quite unconscious of the fact that she regarded him as a dissolute, drunken cowboy with whom Manley ought not to associate.

"That's too bad." His eyes failed to drop guiltily before hers, but continued to regard her calmly. "I'm only going to stay a minute. I came to tell you that there's a scheme to raise-to 'shivaree' you two, tonight. I thought you might want to pull out, along about dark."

Manley looked up at him inquiringly with the eye which was not covered by the lace-edged handkerchief. Valeria seemed startled, just at first. Then she gave Kent a little shock of surprise.

"I have read about such things. A *charivari*, even out here in this uncivilized section of the country, can hardly be dangerous. I really do not think we care to run away, thank you." Her lip curled unmistakably. "Mr. Fleetwood is suffering from a sick headache. He needs rest-not a cowardly night ride."

Naturally Kent admired the spirit she showed, in spite of that eloquent lip, the scorn of which seemed aimed directly at him. But he still faced her steadily.

"Sure. But if I had a headache-like that—I'd certainly burn the earth getting outa town to-night. *Shivarees*"—he stuck stubbornly to his own way of saying it—"are bad for the head. They aren't what you could call silent-not out here in this uncivilized section of the country. They're plumb—" He hesitated for just a fraction of a second, and his resentment of her tone melted into a twinkle of the eyes. "They've got fifty coal-oil cans strung with irons on a rope, and there'll be about ninety-five six-shooters popping, and eight or ten horse-fiddles, and they'll all be yelling to beat four of a kind. They're going," he said quite gravely, "to play the full orchestra. And I don't believe," he added ironically, "it's going to help Mr. Fleetwood's head any."

Valeria looked at him doubtingly with steady, amber-colored eyes before she turned solicitously to readjust the lace-edged handkerchief. Kent seized the opportunity to stare fixedly at Fleetwood and jerk his head meaningly backward, but when, warned by Manley's changing expression, she glanced suspiciously over her shoulder, Kent was standing quietly by the door with his hat in his hand, gazing absently at Walt in his gilt-edged frame upon the gilt easel, and waiting, evidently, for their decision.

"I shall tell them that Mr. Fleetwood is sick-that he has a horrible headache, and mustn't be disturbed."

Kent forgot himself so far as to cough slightly behind his hand. Valeria's eyes sparkled.

"Even out here," she went on cuttingly, "there must be some men who are gentlemen!"

Kent refrained from looking at her, but the blood crept darkly into his tanned cheeks. Evidently she "had it in for him," but he could not see why. He wondered swiftly if she blamed him for Manley's condition.

Fleetwood suddenly sat up, spilling the handkerchief to the floor. When Valeria essayed to push him back he put her hand gently away. He rose and came over to Kent.

"Is this straight goods?" he demanded. "Why don't you stop it?"

"Fred De Garmo's running this show. My influence wouldn't go as far —"

Fleetwood turned to the girl, and his manner was masterful. "I'm going out with Kent-oh, Val, this is Mr. Burnett. Kent, Miss Peyson. I forgot you two aren't acquainted."

From Valeria's manner, they were in no danger of becoming friends. Her acknowledgment was barely perceptible. Kent bowed stiffly.

"I'm going to see about this, Val," continued Fleetwood. "Oh, my head's better —a lot better, really. Maybe we'd better leave town —"

"If your head is better, I don't see why we need run away from a lot of silly noise," Valeria interposed, with merciless logic. "They'll think we're awful cowards."

"Well, I'll try and find out —I won't be gone a minute, dear." After that word, spoken before another, he appeared to be in great haste, and pushed Kent rather unceremoniously through the door. In the dining room, Kent diplomatically included the landlady in the conference, by a gesture of much mystery bringing her in from the kitchen, where she had been curiously peeping out at them.

"Got to let her in," he whispered to Manley, "to keep her face closed."

They murmured together for five minutes. Kent seemed to meet with some opposition from Fleetwood-an aftermath of Valeria's objections to flight-and became brutally direct.

"Go ahead-do as you please," he said roughly. "But you know that bunch. You'll have to show up, and you'll have to set 'em up, and-aw, thunder! By morning you'll be plumb laid out. You'll be headed into one of your four-day jags, and you know it. I was thinking of the girl-but if you don't care, I guess it's none of my funeral. Go to it-but darned if I'd want to start my honeymoon out like that!"

Fleetwood weakened, but still he hesitated. "If I didn't show up —" he began hopefully. But Kent wittered him with a look.

"That bunch will be two-thirds full before they start out. If you don't show up, they'll go up and haul you outa bed-hell, Man! You'd likely start in to kill somebody off. Fred De Garmo don't love you much better than he loves me. You know what him and his friends would do then, I should think." He stopped, and seemed to consider briefly a plan, but shook his head over it. "I could round up a bunch and stand 'em off, maybe-but we'd be shooting each other up, first rattle of the box. It's a whole lot easier for you to get outa town."

"I'll tell somebody you got the bridal chamber," hissed Arline, in a very loud whisper. "That's number two, in front. I can keep a light going and pass back 'n' forth once in a while, to look like you're there. That'll fool 'em good. They'll wait till the light's been out quite a while before they start in. You go ahead and git married at seven, jest as you was going to-and if Kent'll have the team ready somewheres, I can easy sneak you out the back way."

"I couldn't get the team out of town without giving the whole deal away," Kent objected. "You'll have to go horseback.".

"Val can't ride," Fleetwood stated, as if that settled the matter.

"Damn it, she's got to ride!" snapped Kent, losing patience. "Unless you want to stay and go on a toot that'll last a week, most likely."

"Val belongs to the W.C.T.U.," shrugged Fleetwood. "She'd never —"

"Well, it's that or have a fight on your hands you maybe can't handle. I don't see any sense in haggling about going, now you know what to expect. But, of course," he added, with some acrimony, "it's your own business. I don't know what the dickens I'm getting all worked up over it for. Suit yourself." He turned toward the door.

"She could ride my Mollie-and I got a sidesaddle hanging up in the coal shed. She could use that, or a stock saddle, either one," planned Mrs. Hawley anxiously. "You better pull out, Man."

"Hold on, Kent! Don't rush off-we'll go," Fleetwood surrendered. "Val won't like it, but I'll explain as well as I can, without-Say! you stay and see us married, won't you? It's at seven, and —"

Kent's fingers curled around the doorknob. "No, thanks. Weddings and funerals are two bunches of trouble I always ride 'way around. Time enough when you've got to be *it*. Along about nine o'clock you try and get out to the stockyards without letting the whole town see you go, and I'll have the horses there; just beyond the wings, by that pile of ties. You know the place. I'll wait there till ten, and not a minute longer. That'll give you an hour, and you won't need any more time than that if you get down to business. You find out from her what saddle she wants, and you can tell me while I'm eating supper, Mrs. Hawley. I'll 'tend to the rest." He did not wait to hear whether they agreed to the plan, but went moodily down the narrow passage, and entered frowningly the "office." Several men were gathered there, waiting the supper summons. Hawley glanced up from wiping a glass, and grinned.

"Well, did you git the pie?"

"Naw. She said I'd got to wait for mealtime. She plumb chased me out."

Fred De Garmo, sprawled in an armchair and smoking a cigar, lazily fanned the smoke cloud from before his face and looked at Kent attentively.

## Chapter III. A Lady in a Temper

To saddle two horses when the night has grown black and to lead them, unobserved, so short a distance as two hundred yards or so seems a simple thing; and for two healthy young people with full use of their wits and their legs to steal quietly away to where those horses are waiting would seem quite as simple. At the same time, to prevent the successful accomplishment of these things is not difficult, if one but fully understands the designs of the fugitives.

Hawley Hotel did a flourishing business that night. The two long tables in the dining room, usually not more than half filled by those who hungered and were not over-nice concerning the food they ate, were twice filled to overflowing. Mrs. Hawley and the "breed" girl held hasty consultations in the kitchen over the supply, and never was there such a rattling of dishes hurriedly cleansed for the next comer.

Kent managed to find a chair at the first table, and eyed the landlady unobtrusively. But Fred De Garmo sat down opposite, and his eyes were bright and watchful, so that there seemed no possible way of delivering a message undetected-until, indeed, Mrs. Hawley in desperation resorted to strategy, and urged Kent unnecessarily to take another slice of bacon.

"Have some more-it's *side!*" she hissed in his ear, and watched anxiously his face.

"All right," said Kent, and speared a slice with his fork, although his plate was already well supplied with bacon. Then, glancing up, he detected Fred in a thoughtful stare which seemed evenly divided between the landlady and himself. Kent was conscious of a passing, mental discomfort, which he put aside as foolish, because De Garmo could not possibly know what Mrs. Hawley meant. To ease his mind still further he glared insolently at Fred, and then at Polycarp Jenks *te-hee*ing a few chairs away. After that he finished as quickly as possible without exciting remark, and went his way.

He had not, however, been two minutes in the office before De Garmo entered. From that time on through the whole evening Fred was never far distant; wherever he went, Kent could not shake him off though De Garmo never seemed to pay any attention to him, and his presence was always apparently accidental.

"I reckon I'll have to lick that son of a gun yet," sighed Kent, when a glance at the round clock in the hotel office told him that in just twenty minutes it would strike nine; and not a move made toward getting those horses saddled and out to the stockyards.

There was much talk of the wedding, which had taken place quietly in the parlor at the appointed hour, but not a man mentioned a *charivari*. There were many who wished openly that Fleetwood would come out and be sociable about it, but not a hint that they intended to take measures to bring him among them. He had caused a box of cigars to be placed upon the bar of every saloon in town, where men might help themselves at his expense. Evidently he had considered that with the cigars his social obligations were canceled. They smoked the cigars, and, with the same breath, gossiped of him and his affairs.

At just fourteen minutes to nine Kent went out, and, without any attempt at concealment, hurried to the Hawley stables. Half a minute behind him trailed De Garmo, also without subterfuge.

Half an hour later the bridal couple stole away from the rear of the hotel, and, keeping to the shadows, went stumbling over the uneven ground to the stockyards.

"Here's the tie pile," Fleetwood announced, in an undertone, when they reached the place. "You stay here, Val, and I'll look farther along the fence; maybe the horses are down there."

Valeria did not reply, but stood very straight and dignified in the shadow of the huge pile of rotting railroad ties. He was gone but a moment, and came anxiously back to her.

"They're not here," he said, in a low voice. "Don't worry, dear. He'll come —I know Kent Burnett."

"Are you sure?" queried Val sweetly. "From what I have seen of the gentleman, your high estimate of him seems quite unauthorized. Aside from escorting me to the hotel, he has been anything but reliable. Instead of telling you that I was here, or telling me that you were sick, he went straight into a saloon and forgot all about us both. You know that. If he were your friend, why should he immediately begin carousing, instead of —"

"He didn't," Fleetwood defended weakly.

"No? Then perhaps you can explain his behavior. Why didn't he tell me you were sick? Why didn't he tell you I came on that train? Can you tell me that, Manley?"

Manley, for a very good reason, could not; so he put his arms around her and tried to coax her into good humor.

"Sweetheart, let's not quarrel so soon-why, we're only two hours married! I want you to be happy, and if you'll only be brave and —"

"Brave!" Mrs. Fleetwood laughed rather contemptuously, for a bride. "Please to understand, Manley, that I'm not frightened in the least. It's you and that horrid cowboy —*I* don't see why we need run away, like criminals. Those men don't intend to *murder* us, do they?" Her mood softened a little, and she squeezed his arm between her hands. "You dear old silly, I'm not blaming *you*. With your head in such a state, you can't think things out properly, and you let that cowboy influence you against your better judgment. You're afraid I might be annoyed-but, really, Manley, this silly idea of running away annoys me much more than all the noise those fellows could possibly make. Indeed, I don't think I would mind-it would give me a glimpse of the real West; and, perhaps, if they grew too boisterous, and I spoke to them and asked them not to be quite so rough-and, really, they only mean it as a sort of welcome, in their crude way. We could invite some of the nicest in to have cake and coffee-or maybe we might get some ice cream somewhere-and it might turn out a very pleasant little affair. I don't mind meeting them, Manley. The worst of them can't be as bad as that-but, of course, if he's your friend, I suppose I oughtn't to speak too freely my opinion of him!"

Fleetwood held her closely, patted her cheek absently, and tried to think of some effective argument.

"They'll be drunk, sweetheart," he told her, after a silence.

"I don't think so," she returned firmly. "I have been watching the street all the evening. I saw any number of men passing back and forth, and I didn't see one who staggered. And they were all very quiet, considering their rough ways, which one must expect. Why, Manley, you always wrote about these Western men being such fine fellows, and so generous and big-hearted, under their rough exterior. Your letters were full of it-and how chivalrous they all are toward nice women."

She laid her head coaxingly against his shoulder. "Let's go back, Manley. I —*want* to see a *charivari*, dear. It will be fun. I want to write all about it to the girls. They'll be perfectly wild with envy." She struggled with her conventional upbringing. "And even if some of them are slightly under the influence-of liquor, we needn't *meet* them. You needn't introduce those at all, and I'm sure they will understand."

"Don't be silly, Val!" Fleetwood did not mean to be rude, but a faint glimmer of her romantic viewpoint —a viewpoint gained chiefly from current fiction and the stage-came to him and contrasted rather brutally with the reality. He did not know how to make her understand, without incriminating himself. His letters had been rather idealistic, he admitted to himself. They had been written unthinkingly, because he wanted her to like this big land; naturally he had not been too baldly truthful in picturing the place and the people. He had passed lightly over their faults and thrown the limelight on their virtues; and so he had aided unwittingly the stage and the fiction she had read, in giving her a false impression.

Offended at his words and his tone, she drew away from him and glanced wistfully back toward the town, as if she meditated a haughty return to the hotel. She ended by seating herself upon a projecting tie.

"Oh, very well, my lord," she retorted, "I shall try and not be silly, but merely idiotic, as you would have me. You and your friend!" She was very angry, but she was perfectly well-bred, she hoped. "If I might venture a word," she began again ironically, "it seems to me that your friend has been playing a practical joke upon you. He evidently has no intention of bringing any fleet steeds to us. No doubt he is at this moment laughing with his dissolute companions, because we are sitting out here in the dark like two silly chickens!"

"I think he's coming now," Manley said rather stiffly. "Of course, I don't ask you to like him; but he's putting himself to a good deal of trouble for us, and —"

"Wasted effort, so far as I am concerned," Valeria put in, with a chirpy accent which was exasperating, even to a bridegroom very much in love with his bride.

In the darkness that muffled the land, save where the yellow flare of lamps in the little town made a misty brightness, came the click of shod hoofs. Another moment and a man, mounted upon a white horse, loomed indistinct before them, seeming to take substance from the night. Behind him trailed another horse, and for the first time in her life Valeria heard the soft, whispering creak of saddle leather, the faint clank of spur chains, and the whir of a horse mouthing the "cricket" in his bit. Even in her anger, she was conscious of an answering tingle of blood, because this was life in the raw-life such as she had dreamed of in the tight swaddlings of a smug civilization, and had longed for intensely.

Kent swung down close beside them, his form indistinct but purposeful. "I'm late, I guess," he remarked, turning to Fleetwood. "Fred got next, somehow, and —I was detained."

"Where is he?" asked Manley, going up and laying a questioning hand upon the horse, by that means fully recognizing it as Kent's own.

"In the oats box," said Kent laconically. He turned to the girl. "I couldn't get the sidesaddle," he explained apologetically. "I looked where Mrs. Hawley said it was, but I couldn't find it-and I didn't have much time. You'll have to ride a stock saddle."

Valeria drew back a step. "You mean —a man's saddle?" Her voice was carefully polite.

"Why, yes." And he added: "The horse is dead gentle-and a sidesaddle's no good, anyhow. You'll like this better." He spoke, as was evident, purely from a man's viewpoint.

That viewpoint Mrs. Fleetwood refused to share. "Oh, I couldn't ride a man's saddle," she protested, still politely, and one could imagine how her lips were pursed. "Indeed, I'm not sure that I care to leave town at all." To her the declaration did not seem unreasonable or abrupt but she felt that Kent was very much shocked. She saw him turn his head and look back toward the town, as if he half expected a pursuit.

"I don't reckon the oats box will hold Fred very long," he observed meditatively. He added reminiscently to Manley: "I had a deuce of a time getting the cover down and fastened."

"I'm very sorry," said Valeria, with sweet dignity, "that you gave yourself so much trouble —"

"I'm kinda sorry myself," Kent agreed mildly, and Valeria blushed hotly, and was glad he could not see.

"Come, Val-you can ride this saddle, all right. All the girls out here —"

"I did not come West to imitate all the girls. Indeed, I could never think of such a thing. I couldn't possibly-really, Manley! And, you know, it does seem so childish of us to run away —"

Kent moved restlessly, and felt to see if the cinch was tight.

Fleetwood took her coaxingly by the arm. "Come, sweetheart, don't be stubborn. You know —"

"Well, really! If it's a question of obstinacy-You see, I look at the matter in this way: You believe that you are doing what is best for my sake; I don't agree with you-and it does seem as if I should be permitted to judge what I desire." Then her dignity and her sweet calm went down before a flash of real, unpolished temper. "You two can take those nasty horses and ride clear to Dakota, if you want to. I'm going back to the hotel. And I'm going to tell somebody to let that poor fellow out of that box. I think you're acting perfectly horrid, both of you, when I don't want to go!" She actually started back toward the scattered points of light.

She did not, however, get so faraway that she failed to hear Kent's "Well, I'll be damned!" uttered in a tone of intense disgust.

"I don't care," she assured herself, because of the thrill of compunction caused by that one forcible sentence. She had never before in her life heard a man really swear. It affected her very much as would the accidental touch of an electric battery. She walked on slowly, stumbling a little and trying to hear what it was they were saying.

Then Kent passed her, loping back to the town, the led horse shaking his saddle so that it rattled the stirrups like castanets as he galloped. "I don't care," she told herself again very emphatically, because she was quite sure that she did care-or that she would care if only she permitted herself to be so foolish. Manley overtook her then, and drew her hand under his arm to lead her. But he seemed quite sullen, and would not say a word all the way back.

# Chapter IV. The "Shivaree"

Kent jerked open the stable door, led in his horses, turned them into their stalls, and removed the saddles with quick, nervous movements which told plainly how angry he was.

"I'll get myself all excited trying to do her a favor again —I don't think!" he growled in the ear of Michael, his gray gelding. "Think of me getting let down on my face like that! By a woman!"

He felt along the wall in the intense darkness until his fingers touched a lantern, took it down from the nail where it hung, and lighted it. He carried it farther down the rude passage between the stalls, hung it high upon another nail, and turned to the great oats box, from within which came a vigorous thumping and the sound of muttered cursing.

Kent was not in the mood to see the humor of anything in particular. Had he known anything about Pandora's box he might have drawn a comparison very neatly while he stood scowling down at the oats box, for certainly he was likely to release trouble in plenty when he unfastened that lid. He felt of the gun swinging at his hip, just to assure himself that it was there and ready for business in case Fred wanted to shoot, and rapped with his knuckles upon the box, producing instant silence within.

"Don't make so much noise in there," he advised grimly, "not unless you want the whole town to know where you are, and have 'em give you the laugh. And, listen here: I ain't apologizing for what I done, but, all the same, I'm sorry I did it. It wasn't any use. I'd rather be shut up in an oats box all night than get let down like I was-and I'm telling you this so as to start us off even. If you want to fight about it when you come out, all right; you're the doctor. But I'm just as sorry as you are it happened. I lay down my hand right here. I hope you shivaree Man and his wife-and shivaree 'em good. I hope you bust the town wide open."

"Why this sudden change of heart?" came muffled from within.

"Ah-that's my own business. Well, I don't like you a little bit, and you know it; but I'll tell you, just to give you a fair show. I wanted to keep Man sober, and I tried to get him and his wife out of town before that shivaree of yours was pulled off. But the lady wouldn't have it that way. I got let right down on my face, and I'm done. Now you know just where I stand. Maybe I'm a fool for telling you, but I seem to be in the business to-night. Come on out."

He unfastened the big iron hasp, which was showing signs of the strain put upon it, and stepped back watchfully. The thick, oaken lid was pushed up, and Fred De Garmo, rather dusty and disheveled and purple from the close atmosphere of the box and from anger as well, came up like a jack-in-the-box and glared at Kent. When he had stepped out upon the stable floor, however, he smiled rather unpleasantly.

"If you've told the truth," he said maliciously, "I guess the lady has pretty near evened things up. If you haven't —if I don't find them both at the hotel-well-Anyway," he added, with an ominous inflection, "there'll be other days to settle this in!"

"Why, sure. Help yourself, Fred," Kent retorted cheerfully, and stood where he was until Fred had gone out. Then he turned and closed the box. "Between that yellow-eyed dame and the chump that went and left this box wide open for me to tip Fred into," he soliloquized, while he took down the lantern, and so sent the shadows dancing weirdly about him, "I've got a bunch of trouble mixed up, for fair. I wish the son of a gun would fight it out now, and be done with it; but no, that ain't Fred. He'd a heap rather wait and let it draw interest!"

Over in the hotel the "yellow-eyed dame" was doing her unsophisticated best to meet the situation gracefully, and to realize certain vague and rather romantic dreams of her life out West. She meant to be very gracious, for one thing, and to win the chivalrous friendship of every man who came to participate in the rude congratulations that had been planned. Just how she meant to do this she did not know-except that the graciousness would certainly prove a very important factor.

"I'm going to remain downstairs," she told Manley, when they reached the hotel. It was the first sentence she had spoken since he overtook her. "I'm so glad, dear," she added diplomatically, "that you decided to stay. I want to see that funny landlady now, please, and get her to serve coffee and cake to our guests in the parlor. I wish I might have had one of my trunks brought over here; I should like to wear a pretty gown." She glanced down at her tailored suit with true feminine dissatisfaction. "But everything was so-so confused, with your being late, and sick-is your head better, dear?"

Manley, in very few words, assured her that it was. Manley was struggling with his inner self, trying to answer one very important question, and to answer it truthfully: Could he meet "the boys," do his part among them, and still remain sober? That seemed to be the only course open to him now, and he knew himself just well enough to doubt his own strength. But if Kent would help him-He felt an immediate necessity to find Kent.

"You'll find Mrs. Hawley somewhere around," he said hurriedly. "I've got to see Kent—"

"Oh, Manley! Don't have anything to do with that horrid cowboy! He's not-nice. He-he swore, when he must have known I could hear him; and he was swearing about *me*, Manley. Didn't you hear him?" She stood in the doorway and clung to his arm.

"No," lied Manley. "You must have been mistaken, sweetheart."

"Oh, I wasn't; I heard him quite plainly." She must have thought it a terrible thing, for she almost whispered the last words, and she released him with much reluctance. It seemed to her that Manley was in danger of falling among low associates, and that she must protect him in spite of himself. It failed to occur to her that Manley had been exposed to that danger for three years, without any protection whatever.

She was thankful, when he came to her later in the parlor, to learn from him that he had not held any speech with Kent. That was some comfort-and she felt that she needed a little comforting, just then. Her consultation with Arline had been rather unsatisfactory. Arline had told her bluntly that "the bunch" didn't want any coffee and cake. Whisky and cigars, said Arline, without so much as a blush, was what appealed to them fellows. If Manley handed it out liberal enough, they wouldn't bother his bride. Very likely, Arline had assured her, she wouldn't see one of them. That, on the whole, had been rather discouraging. How was she to show herself a gracious lady, forsooth, if no one came near her? But she kept these things jealously tucked away in the remotest corner of her own mind, and managed to look the relief she did not feel.

And, after all, the *charivari*, as is apt to be the case when the plans are laid so carefully, proved a very tame affair. Valeria, sitting rather dismally in the parlor with Mrs. Hawley for company, at midnight heard a banging of tin cans somewhere outside, a fitful popping of six-shooters, and an abortive attempt at a procession coming up the street. But the lines seemed to waver and then break utterly at the first saloon, where drink was to be had for the asking and Manley Fleetwood was pledged to pay, and the rattle of cans was all but drowned in the shouts of laughter and talk which came from the "office," across the hall. For where is the pleasure or the profit in *charivaring* a bridal couple which stays up and waits quite openly for the clamor?

"Is it always so noisy here at night?" asked Valeria faintly when Mrs. Hawley had insisted upon her lying down upon the uncomfortable sofa.

"Well, no-unless a round-up pulls in, or there's a dance, or it's Christmas, or something. It's liable to keep up till two or three o'clock, so the sooner you git used to it, the better off you'll be. I'm going to leave you here, and go to bed-unless you want to go upstairs yourself. Only it'll be noisier than ever up in your room, for it's right over the office, and the way sound travels up is something fierce. Don't you be afraid —I'll lock this door, and if your husband wants to come in he can come through the dining room." She looked at Valeria and hesitated before she spoke the next sentence. "And don't you worry a bit over him, neither. My old man was in the kitchen a minute ago, when I was out there, and he says Man ain't drinking a drop to-night. He's keeping as straight as —"

Valeria sat up suddenly, quite scandalized. "Oh-why, of course Manley wouldn't drink with them! Why-who ever heard of such a thing? The idea!" She stared reproachfully at her hostess.

"Oh, sure! I didn't say such a thing was liable to happen. I just thought you might be-worrying-they're making so much racket in there," stammered Arline.

"Indeed, no. I'm not at all worried, thank you. And please don't let me keep you up any longer, Mrs. Hawley. I am quite comfortable-mentally and physically, I assure you. Good night."

Not even Mrs. Hawley could remain after that. She went out and closed the door carefully behind her, without even finding voice enough to return Valeria's sweetly modulated good night.

"She's got a whole lot to learn," she relieved her feelings somewhat by muttering as she mounted the stairs.

What it cost Manley Fleetwood to abstain absolutely and without even the compromise of "soft" drinks that night, who can say? Three years of free living in Montana had lowered his standard of morality without giving him that rugged strength of mind which makes a man master of himself first of all. He had that day lain, drunken and sleeping, when he should have been at his mental and physical best to meet the girl who would marry him. It was that very defection, perhaps, which kept him sober in the midst of his taunting fellows. Now that Valeria was actually here, and was his wife, he was possessed by the desire to make some sacrifice by which he might prove his penitence. At any cost he would spare her pain and humiliation, he told himself.

He did it, and he did it under difficulty. He was denied the moral support of Kent Burnett, for Kent was sulking over his slight, and would have nothing to say to him. He was jeered unmercifully by Fred De Garmo and his crowd. He was "baptized" by some drunken reveler, so that the stench of spilled whisky filled his nostrils and tortured him the night through. He was urged, he was bullied, he was ridiculed. His head throbbed, his eyeballs burned. But through it all he stayed among them because he feared that if he left them and went to Val, some drunken fool might follow him and shock her with his inebriety. He stayed, and he stayed sober. Val was his wife. She trusted him, and she was ignorant of his sins. If he went to her staggering and babbling incoherent foolishness, he knew it would break her heart.

When the sky was at last showing faint dawn tints and the clamor had worn itself out perforce-because even the leaders were, after all, but men, and there was a limit to their endurance-Manley entered the parlor, haggard enough, it is true, and bearing with him the stale odor of cigars long since smoked, and of the baptism of bad whisky, but also with the air of conscious rectitude which sits so comically upon a man unused to the feeling of virtue.

As is so often the case when one fights alone the good fight and manages to win, he was chagrined to find himself immediately put upon the defensive. Val, as she speedily demonstrated, declined to look upon him as a hero, or as being particularly virtuous. She considered herself rather neglected and abused. She believed that he had stayed away because he was angry with her on account of her refusal to leave town, and she thought that was rather brutal of him. Also, her head ached from tears and lack of sleep, and she hated the town, the hotel-almost she hated Manley himself.

Manley felt the rebuff of her chilling silence when he came in, and when she twitched herself loose from his embrace he came near regretting his extreme virtue. He spent ten minutes trying to explain, without telling all of the truth, and he felt his good opinion of himself slipping from him before her inexorable disfavor.

"Well, I don't blame you for not liking the town, Val," he said at last, rather desperately. "But you mustn't judge the whole country by it. You'll like the ranch, dear. You'll feel as if you were in another world —"

"I hope so," Val interrupted quellingly.

"We'll drive out there just as soon as we have breakfast." He laid his hand diffidently upon her tumbled hair. "I *had* to stay out there with those fellows. I didn't want to —"

"I don't want any breakfast," said Val, getting up and going over to the window-it would seem to avoid his caress. "The odor of that dining room is enough to make one fast forever." She lifted the grimy lace curtain with her finger tips and looked disconsolately out upon the street. "It's just a dirty, squalid little hamlet. I don't suppose the streets have been cleaned or the garbage removed from the back yards since the place was first-founded." She laughed shortly at the idea of "founding" a wretched village like that, but she had no other word at hand.

"*Arline*," she remarked, in a tone of drawling recklessness. "Arline swears. Did you know it? I suppose, of course, you do. She said something that struck me as being shockingly true. She said I'm 'sure having a hell of a honeymoon.'" Then she bit her lips hard, because her eyelids were stinging with the tears she refused to shed in his presence.

"Oh, Val!" From the sofa Manley stared contritely at her back. She must feel terrible, he thought, to bring herself to repeat that sentence-Val, so icily pure in her thoughts and her speech.

Val was blinking her tawny eyes-like the eyes of a lion in color-at the street. Not for the world would she let him see that she wanted to cry! A figure, blurred to indistinctness, appealed in a doorway nearly opposite, stood for a moment looking up at the reddened sky, and came across the street. As the tears were beaten back she saw and recognized him, with a curl of the lip.

"Here comes your cowboy friend-from a saloon, of course." Her voice was lazily contemptuous. "Only his presence in the street was needed to complete the picture of desolation. He has been in a fight, judging from his face. It is all bruised and skinned, and one eye is swollen-ugh! My guide, my adviser-is it possible, Manley, that you couldn't find a *nice* man to meet me at the train?" She turned from the disagreeable sight of Kent and faced her husband. "Are all the men like that? And are all the women like-Arline?"

Manley looked at her dumbly from the sofa. Would Val ever come to understand the place, and the people, he was wondering.

She laughed suddenly. "I'm beginning to feel very sorry for Walt," she said irrelevantly, pointing to the easel and the expressionless crayon portrait staring out from the gilt frame. "He has to stay in this room always. And I believe another two hours would drive me hopelessly insane." The word caught her attention. "Hope!" she laughed ironically. "What imbecile ever thought of hope in the same breath with this place? What they really ought to do is paint that 'Abandon-hope' admonition across the whole front of the depot!"

Manley, because he had lifted his head too suddenly and so sent white-hot irons of pain clashing through his brain, turned sullen. "If you hate it as bad as all that," he said, "why, there'll be a train for the East in about two hours."

Val stiffened perceptibly, though the petulance in her face changed to something wistful. "Do you mean-do you want me to go?" she asked very calmly.

Manley pressed his fingers hard against his temples. "You know I don't. I want you to stay and like the country, and be happy. But-the way you have been talking makes it seem —a-ah!" He dropped his tortured head upon his hands and did not trouble to finish what he had intended to say. Nervous strain, lack of sleep, and a headache to begin with, were taking heavy toll of him. He could not argue with her; he could not do anything except wish he were dead, or that his head would stop aching.

Val took one of her unexpected changes of mood. She went up and laid her cold fingers lightly upon his temples, where she could see the blood beating savagely in the swollen veins. "What a little beast I am!" she murmured contritely. "Shall I get you some coffee, dear? Or some headache tablets, or-You know a cold cloth helped you last evening. Lie down for a little while. There's no hurry about starting, is there? I —I don't hate the place so awfully, Manley. I'm just cross because I couldn't sleep for the noise. Here's a cushion, dear. I think it's stuffed with scrap iron, for there doesn't seem to be anything soft about it except the invitation to 'slumber sweetly,' in red and green silk; but anything is better than the head of that sofa in its natural state."

She arranged the cushion to her own liking, if not to his, and when it was done she bent down impulsively and kissed him on the cheek, blushing vividly the while.

"I won't be nasty and cross any more," she promised. "Now, I'm going to interview Arline. I hear dishes rattling somewhere; perhaps I can get a cup of real coffee for you." At the door she shook her finger at him playfully. "Don't you dare stir off that sofa while I'm gone," she admonished. "And, remember, we're not going to leave town until your head stops aching-not if we stay here a week!"

She insisted upon bringing him coffee and toast upon a tray —a battered old tray, purloined for that purpose from the saloon, if she had only known it-and she informed him, with a pretty, domestic pride, that she had made the toast herself.

"Arline was going to lay slices of bread on top of the stove," she explained. "She said she always makes toast that way, and no one could tell the difference! I never heard of such a thing-did you, Manley? But I've been attending a cooking school ever since you left Fern Hill. I didn't tell you —I wanted it for a surprise. I could have done better with the toast before a wood fire —I think poor Arline was nearly distracted at the way I poked coals down from the grate; but she didn't say anything. Isn't it funny, to have cream in cans! I don't suppose it ever saw a cow-do you? The coffee's pretty bad, isn't it? But wait until we get home! I can make lovely coffee-if you'll get me a percolator. You will, won't you? And I learned now to make the most delicious fruit salad, just before I left. A cousin of Mrs. Forman's taught me how. Could you drink another cup, dear?"

Manley could not, and she deplored the poor quality, although she generously absolved Arline from blame, because there seemed so much to do in that kitchen. She refused to take any breakfast herself, telling him gayly that the odor in the kitchen was both food and drink.

Because he understood a little of her loathing for the place, Manley lied heroically about his headache, so that within an hour they were leaving town, with the two great trunks roped securely to the buckboard behind the seat, and with Val's suitcase placed flat in the front, where she could rest her feet upon it. Val was so happy at the prospect of getting away from the town that she actually threw a kiss in the direction of Arline, standing with her frowsy head, her dough-spotted apron, and her tired face in the parlor door.

Her mood changed immediately, however, for she had no more than turned from waving her hand at Arline, when they met Kent, riding slowly up the street with his hat tilted over the eye most swollen. Without a doubt he had seen her waving and smiling, and so he must have observed the instant cooling of her manner. He nodded to Manley and lifted his hat while he looked at her full; and Val, in the arrogant pride of virtuous young womanhood, let her golden-brown eyes dwell impersonally upon his face; let her white, round chin dip half an inch downward, and then looked past him as if he were a post by the roadside. Afterwards she smiled maliciously when she saw, with a swift, sidelong glance, how he scowled and spurred unnecessarily his gray gelding.

# Chapter V. Cold Spring Ranch

For almost three years the letters from Manley had been headed "Cold Spring Ranch." For quite as long Val had possessed a mental picture of the place —a picture of a gurgly little brook with rocks and watercress and distracting little pools the size of a bathtub, and with a great, frowning boulder —a cliff, almost-at the head. The brook bubbled out and formed a basin in the shadow of the rock. Around it grew trees, unnamed in the picture, it is true, but trees, nevertheless. Below the spring stood a picturesque little cottage. A shack, Manley had written, was but a synonym for a small cottage, and Val had many small cottages in mind, from which she sketched one into her picture. The sun shone on it, and the western breezes flapped white curtains in the windows, and there was a porch where she would swing her hammock and gaze out over the great, beautiful country, fascinating in its very immensity.

Somewhere beyond the cottage —"shack," she usually corrected herself-were the corrals; they were as yet rather impressionistic; high, round, mysterious inclosures forming an effective, if somewhat hazy, background to the picture. She left them to work out their attractive details upon closer acquaintance, for at most they were merely the background. The front yard, however, she dwelt upon, and made aglow with sturdy, bright-hued flowers. Manley had that spring planted sweet peas, and poppies, and pansies, and other things, he wrote her, and they had come up very nicely. Afterward, in a postscript, he answered her oft-repeated questions about the flower garden:

The flowers aren't doing as well as they might. They need your tender care. I don't have much time to pet them along. The onions are doing pretty well, but they need weeding badly.

In spite of that, the flowers bloomed luxuriantly in her mental picture, though she conscientiously remembered that they weren't doing as well as they might. They were weedy and unkempt, she supposed, but a little time and care would remedy that; and was she not coming to be the mistress of all this, and to make everything beautiful? Besides, the spring, and the brook which ran from it, and the trees which shaded it, were the chief attractions.

Perhaps she betrayed a lack of domesticity because she had not been able to "see" the interior of the cottage —"shack" —very clearly. Sunny rooms, white curtains, bright cushions and books, pictures and rugs mingled together rather confusingly in her mind when she dwelt upon the inside of her future home. It would be bright, and cozy, and "homy," she knew. She would love it because it would be hers and Manley's, and she could do with it what she would. She bothered about that no more than she did about the dresses she would be wearing next year.

Cold Spring Ranch! Think of the allurement of that name, just as it stands, without any disconcerting qualification whatever! Any girl with yellow-brown hair and yellow-brown eyes to match, and a dreamy temperament that beautifies everything her imagination touches, would be sure to build a veritable Eve's garden around those three small words.

With that picture still before her mental vision, clear as if she had all her life been familiar with it in reality, she rode beside Manley for three weary hours, across a wide, wide prairie which looked perfectly level when you viewed it as a whole, but which proved all hills and hollows when you drove over it. During those three hours they passed not one human habitation after the first five miles were behind them. There had been a ranch, back there against a reddish-yellow bluff. Val had gazed upon it, and then turned her head away, distressed because human beings could consent to live in such unattractive surroundings. It was bad in its way as Hope, she thought, but did not say, because Manley was talking about his cattle, and she did not want to interrupt him.

After that there had been no houses of any sort. There was a barbed-wire fence stretching away and away until the posts were mere pencil lines against the blue, where the fence dipped over the last hill before the sky bent down and kissed the earth.

The length of that fence was appalling in a vague, wordless way, Val unconsciously drew closer to her husband when she looked at it, and shivered in spite of the midsummer heat.

"You're getting tired." Manley put his arm around her and held her there.

"We're over half-way now. A little longer and we'll be home." Then he bethought him that she might want some preparation for that home-coming. "You mustn't expect much, little wife. It's a bachelor's house, so far. You'll have to do some fixing before it will suit you. You don't look forward to anything like Fern Hill, do you?"

Val laughed, and bent solicitously over the suitcase, which her feet had marred. "Of course I don't. Nothing out here is like Fern Hill. I know our ranch is different from anything I ever knew-but I know just how it will be, and how everything will look."

"Oh! Do you?" Manley looked at her a bit anxiously.

"For three years," Val reminded him, "you have been describing things to me. You told me what it was like when you first took the place. You described everything, from Cold Spring Coulee to the house you built, and the spring under the rock wall, and even the meadow lark's nest you found in the weeds. Of *course* I know."

"It's going to seem pretty rough, at first," he observed rather apologetically.

"Yes-but I shall not mind that. I want it to be rough. I'm tired to death of the smug smooth-ness of my life so far. Oh, if you only knew how I have hated Fern Hill, these last three years, especially since I graduated. Just the same petty little lives lived in the same petty little way, day in and day out. Every Sunday the class in Sunday school, and the bells ringing and the same little walk of four blocks there and back. Every Tuesday and Friday the club meeting-the Merry Maids, and the Mascot, both just alike, where you did the same things. And the same round of calls with mamma, on the same people, twice a month the year round. And the little social festivities-ah, Manley, if you only knew how I tong for something rough and real in my life!" It was very nearly what she said to the tired-faced teacher on the train.

"Well, if that's what you want, you've come to the right place," he told her dryly.

Later, when they drew close to a red coulee rim which he said was the far side of Cold Spring Coulee, she forgot how tired she was, and felt every nerve quiver with eagerness.

Later still, when in the glare of a July sun they drove around a low knoll, dipped into a wide, parched coulee, and then came upon a barren little habitation inclosed in a meager fence of the barbed wire she thought so detestable, she shut her eyes mentally to something she could not quite bring herself to face.

He lifted her out and tumbled the great trunks upon the ground before he drove on to the corrals. "Here's the key," he said, "if you want to go in. I won't be more than a minute or two." He did not look into her face when he spoke.

Val stood just inside the gate and tried to adjust all this to her mental picture. There was the front yard, for instance. A few straggling vines against the porch, and a sickly cluster or two of blossoms-those were the sweet peas, surely. The sun-baked bed of pale-green plants without so much as a bud of promise, she recognized, after a second glance, as the poppies. For the rest, there were weeds against the fence, sun-ripened grass trodden flat, yellow, gravelly patches where nothing grew-and a glaring, burning sun beating down upon it all.

The cottage-never afterward did she think of it by that name, but always as a shack-was built of boards placed perpendicularly, with battens nailed over the cracks to keep out the wind and the snow. At one side was a "lean-to" kitchen, and on the other side was the porch that was just a narrow platform with a roof over it. It was not wide enough for a rocking-chair, to say nothing of swinging a hammock. In the first hasty inspection this seemed to be about all. She was still hesitating before the door when Manley came back from putting up the horses.

"I'm afraid your flowers are a lost cause," he remarked cheerfully. "They were looking pretty good two or three weeks ago. This hot weather has dried them up. Next year we'll have water down here to the house. All these things take time."

"Oh, of course they do." Val managed to smile into his eyes. "Let's see how many dishes you left dirty; bachelors always leave their dishes unwashed on the table, don't they?"

"Sometimes-but I generally wash mine." He led the way into the house, which smelled hot and close, with the odor of food long since cooked and eaten, before he threw all the windows open. The front room was clean-after a man's idea of cleanliness. The floor was covered with an exceedingly dusty carpet, and a rug or two. Her latest photograph was nailed to the wall; and when Val saw it she broke into hysterical laughter.

"You've nailed your colors to the mast," she cried, and after that it was all a joke. The home-made couch, with the calico cushions and the cowhide spread, was a matter for mirth. She sat down upon it to try it, and was informed that chicken wire makes a fine spring. The rickety table, with tobacco, magazines, and books placed upon it in orderly piles, was something to smile over. The chairs, and especially the one cane rocker which went sidewise over the floor if you rocked in it long enough, were pronounced original.

In the kitchen the same masculine idea of cleanliness and order obtained. The stove was quite red, but it had been swept clean. The table was pushed against the only window there, and the back part was filled with glass preserve jars, cans, and a loaf of bread wrapped carefully in paper; but the oilcloth cover was clean-did it not show quite plainly the marks of the last washing? Two frying pans were turned bottom up on an obscure table in an obscure corner of the room, and a zinc water pail stood beside them.

There were other details which impressed themselves upon her shrinking brain, and though she still insisted upon smiling at everything, she stood in the middle of the room holding up her skirts quite unconsciously, as if she were standing at a muddy street crossing, wondering how in the world she was ever going to reach the Other side.

"Isn't it all-deliciously-primitive?" she asked, in a weak little voice, when the smile would stay no longer. "I —love it, dear." That was a lie; more, she was not in the habit of fibbing for the sake of politeness or anything else, so that the words stood for a good deal.

Manley looked into the zinc water pail, took it up, and started for an outer door, rattling the tin dipper as he went. "Want to go up to the spring?" he queried, over his shoulder, "Water's the first thing—I'm horribly thirsty."

Val turned to follow him. "Oh, yes-the spring!" She stopped, however, as soon as she had spoken. "No, dear. There'll be plenty of other times. I'll stay here."

He gave her a glance bright with love and blind happiness in her presence there, and went off whistling and rattling the pail at his side.

Val did not even watch him go. She stood still in the kitchen and looked at the table, and at the stove, and at the upturned frying pans. She watched two great horseflies buzzing against a window-pane, and when she could endure that no longer, she went into the front room and stared vacantly around at the bare walls. When she saw her picture again, nailed fast beside the kitchen door, her face lost a little of its frozen blankness-enough so that her lips quivered until she bit them into steadiness.

She went then to the door and stood looking dully out into the parched yard, and at the wizened little pea vines clutching feebly at their white-twine trellis. Beyond stretched the bare hills with the wavering brown line running down the nearest one-the line that she knew was the trail from town. She was guilty of just one rebellious sentence before she struggled back to optimism.

"I said I wanted it to be rough, but I didn't mean-why, this is just squalid!" She looked down the coulee and glimpsed the river flowing calmly past the mouth of it, a majestic blue belt fringed sparsely with green. It must be a mile away, but it relieved wonderfully the monotony of brown hills, and the vivid coloring brightened her eyes. She heard Manley enter the kitchen, set down the pail of water, and come on to where she stood.

"I'd forgotten you said we could see the river from here," she told him, smiling over her shoulder. "It's beautiful, isn't it? I don't suppose, though, there's a boat within millions of miles."

"Oh, there's a boat down there. It leaks, though. I just use it for ducks, close to shore. Admiring our view? Great, don't you think?"

Val clasped her hands before her and let her gaze travel again over the sweep of rugged hills. "It's—wonderful. I thought I knew, but I see I didn't. I feel very small, Manley; does one ever grow up to it?"

He seemed dimly to catch the note of utter desolation. "You'll get used to all that," he assured her. "I thought I'd reached the jumping-off place, at first. But now-you couldn't dog me outa the country."

He was slipping into the vernacular, and Val noticed it, and wondered dully if she would ever do likewise. She had not yet admitted to herself that Manley was different. She had told herself many times that it would take weeks to wipe out the strangeness born of three years' separation. He was the same, of course; everything else was new and-different. That was all. He seemed intensely practical, and he seemed to feel that his love-making had all been done by letter, and that nothing now remained save the business of living. So, when he told her to rest, and that he would get dinner and show her how a bachelor kept house, she let him go with no reply save that vague, impersonal smile which Kent had encountered at the depot.

While he rattled things about in the kitchen, she stood still in the doorway with her fingers doubled into tight little fists, and stared out over the great, treeless, unpeopled land which had swallowed her alive. She tried to think-and then, in another moment, she was trying not to think.

Glancing quickly over her shoulder, to make sure Manley was too busy to follow her, she went off the porch and stood uncertain in the parched inclosure which was the front yard.

"I may as well see it all, and be done," she whispered, and went stealthily around the corner of the house, holding up her skirts as she had done in the kitchen. There was a dim path beaten in the wiry grass —a path which started at the kitchen door and wound away up the coulee. She followed it. Undoubtedly it would lead her to the spring; beyond that she refused to let her thoughts travel.

In five minutes-for she went slowly-she stopped beside a stock-trampled pool of water and yellow mud. A few steps farther on, a barrel had been sunk in the ground at the base of a huge gray rock; a barrel which filled slowly and spilled the overflow into the mud. There was also a trough, and there was a barrier made of poles and barbed wire to keep the cattle from the barrel. One crawled between two wires, it would seem, to dip up water for the house. There were no trees-not real trees. There were some chokecherry bushes higher than her head, and there were other bushes that did not look particularly enlivening.

With a smile of bitter amusement, she tucked her skirts tightly around her, crept through the fence, and filled a chipped granite cup which stood upon a rock ledge, and drank slowly. Then she laughed aloud.

"The water really *is* cold," she said. "Anywhere else it would be delicious. And that's a spring, I suppose." Mercilessly she was stripping her mind of her illusions, and was clothing it in the harsher weave of reality. "All these hills are Manley's —our ranch." She took another sip and set down the cup. "And so Cold Spring Ranch means-all this."

Down the coulee she heard Manley call. She stood still, pushing back a fallen lock of fine, yellow hair. She turned toward the sound, and the sun in her eyes turned them yellow as the hair above them. She was beautiful, in an odd, white-and-gold way. If her eyes had been blue, or gray-or even brown-she would have been merely pretty; but as they were, that amber tint where one looked for something else struck one unexpectedly and made her whole face unforgettably lovely. However, the color of her eyes and her hair did not interest her then, or make life any easier. She was quite ordinarily miserable and homesick, as she went reluctantly back along the grassy trails The odor of fried bacon came up to her, and she hated bacon. She hated everything.

"I've been to the spring," she called out, resolutely cheerful, as soon as she came in sight of Manley, waiting in the kitchen door; she ran toward him lightly. "However does the water keep so deliciously cool through this hot weather? I don't wonder you call this Cold Spring Ranch."

Manley straightened proudly. "I'm glad you like it; I was afraid you might not, just at first. But you're the right stuff —I might have known it. Not every woman could come out here and appreciate this country right at the start."

Val stopped at the steps, panting a little from her run, and smiled unflinchingly up into his face.

# Chapter VI. Manley's Fire Guard

Hot sunlight, winds as hot, a shimmering heat which distorted objects at a distance and made the sky line a dazzling, wavering ribbon of faded blue; and then the dull haze of smoke which hung over the land, and, without tempering the heat, turned the sun into a huge coppery balloon, which drifted imperceptibly from the east to the west, and at evening time settled softly down upon a parched hilltop and disappeared, leaving behind it an ominous red glow as of hidden fires.

When the wind blew, the touch of it seared the face, as the smoke tang assailed the nostrils. All the world was a weird, unnatural tint, hard to name, never to be forgotten. The far horizons drew steadily closer as the days passed slowly and thickened the veil of smoke. The distant mountains drew daily back into dimmer distance; became an obscure, formless blot against the sky, and vanished completely. The horizon crouched then upon the bluffs across the river, moved up to the line of trees along its banks, blotted them out one day, and impudently established itself half-way up the coulee.

Time ceased to be measured accurately; events moved slowly in an unreal world of sultry heat and smoke and a red sun wading heavily through the copper-brown sky from the east to the west, and a moon as red which followed meekly after.

Men rode uneasily here and there, and when they met they talked of prairie fires and of fire guards and the direction of the wind, and of the faint prospect of rain. Cattle, driven from their accustomed feeding grounds, wandered aimlessly over the still-unburned range, and lowed often in the night as they drifted before the flame-heated wind.

Fifteen miles to the east of Cold Spring Coulee, the Wishbone outfit watched uneasily the deepening haze. Kent and Bob Royden were put to riding the range from the river north and west, and Polycarp Jenks, who had taken a claim where were good water and some shelter, and who never seemed to be there for more than a few hours at a time, because of his boundless curiosity, wandered about on his great, raw-boned sorrel with the white legs, and seemed always to have the latest fire news on the tip of his tongue, and always eager to impart it to somebody.

To the northwest there was the Double Diamond, also sleeping with both eyes open, so to speak. They also had two men out watching the range, though the fires were said to be all across the river. But there was the railroad seaming the country straight through the grassland, and though the company was prompt at plowing fire guards, contract work would always bear watching, said the stockmen, and with the high winds that prevailed there was no telling what might happen.

So Fred De Garmo and Bill Madison patrolled the country in rather desultory fashion, if the truth be known. They liked best to ride to the north and east-which, while following faithfully the railroad and the danger line, would bring them eventually to Hope, where they never failed to stop as long as they dared. For, although they never analyzed their feelings, they knew that as long as they kept their jobs and their pay was forthcoming, a few miles of blackened range concerned them personally not at all. Still, barring a fondness for the trail which led to town, they were not unfaithful to their trust.

One day Kent and Polycarp met on the brink of a deep coulee, and, as is the way of men who ride the dim trails, they stopped to talk a bit.

Polycarp, cracking his face across the middle with his habitual grin, straightened his right leg to its full length, slid his hand with difficulty into his pocket, brought up a dirty fragment of "plug" tobacco, looked it over inquiringly, and pried off the corner with his teeth. When he had rolled it comfortably into his cheek and had straightened his leg and replaced the tobacco in his pocket, he was "all set" and ready for conversation.

Kent had taken the opportunity to roll a cigarette, though smoking on the range was a weakness to be indulged in with much care. He pinched out the blaze of his match, as usual, and then spat upon it for added safety before throwing it away.

"If this heat doesn't let up," he remarked, "the grass is going to blaze up from sunburn."

"It won't need to, if you ask me. I wouldn't be su'prised to see this hull range afire any time. Between you an' me, Kenneth, them Double Diamond fellers ain't watching it as close as they might. I was away over Dry Creek way yesterday, and I seen where there was two different fires got through the company's guards, and kited off across the country. It jest *happened* that the grass give out in that red day soil, and starved 'em both out. They wa'n't *put* out. I looked close all around, and there wasn't nary a track of man or horse. That's their business-ridin' line on the railroad. The section men's been workin' off down the other way, where a culvert got scorched up pretty bad. By granny, Fred 'n' Bill Madison spend might' nigh all their time ridin' the trail to town. They're might' p'ticular about watchin' the railroad between the switches —*he-he!*"

"That's something for the Double Diamond to worry over," Kent rebuffed. He hated that sort of gossip which must speak ill of somebody. "Our winter range lays mostly south and east; we could stop a fire between here and the Double Diamond, even if they let one get past 'em."

Polycarp regarded him cunningly with his little, slitlike eyes. "Mebbe you could," he said doubtfully. "And then again, mebbe you couldn't. Oncet it got past Cold Spring —" He shook his wizened head slowly, leaned, and expectorated gravely.

"Man Fleetwood's keeping tab pretty close over that way."

Polycarp gave a grunt that was half a chuckle. "Man Fleetwood's keeping tab on what runs down his gullet," he corrected. "I seen him an' his wife out burnin' guards t' other day-over on his west line-and, by granny, it wouldn't stop nothing! A toad could jump it —*he-he!*" He sent another stream of tobacco juice afar, with the grave air as before.

"And I told him so. 'Man,' I says, 'what you think you're doing?'

"'Buildin' a fire guard,' he says. 'My wife, Mr. Jenks.'

"'Polycarp Jenks is my cognomen,' I says. 'And I don't want no misterin' in mine. Polycarp's good enough for me,' I says, and I took off my hat and bowed to 'is wife. Funny kinda eyes, she's got-ever take notice? Yeller, by granny! first time I ever seen yeller eyes in a human's face. Mebbe it was the sun in 'em, but they sure was yeller. I dunno as they hurt her looks none, either. Kinda queer lookin', but when you git used to 'em you kinda like 'em.

"'N' I says: 'Tain't half wide enough, nor a third' —spoke right up to 'im! I was thinkin' of the hull blamed country, and I didn't care how he took it. 'Any good, able-bodied wind'll jump a fire across that guard so quick it won't reelize there was any there,' I says.

"Man didn't like it none too well, either. He says to me: 'That guard'll stop any fire I ever saw,' and I got right back at him —*he-he!* 'Man,' I says, 'you ain't never saw a prairie fire' —just like that. 'You wait,' I says, 'till the real thing comes along. We ain't had any fires since you come into the country,' I says, 'and you don't know what they're like. Now, you take my advice and plow another four or five furrows-and plow 'em out, seventy-five or a hundred feet from here,' I says, 'an' make sure you git all the grass burned off between-and do it on a still day,' I says. 'You'll burn up the hull country if you keep on this here way you're doing,' I told him-straight out, just like that. 'And when you do it,' I says, 'you better let somebody know, so's they can come an' help,' I says. ''Tain't any job a man oughta tackle alone,' I says to him. 'Git help, Man, git help.'

"Well, by granny —*he-he!* Man's wife brustled up at me like a —a —" He searched his brain for a simile, and failed to find one. "'I have been helping Manley, Mr. Polycarp Jenks,' she says to me, 'and I flatter myself I have done as well as any *man* could do.' And, by granny! the way them yeller eyes of hern blazed at me —*he-he!* I had to laugh, jest to look at her. Dressed jest like a city girl, by granny! with ruffles on her skirts-to ketch afire if she wasn't mighty keerful! —and a big straw hat tied down with a veil, and kid gloves on her hands, and her yeller hair kinda fallin' around her face-and them yeller eyes snappin' like flames-by granny! if she didn't make as purty a picture as I ever want to set eyes on! Slim and straight, jest like a storybook woman —*he-he!* 'Course, she was all smoke an' dirt; a big flake of burned grass was on her hair, I took notice, and them ruffles was black up to her knees —*he-he!* And she had a big smut on her cheek-but she was right there with her stack of blues, by granny! Settin' into the game like a —a —" He leaned and spat "But burnin' guards ain't no work for a woman to do, an' I told Man so-straight out. 'You git help,' I says. 'I see you're might' near through with this here strip,' I says, 'an' I'm in a hurry, or I'd stay, right now.' And, by granny! if that there wife of Man's didn't up an' hit me another biff—*he-he!*

"'Thank you very much,' she says to me, like ice water. 'When we need your help, we'll be sure to let you know-but at present,' she says, 'we couldn't think of troubling you.' And then, by granny! she turns right around and smiles up at me—*he-he!* Made me feel like somebody'd tickled m' ear with a spear of hay when I was asleep, by granny! Never felt anything like it-not jest with somebody smilin' at me.

"'Polycarp Jenks,' she says to me, 'we do appreciate what you've told us, and I believe you're right,' she says. 'But don't insiniwate I'm not as good a fighter as any man who ever breathed,' she says. 'Manley has another of his headaches to-day—going to town always gives him a sick headache,' she says, 'and I've done nearly all of this my own, lone self,' she says. 'And I'm horribly proud of it, and I'll never forgive you for saying I—' And then, by granny! if she didn't begin to blink them eyes, and I felt like a—a—" He put the usual period to his hesitation.

"Between you an' *me*, Kenneth," he added, looking at Kent slyly, "she ain't having none too easy a time. Man's gone back to drinkin'—I knowed all the time he wouldn't stay braced up very long-lasted about six weeks, from all I c'n hear. Mebbe she reely thinks it's jest headaches ails him when he comes back from town—I dunno. You can't never tell what idees a woman's got tacked away under her hair-from all I c'n gether. I don't p'tend to know nothing about 'em-don't want to know—*he-he!* But I guess," he hinted cunningly, "I know as much about 'em as you do-hey, Kenneth? You don't seem to chase after 'em none, yourself—*he-he!*"

"Whereabouts did Man run his guards?" asked Kent, passing over the invitation to personal confessions.

Polycarp gave a grunt of disdain. "Just on the west rim of his coulee. About forty rod of six-foot guard, and slanted so it'll shoot a fire right into high grass at the head of the coulee and send it kitin' over this way. That's supposin' it turns a fire, which it won't. Six feet—a fall like this here! Why, I never see grass so thick on this range-did you?"

"I wonder, did he burn that extra guard?" Kent was keeping himself rigidly to the subject of real importance.

"No, by granny! he didn't—not unless he done it since yest'day. He went to town for suthin, and he might' nigh forgot to go home—*he-he!* He was there yest'day about three o'clock, an' I says to him—"

"Well, so-long; I got to, be moving." Kent gathered up the reins and went his way, leaving Polycarp just in the act of drawing his "plug" from his pocket, by his usual laborious method, in mental preparation for another half hour of talk.

"If you're ridin' over that way, Kenneth, you better take a look at Man's guard," he called after him. "A good mile of guard, along there, would help a lot if a fire got started beyond. The way he fixed it, it ain't no account at all."

Kent proved by a gesture that he heard him, and rode on without turning to look back. Already his form was blurred as Polycarp gazed after him, and in another minute or two he was blotted out completely by the smoke veil, though he rode upon the level. Polycarp watched him craftily, though there was no need, until he was completely hidden, then he went on, ruminating upon the faults of his acquaintances.

Kent had no intention of riding over to Cold Spring. He had not been there since Manley's marriage, though he had been a frequent visitor before, and unless necessity drove him there, it would be long before he faced again the antagonism of Mrs. Fleetwood. Still, he was mentally uncomfortable, and he felt much resentment against Polycarp Jenks because he had caused that discomfort. What was it to him, if Manley had gone bock to drinking? He asked the question more than once, and he answered always that it was nothing to him, of course. Still, he wished futilely that he had not been quite so eager to cover up Manley's weakness and deceive the girl. He ought to have given her a chance —

A cinder like a huge black snowflake struck him suddenly upon the cheek. He looked up, startled, and tried to see farther into the haze which closed him round. It seemed to him, now that his mind was turned from his musings, that the smoke was thicker, the smell of burning grass stronger, and the breath of wind hotter upon his face. He turned, looked away to the west, fancied there a tumbled blackness new to his sight, and put his horse to a run. If there were fire close, then every second counted; and as he raced over the uneven prairie he fumbled with the saddle string that held a sodden sack tied fast to the saddle, that he might lose no time.

The cinders grew thicker, until the air was filled with them, like a snowstorm done in India ink. A little farther and he heard a faint crackling; topped a ridge and saw not far ahead, a dancing, yellow line. His horse was breathing heavily with the pace he was keeping, but Kent, swinging away from the onrush of flame and heat, spurred him to a greater speed. They neared the end of the crackling, red line, and as Kent swung in behind it upon the burned ground, he saw several men beating steadily at the flames.

He was hardly at work when Polycarp came running up and took his place beside him; but beyond that Kent paid no attention to the others, though he heard and recognized the voice of Fred De Garmo calling out to some one. The smoke which rolled up in uneven volumes as the wind lifted it and bore it away, or let it suck backward as it veered for an instant, blinded him while he fought. He heard other men gallop up, and after a little some one clattered up with a wagon filled with barrels of water. He ran to wet his sack, and saw that it was Blumenthall himself, foreman of the Double Diamond, who drove the team.

"Lucky it ain't as windy as it was yesterday and the day before," Blumenthall cried out, as Kent stepped upon the brake block to reach a barrel. "It'd sweep the whole country if it was."

Kent nodded, and ran back to the fire, trailing the dripping sack after him. As he passed Polycarp and another, he heard Polycarp saying something about Man Fleetwood's fire guard; but he did not stop to hear what it was. Polycarp was always talking, and he didn't always keep too closely to facts.

Then, of a sudden, he saw men dimly when he glanced down the leaping fire line, and he knew that the fire was almost conquered. Another frenzied minute or two, and he was standing in a group of men, who dropped their charred, blackened fragments of blanket and bags, and began to feel for their smoking material, while they stamped upon stray embers which looked live enough to be dangerous.

"Well, she's out," said a voice, "But it did look for a while as if it'd get away in spite of us."

Kent turned away, wiping an eye which held a cinder fast under the lid. It was Fred De Garmo who spoke.

"If somebody'd been watchin' the railroad a leetle might closer—" Polycarp began, in his thin, rasping voice.

Fred cut him short. "I thought you laid it to Man Fleetwood, burning fire guards," he retorted. "Keep on, and you'll get it right pretty soon. This never come from the railroad; you can gamble on that."

Blumenthall had left his team and come among them. "If you want to know how it started, I can tell you. Somebody dropped a match, or a cigarette, or something, by the trail up here a ways. I saw where it started when I went to Cold Spring after the last load of water. And if I knew who it was—"

Polycarp launched his opinion first, as usual. "Well, I don't *know* who done it-but, by granny! I can might' nigh guess who it was. There's jest one man that I know of been traveling that trail lately when he wa'n't in his sober senses—"

Here Manley Fleetwood rode up to them, coughing at the soot his horse kicked up. "Say! you fellows come on over to the house and have something to eat-and," he added significantly, "something *wet*. I told my wife, when I saw the fire, to make plenty of coffee, for fighting fire's hungry work, let me tell. Come on-no hanging back, you know. There'll be lots of coffee, and I've got a quart of something better cached in the haystack!"

As he had said, fighting fire is hungry work, and none save Blumenthall, who was dyspeptic and only ate twice a day, and then of certain foods prepared by himself, declined the invitation.

# Chapter VII. Val's New Duties

To Val the days of heat and smoke, and the isolation, had made life seem unreal, like a dream which holds one fast and yet is absurd and utterly improbable. Her past was pushed so far from her that she could not even long for it as she had done during the first few weeks. There were nights of utter desolation, when Manley was in town upon some errand which prevented his speedy return-nights when the coyotes howled much louder than usual, and she could not sleep for the mysterious snapping and creaking about the shack, but lay shivering with fear until dawn; but not for worlds would she have admitted to Manley her dread of staying alone. She believed it to be necessary, or he would not require it of her, and she wanted to be all that he expected her to be. She was very sensitive, in those days, about doing her whole duty as a wife-the wife of a Western rancher.

For that reason, when Manley shouted to her the news of the fire as he galloped past the shack, and told her to have something for the men to eat when the fire was out, she never thought of demurring, or explaining to him that there was scarcely any wood, and that she could not cook a meal without fuel. Instead, she waved her hand to him and let him go; and when he was quite out of sight she went up to the corrals to see if she could find another useless pole, or a broken board or two which her slight strength would be sufficient to break up with the axe. Till she came to Montana, Val had never taken an axe in her hands; but its use was only one of the many things she must learn, of which she had all her life been ignorant.

There was an old post there, lying beside a rusty, overturned plow. More than once she had stopped and eyed it speculatively, and the day before she had gone so far as to lift an end of it tentatively; but she had found it very heavy, and she had also disturbed a lot of black bugs that went scurrying here and there, so that she was forced to gather her skirts close about her and run for her life.

Where Manley had built his hayrack she had yesterday discovered some ends of planking hidden away in the rank, ripened weeds and grass. She went there now, but there were no more, look closely as she might. She circled the evil-smelling stable in discouragement, picked up one short piece of rotten board, and came back to the post. As she neared it she involuntarily caught her skirts and held them close, in terror of the black bugs.

She eyed it with extreme disfavor, and finally ventured to poke it with her slipper toe; one lone bug scuttled out and away in the tall weeds. With the piece of board she turned it over, stared hard at the yellowed grass beneath, discovered nothing so very terrifying after all, and, in pure desperation, dragged the post laboriously down to the place where had been the woodpile. Then, lifting the heavy axe, she went awkwardly to work upon it, and actually succeeded, in the course of half an hour or so, in worrying an armful of splinters off it.

She started a fire, and then she had to take the big zinc pail and carry some water down from the spring before she could really begin to cook anything. Manley's work, every bit of it-but then Manley was so very busy, and he couldn't remember all these little things, and Val hated to keep reminding him. Theoretically, Manley objected to her chopping wood or carrying water, and always seemed to feel a personal resentment when he discovered her doing it. Practically, however, he was more and more often making it necessary for her to do these things.

That is why he returned with the fire fighters and found Val just laying the cloth upon the table, which she had moved into the front room so that there would be space to seat her guests at all four sides. He frowned when he looked in and saw that they must wait indefinitely, and her cheeks took on a deeper shade of pink.

"Everything will be ready in ten minutes," she hurriedly assured him. "How many are there, dear?"

"Eight, counting myself," he answered gruffly. "Get some clean towels, and we'll go up to the spring to wash; and try and have dinner ready when we get back-we're half starved." With the towels over his arm, he led the way up to the spring. He must have taken the trail which led past the haystack, for he returned in much better humor, and introduced the men to his wife with the genial air of a host who loves to entertain largely.

Val stood back and watched them file in to the table and seat themselves with a noisy confusion. Unpolished they were, in clothes and manner, though she dimly appreciated the way in which they refrained from looking at her too intently, and the conscious lowering of their voices while they talked among themselves.

They did, however, glance at her surreptitiously while she was moving quietly about, with her flushed cheeks and her yellow-brown hair falling becomingly down at the temples because she had not found a spare minute in which to brush it smooth, and her dainty dress and crisp, white apron. She was not like the women they were accustomed to meet, and they paid her the high tribute of being embarrassed by her presence.

She poured coffee until all the cups were full, replenished the bread plate and brought more butter, and hunted the kitchen over for the can opener, to punch little holes in another can of condensed cream; and she rather astonished her guests by serving it in a beautiful cut-glass pitcher instead of the can in which it was bought.

They handled the pitcher awkwardly because of their mental uneasiness, and Val shared with them their fear of breaking it, and was guilty of an audible sigh of relief when at last it found safety upon the table.

So perturbed was she that even when she decided that she could do no more for their comfort and retreated to the kitchen, she failed to realize that the one extra plate meant an absent guest, and not a miscount in placing them, as she fancied.

She remembered that she would need plenty of hot water to wash all those dishes, and the zinc pail was empty; it always was, it seemed to her, no matter how often she filed it. She took the tin dipper out of it, so that it would not rattle and betray her purpose to Manley, sitting just inside the door with his back toward her, and tiptoed quite guiltily out of the kitchen. Once well away from the shack, she ran.

She reached the spring quite out of breath, and she actually bumped into a man who stood carefully rinsing a bloodstained handkerchief under the overflow from the horse trough. She gave a little scream, and the pail went rolling noisily down the steep bank and lay on its side in the mud.

Kent turned and looked at her, himself rather startled by the unexpected collision. Involuntarily he threw out his hand to steady her. "How do you do, Mrs. Fleetwood?" he said, with all the composure he could muster to his aid. "I'm afraid I scared you. My nose got to bleeding-with the heat, I guess. I just now managed to stop it." He did not consider it necessary to explain his presence, but he did feel that talking would help her recover her breath and her color. "It's a plumb nuisance to have the nosebleed so much," he added plaintively.

Val was still trembling and staring at him with her odd, yellow-brown eyes. He glanced at her swiftly, and then bent to squeeze the water from his handkerchief; but his trained eyes saw her in all her dainty allurement; saw how the coppery sunlight gave a strange glint to her hair, and how her eyes almost matched it in color, and how the pupils had widened with fright. He saw, too, something wistful in her face, as though life was none too kind to her, and she had not yet abandoned her first sensation of pained surprise that it should treat her so.

"That's what I get for running," she said, still panting a little as she watched him. "I thought all the men were at the table, you see. Your dinner will be cold, Mr. Burnett."

Kent was a bit surprised at the absence of cold hauteur in her manner; his memory of her had been so different.

"Well, I'm used to cold grub," he smiled over his shoulder. "And, anyway, when your nose gets to acting up with you, it's like riding a pitching horse; you've got to pass up everything and give it all your time and attention." Then, with the daring that sometimes possessed him like a devil, he looked straight at her.

"Sure you intend to give me my dinner?" he quizzed, his lips' lifting humorously at the corners. "I kinda thought, from the way you turned me down cold when we met before, you'd shut your door in my face if I came pestering around. How *about* that?"

Little flames of light nickered in her eyes. "You are the guest of my husband, here by his invitation," she answered him coldly. "Of course I shall give you your dinner, if you want any."

He inspected his handkerchief critically, decided that it was not quite clean, and held it again under the stream of water. "If I want it-yes," he drawled maliciously. "Maybe I'm not sure about that part. Are you a pretty fair cook?"

"Perhaps you'd better interview your friends," she retorted, "if you are so very fastidious. I —" She drew her brows together, as if she was in doubt as to the proper method of dealing with this impertinence. She suspected that he was teasing her purposely, but still —

"Oh, I can eat 'most any old thing," he assured her, with calm effrontery. "You look as if you'd learn easy, and Man ain't the worst cook I ever ate after. If he's trained you faithful, maybe it'll be safe to take a change. How *about* that? Can you make sour-dough bread yet?"

"No!" she flung the word at him. "And I don't want to learn," she added, at the expense of her dignity.

Kent shook his head disapprovingly. "That sure ain't the proper spirit to show," he commented. "Man must have to beat you up a good deal, if you talk back to *him* that way." He eyed her sidelong. "You're a real little wolf, aren't you?" He shook his head again solemnly, and sighed. "A fellow sure must build himself lots of trouble when he annexes a wife —a wife that won't learn to make sour-dough bread, and that talks back. I'm plumb sorry for Man. We used to be pretty good friends —" He stopped short, his face contrite.

Val was looking away, and she was winking very fast. Also, her lips were quivering unmistakably, though she was biting them to keep them steady.

Kent stared at her helplessly. "Say! I never thought you'd mind a little joshing," he said gently, when the silence was growing awkward. "I ought to be killed! You-you must get awful lonesome —"

She turned her face toward him quickly, as if he were the first person who had understood her blank loneliness. "That," she told him, in an odd, hesitating manner, "atones for the-the 'joshing.' No one seems to realize —"

"Why don't you get out and ride around, or do something beside stick right here in this coulee like a —a cactus?" he demanded, with a roughness that somehow was grateful to her. "I'll bet you haven't been a mile from the ranch since Man brought you here. Why don't you go to town with him when he goes? It'd be a whole lot better for you-for both of you. Have you got acquainted with any of the women here yet? I'll gamble you haven't!" He was waving the handkerchief gently like a flag, to dry it.

Val watched him; she had never seen any one hold a handkerchief by the corners and wave it up and down like that for quick drying, and the expedient interested her, even while she was wondering if it was quite proper for him to lecture her in that manner. His scolding was even more confusing than his teasing.

"I've been down to the river twice," she defended weakly, and was angry with herself that she could not find words with which to quell him.

"Really?" He down at her indulgently. "How did you ever manage to get so far? It must be all of half a mile!"

"Oh, you're perfectly horrible!" she flashed suddenly. "I don't see how it can possibly concern you whether I go anywhere or not."

"It does, though. I'm a lot public-spirited. I hate to see taxes go up, and every lunatic that goes to the asylum costs the State just that much more. I don't know an easier recipe for going crazy than just to stay off alone and think. It's a fright the way it gets sheep-herders, and such."

"I'm *such*, I suppose!"

Kent glanced at her, approved mentally of the color in her cheeks and the angry light in her eyes, and laughed at her quite openly.

"There's nothing like getting good and mad once in a while, to take the kinks out of your brain," he observed. "And there's nothing like lonesomeness to put 'em in. A good fighting mad is what you need, now and then; I'll have to put Man next, I guess. He's too mild."

"No one could accuse you of that," she retorted, laughing a little in spite of herself. "If I were a man I should want to blacken your eyes —" And she blushed hotly at being betrayed into a personality which seemed to her undignified, and, what was worse, unrefined. She turned her back squarely toward him, started down the path, and remembered that she had not filled the water bucket, and that without it she could not consistently return to the house.

Kent interpreted her glance, went sliding down the steep bank and recovered the pail; he was laughing to himself while he rinsed and filled it at the spring, but he made no effort to explain his amusement. When he came back to where she stood watching him, Val gave her head a slight downward tilt to indicate her thanks, turned, and led the way back to the house without a word. And he, following after, watched her slim figure swinging lightly down the hill before him, and wondered vaguely what sort of a hell her life was going to be, out here where everything was different from what she had been accustomed to, and where she did not seem to "fit into the scenery," as he put it.

"You ought to learn to ride horseback," he advised unexpectedly.

"Pardon me-you ought to learn to wait until your advice is wanted," she replied calmly, without turning her head. And she added, with a sort of defiance: "I do not feel the need of either society or diversion, I assure you; I am perfectly contented."

"That's real nice," he approved. "There's nothing like being satisfied with what's handed out to you." But, though he spoke with much unconcern, his tone betrayed his skepticism.

The others had finished eating and were sitting upon their heels in the shade of the house, smoking and talking in that desultory fashion common to men just after a good meal. Two or three glanced rather curiously at Kent and his companion, and he detected the covert smile on the scandal-hungry face of Polycarp Jenks, and also the amused twist of Fred De Garmo's lips. He went past them without a sign of understanding, set the water pail down in its proper place upon a bench inside the kitchen door, tilted his hat to Val, who happened to be looking toward him at that moment, and went out again.

"What's the hurry, Kenneth?" quizzed Polycarp, when Kent started toward the corral.

"Follow my trail long enough and you'll find out-maybe," Kent snapped in reply. He felt that the whole group was watching hum, and he knew that if he looked back and caught another glimpse of Fred De Garmo's sneering face he would feel compelled to strike it a blow. There would be no plausible explanation, of course, and Kent was not by nature a trouble hunter; and so he chose to ride away without his dinner.

While Polycarp was still wondering audibly what was the matter, Kent passed the house on his gray, called "So-long, Man," with scarcely a glance at his host, and speedily became a dim figure in the smoke haze.

"He must be runnin' away from you, Fred," Polycarp hinted, grinning cunningly. "What you done to him-hey?"

Fred answered him with an unsatisfactory scowl. "You sure would be wise, if you found out everything you wanted to know," he said contemptuously, after an appreciable Wait. "I guess we better be moving along, Bill." He rose, brushed off his trousers with a downward sweep of his hands, and strolled toward the corrals, followed languidly by Bill Madison.

As if they had been waiting for a leader, the others rose also and prepared to depart. Polycarp proceeded, in his usual laborious manner, to draw his tobacco from his pocket, and pry off a corner.

"Why don't you burn them guards now, Manley, while you got plenty of help?" he suggested, turning his slit-lidded eyes toward the kitchen door, where Val appeared for an instant to reach the broom which stood outside.

"Because I don't want to," snapped Manley: "I've got plenty to do without that."

"Well, they ain't wide enough, nor long enough, and they don't run in the right direction-if you ask me." Polycarp spat solemnly off to the right.

"I don't ask you, as it happens." Manley turned and went into the home.

Polycarp looked quizzically at the closed door. "He's mighty touchy about them guards, for a feller that thinks they're all right —*he-he!*" he remarked, to no one in particular. "Some of these days, by granny, he'll wisht he'd took my advice!"

Since no one gave him the slightest attention, Polycarp did not pursue the subject further. Instead, with both ears open to catch all that was said, he trailed after the others to the corral. It was a matter of instinct, as well as principle, with Polycarp Jenks, to let no sentence, however trivial, slip past his hearing and his memory.

# Chapter VIII. The Prairie Fire

A calamity expected, feared, and guarded against by a whole community does sometimes occur, and with a suddenness which finds the victims unprepared in spite of all their elaborate precautions. Compared with the importance of saving the range from fire, it was but a trivial thing which took nearly every man who dwelt in Lonesome Land to town on a certain day when the wind blew free from out the west. They were weary of watching for the fire which did not come licking through the prairie grass, and a special campaign train bearing a prospective President of our United States was expected to pass through Hope that afternoon.

Since all trains watered at the red tank by the creek, there would be a five-minute stop, during which the prospective President would stand upon the rear platform and deliver a three-minute address —a few gracious words to tickle the self-esteem of his listeners-and would employ the other two minutes in shaking the hand of every man, woman, and child who could reach him before the train pulled out. There would be a cheer or two given as he was borne away-and there would be something to talk about afterward in the saloons. Scarce a man of then had ever seen a President, and it was worth riding far to look upon a man who even hoped for so exalted a position.

Manley went because he intended to vote for the man, and called it an act of loyalty to his party to greet the candidate; also because it took very little, now that haying was over and work did not press, to start him down the trail in the direction of Hope.

At the Blumenthall ranch no man save the cook remained at home, and he only because he had a boil on his neck which sapped his interest in all things else. Polycarp Jenks was in town by nine o'clock, and only one man remained at the Wishbone. That man was Kent, and he stayed because, according to his outraged companions, he was an ornery cuss, and his bump of patriotism was a hollow in his skull. Kent had told them, one and all, that he wouldn't ride twenty-five miles to shake hands with the Deity Himself-which, however, is not a verbatim report of his statement. The prospective President had not done anything so big, he said, that a man should want to break his neck getting to town just to watch him go by. He was dead sure he, for one, wasn't going to make a fool of himself over any swell-headed politician.

Still, he saddled and rode with his fellows for a mile or two, and called them unseemly names in a facetious tone; and the men of the Wishbone answered his taunts with shrill yells of derision when he swung out of the trail and jogged away to the south, and finally passed out of sight in the haze which still hung depressingly over the land.

Oddly enough, while all the able-bodied men save Kent were waiting hilariously in Hope to greet, with enthusiasm, the brief presence of the man who would fain be their political chief, the train which bore him eastward scattered fiery destruction abroad as it sped across their range, four minutes late and straining to make up the time before the next stop.

They had thought the railroad safe at last, what with the guards and the numerous burned patches where the fire had jumped the plowed boundary and blackened the earth to the fence which marked the line of the right of way, and, in some places, had burned beyond. It took a flag-flying special train of that bitter Presidential campaign to find a weak spot in the guard, and to send a spark straight into the thickest bunch of wiry sand grass, where the wind could fan it to a blaze and then seize it and bend the tall flame tongues until they licked around the next tuft of grass, and the next, and the next-until the spark was grown to a long, leaping line of fire, sweeping eastward with the relentless rush of a tidal wave upon a low-lying beach.

Arline Hawley was, perhaps, the only citizen of Hope who had deliberately chosen to absent herself from the crowd standing, in perspiring expectation, upon the depot platform. She had permitted Minnie, the "breed" girl, to go, and had even grudgingly consented to her using a box of cornstarch as first aid to her complexion. Arline had not approved, however, of either the complexion or the occasion.

"What you want to go and plaster your face up with starch for, gits me," she had criticised frankly. "Seems to me you're homely enough without lookin' silly, into the bargain. Nobody's going to look at you, no matter what you do. They're out to rubber at a higher mark than you be. And what they expect to see so great, gits me. He ain't nothing but a man—and, land knows, men is common enough, and ornery enough, without runnin' like a band of sheep to see one. I don't see as he's any better, jest because he's runnin' for President; if he gits beat, he'll want to hide his head in a hole in the ground. Look at my Walt. *He* was the biggest man in Hope, and so swell-headed he wouldn't so much as pack a bucket of water all fall, or chop up a tie for kindlin'—till the day after 'lection. And what was he then but a frazzled-out back number, that everybody give the laugh—till he up and blowed his brains out! Any fool can *run* for President—it's the feller that gits there that counts.

"Say, that red-white-'n'-blue ribbon sure looks fierce on that green dress—but I reckon blood will tell, even if it's Injun blood. G'wan, or you'll be late and have your trouble for your pay. But hurry back soon's the agony's over; the bread'll be ready to mix out."

Even after the girl was gone, her finery a-flutter in the sweeping west wind, Arline muttered aloud her opinion of men, and particularly of politicians who rode about in special trains and expected the homage of their fellows.

She was in the back yard, taking her "white clothes" off the line, when the special came puffing slowly into town. To emphasize her disapproval of the whole system of politics, she turned her back square toward it, and laid violent hold of a sheet. There was a smudge of cinders upon its white surface, and it crushed crisply under her thumb with the unmistakable feel of burned grass.

"Now, what in time—" began Arline aloud, after the manner of women whose tongues must keep pace with their thoughts. "That there feels fresh and"—with a sniff at the spot— "*smells* fresh."

With the wisdom of much experience she faced the hot wind and sniffed again, while her eyes searched keenly the sky line, which was the ragged top of the bluff marking the northern boundary of the great prairie land. A trifle darker it was there, and there was a certain sullen glow discernible only to eyes trained to read the sky for warning signals of snow, fire, and flood.

"That's a fire, and it's this side of the river. And if it is, then the railroad set it, and there ain't a livin' thing to stop it. An' the wind's jest right—" A curdled roll of smoke showed plainly for a moment in the haze. She crammed her armful of sheets into the battered willow basket, threw two clothespins hastily toward the same receptacle, and ran.

The special had just come to a stop at the depot. The cattlemen, cowboys, and townspeople were packed close around the rear of the train, their backs to the wind and the disaster sweeping down upon them, their browned faces upturned to the sleek, carefully groomed man in the light-gray suit, with a flaunting, prairie sunflower ostentatiously displayed in his buttonhole and with his campaign smile upon his lips and dull boredom looking out of his eyes.

"Ladies and gentlemen," he was saying, as he smiled, "you favoured ones whose happy lot it is to live in the most glorious State of our glorious union, I greet you, and I envy you—"

Arline, with her soiled kitchen apron, her ragged coil of dust-brown hair, her work-drawn face and faded eyes which blazed with excitement, pushed unceremoniously through the crowd and confronted him undazzled.

"Mister Candidate, you better move on and give these men a chancet to save their prope'ty," she cried shrilly. "They got something to do besides stand around here and listen at you throwin' campaign loads. The hull country's afire back of us, and the wind bringin' it down on a long lope."

She turned from the astounded candidate and glared at the startled crowd, every one of whom she knew personally.

"I must say I got my opinion of a bunch that'll stand here swallowin' a lot of hot air, while their coat tails is most ready to ketch afire!" Her voice was rasping, and it carried to the farthest of them. "You make me *tired!* Political slush, all of it—and the hull darned country a-blazin' behind you!"

The crowd moved uneasily, then scattered away from the shelter of the depot to where they could snuff inquiringly the wind, like dogs in the leash.

"That's right," yelled Blumenthall, of the Double Diamond. "There's a fire, sure as hell!" He started to run.

The man behind him hesitated but a second, then gripped his hat against the push of the wind, and began running. Presently men, women, and children were running, all in one direction.

The prospective President stood agape upon the platform of his bunting-draped car, his chosen allies grouped foolishly around him. It was the first time men had turned from his presence with his gracious, flatteringly noncommittal speech unuttered, his hand unshaken, his smiling, bowing departure unmarked by cheers growing fainter as he receded. Only Arline tarried, her thin fingers gripping the arm of her "breed girl," lest she catch the panic and run with the others.

Arline tilted back her head upon her scrawny shoulders and eyed the prospective President with antagonism unconcealed.

"I got something to say to you before you go," she announced, in her rasping voice, with its querulous note. "I want to tell you that the chances are a hundred to one you set that fire yourself, with your engine that's haulin' you around over the country, so you can jolly men into votin' for you. Your train's the only one over the road since noon, and that fire started from the railroad. The hull town's liable to burn, unless it can be stopped the other side the creek, to say nothing of the range, that feeds our stock, and the hay, and maybe houses-and maybe *people!*"

She caught her breath, and almost shrieked the last three words, as a dreadful probability flashed into her mind.

"I know a woman-just a girl-and she's back there twenty mile —*alone*, and her man's here to look at you go by! I hope you git beat, just for that!

"If this town ketches afire and burns up, I hope you run into the ditch before you git ten mile! If you was a man, and them fellers with you was men, you'd hold up your train and help save the town. Every feller counts, when it comes to fightin' fire."

She stopped and eyed the group keenly. "But you won't. I don't reckon you ever done anything with them hands in your life that would grind a little honest dirt into your knuckles and under them shiny nails!"

The prospective President turned red to his ears, and hastily removed his immaculate hands from where they had been resting upon the railing. And he did not hold up the train while he and his allies stopped to help save the town. The whistle gave a warning toot, the bell jangled, and the train slid away toward the next town, leaving Arline staring, tight-lipped, after it.

"The darned chump-he'd 'a' made votes hand over fist if he'd called my bluff; but, I knew he wouldn't, soon as I seen his face. He ain't man enough."

"He's real good-lookin'," sighed Minnie, feebly attempting to release her arm from the grasp of her mistress. "And did you notice the fellow with the big yellow mustache? He kept eyin' me —"

"Well, I don't wonder-but it ain't anything to your credit," snapped Arline, facing her toward the hotel, "You do look like sin a-flyin', in that green dress, and with all that starch on your face. You git along to the house and mix that bread, first thing you do, and start a fire. And if I ain't back by that time, you go ahead with the supper; you know what to git. We're liable to have all the tables full, so you set all of 'em."

She was hurrying away, when the girl called to her.

"Did you mean Mis' Fleetwood, when you said that about the woman burning? And do you s'pose she's really in the fire?"

"You shut up and go along!" cried Arline roughly, under the stress of her own fears. "How in time's anybody going to tell, that's twenty miles away?"

She left the street and went hurrying through back yards and across vacant lots, crawled through a wire fence, and so reached, without any roundabout method, the trail which led to the top of the bluff, where the whole town was breathlessly assembling. Her flat-chested, un-corseted figure merged into the haze as she half trotted up the steep road, swinging her arms like a man, her skirts flapping in the wind. As she went, she kept muttering to herself:

"If she really is caught by the fire-and her alone-and Man more'n half drunk —" She whirled, and stood waiting for the horseman who was galloping up the trail behind her. "You going home, Man? You don't think it could git to your place, do you?" She shouted the questions at him as he pounded past.

Manley, sallow white with terror, shook his head vaguely and swung his heavy quirt down upon the flanks of his horse. Arline lowered her head against the dust kicked into her face as he went tearing past her, and kept doggedly on. Some one came rattling up behind her with empty barrels dancing erratically in a wagon, and she left the trail to make room. The hostler from their own stable it was who drove, and at the creek ahead of them he stopped to fill the barrels. Arline passed him by and kept on.

At the brow of the hill the women and children were gathered in a whimpering group. Arline joined them and gazed out over the prairie, where the smoke was rolling toward them, and, lifting here and there, let a flare of yellow through.

"It'll show up fine at dark," a fat woman in a buggy remarked. "There's nothing grander to look at than a prairie fire at night. I do hope," she added weakly, "it don't do no great damage!"

"Oh, it won't," Arline cut in, with savage sarcasm, panting from her climb. "It's bound to sweep the hull country slick an' clean, and maybe burn us all out-but that won't matter, so long as it looks purty after dark!"

"They say it's a good ten mile away yet," another woman volunteered encouragingly. "They'll git it stopped, all right. There's lots of men here to fight it, thank goodness!"

Arline moved on to where a plow was being hurriedly unloaded from a wagon, the horses hitched to it, and a man already grasping the handles in an aggressive manner. As she came up he went off, yelling his opinions and turning a shallow, uneven furrow for a back fire. Within five minutes another plow was tearing up the sod in an opposite direction.

"If it jumps here, or they can't turn it, the creek'll help a lot," some one was yelling.

The plowed furrows lengthened, the horses sweating and throwing their heads up and down with the discomfort of the pace they must keep. Whiplashes whistled and the drivers urged them on with much shouting. Blumenthall, cut off, with his men, from reaching his own ranch, was directing a group about to set a back fire. His voice boomed as if he were shouting across a milling herd. A roll of his eye brought his attention momentarily from the work, and he ran toward a horseman who was gesticulating wildly and seemed on the point of riding straight toward the fire.

"Hi! Fleetwood, we need you here!" he yelled. "You can't get home now, and you know it. The fire's past your place already; you'd have to ride through it, you fool! Hey? Your wife home alone —*alone!*"

He stood absolutely still and stared out to the southwest, where the smoke cloud was rolling closer with every breath. He drew his fingers across his forehead and glanced at the men around him, also stunned into inactivity by the tragedy behind the words.

"Well-get to work, men. We've got to save the town. Fine time to burn guards-when a fire's loping up on you! But that's the way it goes, generally. This ought to've been done a month ago. Put it off and put it off-while they haggle over bids-Brinberg, you and I'll string the fire. The rest of you watch it don't jump back. And, say!" he shouted to the group around Manley. "Don't let that crazy fool start off now. Put him to work. Best thing for him. But-my God, that's awful!" He did not shout the last sentence. He spoke so that only the nearest man heard him-heard, and nodded dumb assent.

Manley raged, sitting helpless there upon his horse. They would not let him ride out toward that sweeping wave of fire. He could not have gone five miles toward home before he met the flames. He stood in the stirrups and shook his fists impotently. He strained his eyes to see what it was impossible for him to see-his ranch and Val, and how they had fared. He pictured mentally the guard he had burned beyond the coulee to protect them from just this danger, and his heart squeezed tight at the realization of his own shiftlessness. That guard! A twelve-foot strip of half-burned sod, with tufts of grass left standing here and there-and he had meant to burn it wider, and had put it off from day to day, until now. *Now!*

His clenched fist dropped upon the saddle horn, and he stared dully at the rushing, rolling smoke and fire. It was not *that* he saw-it was Val, with cinder-blackened ruffles, grimy face, and yellow hair falling in loose locks upon her cheeks-locks which she must stop to push out of her eyes, so that she could see where to swing the sodden sack while she helped him-him, Manley, who had permitted her to do work it for none but a man's hard muscles, so that he might finish the sooner and ride to town upon some flimsy pretext. And he could not even reach her now-or the place where she had been!

The group had thinned around him, for there was something to do besides give sympathy to a man bereaved. Unless they bestirred themselves, they might all be in need of sympathy before the day was done. Manley took his eyes from the coming fire and glanced around him, saw that he was alone, and, with a despairing oath, wheeled his horse and raced back down the hill to town, as if fiends rode behind the saddle.

At the saloon opposite the Hawley Hotel he drew up; rather, his horse stopped there of his own accord, as if he were quite at home at that particular hitching pole. Manley dismounted heavily and lurched inside. The place was deserted save for Jim, who was paid to watch the wares of his employer, and was now standing upon a chair at the window, that he might see over the top of Hawley's coal shed and glimpse the hilltop beyond. Jim stepped down and came toward him.

"How's the fire?" he demanded anxiously. "Think she'll swing over this way?"

But Manley had sunk into a chair and buried his face in his arms, folded upon a whisky-spotted card table.

"Val-my Val!" he wailed, "Back there alone-get me a drink," he added thickly, "or I'll go crazy!"

Jim hastily poured a full glass, and stood over him anxiously.

"Here it is. Drink 'er down, and brace up. What you mean? Is your wife —"

Manley lifted his head long enough to gulp the whisky, then dropped it again upon his arms and groaned.

## Chapter IX. Kent to the Rescue

The fire had been burning a possible half-hour when Kent, jogging aimlessly toward a log ridge with the lazy notion of riding to the top and taking a look at the country to the west before returning to the ranch, first smelled the stronger tang of burned grass and swung instinctively into the wind. He galloped to higher ground, and, trained by long watching of the prairie to detect the smoke of a nearer fire in the haze of those long distant, saw at once what must have happened, and knew also the danger. His horse was fresh, and he raced him over the uneven prairie toward the blaze.

It was tearing straight across the high ground between Dry Creek and Cold Spring Coulee when he first saw it plainly, and he altered his course a trifle. The roar of it came faintly on the wind, like the sound of storm-beaten surf pounding heavily upon a sand bar when the tide is out, except that this roar was continuous, and was full of sharp cracklings and sputterings; and there was also the red line of flame to visualize the sound.

When his eyes first swept the mile-long blaze, he felt his helplessness, and cursed aloud the man who had drawn all the fighting force from the prairie that day. They might at least have been able to harry it and hamper it and turn the savage sweep of it into barren ground upon some rock-bound coulee's rim. If they could have caught it at the start, or even in the first mile of its burning-or, even now, if Blumenthall's outfit were on the spot-or if Manley Fleetwood's fire guards held it back-He hoped some of them had stayed at home, so that they could help fight it.

In that brief glimpse before he rode down into a hollow and so lost sight of it, he knew that the fire they had fought and vanquished before had been a puny blaze compared with this one. The ground it had burned was not broad enough to do more than check this fire temporarily. It would simply burn around the blackened area and rush on and on, until the bend of the river turned it back to the north, where the river's first tributary stream would stop it for good and all. But before that happened it would have done its worst-and its worst was enough to pale the face of every prairie dweller.

Once more he caught sight of the fire as he was riding swiftly across the level land to the east of Cold Spring Coulee. He was going to see if Manley's fire guards were any good, and if anyone was there ready to fight it when it came up; they could set a back fire from the guards, he thought, even if the guards themselves were not wide enough to hold the main fire.

He pounded heavily down the long trail into the coulee, passed close by the house with a glance sidelong to see if anybody was in sight there, rounded the corral to follow the trail which wound zigzag up the farther coulee wall, and overtook Val, running bareheaded up the hill, dragging a wet sack after her. She was panting already from the climb, and she had on thin slippers with high heels, he noticed, that impeded her progress and promised a sprained ankle before she reached the top. Kent laughed grimly when he overtook her; he thought it was like a five-year-old child running with a cup of water to put out a burning house.

"Where do you think you're going with that sack?" he called out, by way of greeting.

She turned a pale, terrified face toward him, and reached up a hand mechanically to push her fair hair out of her eyes. "So much smoke was rolling into the coulee," she panted, "and I knew there must be a fire. And I've never felt quite easy about our guards since Polycarp Jenks said-Do you know where it is-the fire?"

"It's between here and the railroad. Give me that sack, and you go on back to the house. You can't do any good." And when she handed the sack up to him and then kept on up the hill, he became autocratic in his tone. "Go on back to the house, I tell you!"

"I shall not do anything of the kind," she retorted indignantly, and Kent gave a snort of disapproval, kicked his horse into a lunging gallop, and left her.

"You'll spoil your complexion," he cried over his shoulder, "and that's about all you will do. You better go back and get a parasol."

Val did not attempt to reply, but she refused to let his taunts turn her back, and kept stubbornly climbing, though tears of pure rage filled her eyes and even slipped over the lids to her cheeks. Before she had reached the top, he was charging down upon her again, and the pallor of his face told her much.

"All hell couldn't stop that fire!" he cried, before he was near her, and the words were barely distinguishable in the roar which was growing louder and more terrifying. *"Get back!* You want to stand there till it comes down on you?" Then, just as he was passing, he saw how white and trembling she was, and he pulled up, with Michael sliding his front feet in the loose soil that he might stop on that steep slope.

"You don't want to go and faint," he remonstrated in a more kindly tone, vaguely conscious that he had perhaps seemed brutal. "Here, give me your hand, and stick your toe in the stirrup. Ah, don't waste time trying to make up your mind-up you come! Don't you want to save the house and corrals-and the haystacks? We've got our work cut out, let me tell you, if we do it."

He had leaned and lifted her up bodily, helped her to put her foot in the stirrup from which he had drawn his own, and he held her beside him while he sent Michael down the trail as fast as he dared. It was a good deal of a nuisance, having to look after her when seconds were so precious, but he couldn't go on and leave her, though she might easily have reached the bottom as soon as he if she had not been so frightened. He was afraid to trust her; she looked, to him, as if she were going to faint in his arms.

"You don't want to get scared," he said, as calmly as he could. "It's back two or three miles on the bench yet, and I guess we can easy stop it from burning anything but the grass. It's this wind, you see. Manley went to town, I suppose?"

"Yes," she answered weakly. "He went yesterday, and stayed over. I'm all alone, and I didn't know what to do, only to go up and try —"

"No use, up there."

They were at the corral gate then, and he set her down carefully, then dismounted and turned Michael into the corral and shut the gate.

"If we can't step it, and I ain't close by, I wish you'd let Michael out," he said hurriedly, his eyes taking in the immediate surroundings and measuring the danger which lurked in weeds, grass, and scattered hay. "A horse don't have much show when he's shut up, and-Out there where that dry ditch runs, we'll back-fire. You take this sack and come and watch out my fire don't jump the ditch. We'll carry it around the house, just the other side the trail." He was pulling a handful of grass for a torch, and while he was twisting it and feeling in his pocket for a match, he looked at her keenly. "You aren't going to get hysterics and leave me to fight it alone, are you?" he challenged.

"I hope I'm not quite such a silly," she answered stiffly, and he smiled to himself as he ran along the far side of the ditch with his blazing tuft of grass, setting fire to the tangled, brown mat which covered the coulee bottom.

Val followed slowly behind him, watching that the blaze did not blow back across the ditch, and beating it out when it seemed likely to do so. Now that she could actually do something, she was no more excited than he, if one could judge by her manner. She did look sulky, however, at his way of treating her.

To back-fire on short notice, with no fresh-turned furrow of moist earth, but only a shallow little dry ditch with the grass almost meeting over its top in places, is ticklish business at best. Kent went slowly, stamping out incipient blazes that seemed likely to turn unruly, and not trusting Val any more than he was compelled to do. She was a woman, and Kent's experience with women of her particular type had not been extensive enough to breed confidence in an emergency like this.

He had no more than finished stringing his line of fire in the irregular half circle which enclosed house, corral, stables, and haystacks, and had for its eastern half the muddy depression which, in seasons less dry, was a fair-sized creek fed by the spring, when a jagged line of fire with an upper wall of tumbling, brown smoke, leaped into view at the top of the bluff.

One thing was in his favor: The grass upon the hillside was scantier than on the level upland, and here and there were patches of yellow soil absolutely bare of vegetation, where a fire would be compelled to halt and creep slowly around. Also, fire usually burns slower down a hill than over a level. On the other hand, the long, seamlike depressions which ran to the top were filled with dry brush, and even the coulee bottom had clumps of rosebushes and wild currant, where the flames would revel briefly.

But already the black, smoking line which curved around the haystacks to the north, and around the house toward the south, was widening with every passing second.

Val had a tub half filled with water at the house, and that helped amazingly by making it possible to keep the sacks wet, so that every blow counted as they beat out the ragged tongues of flame which, in that wind, would jump here and there the ditch and the road, and go creeping back toward the stacks and the buildings. For it was a long line they were guarding, and there was a good deal of running up and down in their endeavor to be in two places at once.

Then Val, in turning to strike a new-born flame behind her, swept her skirt across a tuft of smoldering grass and set herself afire. With the excitement of watching all points at once, and with the smoke and smell of fire all about her, she did not see what had happened, and must have paid a frightful penalty if Kent had not, at that moment, been running past her to reach a point where a blaze had jumped the ditch.

He swerved, and swung a newly wet sack around her with a force which would have knocked her down if he had not at the same time caught and held her. Val screamed, and struggled in his arms, and Kent knew that it was of him she was afraid. As soon as he dared, he released her and backed away sullenly.

"Sorry I didn't have time to say please-you were just ready to go up in smoke," he flung savagely over his shoulder. But he found himself shaking and weak, so that when he reached the blaze he must beat out, the sack was heavy as lead. "Afraid of *me* —women sure do beat hell!" he told himself, when he was a bit steadier. He glanced back at her resentfully. Val was stooping, inspecting the damage done to her dress. She stood up, looked at him, and he saw that her face was white again, as it had been upon the hillside.

A moment later he was near her again.

"Mr. Burnett, I'm —ashamed-but I didn't know, and you-you startled me," she stopped him long enough to confess, though she did not meet his eyes. "You saved —"

"You'll be startled worse, if you let the fire hang there in that bunch of grass," he interrupted coolly. "Behind you, there."

She turned obediently, and swung her sack down several times upon a smoldering spot, and the incident was closed.

Speedily it was forgotten, also. For with the meeting of the fires, which they stood still to watch, a patch of wild rosebushes was caught fairly upon both sides, and flared high, with a great snapping and crackling. The wind seized upon the blaze, flung it toward them like a great, yellow banner, and swept cinders and burning twigs far out over the blackened path of the back fire. Kent watched it and hardly breathed, but Val was shielding her face from the searing heat with her arms, and so did not see what happened then. A burning branch like a long, flaming dagger flew straight with the wind and lighted true as if flung by the hand of an enemy. A long, neatly tapered stack received it fairly, and Kent's cry brought Val's arms down, and her scared eyes staring at him.

"That settles the hay," he exclaimed, and raced for the stacks knowing all the while that he could do nothing, and yet panting in his hurry to reach the spot.

Michael, trampling uneasily in the corral, lifted his head and neighed shrilly as Kent passed him on the run. Michael had watched fearfully the fire sweeping down upon him, and his fear had troubled Val not a little. When she saw Kent pass the gate, she hurried up and threw it open, wondering a little that Kent should forget his horse. He had told her to see that he was turned loose if the fire could not be stopped-and now he seemed to have forgotten it.

Michael, with a snort and an upward toss of his head to throw the dragging reins away from his feet, left the corral with one jump, and clattered away, past the house and up the hill, on the trail which led toward home. Val stood for a moment watching him. Could he out-run the fire? He was holding his head turned to one side now, so that the reins dangled away from his pounding feet; once he stumbled to his knees, but he was up in a flash, and running faster than ever. He passed out of sight over the hill, and Val, with eyes smarting and cheeks burning from the heat, drew a long breath and started after Kent.

Kent was backing, step by step, away from the heat of the burning stacks. The roar, and the crackle, and the heat were terrific; it was as if the whole world was burning around them, and they only were left. A brand flew low over Val's head as she ran staggeringly, with a bewildered sense that she must hurry somewhere and do something immediately, to save something which positively must be saved. A spark from the brand fell upon her hand, and she looked up stupidly. The heat and the smoke were choking her so that she could scarcely breathe.

A new crackle was added to the uproar of flames. Kent, still backing from the furnace of blazing hay, turned, and saw that the stable, with its roof of musty hay, was afire. And, just beyond, Val, her face covered with her sooty hands, was staggering drunkenly. He reached her as she fell to her knees.

"I —can't —fight-any more," she whispered faintly.

He picked her up in his arms and hesitated, his face toward the house; then ran straight away from it, stumbled across the dry ditch and out across the blackened strip which their own back fire had swept clean of grass. The hot earth burned his feet through the soles of his riding boots, but the wind carried the heat and the smoke away, behind them. Clumps of bushes were still burning at the roots, but he avoided them and kept on to the far side hill, where a barren, yellow patch, with jutting sandstone rocks, offered a resting place. He set Val down upon a rock, placed himself beside her so that she was leaning against him, and began fanning her vigorously with his hat.

"Thank the Lord, we're behind that smoke, anyhow," he observed, when he could get his breath. He felt that silence was not good for the woman beside him, though he doubted much whether she was in a condition to understand him. She was gasping irregularly, and her body was a dead weight against him. "It was sure fierce, there, for a few minutes."

He looked out across the coulee at the burning stables, and waited for the house to catch. He could not hope that it would escape, but he did not mention the probability of its burning.

"Keep your eyes shut," he said. "That'll help some, and soon as we can we'll go to the spring and give our faces and hands a good bath." He untied his silk neckerchief, shook out the cinders, and pressed it against her closed eyes. "Keep that over 'em," he commanded, "till we can do better. My eyes are more used to smoke than yours, I guess. Working around branding fires toughens 'em some."

Still she did not attempt to speak, and she did not seem to have energy enough left to keep the silk over her eyes. The wind blew it off without her stirring a finger to prevent, and Kent caught it just in time to save it from sailing away toward the fire. After that he held it in place himself, and he did not try to keep talking. He sat quietly, with his arm around her, as impersonal in the embrace as if he were holding a strange partner in a dance, and watched the stacks burn, and the stables. He saw the corral take fire, rail by rail, until it was all ablaze. He saw hens and roosters running heavily, with wings dragging, until the heat toppled them over. He saw a cat, with white spots upon its sides, leave the bushes down by the creek and go bounding in terror to the house.

And still the house stood there, the curtains flapping in and out through the open windows, the kitchen door banging open and shut as the gusts of wind caught it. The fire licked as close as burned ground and rocky creek bed would let it, and the flames which had stayed behind to eat the spare gleanings died, while the main line raged on up the hillside and disappeared in a huge, curling wave of smoke. The stacks burned down to blackened, smoldering butts. The willows next the spring, and the chokecherries and wild currants withered in the heat and waved charred, naked arms impotently in the wind. The stable crumpled up, flared, and became a heap of embers. The corral was but a ragged line of smoking, half-burned sticks and ashes. Spirals of smoke, like dying camp fires, blew thin ribbons out over the desolation.

Kent drew a long breath and glanced down at the limp figure in his arms. She lay so very still that in spite of a quivering breath now and then he had a swift, unreasoning fear she might be dead. Her hair was a tangled mass of gold upon her head, and spilled over his arm. He carefully picked a flake or two of charred grass from the locks on her temples, and discovered how fine and soft was the hair. He lifted the grimy neckerchief from her eyes and looked down at her face, smoke-soiled and reddened from the heat. Her lips were drooped pitifully, like a hurt child. Her lashes, he noticed for the first time, were at least four shades darker than her hair. His gaze traveled on down her slim figure to her ringed fingers lying loosely in her lap, a long, dry-looking blister upon one hand near the thumb; down to her slippers, showing beneath her scorched skirt. And he drew another long breath. He did not know why, but he had a strange, fleeting sense of possession, and it startled him into action.

"You gone to sleep?" he called gently, and gave her a little shake. "We can get to the spring now, if you feel like walking that far; if you don't, I reckon I'll have to carry you-for I sure do want a drink!"

She half lifted her lashes and let them drop again, as if life were not worth the effort of living. Kent hesitated, set his lips tightly together, and lifted her up straighter. His eyes were intent and stern, as though some great issue was at stake, and he must rouse her at once, in spite of everything.

"Here, this won't do at all," he said-but he was speaking to himself and his quivering nerves, more than to her.

She sighed, made a conscious effort, and half opened her eyes again. But she seemed not to share his anxiety for action, and her mental and physical apathy were not to be mistaken. The girl was utterly exhausted with fire-fighting and nervous strain.

"You seem to be all in," he observed, his voice softly complaining. "Well, I packed you over here, and I reckon I better pack you back again-if you *won't* try to walk."

She muttered something, of which Kent only distinguished "a minute." But she was still limp, and absolutely without interest in anything, and so, after a moment of hesitation, he gathered her up in his arms and carried her back to the house, kicked the door savagely open, took her in through the kitchen, and laid her down upon the couch, with a sigh of relief that he was rid of her.

The couch was gay with a bright, silk spread of "crazy" patchwork, and piled generously with dainty cushions, too evidently made for ornamental purposes than for use. But Kent piled the cushions recklessly around her, tucked her smudgy skirts close, went and got a towel, which he immersed recklessly in the water pail, and bathed her face and hands with clumsy gentleness, and pushed back her tangled hair. The burn upon her hand showed an angry red around the white of the blister, and he laid the wet towel carefully upon it. She did not move.

He was a man, and he had lived all his life among men. He could fight anything that was fightable. He could save her life, but after this slight attention to her comfort he had reached the limitations set by his purely masculine training. He lowered the shades so that the room was dusky and as cool as any other place in that fire-tortured land, and felt that he could no do more for her.

He stood for a moment looking down at the inert, grimy little figure stretched out straight, like a corpse, upon the bright-hued couch, her eyes closed and sunken, with blue shadows beneath, her lips pale and still with that tired, pitiful droop. He stooped and rearranged the wet towel on her burned hand, held his face close above hers for a second, sighed, frowned, and tiptoed out into the kitchen, closing the door carefully behind him.

# Chapter X. Desolation

For more than two hours Kent sat outside in the shade of the house, and stared out over the black desolation of the coulee. His horse was gone, so that he could not ride anywhere-and there was nowhere in particular to ride. For twenty miles around there was no woman whom he could bring to Val's assistance, even if he had been sure that she needed assistance. Several times he tiptoed into the kitchen, opened the door into the front room an inch or so, and peered in at her. The third time, she had relaxed from the corpselike position, and had thrown an arm up over her face, as if she were shielding her eyes from something. He took heart at that, and went out and foraged for firewood.

There was a hard-beaten zone around the corral and stables, which had kept the fire from spreading toward the house, and the wind had borne the sparks and embers back toward the spring, so that the house stood in a brown oasis of unburned grass and weeds, scanty enough, it is true, but yet a relief from the dead black surroundings.

The woodpile had not suffered. A chopping block, a decrepit sawhorse, an axe, and a rusty bucksaw marked the spot; also three ties, hacked eloquently in places, and just five sticks of wood, evidently chopped from a tie by a man in haste. Kent looked at that woodpile, and swore. He had always known that Manley had an aversion to laboring with his hands, but he was unprepared for such an exhibition of shiftlessness.

He savagely attacked the three ties, chopped them into firewood, and piled them neatly, and then, walking upon his toes, he made a fire in the kitchen stove, filled the woodbox, the teakettle, and the water pail, sat out in the shade until he heard the kettle boiling over on the stove, took another peep in at Val, and then, moving as quietly as he could, proceeded to cook supper for them both.

He had been perfectly familiar with the kitchen arrangements in the days when Manley was a bachelor, and it interested him and filled him with a respectful admiration for woman in the abstract and for Val in particular, to see how changed everything was, and how daintily clean and orderly. Val's smooth, white hands, with their two sparkly rings and the broad wedding band, did not suggest a familiarity with actual work about a house, but the effect of her labor and thought confronted him at every turn.

"You can see your face in everything you pick up that was made to shine," he commented, standing for a moment while he surveyed the bottom of a stewpan. "She don't look it, but that yellow-eyed little dame sure knows how to keep house." Then he heard her cough, and set down the stewpan hurriedly and went to see if she wanted anything.

Val was sitting upon the couch, her two hands pushing back her hair, gazing stupidly around her.

"Everything's all ready but the tea," Kent announced, in a perfectly matter-of-fact tone. "I was just waiting to see how strong you want it."

Val turned her yellow-brown eyes upon him in bewilderment. "Why, Mr. Burnett-maybe I wasn't dreaming, then. I thought there was a fire. Was there?"

Kent grinned. "Kinda. You worked like a son of a gun, too-till there wasn't any more to do, and then you laid 'em down for fair. You were all in, so I packed you in and put you there where you could be comfortable. And supper's ready-but how strong do you want your tea? I kinda had an idea," he added lamely, "that women drink tea, mostly. I made coffee for myself."

Val let herself drop back among the pretty pillows. "I don't want any. If there was a fire," she said dully, "then it's true. Everything's all burned up. I don't want any tea. I want to die!"

Kent studied her for a moment. "Well, in that case-shall I get the axe?"

Val had closed her eyes, but she opened them again. "I don't care what you do," she said.

"Well, I aim to please," he told her calmly. "What *I'd* do, in your place, would be to go and put on something that ain't all smoked and scorched like a —a ham, and then I'd sit up and drink some tea, and be nice about it. But, of course, if you want to cash in —"

Val gave a sob. "I can't help it—I'd just as soon be dead as alive. It was bad enough before-and now everything's burned up-and all Manley's nice-ha-ay—"

"Well," Kent interrupted mercilessly, "I've heard of women doing all kinds of fool things-but this is the first time I ever knew one to commit suicide over a couple of measly haystacks!" He went out and slammed the door so that the house shook, and tramped three times across the kitchen floor. "That'll make her so mad at me she won't think about anything else for a while," he reasoned shrewdly. But all the while his eyes were shiny, and when he winked, his lashes became unaccountably moist. He stopped and looked out at the blackened coulee. "Shut into this hole, week after week, without a woman to speak to-it must be-damned tough!" he muttered.

He tiptoed up and laid his ear against the inner door, and heard a smothered sobbing inside. That did not sound as if she were "mad," and he promptly cursed himself for a fool and a brute. With his own judgment to guide him, he brewed some very creditable tea, sugared and creamed it lavishly, browned a slice of bread on top of the stove-blowing off the dust beforehand-after Arline's recipe for making toast, buttered it until it dripped oil, and carried it in to her with the air of a man who will have peace even though he must fight for it. The forlorn picture she made, lying there with her face buried in a pink-and-blue cushion, and with her shoulders shaking with sobs, almost made him retreat, quite unnerved. As it was, he merely spilled a third of the tea and just missed letting the toast slide from the plate to the floor; when he had righted his burden he had recovered his composure to a degree.

"Here, this won't do at all," he reproved, pulling a chair to the couch by the simple method of hooking his toe under a round and dragging it toward him. "You don't want Man to come and catch you acting like this. He's liable to feel pretty blue himself, and he'll need some cheering up-don't you think? I don't know for sure-but I've always been kinda under the impression that's what a man gets a wife for. Ain't it? You don't want to throw down your cards now. You sit up and drink this tea, and eat this toast, and I'll gamble you'll feel about two hundred per cent better.

"Come," he urged gently, after a minute. "I never thought a nervy little woman like you would give up so easy. I was plumb ashamed of myself, the way you worked on that back fire. You had me going, for a while. You're just tired out, is all ails you. You want to hurry up and drink this, before it gets cold. Come on. I'm liable to feel, insulted if you pass up my cooking this way."

Val choked back the tears, and, without taking her face from the pillow, put out the burned hand gropingly until it touched his knee.

"Oh, you-you're good," she said brokenly. "I used to think you were-horrid, and I'm a—ashamed. You're good, and I—"

"Well, I ain't going to be good much longer, if you don't get your head outa that pillow and drink this tea!" His tone was amused and half impatient. But his face-more particularly his eyes-told another story, which perhaps it was as well she did not read. "I'll be dropping the blamed stuff in another minute. My elbow's plumb getting a cramp in it," he added complainingly.

Val made a sound half-way between a sob and a laugh, and sat up. With more haste than the occasion warranted, Kent put the tea and toast on the chair and started for the kitchen.

"I was bound you'd eat before I did," he explained, "and I could stand a cup of coffee myself. And, say! If there's anything more you want, just holler, and I'll come on the long lope."

Val took up the teaspoon, tasted the tea, and then regarded the cup doubtfully. She never drank sugar in her tea. She wondered how much of it he had put in. Her head ached frightfully, and she felt weak and utterly hopeless of ever feeling different.

"Everything all right?" came Kent's voice from the kitchen.

"Yes," Val answered hastily, trying hard to speak with some life and cheer in her tone. "It's lovely-all of it."

"Want more tea?" It sounded, out there, as though he was pushing back his chair to rise from the table.

"No, no, this is plenty." Val glanced fearfully toward the kitchen door, lifted the teacup, and heroically drank every drop. It was, she considered, the least that she could do.

When he had finished eating he came in, and found her nibbling apathetically at the toast. She looked up at him with an apology in her eyes.

"Mr. Burnett, don't think I am always so silly," she began, leaning back against the piled pillows with a sigh. "I have always thought that I could bear anything. But last night I didn't sleep much. I dreamed about fires, and that Manley was-dead-and I woke up in a perfect horror. It was only ten o'clock. So then I sat up and tried to read, and every five minutes I would go out and look at the sky, to see if there was a glow anywhere. It was foolish, of course. And I didn't sleep at all to-day, either. The minute I would lie down I'd imagine I heard a fire roaring. And then it came. But I was all used up before that, so I wasn't really —I must have fainted, for I don't remember getting into the house-and I do think fainting is the silliest thing! I never did such a thing before," she finished abjectly.

"Oh, well—I guess you had a license to faint if you felt that way," he comforted awkwardly. "It was the smoke and the heat, I reckon; they were enough to put a crimp in anybody. Did Man say about when he would be back? Because I ought to be moving along; it's quite a walk to the Wishbone."

"Oh-you won't go till Manley comes! Please! I —I'd go crazy, here alone, and-and he might not come-he's frequently detained. I —I've such a horror of fires —" She certainly looked as if she had. She was sitting up straight, her hands held out appealingly to him, her eyes big and bright.

"Sure I won't go if you feel that way about it." Kent was half frightened at her wild manner. "I guess Man will be along pretty soon, anyway. He'll hit the trail as soon as he can get behind the fire, that's a cinch. He'll be worried to death about you. And you don't need to be afraid of prairie fires any more, Mrs. Fleetwood; you're safe. There can't be any more fires till next year, anyway; there's nothing left to burn." He turned his face to the window and stared out somberly at the ravaged hillside. "Yes-you're dead safe, now!"

"I'm such a fool," Val confessed, her eyes also turning to the window, "If you want to go, I —" Her mouth was quivering, and she did not finish the sentence.

"Oh, I'll stay till Man comes. He's liable to be along any time, now." He glanced at her scorched, smoke-stained dress. "He'll sure think you made a hand, all right!"

Val took the hint, and blushed with true feminine shame that she was not looking her best. "I'll go and change," she murmured, and rose wearily. "But I feel as if the world had been 'rolled up in a scroll and burned,' as the Bible puts it, and as if nothing matters any more."

"It does, though. We'll all go right along living the same as ever, and the first snow will make this fire seem as old as the war-except to the cattle; they're the ones to get it in the neck this winter."

He went out and walked aimlessly around in the yard, and went over to the smoking remains of the stable, and to the heap of black ashes where the stacks had been. Manley would be hard hit, he knew. He wished he would hurry and come, and relieve him of the responsibility of keeping Val company. He wondered a little, in his masculine way, that women should always be afraid when there was no cause for fear. For instance, she had stayed alone a good many times, evidently, when there was real danger of a fire sweeping down upon her at any hour of the day or night; but now, when there was no longer a possibility of anything happening, she had turned white and begged him to stay-and Val, he judged shrewdly, was not the sort of woman who finds it easy to beg favors of anybody.

There came a sound of galloping, up on the hill, and he turned quickly. Dull dusk was settling bleakly down upon the land, but he could see three or four horsemen just making the first descent from the top. He shouted a wordless greeting, and heard their answering yells. In another minute or two they were pulling up at the house, where he had hurried to meet them. Val, tucking a side comb hastily into her freshly coiled hair, her pretty self clothed all in white linen, appeased eagerly in the doorway.

"Why-where's Manley?" she demanded anxiously.

Blumenthall was dismounting near her, and he touched his hat before he answered. "We were on the way home, and we thought we'd better ride around this way and see how you came out," he evaded. "I see you lost your hay and buildings-pretty close call for the house, too, I should judge. You must have got here in time to do something, Kent."

"But where's Manley?" Val was growing pale again. "Has anything happened? Is he hurt? Tell me!"

"Oh, he's all right, Mrs. Fleetwood." Blumenthall glanced meaningly at Kent-and Fred De Garmo, sitting to one side of his saddle, looked at Polycarp Jenks and smiled slightly. "We left town ahead of him, and knocked right along."

Val regarded the group suspiciously. "He's coming, then, is he?"

"Oh, certainly. Glad you're all right, Mrs. Fleetwood. That was an awful fire-it swept the whole country clean between the two rivers, I'm afraid. This wind made it bad." He was tightening his cinch, and now he unhooked the stirrup from the horn and mounted again. "We'll have to be getting along-don't know, yet, how we came out of it over to the ranch. But our guards ought to have stopped it there." He looked at Kent. "How did the Wishbone make it?" he inquired.

"I was just going to ask you if you knew," Kent replied, scowling because he saw Fred looking at Val in what he considered an impertinent manner. "My horse ran off while I was fighting fire here, so I'm afoot. I was waiting for Man to show up."

"You'll git all of that you want —*he-he!*" Polycarp cut in tactlessly. "Man won't git home t'-night-not unless —"

"Aw, come on." Fred started along the charred trail which led across the coulee and up the farther side. Blumenthall spoke a last, commonplace sentence or two, just to round off the conversation and make the termination not too abrupt, and they rode away, with Polycarp glancing curiously back, now and then, as though he was tempted to stay and gossip, and yet was anxious to know all that had happened at the Double Diamond.

"What did Polycarp Jenks mean-about Manley not coming to-night?" Val was standing in the doorway, staring after the group of horsemen.

"Nothing, I guess, Polycarp never does mean anything half the time; he just talks to hear his head roar. Man'll come, all right. This bunch happened to beat him out, is all."

"Oh, do you think so? Mr. Blumenthall acted as if there was something —"

"Well, what can you expect of a man that lives on oatmeal mush and toast and hot water?" Kent demanded aggressively. "And Fred De Garmo is always grinning and winking at somebody; and that other fellow is a Swede and got about as much sense as a prairie dog-and Polycarp is an old granny gossip that nobody ever pays any attention to. Man won't stay in town-hell be too anxious."

"It's terrible," sighed Val, "about the hay and the stables. Manley will be so discouraged-he worked so hard to cut and stack that hay. And he was just going to gather the calves together and put them in the river field, in a couple of weeks-and now there isn't anything to feed them!"

"I guess he's coming; I hear somebody." Kent was straining his eyes to see the top of the hill, where the dismal sight shadows lay heavily upon the dismal black earth. "Sounds to me like a rig, though. Maybe he drove out." He left her, went to the wire gate which gave egress from the tiny, unkempt yard, and walked along the trail to meet the newcomer.

"You stay there," he called back, when he thought he heard Val following him. "I'm just going to tell him you're all right. You'll get that white dress all smudged up in these ashes."

In the narrow little gully where the trail crossed the half-dry channel from the spring he met the rig. The driver pulled up when he caught sight of Kent.

"Who's that? Did she git out of it?" cried Arline Hawley, in a breathless undertone, "Oh-it's you, is it, Kent? I couldn't stand it —I just had to come and see if she's alive. So I made Hank hitch right up-as soon as we knew the fire wasn't going to git into all that brush along the creek, and run down to the town-and bring me over. And the way —"

"But where's Man?" Kent laid a hand upon the wheel and shot the question into the stream of Arline's talk.

"Man! I dunno what devil gits into men sometimes. Man went and got drunk as a fool soon as he seen the fire and knew what coulda happened out here. Started right in to drownd his sorrows before he made sure whether he had any to drown! If that ain't like a man, every time! Time we all got back to town, and the fire was kiting away from us instead of coming up toward us, he was too drunk to do anything. He must of poured it down him by the quart. He —"

"Manley! Is that you, dear?" It was Val, a slim, white figure against the blackness all around her, coming down the trail to see what delayed them. "Why don't you come to the house? There *is* a house, you know. We aren't quite burned out. And I'm all right, so there's no need to worry any more."

"Now, ain't that a darned shame?" muttered Arline wrathfully to Kent. "A feller that'll drink when he's got a wife like that had oughta be hung!

"It's me, Arline Hawley!" She raised her voice to its ordinary shrill level. "It ain't just the proper time to make a call, I guess, but it's better late than never. Man, he was took with one of his spells, so I told him I'd come on out and take you back to town. How are you, anyhow? Scared plumb to death, I'll bet, when that fire come over the hill. You needn't 'a' tramped clear down here-we was coming on to the house in a minute. I got to chewin' the rag with Kent. Git in; you might as well ride back to the house, now you're here."

"Manley didn't come?" Val was standing beside the rig, near Kent. Her white-clothed figure was indistinct, and her face obscured in the dark. Her voice was quiet-lifelessly quiet. "Is he sick?"

"Well-of course has nerves was all upset —"

"Oh! Then he *is* sick?"

"Well-nothing dangerous, but-he wasn't feelin' well, so I thought I'd come out and take you back with me."

"Oh!"

"Man was awful worried; you mustn't think he wasn't. He was pretty near crazy, for a while."

"Oh, yes, certainly."

"Get in and ride. And you mustn't worry none about Man, nor feel hurt that he didn't come. He felt so bad —"

"I'll walk, thank you; it's only a few steps. And I'm not worried at all. I quite understand."

The team started on slowly, and Mrs. Hawley turned in the seat so that she could continue talking without interruption to the two who walked behind. But it was Kent who answered her at intervals, when she asked a direct question or appeared to be waiting for some comment. Betweenwhiles he was wondering if Val did, after all, understand. She knew so little of the West and its ways, and her faith in Manley was so firm and unquestioning, that he felt sure she was only hurt at what looked very much like an indifference to her welfare. He suspected shrewdly that she was thinking what she would have done in Manley's place, and was trying to reconcile Mrs. Hawley's assurances that Manley was not actually sick or disabled with the blunt fact that he had stayed in town and permitted others to come out to see if she were alive or dead.

And Kent had another problem to solve. Should he tell her the truth? He had never ceased to feel, in some measure, responsible for her position. And she was sure to discover the truth before long; not even her innocence and her ignorance of life could shield her from that knowledge. He let a question or two of Arline's go unanswered while he struggled for a decision, but when they reached the house, only one point was dearly settled in his mind. Instead of riding as far as he might, and then walking across the prairie to the Wishbone, he intended to go on to town with them —"to see her through with it."

## Chapter XI. Val's Awakening

Val stood just inside the door of the hotel parlor and glanced swiftly around at the place of unpleasant memory.

"No, I must see Manley before I can tell you whether we shall want to stay or not," she replied to Arline's insistence that she "go right up to a room" and lie down. "I feel quite well, and you must not bother about me at all. If Mr. Burnett will be good enough to send Manley to me —I must see him first of all." It was Val in her most unapproachable mood, and Arline subsided before it.

"Well, then, I'll go and send word to Man, and see about some supper for us. I feel as if *I* could eat ten-penny nails!" She went out into the hall, hesitated a moment, and then boldly invaded the "office."

"Say! have you got Man rounded up yit?" she demanded of her husband. "And how is he, anyhow? That girl ain't got the first idea of what ails him-how anybody with the brains and education she's got can be so thick-headed gits me. Jim told me Man's been packing a bottle or two home with him every trip he's made for the last month-and she don't know a thing about it. I'd like to know what 'n time they learn folks back East, anyhow; to put their eyes and their sense in their pockets, I guess, and go along blind as bats. Where's Kent at? Did he go after him? She won't do nothing till she sees Man —"

At that moment Kent came in, and his disgust needed no words. He answered Mrs. Hawley's inquiring look with a shake of the head.

"I can't do anything with him," he said morosely. "He's so full he don't know he's got a wife, hardly. You better go and tell her, Mrs. Hawley. Somebody's got to."

"Oh, my heavens!" Arline clutched at the doorknob for moral support. "I could no more face them yellow eyes of hern when they blaze up-you go tell her yourself, if you want her told. I've got to see about some supper for us. I ain't had a bite since dinner, and Min's off gadding somewheres —" She hurried away, mentally washing her hands of the affair. "Women's got to learn some time what men is," she soliloquized, "and I guess she ain't no better than any of the rest of us, that she can't learn to take her medicine-but *I* ain't goin' to be the one to tell her what kinda fellow she's tied to. My stunt'll be helpin' her pick up the pieces and make the best of it after she's told."

She stopped, just inside the dining room, and listened until she heard Kent cross the hall from the office and open the parlor door. "Gee! It's like a hangin'," she sighed. "If she wasn't so plumb innocent —" She started for the door which opened into the parlor from the dining room, strongly tempted to eavesdrop. She did yield so far as to put her ear to the keyhole, but the silence within impressed her strangely, and she retreated to the kitchen and closed the door tightly behind her as the most practical method of bidding Satan begone.

The silence in the parlor lasted while Kent, standing with his back against the door, faced Val and meditated swiftly upon the manner of his telling.

"Well?" she demanded at last. "I am still waiting to see Manley. I am not quite a child, Mr. Burnett. I know something is the matter, and you-if you have any pity, or any feeling of friendship, you will tell me the truth. Don't you suppose I know that Arline was —*lying* to me all the time about Manley? You helped her to lie. So did that other man. I waited until I reached town, where I could do something, and now you must tell me the truth. Manley is badly hurt, or he is dead. Tell me which it is, and take me to him." She spoke fast, as if she was afraid she might not be able to finish, though her voice was even and low, it was also flat and toneless with her effort to seem perfectly calm and self-controlled.

Kent looked at her, forgot all about leading up to the truth by easy stages, as he had intended to do, and gave it to her straight. "He ain't either one," he said. "He's drunk!"

Val stared at him. "Drunk!" He could see how even her lips shrank from the word. She threw up her head. "That," she declared icily, "I know to be impossible!"

"Oh, do you? Let me tell you that's *never* impossible with a man, not when there's whisky handy."

"Manley is not that sort of a man. When he left me, three years ago, he promised me never to frequent places where liquor is sold. He never had touched liquor; he never was tempted to touch it. But, just to be doubly sure, he promised me, on his honor. He has never broken that promise; I know, because he told me so." She made the explanation scornfully, as if her pride and her belief in Manley almost forbade the indignity of explaining. "I don't know why you should come here and insult me," she added, with a lofty charity for his sin.

"I don't see how it can insult you," he contended. "You're got a different way of looking at things, but that won't help you to dodge facts. Man's drunk. I said it, and I mean it. It ain't the first time, nor the second. He was drunk the day you came, and couldn't meet the train. That's why I met you. I ought to've told you, I guess, but I hated to make you feel bad. So I went to work and sobered him up, and sent him over to get married. I've always been kinda sorry for that. It was a low-down trick to play on you, and that's a fact. You ought to've had a chance to draw outa the game, but I didn't think about it at the time. Man and I have always been pretty good friends, and I was thinking of *his* side of the case. I thought he'd straighten up after he got married; he wasn't such a hard drinker-only he'd go on a toot when he got into town, like lots of men. I didn't think it had such a strong hold on him. And I knew he thought a lot of you, and if you went back on him it'd hit him pretty hard. Man ain't a bad fellow, only for that. And he's liable to do better when he finds out you know about it. A man will do 'most anything for a woman he thinks a lot of."

"Indeed!" Val was sitting now upon the red plush chair. Her face was perfectly colorless, her manner frozen. The word seemed to speak itself, without having any relation whatever to her thoughts and her emotions.

Kent waited. It seemed to him that she took it harder than she would have taken the news that Manley was dead. He had no means of gauging the horror of a young woman who has all her life been familiar with such terms as "the demon rum," and who has been taught that "intemperance is the doorway to perdition"; a young woman whose life has been sheltered jealously from all contact with the ugly things of the world, and who believes that she might better die than marry a drunkard. He watched her unobtrusively.

"Anyway, it was worrying over you that made him get off wrong to-day," he ventured at last, as a sort of palliative. "They say he was going to start home right in the face of the fire, and when they wouldn't let him, he headed straight for a saloon and commenced to pour whisky down him. He thought sure you-he thought the fire would —"

"I see," Val interrupted stonily. "For the very doubtful honor of shaking the hand of a politician, he left me alone to face as best I might the possibility of burning alive; and when it seemed likely that the possibility had become a certainty, he must celebrate his bereavement by becoming a beast. Is that what you would have me believe of my husband?"

"That's about the size of it," Kent admitted reluctantly. "Only I wouldn't have put it just that way, maybe."

"Indeed! And how would you pit it, then?"

Kent leaned harder against the door, and looked at her curiously. Women, it seemed to him, were always going to extremes; they were either too soft and meek, or else they were too hard and unmerciful.

"How would you put it? I am rather curious to know your point of view."

"Well, I know men better than you do, Mrs. Fleetwood. I know they can do some things that look pretty rotten on the surface, and yet be fairly decent underneath. You don't know how a habit like that gets a fellow just where he's weakest. Man ain't a beast. He's selfish and careless, and he gives way too easy, but he thinks the world of you. Jim says he cried like a baby when he came into the saloon, and acted like a crazy man. You don't want to be too hard on him. I've an idea this will learn him a lesson. If you take him the right way, Mrs. Fleetwood, the chances are he'll quit drinking."

Val smiled. Kent thought he had never before seen a smile like that, and hoped he never would see another. There was in it neither mercy nor mirth, but only the hard judgment of a woman who does not understand.

"Will you bring him to me here, Mr. Burnett? I do not feel quite equal to invading a saloon and begging him, on my knees, to come-after the conventional manner of drunkards' wives. But I should like to see him."

Kent stared. "He ain't in any shape to argue with," he remonstrated. "You better wait a while."

She rested her chin upon her hands, folded upon the high chair back, and gazed at him with her tawny eyes, that somehow reminded Kent of a lioness in a cage. He thought swiftly that a lioness would have as much mercy as she had in that mood.

"Mr. Burnett," she began quietly, when Kent's nerves were beginning to feel the strain of her silent stare, "I want to see Manley *as he is now*. I will tell you why. You aren't a woman, and you never will understand, but I shall tell you; I want to tell *somebody*.

"I was raised well-that sounds queer, but modesty forbids more. At any rate, my mother was very careful about me. She believed in a girl marrying and becoming a good wife to a good man, and to that end she taught me and trained me. A woman must give her all-her life, her past, present, and future-to the man she marries. For three years I thought how unworthy I was to be Manley's wife. *Unworthy*, do you hear? I slept with his letters under my pillow." The self-contempt in her tone! "I studied the things I thought would make me a better companion out here in the wilderness. I practiced hours and hours every day upon my violin, because Manley had admired my playing, and I thought it would please him to have me play in the firelight on winter evenings, when the blizzards were howling about the house! I learned to cook, to wash clothes, to iron, to sweep, and to scrub, and to make my own clothes, because Manley's wife would live where she could not hire servants to do these things. I lived a beautiful, picturesque dream of domestic happiness.

"I left my friends, my home, all the things I had been accustomed to all my life, and I came out here to live that dream!" She laughed bitterly.

"You can easily guess how much of it has come true, Mr. Burnett. But you don't know what it costs a girl to come down from the clouds and find that reality is hard and ugly-from dreaming of a cozy little nest of a home, and the love and care of-of Manley, to the reality-to carrying water and chopping wood and being left alone, day after day, and to find that his love only meant-Oh, you don't know how a woman clings to her ideals! You don't know how I have dung to mine. They have become rather tattered, and I have had to mend them often, but I have clung to them, even though they do not resemble much the dreams I brought with me to this horrible country.

"But if it's true, what you tell me-if Manley himself is another disillusionment-if beyond his selfishness and his carelessness he is a drunken brute whom I can't even respect, then I'm done with my ideals. I want to see him just as he is. I want to see him once without the halo I have kept shining all these months. I've got my life to live-but I want to face facts and live facts. I can't go on dreaming and making believe, after this." She stopped and looked at him speculatively, absolutely without emotion.

"Just before I left home," she went on in the same calm quiet, "a girl showed me some verses written by a very wicked man. At least, they say he is very wicked-at any rate, he is in jail. I thought the verses horrible and brutal; but now I think the man must be very wise. I remember a few lines, and they seem to me to mean Manley.

> "For each man kills the thing he loves —
> Some do it with a bitter look,
> Some with a flattering word;
> The coward does it with a kiss,
> The brave man with a sword.

"I don't remember all of it, but there was another line or two:

> "The kindest use a knife, because
> The dead so soon grow cold.

"I wish I had that poem now —I think I could understand it. I think —"

"I think you've got talking hysterics, if there is such a thing," Kent interrupted harshly. "You don't know half what you're saying. You've had a hard day, and you're all tired out, and everything looks outa focus. I know —I've seen men like that sometimes when some trouble hit 'em hard and unexpected. What you want is sleep; not poetry about killing people. A man, in the shape you are in, takes to whisky. You're taking to graveyard poetry-and, if you ask *me*, that's worse than whisky. You ain't normal. What you want to do is go straight to bed. When you wake up in the morning you won't feel so bad. You won't have half as many troubles as you've got now."

"I knew you wouldn't understand it," Val remarked coldly, still staring at him with her chin on her hands.

"You won't yourself, to-morrow morning," Kent declared unsympathetically, and called Mrs. Hawley from the kitchen. "You better put Mrs. Fleetwood to bed," he advised gruffly. "And if you've got anything that'll make her sleep, give her a dose of it. She's so tired she can't see straight." He was nearly to the outside door when Val recovered her speech.

"You men are all alike," she said contemptuously. "You give orders and you consider yourselves above all the laws of morality or decency; in reality you are beneath them. We shouldn't expect anything of the lower animals! How I *despise* men!"

"Now you're *talking*," grinned Kent, quite unmoved. "Whack us in a bunch all you like-but don't make one poor devil take it all. Men as a class are used to it and can stand it." He was laughing as he left the room, but his amusement lasted only until the door was closed behind him. "Lord!" he exclaimed, and drew a deep breath. "I'd sure hate to have that little woman say all them things about *me!*" and glanced involuntarily over his shoulder to where a crack of light showed under the faded green shade of one of the parlor windows.

He crossed the street and entered the saloon where Manley was still drinking heavily, his face crimson and blear-eyed and brutalized, his speech thickened disgustingly. He was sprawled in an armchair, waving an empty glass in an erratic attempt to mark the time of a college ditty six or seven years out of date, which he was trying to sing. He leered up at Kent.

"Wife 'sall righ'," he informed him solemnly. "Knew she would be-fine guards's got out there. 'Sall righ' —somebody shaid sho. Have a drink."

Kent glowered down at him, made a swift, mental decision, and pipped him by the shoulder. "You come with me," he commanded. "I've got something important I want to tell you. Come on-if you can walk."

"'Course I c'n walk all righ'. Shertainly I can walk. Wha's makes you think I can't walk? Want to inshult me? 'Sall my friends here-no secrets from my friends. Wha's want tell me? Shay it here."

Kent was a big man; that is to say, he was tall, well-muscled and active. But so was Manley. Kent tried the power of persuasion, leaving force as a last, doubtful result. In fifteen minutes or thereabouts he had succeeded in getting Manley outside the door, and there he balked.

"Wha's matter wish you?" he complained, pulling back. "C'm on back 'n' have drink. Wha's wanna tell me?"

"You wait. I'll tell you all about it in a minute. I've got something to show you, and I don't want the bunch to get next. Savvy?"

He had a sickening sense that the subterfuge would not have deceived a five-year-old child, but it was accepted without question.

He led Manley stumbling up the street, evading a direct statement as to his destination, pulled him off the board walk, and took him across a vacant lot well sprinkled with old shoes and tin cans. Here Manley fell down, and Kent's patience was well tested before he got him up and going again.

"Where y' goin'?" Manley inquired pettishly, as often as he could bring his tongue to the labor of articulation.

"You wait and I'll show you," was Kent's unvaried reply.

At last he pushed open a door and led his victim into the darkness of a small, windowless building. "It's in here-back against the wall, there," he said, pulling Manley after him. By feeling, and by a good sense of location, he arrived at a rough bunk built against the farther wall, with a blanket or two upon it.

"There you are," he announced grimly. "You'll have a sweet time getting anything to drink here, old boy. When you're sober enough to face your wife and have some show of squaring yourself with her, I'll come and let you out." He had pushed Manley down upon the bunk, and had reached the door before the other could get up and come at him. He pulled the door shut with a slam, slipped a padlock into the staple, and snapped it just before Manley lurched heavily against it. He was cursing as well as he could-was Manley, and he began kicking like an unruly child shut into a closet.

"Aw, let up," Kent advised him, through a crack in the wall. "Want to know where you are? Well, you're in Hawley's ice house; you know it's a fine place for drunks to sober up in; it's awful popular for that purpose. Aw, you can't do any business kicking-that's been tried lots of times. This is sure well built, for an ice house. No, I can't let you out. Couldn't possibly, you know. I haven't got the key-old lady Hawley has got it, and she's gone to bed hours ago. You go to sleep and forget about it. I'll talk to you in the morning. Good night, and pleasant dreams!"

The last thing Kent heard as he walked away was Manley's profane promise to cut Kent's heart out very early the next day.

"The darned fool," Kent commented, as he stopped in the first patch of lamplight to roll a cigarette. "He ain't got another friend in town that'd go to the trouble I've gone to for him. He'll realize it, too, when all that whisky quits stewing inside him."

# Chapter XII. A Lesson in Forgiveness

"Well, old-timer, how you coming? You sure do sleep sound-this is the third time I've come to tell you breakfast is ready and then some. You'll get the bottom of the coffeepot, for fair, if you don't hustle." Kent left the door of the ice house wide open behind him, so that the warmth of mid-morning swept in to do battle with the chill and damp of wet sawdust and buried ice.

Manley rolled over so that he faced his visitor, and his reply was abusive in the extreme. Kent waited, with an air of impersonal interest, until he was done and had turned his face away as though the subject was quite exhausted.

"Well, now you've got that load off your mind, come on over and get a cup of coffee. But while you're thinking about whether you want anything but my heart's blood, I'm going to speak right up and tell you a few things that commonly ain't none of my business.

"Do you know your wife came within an ace of burning to death yesterday?" Manley sat up with a jerk and glared at him. "Do you know you're burned out, slick and clean-all except the shack? Hay, stables, corral, wagons, chickens —" Kent spread his hands in a gesture including all minor details. "I rode over there when I saw the fire coming, and it's lucky I did, old-timer. I back-fired and saved the house-and your wife-from going up in smoke. But everything else went. Let that sink into your system, will you? And just see if you can draw a picture of what woulda happened if nobody had showed up-if that fire had hit the coulee with nobody there but your wife. Why, I run onto her half-way up the bluff, packing a wet sack, to fight it at the fire guards I Now, Man, it ain't any credit to, *you* that the worst didn't happen. I'd sure like to tell you what I think of a fellow that will leave a woman out there, twenty miles from town and ten from the nearest neighbor-and them not at home-to take a chance on a thing like that; but I can't. I never learned words enough.

"There's another thing. Old lady Hawley took more interest in her than you did; she drove out there to see how about it, as soon as the fire had burned on past and left the trail safe. And it didn't look good to her-that little woman stuck out there all by herself. She made her pack up some clothes, and brought her to town with her. She didn't want to come; she had an idea that she ought to stay with it till you showed up. But the only original Hawley is sure all right! She talked your wife plumb outa the house and into the rig, and brought her to town. She's over to the hotel now."

"Val at the hotel? How long has she been there?" Manley began smoothing his hair and his crumpled clothes with his hands, "Good heavens! You told her I'd gone on out, and had missed her on the trail, didn't you, Kent? She doesn't know I'm in town, does she? You always were a good fellow —I haven't forgotten how you —"

"Well, you can forget it now. I didn't tell her anything like that. I didn't think of it, for one thing. She knew all the time that you were in town. I'm tired of lying to her. I told her the truth. I told her you were drunk."

Manley's jaw dropped. "You-you told her —"

"Ex-actly. I told her you were drunk." Kent nodded gravely, and his lips curled as he watched the other cringe. "She called me a liar," he added, with a certain reminiscent amusement.

Manley brightened. "That's Val-once she believes in a person she's loyal as —"

"She ain't now," Kent interposed dryly. "When I let up she was plumb convinced. She knows now what ailed you the day she came and you didn't meet her."

"You dirty cur! And I thought you were a friend. You —"

"You thought right-until you got to rooting a little too deep in the mud, old-timer. And let me tell you something. I was your friend when I told her. She's got to know-you couldn't go on like this much longer without having her get wise; she ain't a fool. The thing for you to do now is to buck up and let her reform you. I've always heard that women are tickled plumb to death when they can reform a man. You go on over there and make your little talk, and then buckle down and live up to it. Savvy? That's your only chance now. It'll work, too.

"You *ought* to straighten up, Man, and act white! Not just to square yourself with her, but because you're going downhill pretty fast, if you only knew it. You ain't anything like you were two years ago, when we bached together. You've got to brace up pretty sudden, or you'll be so far gone you can't climb back. And when a man has got a wife to look after, it seems to me he ought to be the best it's in him to be. You were a fine fellow when you first hit the country-and she thought she was getting that same fine fellow when she came away out here to marry you. It ain't any of my business-but do you think you're giving her a square deal?" He waited a minute, and spoke the next sentence with a certain diffidence. "I'll gamble you haven't been disappointed in *her*."

"She's an angel-and I'm a beast!" groaned Manley, with the exaggerated self-abasement which so frequently follows close upon the heels of intoxication. "She'll never forgive a thing like that-the best thing I can do is to blow my brains out!"

"Like Walt. And have your picture enlarged and put in a gold frame, and hubby number two learning his morals from your awful example," elaborated Kent, in much the same tone he had employed when Val, only the day before, had rashly expressed a wish for a speedy death.

Manley sat up straighter and sent a look of resentment toward the man who bantered when he should have sympathized. "It's all a big joke with you, of course," he flared weakly. "You're not married-to a perfect woman; a woman who never did anything wrong in her life, and can't understand how anybody should want to, and can't forgive him when he does. She expects a man to be a saint. Why, I don't even smoke in the house-and she doesn't dream I'd ever swear, under any circumstances.

"Why, Kent, a fellow's *got* to go to town and turn himself loose sometimes, when he lives in a rarified atmosphere of refined morality, and listens to Songs Without Words and weepy classics on the violin, and never a thing to make your feet tingle. She doesn't believe in public dances, either. Nor cards. She reads 'The Ring and the Book' evenings, and wants to discuss it and read passages of it to me. I used to take some interest in those things, and she doesn't seem to see I've changed. Why, hang it, Kent, Cold Spring Coulee's no place for Browning-he doesn't fit in. All that sort of thing is a thousand miles behind me-and I've got to —" He stopped short and brooded, his eyes upon the dank sawdust at his feet.

"I'm a beast," he repeated rather lugubriously. "She's an angel-an Eastern-bred angel. And let me tell you, Kent, all that's pretty hard to live up to!"

Kent looked down at him meditatively, wondering if there was not a good deal of truth and justice in Manley's argument. But his sympathies had already gone to the other side, and Kent was not the man to make an emotional pendulum of himself.

"Well, what you going to do about it?" he asked, after a short silence.

For answer Manley rose to his feet with a certain air of determination, which flamed up oddly above his general weakness, like the last sputter of a candle burned down. "I'm going over and take my medicine-face the music," he said almost sullenly, "She's too good for me —I always knew it. And I haven't treated her right —I've left her out there alone too much. But she wouldn't come to town with me-she said she couldn't endure the sight of it. What could I do? *I* couldn't stay out there all the time; there were times when I had to come. She didn't seem to mind staying alone. She never objected. She was always sweet sad good-natured —and shut up inside of herself. She just gives you what she pleases of her mind, and the rest she hides —"

Kent laughed suddenly. "You married men sure do have all kinds of trouble," he remarked. "A fellow like me can go on a jamboree any time he likes, and as long as he likes, and it don't concern anybody but himself-and maybe the man he's working for; and look at you, scared plumb silly thinking of what your wife's going to say about it. If you ask me, I'm going to trot alone; I'd rather be lonesome than good, any old time."

That, however, did not tend to raise Manley's spirits any. He entered the hotel with visible reluctance, looked into the parlor, and heaved a sigh of relief when he saw that it was empty, wavered at the foot of the steep, narrow stairs, and retreated to the dining room, with Kent at his heels knowing that the matter had passed quite beyond his help or hindrance and had entered that mysterious realm of matrimony where no unwedded man or woman may follow and yet is curious enough to linger.

Just inside the door Manley stopped so suddenly that Kent bumped against him. Val, sweet and calm and cool, was sitting just where the smoke-dimmed sunlight poured in through a window upon her, and a breeze came with it and stirred her hair. She had those purple shadows under her eyes which betray us after long, sleepless hours when we live with our troubles and the world dreams around us; she had no color at all in her cheeks, and she had that aloofness of manner which Manley, in his outburst, had described as being shut up inside herself. She glanced up at them, just as she would have done had they both been strangers, and went on sugaring her coffee with a dainty exactness which, under the circumstances, seemed altogether too elaborate to be unconscious.

"Good morning," she greeted them quietly. "I think we must be the laziest people in town; at any rate, we seem to be the latest risers."

Kent stared at her frankly, so that she flushed a little under the scrutiny. Manley consciously avoided looking at her, and muttered something unintelligible while he pulled out a chair three places distant from her.

Val stole a sidelong, measuring look at her husband while she took a sip of coffee, and then her eyes turned upon Kent. More than ever, it seemed to him, they resembled the eyes of a lioness watching you quietly from the corner of her cage. You could look at them, but you could not look into them. Always they met your gaze with a baffling veil of inscrutability. But they were darker than the eyes of a lioness; they were human eyes; woman eyes-alluring eyes. She did not say a word, and, after a brief stare which might have meant almost anything, she turned to her plate of toast and broke away the burned edges of a slice and nibbled at the passable center as if she had no trouble beyond a rather unsatisfactory breakfast.

It was foolish, it was childish for three people who knew one another very well, to sit and pretend to eat, and to speak no word; so Kent thought, and tried to break the silence with some remark which would not sound constrained.

"It's going to storm," he flung into the silence, like chucking a rock into a pond.

"Do you think so?" Val asked languidly, just grazing him with a glance, in that inattentive way she sometimes had. "Are you going out home-or to what's left of it-to-day, Manley?" She did not look at him at all, Kent observed.

"I don't know —I'll have to hire a team —I'll see what —"

"Mrs. Hawley thinks we ought to stay here for a few days-or that I ought-while you make arrangements for building a new stable, and all that."

"If you want to stay," Manley agreed rather eagerly, "why, of course, you can. There's nothing out there to —"

"Oh, it doesn't matter in the slightest degree where I stay. I only mentioned it because I promised her I would speak to you about it." There was more than languor in her tone.

"They're going to start the fireworks pretty quick," Kent mentally diagnosed the situation and rose hurriedly. "Well, I've got to hunt a horse, myself, and pull out for the Wishbone," he explained gratuitously. "Ought to've gone last night. Good-bye." He closed the door behind him and shrugged his shoulders. "Now they can fight it out," he told himself. "Glad *I* ain't a married man!"

However, they did not fight it out then. Kent had no more than reached the office when Val rose, hoped that Manley would please excuse her, and left the room also. Manley heard her go up-stairs, found out from Arline what was the number of Val's room, and followed her. The door was locked, but when he rapped upon it Val opened it an inch and held it so.

"Val, let me in. I want to talk with you. I —God knows how sorry I am —"

"If He does, that ought to be sufficient," she answered coldly. "I don't feel like talking now-especially upon the subject you would choose. You're a man, supposedly. You must know what it is your duty to do. Please let us not discuss it-now or ever.

"But, Val —"

"I don't want to talk about it, I tell you! I won't —I *can't*. You must do without the conventional confession and absolution. You must have some sort of conscience-let that receive your penitence." She started to close the door, but he caught it with his hand.

"Val-do you hate me?"

She looked at him for a moment, as if she were trying to decide. "No," she said at last, "I don't think I do; I'm quite sure that I do not. But I'm terribly hurt and disappointed." She closed the door then and turned the key.

Manley stood for a moment rather blankly before it, then put his hands as deep in his pockets as they would go, and went slowly down the stairs. At that moment he did not feel particularly penitent. She would not listen to "the conventional confession!"

"That girl can be hard as nails!" he muttered, under his breath.

He went into the office, got a cigar, and lighted it moodily. He glanced at the bottles ranged upon the shelves behind the bar, drew in his breath for speech, let it go in a sigh, and walked out. He knew perfectly well what Val had meant. She had deliberately thrown him back upon his own strength. He had fallen by himself, he must pick himself up; and she would stand back and watch the struggle, and judge him according to his failure or his success. He had a dim sense that it was a dangerous experiment.

He looked for Kent, found him just as he was mounting at the stables, and let him go almost without a word. After all, no one could help him. He stood there smoking after Kent had gone, and when his cigar was finished he wandered back to the hotel. As was always the case after hard drinking, he had a splitting headache. He got a room as close to Val's as he could, shut himself into it, and gave himself up to his headache and to gloomy meditation. All day he lay upon the bed, and part of the time he slept. At supper time he rapped upon Val's door, got no answer, and went down alone, to find her in the dining room. There was an empty chair beside her, and he took it as his right. She talked a little-about the fire and the damage it had done. She said she was worried because she had forgotten to bring the cat, and what would it find to eat out there?

"Everything's burned perfectly black for miles and miles, you know," she reminded him.

They left the room together, and he followed her upstairs and to her door. This time she did not shut him out, and he went in and sat down by the window, and looked out upon the meager little street. Never, in the years he had known her, had she been so far from him. He watched her covertly while she searched for something in her suit case.

"I'm afraid I didn't bring enough clothes to last more than a day or two," she remarked. "I couldn't seem to think of anything that night. Arline did most of the packing for me. I'm afraid I misjudged that woman, Manley; there's a good deal to her, after all. But she *is* funny."

"Val, I want to tell you I'm going to-to be different. I've been a beast, but I'm going to —" So much he had rushed out before she could freeze him to silence again.

"I hope so," she cut in, as he hesitated, "That is something you must judge for yourself, and do by yourself. Do you think you will be able to get a team tomorrow?"

"Oh-to hell with a team!" Manley exploded.

Val dropped her hairbrush upon the floor. "Manley Fleetwood! Has it come to that, also? Isn't it enough to —" She choked. "Manley, you can be a —a drunken sot, if you choose —I've no power to prevent you; but you shall not swear in my presence. I thought you had some of the instincts of a gentleman, but —" She set her teeth hard together. She was white around the mouth, and her whole, slim body was aquiver with outraged dignity.

There was something queer in Manley's eyes as he looked at her, the length of the tiny room between them.

"Oh, I beg your pardon. I remember, now, your Fern Hill ethics. I may *go* to hell, for all of you-you will simply hold back your immaculate, moral skirts so that I may pass without smirching them; but I must not mention my destination-that is so unrefined!" He got up from the chair, with a laugh that was almost a snort. "You refuse to discuss a certain subject, though it's almost a matter of life and death with me; at least, it was. Your happiness and my own was at stake, I thought. But it's all right —I needn't have worried about it. I still have some of the instincts of a gentleman, and your pure ears shall not be offended by any profanity or any disagreeable 'conventional confessions.' The absolution, let me say, I expected to do without." He started, full of some secret intent, for the door.

Val humanized suddenly. By the time his fingers touched the door knob she had read his purpose, had readied his side, and was clutching his arm with both her hands.

"Manley Fleetwood, what are you going to do?" She was actually panting with the jump of her heart.

He turned the knob, so that the latch clicked. "Get drunk. Be the drunken sot you expect me to be. Go to that vulgar place which I must not mention in your presence. Let go my arm, Val."

She was all woman, then. She pulled him away from the door and the unnamed horror which lay outside. She was not the crying sort, but she cried, just the same-heartbrokenly, her head against his shoulder, as if she herself were the sinner. She clung to him, she begged him to forgive her hardness.

She learned something which every woman must learn if she would keep a little happiness in her life: she learned how to forgive the man she loved, and to trust him afterward.

# Chapter XIII. Arline Gives a Dance

A house, it would seem, is almost the least important part of a ranch; one can camp, with frying pan and blankets, in the shade of a bush or the shelter of canvas. But to do anything upon a ranch, one must have many things-burnable things, for the most part, as Manley was to learn by experience when he left Val at the hotel and rode out, the next day, to Cold Spring Coulee.

To ride over twenty miles of blackness is depressing enough in itself, but to find, at the end of the journey, that one's work has all gone for nothing, and one's money and one's plans and hopes, is worse than depressing. Manley sat upon his horse and gazed rather blankly at the heap of black cinders that had been his haystacks, and at the cold embers where had stood his stables, and at the warped bits of iron that had been his buckboard, his wagon, his rake and mower-all the things he had gathered around him in the three years he had spent upon the place.

The house merely emphasized his loss. He got down, picked up the cat, which was mewing plaintively beside his horse, snuggled it into his arm, and remounted. Val had told him to be sure and find the cat, and bring it back with him. His horses and his cattle-not many, to be sure, in that land of large holdings-were scattered, and it would take the round-up to gather them together again. So the cat, and the horse he rode, the bleak coulee, and the unattractive little house with its three rooms and its meager porch, were all that he could visualize as his worldly possessions. And when he thought of his bank account he winced mentally. Before snow fell he would be debt-ridden, the best he could do. For he must have a stable, and corral, and hay, and a wagon, and-he refused to remind himself of all the things he must have if he would stay on the ranch.

His was not a strong nature at best, and now he shrank from facing his misfortune and wanted only to get away from the place. He loped his horse half-way up the hill, which was not merciful riding. The half-starved cat yowled in his arms, and struck her claws through his coat till he felt the prick of them, and he swore; at the cat, nominally, but really at the trick fate had played upon him.

For a week he dallied in town, without heart or courage though Val urged him to buy lumber and build, and cheered him as best she could. He did make a half-hearted attempt to get lumber to the place, but there seemed to be no team in town which he could hire. Every one was busy, and put him off. He tried to buy hay of Blumenthall, of the Wishbone, of every man he met who had hay. No one had any hay to sell, however. Blumenthall complained that he was short, himself, and would buy if he could, rather than sell. The Wishbone foreman declared profanely-that hay was going to be worth a dollar a pound to *them*, before spring. They were all sorry for Manley, and told him he was "sure playing tough luck," but they couldn't sell any hay, that was certain.

"But we must manage somehow to fix the place so we can live on it this winter," Val would insist, when he told her how every move seemed blocked. "You're very brave, dear, and I'm proud of the way you are holding out-but Hope is not a good place for you. It would be foolish to stay in town. Can't you buy enough hay here in town-baled hay from the store-to keep our horses through the winter?"

"Well, I tried," Manley responded gloomily. "But Brinberg is nearly out. He's expecting a carload in, but it hasn't come yet. He said he'd let me know when it gets here."

Meanwhile the days slipped away, and imperceptibly the heat and haze of the fires gave place to bright sunlight and chill winds, and then to the chill winds without the sunshine. One morning the ground was frozen hard, and all the roofs gleamed white with the heavy frost. Arline bestirred herself, and had a heating stove set up in the parlor, and Val went down to the dry heat and the peculiar odor of a rusted stove in the flush of its first fire since spring.

The next day, as she sat by her window up-stairs, she looked out at the first nip of winter. A few great snowflakes drifted down from the slaty sky; a puff of wind sent them dancing down the street, shook more down, and whirled them giddily. Then the storm came and swept through the little street and whined lonesomely around the hotel.

Over at the saloon —"Pop's Place," it proclaimed itself in washed-out lettering-three tied horses circled uneasily until they were standing back to the storm, their bodies hunched together with the chill of it, their tails whipping between their legs. They accentuated the blank dreariness of the empty street. The snow was whitening their rumps and clinging, in tiny drifts, upon the saddle skirts behind the cantles.

All the little hollows of the rough, frozen ground were filling slowly, making white patches against the brown of the earth-patches which widened and widened until they met, and the whole street was blanketed with fresh, untrodden snow. Val shivered suddenly, and hurried down-stairs where the air was warm and all a-steam with cooking, and the odor of frying onions smote the nostrils like a blow in the face.

"I suppose we must stay here, now, till the storm is over," she sighed, when she met Manley at dinner. "But as soon as it clears we must go back to the ranch. I simply cannot endure another week of it."

"You're gitting uneasy —I seen that, two or three days ago," said Arline, who had come into the dining room with a tray of meat and vegetables, and overheard her. "You want to stay, now, till after the dance. There's going to be a dance Friday night, you know-everybody's coming. You got to wait for that."

"I don't attend public dances," Val stated calmly. "I am going home as soon as the storm clears-if Manley can buy a little hay, and find our horses, and get some sort of a driving vehicle."

"Well, if he can't, maybe he can round up a *ridin"* vee-hicle," Arline remarked dryly, placing the meat before Manley, the potatoes before Val, and the gravy exactly between the two, with mathematical precision. "I'm givin' that dance myself. You'll have to go —I'm givin' it in your honor."

"In-my-why, the *idea!* It's good of you, but —"

"And you're goin', and you're goin' to take your vi'lin over and play us some pieces. I tucked it into the rig and brought it in, on purpose. I planned out the hull thing, driving out to your place. In case you wasn't all burned up, I made up my mind I was going to give you a dance, and git you acquainted with folks. You needn't to hang back —I've told everybody it was in your honor, and that you played the vi'lin swell, and we'd have some real music. And I've sent to Chinook for the dance music-harp, two fiddles, and a coronet-and you ain't going to stall the hull thing now. I didn't mean to tell you till the last minute, but you've got to have time to mate up your mind you'll go to a public dance for oncet in your life. It ain't going to hurt you none. I've went, ever sence I was big enough to reach up and grab holt of my pardner-and I'm every bit as virtuous as you be. You're going, and you'n Man are going to head the grand march."

Val's face was flushed, her lips pursed, and her eyes wide. Plainly she was not quite sure whether she was angry, amused, or insulted. She descended straight to a purely feminine objection.

"But I haven't a thing to wear, and —"

"Oh, yes, you have. While you was dillydallying out in the front room, that night, wondering whether you'd have hysterics, or faint, or what all, I dug deep in that biggest trunk of yourn, and fished up one of your party dresses-white satin, it is, with embroid'ry all up 'n' down the front, and slimpsy lace; it's kinda low-'n'-behold-one of them —"

"My white satin-why, Mrs. Hawley! That-you must have brought the gown I wore to my farewell club reception. It has a train, and-why, the *idea!*"

"You can cut off the trail-you got plenty of time-or you can pin it up. I didn't have time that night to see how the thing was made, and I took it because I found white skirts and stockin's, and white satin slippers to go with it, right handy. You're a bride, and white'll be suitable, and the dance is in your honor. Wear it just as it is, fer all me. Show the folks what real clothes look like. I never seen a woman dressed up that way in my hull life. You wear it, Val, trail 'n' all. I'll back you up in it, and tell folks it's my idee, and not yourn."

"I'm not in the habit of apologizing to people for the clothes I wear." Val lifted her chin haughtily. "I am not at all sure that I shall go. In fact, I —"

"Oh, you'll go!" Arline rested her arms upon her bony hips and snapped her meager jaws together. "You'll go, if I have to carry you over. I've sent for fifteen yards of buntin' to decorate the hall with. I ain't going to all that trouble for nothing. I ain't giving a dance in honor of a certain person, and then let that person stay away. You-why, you'd queer yourself with the hull country, Val Fleetwood! You ain't got the least sign of an excuse You got the clothes, and you ain't sick. There's a reason why you got to show up. I ain't going into no details at present, but under the circumstances, it's *advisable*." She smelled something burning then, and bolted for the kitchen, where her sharp, rather nasal voice was heard upbraiding Minnie for some neglect.

Polycarp Jenks came in, eyed Val and Manley from under one lifted, eyebrow, smiled skinnily, and pulled out a chair with a rasping noise, and sat down facing them. Instinctively Val refrained from speaking her mind about Arline and her dance before Polycarp, but afterward, in their own room, she grew rather eloquent upon the subject. She would not go. She would not permit that woman to browbeat her into doing what she did not want to do, she said. In her honor, indeed! The impertinence of going to the bottom of her trunk, and meddling with her clothes-with that reception gown, of all others! The idea of wearing that gown to a frontier dance-even if she consented to go to such a dance! And expecting her to amuse the company by playing "pieces" on the violin!

"Well, why not?" Manley was sitting rather apathetically upon the edge of the bed, his arms resting upon his knees, his eyes moodily studying the intricate rose pattern in the faded Brussels carpet. They were the first words he had spoken; one might easily have doubted whether he had heard all Val said.

"Why not? Manley Fleetwood, do you mean to tell me —"

"Why not go, and get acquainted, and quit feeling that you're a pearl cast among swine? It strikes me the Hawley person is pretty level-headed on the subject. If you're going to live in this country, why not quit thinking how out of place you are, and how superior, and meet us all on a level? It won't hurt you to go to that dance, and it won't hurt you to play for them, if they want you to. You *can* play, you know; you used to play at all the musical doings in Fern Hill, and even in the city sometimes. And, let me tell you, Val, we aren't quite savages, out here. I've even suspected, sometimes, that we're just as good as Fern Hill."

"We?" Val looked at him steadily. "So you wish to identify yourself with these people-with Polycarp Jenks, and Arline Hawley, and —"

"Why not? They're shaky on grammar, and their manners could stand a little polish, but aside from that they're exactly like the people you've lived among all your life. Sure, I wish to identify myself with them. I'm just a rancher-pretty small punkins, too, among all these big outfits, and you're a rancher's wife. The Hawley person could buy us out for cash to-morrow, if she wanted to, and never miss the money. And, Val, she's giving that dance in your honor; you ought to appreciate that. The Hawley doesn't take a fancy to every woman she sees-and, let me tell you, she stands ace-high in this country. If she didn't like you, she could make you wish she did."

"Well, upon my word! I begin to suspect you of being a humorist, Manley. And even if you mean that seriously-why, it's all the funnier." To prove it, she laughed.

Manley hesitated, then left the room with a snort, a scowl, and a slam of the door; and the sound of Val's laughter followed him down the stairs.

Arline came up, her arms full of white satin, white lace, white cambric, and the toes of two white satin slippers showing just above the top of her apron pockets. She walked briskly in and deposited her burden upon the bed.

"My! them's the nicest smellin' things I ever had a hold of," she observed. "And still they don't seem to smell, either. Must be a dandy perfumery you've got. I brought up the things, seein' you know they're here. I thought you could take your time about cuttin' off the trail and fillin' in the neck and sleeves."

She sat down upon the foot of the bed, carefully tucking her gingham apron close about her so that it might not come in contact with the other.

"I never did see such clothes," she sighed. "I dunno how you'll ever git a chancet to wear 'em out in this country-seems to me they're most too pretty to wear, anyhow, I can git Marthy Winters to come over and help you-she does sewin' —and you can use my machine any time you want to. I'd take a hold myself if I didn't have all the baking to do for the dance. That Min can't learn nothing, seems like. I can't trust her to do a thing, hardly, unless I stand right over her. Breed girls ain't much account ever; but they're all that'll work out, in this country, seems like. Sometimes I swear I'll git a Chink and be done with it-only I got to have somebody I can talk to oncet in a while. I couldn't never talk to a Chink-they don't seem hardly human to me. Do they to you?

"And say! I've got some allover lace-it's eecrue-that you can fill in the neck with; you're welcome to use it-there's most a yard of it, and I won't never find a use for it. Or I was thinkin', there'll be enough cut off'n the trail to make a gamp of the satin, sleeves and all." She lifted the shining stuff with manifest awe. "It does seem a shame to put the shears to it-but you never'll git any wear out of it the way it is, and I don't believe —"

"Mis' *Hawley!*" shrilled the voice of Minnie at the foot of the stairs. "There's a couple of *drummers* off'n the *train*, 'n' they want *supper*, 'n' what'll I *give* 'em?"

"My heavens! That girl'll drive me crazy, sure!" Arline hurried to the door. "Don't take the roof off'n the house," she cried querulously down the stairway. "I'm comin'."

Val had not spoken a word. She went over to the bed, lifted a fold of satin, and smiled down at it ironically. "Mamma and I spent a whole month planning and sewing and gloating over you," she said aloud. "You were almost as important as a wedding gown; the club's farewell reception —'To what base uses we do —'"

"Oh, here's your slippers!" Arline thrust half her body into the room and held the slippers out to Val. "I stuck 'em into my pockets to bring up, and forgot all about 'em, mind you, till I was handin' the drummers their tea. And one of 'em happened to notice 'em, and raised right up outa his chair, an' said: 'Cind'rilla, sure as I live! Say, if there's a foot in this town that'll go into them slippers, for God's sake introduce me to the owner!' I told him to mind his own business. Drummers do get awful fresh when they think they can get away with it." She departed in a hurry, as usual.

Every day after that Arline talked about altering the satin gown. Every day Val was noncommittal and unenthusiastic. Occasionally she told Arline that she was not going to the dance, but Arline declined to take seriously so preposterous a declaration.

"You want to break a leg, then," she told Val grimly on Thursday. "That's the only excuse that'll go down with this bunch. And you better git a move on-it comes off to-morrer night, remember."

"I won't go, Manley!" Val consoled herself by declaring, again and again. "The idea of Arline Hawley ordering me about like a child! Why should I go if I don't care to go?"

"Search me." Manley shrugged his shoulders. "It isn't so long, though, since you were just as determined to stay and have the shivaree, you remember."

"Well, you and Mr. Burnett tried to do exactly what Arline is doing. You seemed to think I was a child, to be ordered about."

At the very last minute-to be explicit, an hour before the hall was lighted, several hours after smoke first began to rise from the chimney, Val suddenly swerved to a reckless mood. Arline had gone to her own room to dress, too angry to speak what was in her mind. She had worked since five o'clock that morning. She had bullied Val, she had argued, she had begged, she had wheedled. Val would not go. Arline had appealed to Manley, and Manley had assured her, with a suspicious slurring of his *esses* that he was out of it, and had nothing to say. Val, he said, could not be driven.

It was after Arline had gone to her room and Manley had returned to the "office" that Val suddenly picked up her hairbrush and, with an impish light in her eyes, began to pile her hair high upon her head. With her lips curved to match the mockery of her eyes, she began hurriedly to dress. Later, she went down to the parlor, where four women from the neighboring ranches were sitting stiffly and in constrained silence, waiting to be escorted to the hall. She swept in upon them, a glorious, shimmery creature all in white and gold. The women steed, wavered, and looked away-at the wall, the floor, at anything but Val's bare, white shoulders and arms as white. Arline had forgotten to look for gloves.

Val read the consternation in their weather-tanned faces, and smiled in wicked enjoyment. She would shock all of Hope; she would shock even Arline, who had insisted upon this. Like a child in mischief, she turned and went rustling down the ball to the dining room. She wanted to show Arline. She had not thought of the possibility of finding any one but Arline and Minnie there, so that she was taken slightly aback when she discovered Kent and another man eating a belated supper.

Kent looked up, eyed her sharply for just an instant, and smiled.

"Good evening, Mrs. Fleetwood," he said calmly. "Ready for the ball, I see. We got in late." He went on spreading butter upon his bread, evidently quite unimpressed by her magnificence.

The other man stared fixedly at his plate. It was a trifle, but Val suddenly felt foolish and ashamed. She took a step or two toward the kitchen, then retreated; down the hall she went, up the stairs and into her own room, the door of which she shut and locked.

"Such a fool!" she whispered vehemently, and stamped her white-shod foot upon the carpet. "He looked perfectly disgusted-and so did that other man. And no wonder. Such-it's *vulgar*, Val Fleetwood! It's just ill-bred, and coarse, and horrid!" She threw herself upon the bed and put her face in the pillow.

Some one-she thought it sounded like Manley-came up and tried the door, stood a moment before it, and went away again. Arline's voice, sharpened with displeasure, she heard speaking to Minnie upon the stairs. They went down, and there was a confusion of voices below. In the street beneath her window footsteps sounded intermittently, coming and going with a certain eagerness of tread. After a time there came, from a distance, the sound of violins and the "coronet" of which Arline had been so proud; and mingled with it was an undercurrent of shuffling feet, a mere whisper of sound, cut sharply now and then by the sharp commands of the floor manager. They were dancing-in her honor. And she was a fool; a proud, ill-tempered, selfish fool..

With one of her quick changes of mood she rose, patted her hair smooth, caught up a wrap oddly inharmonious with the gown and slippers, looped her train over her arm, tool her violin, and ran lightly down-stairs. The parlor, the dining room, the kitchen were deserted and the lights turned low. She braced herself mentally, and, flushing at the unaccustomed act, rapped timidly upon the door which opened into the office-which by that time she knew was really a saloon. Hawley himself opened the door, and in his eyes bulged at sight of her.

"Is Mr. Fleetwood here? I—I thought, after all, I'd go to the dance," she said, in rather a timid voice, shrinking back into the shadow.

"Fleetwood? Why, I guess he's gone on over. He said you wasn't going. You wait a minute. I—here, Kent! You take Mrs. Fleetwood over to the hall. Man's gone."

"Oh, no! I—really, it doesn't matter—"

But Kent had already thrown away his cigarette and come out to her, closing the door immediately after him.

"I'll take you over—I was just going, anyway," He assured her, his eyes dwelling upon her rather intently.

"Oh—I wanted Manley. I—I hate to go-like this, it seems so-so queer, in this place. At first I—I thought it would be a joke, but it isn't; it's silly and, —and ill-bred. You-everybody will be shocked, and —"

Kent took a step toward her, where she was shrinking against the stairway. Once before she had lost her calm composure and had let him peep into her mind. Then it had been on account of Manley; now, womanlike, it was her clothes.

"You couldn't be anything but all right, if you tried," he told her, speaking softly. "It isn't silly to look the way the Lord meant you to look. You-you-oh, you needn't worry-nobody's going to be shocked very hard." He reached out and took the violin from her; took also her arm and opened the outer door. "You're late," he said, speaking in a more commonplace tone. "You ought to have overshoes, or something-those white slippers won't be so white time you get there. Maybe I ought to carry you."

"The idea!" she stepped out daintily upon the slushy walk.

"Well, I can take you a block or two around, and have sidewalk all the way; that'll help some. Women sure are a lot of bother —I'm plumb sorry for the poor devils that get inveigled into marrying one."

"Why, Mr. Burnett! Do you always talk like that? Because if you do, I don't wonder —"

"No," Kent interrupted, looking down at her and smiling grimly, "as it happens, I don't. I'm real nice, generally speaking. Say! this is going to be a good deal of trouble, do you know? After you dance with hubby, you've got to waltz with me."

"*Got* to?" Val raised her eyebrows, though the expression was lost upon him.

"Sure. Look at the way I worked like a horse, saving your life-and the cat's —and now leading you all over town to keep those nice white slippers clean! By rights, you oughtn't to dance with anybody else. But I ain't looking for real gratitude. Four or five waltzes is all I'll insist on, but —" His tone was lugubrious in the extreme.

"Well, I'll waltz with you once-for saving the cat; and once for saving the slippers. For saving me, I'm not sure that I thank you." Val stepped carefully over a muddy spot on the walk. "Mr. Burnett, you-really, you're an awfully queer man."

Kent walked to the next crossing and helped her over it before he answered her. "Yes," he admitted soberly then, "I reckon you're right. I am-queer."

# Chapter XIV. A Wedding Present

Sunday it was, and Val had insisted stubbornly upon going back to the ranch; somewhat to her surprise, if one might judge by her face, Arline Hawley no longer demurred, but put up lunch enough for a week almost, and announced that she was going along. Hank would have to drive out, to bring back the team, and she said she needed a rest, after all the work and worry of that dance. Manley, upon whose account it was that Val was so anxious, seemed to have nothing whatever to say about it. He was sullenly acquiescent-as was perhaps to be expected of a man who had slipped into his old habits and despised himself for doing so, and almost hated his wife because she had discovered it and said nothing. Val was thankful, during that long, bleak ride over the prairie, for Arline's incessant chatter. It was better than silence, when the silence means bitter thoughts.

"Now," said Arline, moving excitedly in her seat when they neared Cold Spring Coulee, "maybe I better tell you that the folks round here has kinda planned a little su'prise for you. They don't make much of a showin' about bein' neighborly-not when things go smooth-but they're right there when trouble comes. It's jest a little weddin' present-and if it comes kinda late in the day, why, you don't want to mind that. My dance that I gave was a weddin' party, too, if you care to call it that. Anyway, it was to raise the money to pay for our present, as far as it went-and I want to tell you right now, Val, that you was sure the queen of the ball; everybody said you looked jest like a queen in a picture, and I never heard a word ag'inst your low-neck dress. It looked all right on *you*, don't you see? On me, for instance, it woulda been something fierce. And I'm real glad you took a hold and danced like you did, and never passed nobody up, like some woulda done. You'll be glad you did, now you know what it was for. Even danced with Polycarp Jenks-and there ain't hardly any woman but what'll turn *him* down; I'll bet he tromped all over your toes, didn't he?"

"Sometimes," Val admitted. "What about the surprise you were speaking of, Mrs. Hawley?"

"It does seem as if you might call me Arline," she complained irrelevantly. "We're comin' to that-don't you worry."

"Is it —a piano?"

"My lands, no! You don't need a fiddle and a piano both, do you? Man, what'd you rather have for a weddin' present?"

Manley, upon the front seat beside Hank, gave his shoulders an impatient twitch. "Fifty thousand dollars," he replied glumly.

"I'm glad you're real modest about it," Arline retorted sharply. She was beginning to tell herself quite frequently that she "didn't have no time for Man Fleetwood, seeing he wouldn't brace up and quit drinkin."

Val's lips curled as she looked at Manley's back. "What I should like," she said distinctly, "is a great, big pile of wood, all cut and ready for the stove, and water pails that never would go empty. It's astonishing how one's desires eventually narrow down to bare essentials, isn't it? But as we near the place, I find those two things more desirable than a piano!" Then she bit her lip angrily because she had permitted herself to give the thrust.

"Why, you poor thing! Man Fleetwood, do you —"

Val impulsively caught her by the arm. "Oh, hush! I was only joking," she said hastily. "I was trying to balance Manley's wish for fifty thousand dollars, don't you see? It was stupid of me, I know." She laughed unconvincingly. "Let me guess what the surprise is. First, is it large or small?"

"Kinda big," tittered Arline, falling into the spirit of the joke.

"Bigger than a —wait, now. A sewing machine?"

Arline covered her mouth with her hand and nodded dumbly.

"You say all the neighbors gave it and the dance helped pay for it-let me see. Could it possibly be-what in the world could it be? Manley, help me guess! Is it something useful, or just something nice?"

"Useful," said Arline, and snapped her jaws together as if she feared to let another word loose.

"Larger than a sewing machine, and useful." Val puckered her brows over the puzzle. "And all the neighbors gave it. Do you know, I've been thinking all sorts of nasty things about our poor neighbors, because they refused to sell Manley any hay. And all the while they were planning this sur —" She never finished that sentence, or the word, even.

With a jolt over a rock, and a sharp turn to the right, Hank had brought them to the very brow of the hill, where they could look down into the coulee, and upon the house standing in its tiny, unkempt yard, just beyond the sparse growth of bushes which marked the spring creek. Involuntarily every head turned that way, and every pair of eyes looked downward. Hank chirped to the horses, threw all his weight upon the brake, and they rattled down the grade, the brake block squealing against the rear wheels. They were half-way down before any one spoke. It was Val, and she almost whispered one word:

"Manley!"

Arline's eyes were wet, and there was a croak in her voice when she cried jubilantly: "Well, ain't that better 'n a sewin' machine-or a piano?"

But Val did not attempt an answer. She was staring-staring as if she could not convince herself of the reality. Even Manley was jarred out of his gloomy meditations, and half rose in the seat that he might see over Hank's shoulder.

"That's what your neighbors have done," Arline began eagerly, "and they nearly busted tryin' to git through in time, and to keep it a dead secret. They worked like whiteheads, lemme tell you, and never even stopped for the storm. The night of the dance I heard all about how they had to hurry. And I guess Kent's there an' got a fire started, like I told him to. I was afraid it might be colder'n what it is. I asked him if he wouldn't ride over an' warm up the house t'day-and I see there's a smoke, all right." She looked at Manley, and then turned to Val. "Well, ain't you goin' to say anything? You dumb, both of you?"

Val took a deep breath. "We should be dumb," she said contritely. "We should go down on our knees and beg their pardon and yours —I especially. I think I've never in my life felt quite so humbled-so overwhelmed with the goodness of my fellows, and my own unworthiness. I —I can't put it into words-all the resentment I have felt against the country and the people in it-as if-oh, tell them all how I want them to forgive me for-for the way I have felt. And —*Arline* —"

"There, now —I didn't bargain for you to make it so serious," Arline expostulated, herself near to crying. "It ain't nothing much-us folks believe in helpin' when help's needed, that's all. For Heaven's sake, don't go 'n' cry about it!"

Hank pulled up at the gate with a loud *whoa* and a grip of the brake. From the kitchen stovepipe a blue ribbon of smoke waved high in the clear air. Kent appeared, grinning amiably, in the doorway, but Val was looking beyond, and scarcely saw him-beyond, where stood a new stable upon the ashes of the old; a new corral, the posts standing solidly in the holes dug for those burned away, a new haystack-when hay was almost priceless! A few chickens wandered about near the stable, and Val recognized them as Arline's prized Plymouth Rocks. Small wonder that she and Manley were stunned to silence. Manley still looked as if some one had dealt him an unexpected blow in the face. Val was white and wide-eyed.

Together they walked out to the stable. When they stopped, she put her hand timidly upon his aim. "Dear," she said softly, "there is only one way to thank them for this, and that is to be the very best it is in us to be. We will, won't we? We-we haven't been our best, but we'll start in right now. Shall we, Manley?"

Manley looked down at her for a moment, saying nothing.

"Shall we, Manley? Let us start now, and try again. Let's play the fire burned up our old selves, and we're all new, and strong-shall we? And we won't feel any resentment for what is past, but we'll work together, and think together, and talk together, without any hidden thing we can't discuss freely. Please, Manley!"

He knew what she meant, well enough. For the last two days he had been drinking again. On the night of the dance he had barely kept within the limit of decent behavior. He had read

Val's complete understanding and her disgust the morning after-and since then they had barely spoken except when speech was necessary. Oh, he knew what she meant! He stood for another minute, and she let go his arm and stood apart, watching his face.

A good deal depended upon the next minute, and they both knew it, and hardly breathed. His hand went slowly into a deep pocket of his overcoat, his fingers closed over something, and drew it reluctantly to the light. Shamefaced, he held it up for her to see —a flat bottle of generous size, full to within a inch of the cork with a pale, yellow liquid.

"There-take it, and break it into a million pieces," he said huskily. "I'll try again."

Her yellow-brown eyes darkened perceptibly. "Manley Fleetwood, *you* must throw it away. This is your fight-be a man and *fight*."

"Well-there! May God damn me forever if I touch liquor again! I'm through with the stuff for keeps!" He held the bottle high, without looking at it, and sent it crashing against the stable door.

"Manley!" She stopped her ears, aghast at his words, but for all that her eyes were ashine. She went up to him and put her arms around him. "Now we can start all over again," she said. "We'll count our lives from this minute, dear, and we'll keep them clean and happy. Oh, I'm so glad! So glad and so proud, dear!"

Kent had got half-way down the path from the house; he stopped when Manley threw the bottle, and waited. Now he turned abruptly and retraced his steps, and he did not look particularly happy, though he had been smiling when he left the kitchen.

Arline turned from the window as he entered.

"Looks like Man has swore off ag'in," she observed dryly. "Well, let's hope 'n' pray he stays swore off."

## Chapter XV. A Compact

The blackened prairie was fast hiding the mark of its fire torture under a cloak of tender new grass, vividly green as a freshly watered, well-kept lawn. Meadow larks hopped here and there, searching long for a sheltered nesting place, and missing the weeds where they were wont to sway and swell their yellow breasts and sing at the sun. They sang just as happily, however, on their short, low flights over the levels, or sitting upon gray, half-buried boulders upon some barren hilltop. Spring had come with lavish warmth. The smoke of burning ranges, the bleak winter with its sweeping storms of snow and wind, were pushed info the past, half forgotten in this new heaven and new earth, when men were glad simply because they were alive.

On a still, Sunday morning-that day which, when work does not press, is set apart in the range land for slight errands, attention to one's personal affairs, and to the pursuit of pleasure-Kent jogged placidly down the long hill into Cold Spring Coulee and pulled up at the familiar little unpainted house of rough boards, with its incongruously dainty curtains at the windows and its tiny yard, green and scrupulously clean.

The cat with white spots on its sides was washing its face on the kitchen doorstep. Val was kneeling beside the front porch, painstakingly stringing white grocery twine upon nails, which she drove into the rough posts with a small rock. The primitive trellis which resulted was obviously intended for the future encouragement of the sweet-pea plants just unfolding their second clusters of leaves an inch above ground. She did not see Kent at first, and he sat quiet in the saddle, watching her with a flicker of amusement in his eyes; but in a moment she struck her finger and sprang up with a sharp little cry, throwing the rock from her.

"Didn't you know that was going to happen, sooner or later?" Kent inquired, and so made known his presence.

"Oh-how do you do?" She came smiling down to the gate, holding the hurt finger tightly clasped in the other hand. "How comes it you are riding this way? Our trail is all growing up to grass, so few ever travel it."

"We're all hard-working folks these days. Where's Man?"

"Manley is down to the river, I think." She rested both arms upon the gatepost and regarded him with her steady eyes. "If you can wait, he will be back soon. He only went to see if the river is fordable. He thinks two or three of our horses are on the other side, and he'd like to get them. The river has been too high, but it's lowering rather fast. Won't you come in?" She was pleasant, she was unusually friendly, but Kent felt vaguely that, somehow, she was different.

He had not seen her for three months. Just after Christmas he had met her and Manley in town, when he was about to leave for a visit to his people in Nebraska. He had returned only a week or so before, and, if the truth were known, he was not displeased at the errand which brought him this way. He dismounted, and when she moved away from the gate he opened it and went in.

"Well," he began lightly, when he was seated upon the floor of the porch and she was back at her trellis, "and how's the world been using you? Had any more calamities while I've been gone?"

She busied herself with tying together two pieces of string, so that the whole would reach to a certain nail driven higher than her head. She stood with both hands uplifted, and her face, and her eyes; she did not reply for so long that Kent began to wonder if she had heard him. There was no reason why he should watch her so intently, or why he should want to get up and push back the one lock of hair which seemed always in rebellion and always falling across her temple by itself.

He was drifting into a dreamy wonder that all women with yellow-brown hair should not be given yellow-brown eyes also, and to wishing vaguely that it might be his luck to meet one some time-one who was not married-when she looked down at him quite unexpectedly. He was startled, and half ashamed, and afraid that she might not like what he, had been thinking.

She was staring straight into his eyes, and he knew that she was thinking of something that affected her a good deal.

"Unless it's a calamity to discover that the world is-what it is, and people in it are-what they are, and that you have been a blind idiot. Is that a calamity, Mr. Cowboy? Or is it a blessing? I've been wondering."

Kent discovered, when he started to speak, that he had run short of breath. "I reckon that depends on how the discovery pans out," he ventured, after a moment. He was not looking at her then. For some reason, unexplained to himself, he felt that it wasn't right for him to look at her; nor wise; nor quite pleasant in its effect. He did not know exactly what she meant, but he knew very well that she meant something more than to make conversation.

"That," she said, and gave a little sigh —"that takes so long-don't you know? The panning out, as you call it. It's hard to see things very clearly, and to make a decision that you know is going to stand the test, and then-just sit down and fold your hands, because some sordid, petty little reason absolutely prevents your doing anything. I hate waiting for anything. Don't you? When I want to do a thing, I want to do it immediately. These sweet-peas —now I've fixed the trellis for them to climb upon, I resent it because they don't take hold right now. Nasty little things-two inches high, when they should be two yards, and all covered with beautiful blossoms."

"Not the last of April," he qualified. "Give 'em a fair chance, can't you? They'll make it, all right; things take time."

She laughed surrenderingly, and came and sat down upon the porch near him, and tapped a slipper toe nervously upon the soft, green sod.

"Time! Yes —" She threw back her head and smiled at him brightly-and appealingly, it seemed to Kent. "You remember what you told me once-about sheep-herders and *such* going crazy out here? The *such* is sometimes ready to agree with you." She turned her head with a quick impatience. "Such is learning to ride a horse," she informed him airily. "Such does it on the sly-and she fell off once and skinned her elbow, and she-well, Such hasn't any sidesaddle-but she's learning, 'by granny!'"

Kent laughed unsteadily, and looked sidelong at her with eyes alight. She matched the glance for just about one second, and turned her eyes away with a certain consciousness that gave Kent a savage delight. Of a truth, she was different! She was human, she was intolerably alluring. She was not the prim, perfectly well-bred young woman he had met at the train. Lonesome Land was doing its work. She was beginning to think as an individual-as a woman; not merely as a member of conventional society.

"Such is beginning to be the proper stuff —'by granny," he told her softly.

He was afraid his tone had offended her. She rose, and her color flared and faded. She leaned slightly against the post beside her, and, with a hand thrown up and half shielding her face, she stared out across the coulee to the hill beyond.

"Did you —I feel like a fool for talking like this, but one sometimes clutches at the least glimmer of sympathy and-and understanding, and speaks what should be kept bottled up inside, I suppose. But I've been bottled up for so *long* —" She struck her free hand suddenly against her lips, as if she would apply physical force to keep them from losing all self-control. When she spoke again, her voice was calmer. "Did you ever get to the point, Mr. Cowboy, where you-you dug right down to the bottom of things, and found that you must do something or go mad-and there wasn't a thing you could do? Did you ever?" She did not turn toward him, but kept her eyes to the hills. When he did not answer, however, she swung her head slowly and looked down at him, where he sat almost at her feet.

Kent was leaning forward, studying the gashes he had cut in the sod with his spurs. His brows were knitted close.

"I kinda think I'm getting there pretty fast," he owned gravely when he felt her gaze upon him. "Why?"

"Oh-because you can understand how one must speak sometimes. Ever since I came, you have been—I don't know-different. At first I didn't like you at all; but I could see you were different. Since then-well, you have now and then said something that made me see one could speak to you, and you would understand. So I—" She broke off suddenly and laughed an apology. "Am I boring you dreadfully? One grows so self-centered living alone. If you aren't interested —"

"I am." Kent was obliged to clear his throat to get those two words out. "Go on. Say all you want to say."

She laughed again wearily. "Lately," she confessed nervously, "I've taken to telling my thoughts to the cat. It's perfectly safe, but, after all, it isn't quite satisfying." She stopped again, and stood silent for a moment.

"It's because I am alone, day after day, week in and week out," she went on. "In a way, I don't mind it-under the circumstances I prefer to be alone, really. I mean, I wouldn't want any of my people near me. But one has too much time to think. I tell you this because I feel I ought to let you know that you were right that time; I don't suppose you even remember it! But I do. Once last fall-the first time you came to the ranch-you know, the time I met you at the spring, you seemed to see that this big, lonesome country was a little too much for me. I resented it then. I didn't want any one to tell me what I refused to admit to myself. I was trying so hard to like it-it seemed my only hope, you see. But now I'll tell you you were right.

"Sometimes I feel very wicked about it. Sometimes I don't care. And sometimes I —I feel I shall go crazy if I can't talk to some one. Nobody comes here, except Polycarp Jenks. The only woman I know really well in the country is Arline Hawley. She's good as gold, but-she's intensely practical; you can't tell her your troubles-not unless they're concrete and have to do with your physical well-being. Arline lacks imagination." She laughed again shortly.

"I don't know why I'm taking it for granted you don't," she said. "You think I'm talking pore nonsense, don't you, Mr. Cowboy?" She turned full toward him, and her yellow-brown eyes challenged him, begged him for sympathy and understanding, held him at bay-but most of all they set his blood pounding sullenly in his veins. He got unsteadily to his feet.

"You seem to pass up a lot of things that count, or you wouldn't say that," he reminded her huskily. "That night in town, just after the fire, for instance. And here, that same afternoon. I tried to jolly you out of feeling bad, both those times; but you know I understood. You know damn' *well* I understood! And you know I was sorry. And if you don't know, I'd do anything on God's green earth —" He turned sharply away from her and stood kicking savagely backward at a clod with his rowel. Then he felt her hand touch his arm, and started. After that he stood perfectly still, except that he quivered like a frightened horse.

"Oh, it doesn't mean much to you-you have your life, and you're a man, and can do things when you want to. But I do so need a friend! Just somebody who understands, to whom I can talk when that is the only thing will keep me sane. You saved my life once, so I feel-no, I don't mean that. It isn't because of anything you did; it's just that I feel I can talk to you more freely than to any one I know. I don't mean whine. I hope I'm not a whiner. If I've blundered, I'm willing to-to take my medicine, as you would say. But if I can feel that somewhere in this big, empty country just one person will always feel kindly toward me, and wish me well, and be sorry for we when I —when I'm miserable, and —" She could not go on. She pressed her lips together tightly, and winked back the tears.

Kent faced about and laid both his hands upon her shoulders. His face was very tender and rather sad, and if she had only understood as well as he did —. But she did not.

"Little woman, listen here," he said. "You're playing hard luck, and I know it; maybe I don't know just how hard-but maybe I can kinda give a guess. If you'll think of me as your friend-your pal, and if you'll always tell yourself that your pal is going to stand by you, no matter what comes, why-all right." He caught his breath.

She smiled up at him, honestly pleased, wholly without guile-and wholly blind. "I'd rather have such a friend, just now, than anything I know, except —. But if your sweetheart should object-could you —"

His fingers gripped her shoulders tighter for just a second, and he let her go. "I guess that part'll be all right," he rejoined in a tone she could not quite fathom. "I never had one in m' life."

"Why, you poor thing!" She stood back and tilted her head at him. "You poor —*pal*. I'll have to see about that immediately. Every young man wants a sweetheart-at least, all the young men I ever knew wanted one, and —"

"And I'll gamble they all wanted the same one," he hinted wickedly, feeling himself unreasonably happy over something he could not quite put into words, even if he had dared.

"Oh, no. Hardly ever the same one, luckily. Do you know-pal, I've quite forgotten what it was all about-the unburdening of my soul, I mean. After all, I think I must have been just lonesome. The country is just as big, but it isn't quite so-so *empty*, you see. Aren't you awfully vain, to see how you have peopled it with your friendship?" She clasped her hands behind her and regarded him speculatively. "I hope, Mr. Cowboy, you're in earnest about this," she observed doubtfully. "I hope you have imagination enough to see it isn't silly, because if I suspected you weren't playing fair, and would go away and laugh at me, I'd —scratch-you." She nodded her head slowly at him. "I've always been told that, with tiger eyes, you find the disposition of a tiger. So if you don't mean it, you'd better let me know at once."

Kent brought the color into her cheeks with his steady gaze. "I was just getting scared *you* didn't mean it," he averred. "If my pal goes back on me-why, Lord help her!"

She took a slow, deep breath. "How is it you men ratify a solemn agreement?" she puzzled. "Oh, yes." With a pretty impulse she held out her right hand, half grave, half playful. "Shake on it, pal!"

Kent took her hand and pressed it as hard as he dared. "You're going to be a dandy little chum," he predicted gamely. "But let me tell you right now, if you ever get up on your stilts with me, there's going to be all kinds of trouble. You call me Kent-that is," he qualified, with a little, unsteady laugh, "when there ain't any one around to get shocked."

"I suppose this *isn't* quite conventional," she conceded, as if the thought had just then occurred to her. "But, thank goodness, out here there aren't any conventions. Every one lives as every one sees fit. It isn't the best thing for some people," she added drearily. "Some people have to be bolstered up by conventions, or they can't help miring in their own weaknesses. But we don't; and as long as we understand —" She looked to him for confirmation.

"As long as we understand, why, it ain't anybody's business but our own," he declared steadily.

She seemed relieved of some lingering doubt. "That's exactly it. I don't know why I should deny myself a friend, just because that friend happens to be a man, and I happen to be-married. I never did have much patience with the rule that a man must either be perfectly indifferent, or else make love. I'm so glad you-understand. So that's all settled," she finished briskly, "and I find that, as I said, it isn't at all necessary for me to unburden my soul."

They stood quiet for a moment, their thoughts too intangible for speech.

"Come inside, won't you?" she invited at last, coming back to everyday matters. "Of course you're hungry-or you ought to be. You daren't run away from my cooking this time, Mr. Cowboy. Manley will be back soon, I think. I must get some lunch ready."

Kent replied that he would stay outside and smoke, so she left him with a fleeting smile, infinitely friendly and confiding and glad. He turned and looked after her soberly, gave a great sigh, and reached mechanically for his tobacco and papers; thoughtfully rolled a cigarette, lighted it, and held the match until it burned quite down to his thumb and fingers. "Pals!" he said just under his breath, for the mere sound of the word. "All right-pals it is, then."

He smoked slowly, listening to her moving about in the house. Her steps came nearer. He turned to look.

"What was it you wanted to see Manley about?" she asked him from the doorway. "I just happened to wonder what it could be."

"Well, the Wishbone needs men, and sent me over to tell him he can go to work. The wagons are going to start to-morrow. He'll want to gather his cattle up, and of course we know about how he's fixed-for saddle horses and the like. He can work for the outfit and draw wages, and get his cattle thrown back on this range and his calves branded besides. Get paid for doing what he'll have to do anyhow, you see."

"I see." Val pushed back the rebellious lock of hair. "Of course you suggested the idea to the Wishbone. You're always doing something—"

"The outfit is short-handed," he reiterated. "They need him. They ain't straining a point to do Man a favor-don't you ever think it! Well-he's coming," he broke off, and started to the gate.

Manley clattered up, vociferously glad to greet him. Kent, at his urgent invitation, led his horse to the stable and turned him into the corral, unsaddled and unbridled him so that he could eat. Also, he told his errand. Manley interrupted the conversation to produce a bottle of whisky from a cunningly concealed hole in the depleted haystack, and insisted that Kent should take a drink. Kent waved it off, and Manley drew the cork and held the bottle to his own lips.

As he stood there, with his face uplifted while the yellow liquor gurgled down his throat, Kent watched him with a curiously detached interest. So that's how Manley had kept his vow! he was thinking, with an impersonal contempt. Four good swallows-Kent counted them.

"You're hitting it pretty strong, Man, for a fellow that swore off last fall," he commented aloud.

Manley took down the bottle, gave a sigh of pure, animal satisfaction, and pushed the cork in with an unconsciously regretful movement.

"A fellow's got to get something out of life," he defended peevishly. "I've had pretty hard luck-it's enough to drive a fellow to most any kind of relief. Burnt out, last fall-cattle scattered and calves running the range all winter—I haven't got stock enough to stand that sort of a deal, Kent. No telling where I stand now on the cattle question. I did have close to a hundred head-and three of my best geldings are missing—a poor man can't stand luck like that. I'm in debt too-and when you've got an iceberg in the house-when a man's own wife don't stand by him-when he can't get any sympathy from the very one that ought to-but, then, I hope I'm a gentleman; I don't make any kick against *her* —my domestic affairs are my own affairs. Sure. But when your wife freezes up solid —" He held the bottle up and looked at it. "Best friend I've got," he finished, with a whining note in his voice.

Kent turned away disgusted. Manley had coarsened. He had "slopped down" just when he should have braced up and caught the fighting spirit-the spirit that fights and overcomes obstacles. With a tightening of his chest, he thought of his "pal," tied for life to this whining drunkard. No wonder she felt the need of a friend!

"Well, are you going out with the Wishbone?" he asked tersely, jerking his thoughts back to his errand. "If you are, you'll need to go over there to-night —the wagons start out to-morrow. Maybe you better ride around by Polly's place and have him come over here, once in a while, to look after things. You can't leave your wife alone without somebody to kinda keep an eye out for her, you know. Polycarp ain't going to ride this spring; he's got rheumatism, or some darned thing. But he can chop what wood she'll need, and go to town for her once in a while, and make sure she's all right. You better leave your gentlest horse here for her to use, too. She can't be left afoot out here."

Manley was taking another long swallow from the bottle, but he heard.

"Why, sure —I never thought about that. I guess maybe I *had* better get Polycarp. But Val could make out all right alone. Why, she's held it down here for a week at a time-last winter, when I'd forgot to come home" —he winked shamelessly —"or a storm would come up so I couldn't get home. Val isn't like some fool women, I'll say that much for her. She don't care whether I'm around or not; fact is, sometimes I think she's better pleased when I'm gone. But you're right —I'll see Polycarp and have him come over once in a while. Sure. Glad you spoke of it. You always had a great head for thinking about other people, Kent. You ought to get married."

"No, thanks," Kent scowled. "I haven't got any grudge against women. The world's full of men ready and willing to give 'em a taste of pure, unadulterated hell."

Manley stared at him stupidly, and then laughed doubtfully, as if he felt certain of having, by his dullness, missed the point of a very good joke.

After that the time was filled with the preparations for Manley's absence. Kent did what he could to help, and Val went calmly about the house, packing the few necessary personal belongings which might be stuffed into a "war bag" and used during round-up. Beyond an occasional glance of friendly understanding, she seemed to have forgotten the compact she had made with Kent.

But when they were ready to ride away, Kent purposely left his gloves lying upon the couch, and remembered them only after Manley was in the saddle. So he went back, and Val followed him into the room. He wanted to say something-he did not quite know what-something that would bring them a little closer together, and keep them so; something that would make her think of him often and kindly. He picked up his gloves and held out his hand to her-and then a diffidence seized his tongue. There was nothing he dared say. All the eloquence, all the tenderness, was in his eyes.

"Well-good-by, pal. Be good to yourself," he said simply.

Val smiled up at him tremulously. "Good-by, my one friend. Don't —don't get hurt!"

Their clasp tightened, their hands dropped apart rather limply. Kent went out and got upon his horse, and rode away beside Manley, and talked of the range and of the round-up and of cattle and a dozen other things which interest men. But all the while one exultant thought kept reiterating itself in his mind: "She never said that much to *him!* She never said that much to *him!*"

# Chapter XVI. Manley's New Tactics

To the east, to the south, to the north went the riders of the Wishbone, gathering the cattle which the fires had driven afar. No rivers stopped them, nor mountains, nor the deep-scarred coulees, nor the plains. It was Manley's first experience in real round-up work, for his own little herd he had managed to keep close at home, and what few strayed afar were turned back, when opportunity afforded, by his neighbors, who wished him well. Now he tasted the pride of ownership to the full, when a VP cow and her calf mingled with the milling Wishbones and Double Diamonds. He was proud of his brand, and proud of the sentiment which had made him choose Val's initials. More than once he explained to his fellows that VP meant Val Peyson, and that he had got it recorded just after he and Val were engaged. He was not sentimental about her now, but he liked to dwell upon the fact that he had been; it showed that he was capable of fine feeling.

More dominant, however, as the weeks passed and the branding went on, became the desire to accumulate property-cattle. The Wishbone brand went scorching through the hair of hundreds of calves, while the VP scared tens. It was not right. He felt, somehow, cheated by fate. He mentally figured the increase of his herd, and it seemed to him that it took a long while, much longer than it should, to gain a respectable number in that manner. He cast about in his mind for some rich acquaintance in the East who might be prevailed upon to lend him capital enough to buy, say, five hundred cows. He began to talk about it occasionally when the boys lay around in the evenings.

"You want to ride with a long rope," suggested Bob Royden, grinning openly at the others. "That's the way to work up in the cow business. Capital nothing! You don't get enough excitement buying cattle; you want to steal 'em. That's what I'd do if I had a brand of my own and all your ambitions to get rich."

"And get sent up," Manley rounded out the situation. "No, thanks." He laughed. "It's a better way to get to the pen than it is to get rich, from all accounts."

Sandy Moran remembered a fellow who worked a brand and kept it up for seven or eight years before they caught him, and he recounted the tale between puffs at his cigarette. "Only they didn't catch him" he finished. "A puncher put him wise to what was in the wind, and he sold out cheap to a tenderfoot and pulled his freight. They never did locate him." Then, with a pointed rock which he picked up beside him, he drew a rude diagram or two in the dirt. "That's how he done it," he explained. "Pretty smooth, too."

So the talk went on, as such things will, idly, without purpose save to pass the time. Shop talk of the range it was. Tales of stealing, of working brands, and of branding unmarked yearlings at weaning time. Of this big cattleman and that, who practically stole whole herds, and thereby took long strides toward wealth. Range scandals grown old; range gossip all of it, of men who had changed a brand or made one, using a cinch ring at a tiny fire in a secluded hollow, or a spur, or a jackknife; who were caught in the act, after the act, or merely suspected of the crime. Of "sweat" brands, blotched brands, brands added to and altered, of trials, of shootings, of hangings, even, and "getaways" spectacular and humorous and pathetic.

Manley, being in a measure a pilgrim, and having no experience to draw upon, and not much imagination, took no part in the talk, except that he listened and was intensely interested. Two months of mingling with men who talked little else had its influence.

That fall, when Manley had his hay up, and his cattle once more ranging close, toward the river and in the broken country bounded upon the west by the fenced-in railroad, three calves bore the VP brand-three husky heifers that never had suckled a VP mother. So had the range gossip, sown by chance in the soil of his greed of gain and his weakening moral fiber, borne fruit.

The deed scared him sober for a month. For a month his color changed and his blood quickened whenever a horseman showed upon the rim of Cold Spring Coulee. For a month he never left the ranch unless business compelled him to do so, and his return was speedy, his eyes anxious until he knew that all was well. After that his confidence returned. He grew more secretive, more self-assured, more at ease with his guilt. He looked the Wishbone men squarely in the eye, and it seldom occurred to him that he was a thief; or if it did, the word was but a synonym for luck, with shrewdness behind. Sometimes he regretted his timidity. Why three calves only? In a deep little coulee next the river—a coulee which the round-up had missed-had been more than three. He might have doubled the number and risked no more than for the three. The longer he dwelt upon that the more inclined he was to feel that he had cheated himself.

That fall there were no fires. It would be long before men grew careless when the grass was ripened and the winds blew hot and dry from out the west. The big prairie which lay high between the river and Hope was dotted with feeding cattle. Wishbones and Double Diamonds, mostly, with here and there a stray.

Manley grew wily, and began to plan far in advance. He rode here and there, quietly keeping his own cattle well down toward the river. There was shelter there, and feed, and the idea was a good one. Just before the river broke up he saw to it that a few of his own cattle, and with them some Wishbone cows and a steer or two, were ranging in a deep, bushy coulee, isolated and easily passed by. He had driven them there, and he left them there. That spring he worked again with the Wishbone.

When the round-up swept the home range, gathering and branding, it chanced that his part of the circle took him and Sandy Moran down that way. It was hot, and they had thirty or forty head of cattle before them when they neared that particular place.

"No need going down into the breaks here," he told Sandy easily. "I've been hazing out everything I came across lately. They were mostly my own, anyway. I believe I've got it pretty well cleaned up along here."

Sandy was not the man to hunt hard riding. He went to the rim of the coulee and looked down for a minute. He saw nothing moving, and took Manley's word for it with no stirring of his easy-going conscience. He said all right, and rode on.

## Chapter XVII. Val Becomes an Author

Quite as marked had been the change in Val that year. Every time Kent saw her, he recognized the fact that she was a little different; a little less superior in her attitude, a little more independent in her views of life. Her standards seemed slowly changing, and her way of thinking. He did not see her often, but when he did the mockery of their friendship struck him more keenly, his inward rebellion against circumstances grew more bitter. He wondered how she could be so blind as to think they were just pals, and no more. She did think so. All the little confidences, all the glances, all the smiles, she gave and received frankly, in the name of friendship.

"You know, Kent, this is my ideal of how people should be," she told him once, with a perfectly honest enthusiasm. "I've always dreamed of such a friendship, and I've always believed that some day the right man would come along and make it possible. Not one in a thousand could understand and meet one half-way —"

"They'd be liable to go farther," Kent assented dryly.

"Yes. That's just the trouble. They'd spoil an ideal friendship by falling in love."

"Darned chumps," Kent classed them sweepingly.

"Exactly. Pal, your vocabulary excites my envy. It's so forcible sometimes."

Kent grinned reminiscently. "It sure is, old girl."

"Oh, I don't mean necessarily profane. I wonder what your vocabulary will do to the secret I'm going to tell you." The sweet-peas had reached the desired height and profusion of blossoms, thanks to the pails and pails of water Val had carried and lavished upon them, and she was gathering a handful of the prettiest blooms for him. Her cheeks turned a bit pinker as she spoke, and her hesitation raised a wild hope briefly in Kent's heart.

"What is it?" He had to force the words out.

"I —I hate to tell, but I want you to-to help me."

"Well?" To Kent, at that moment, she was not Manley's wife; she was not any man's wife; she was the girl he loved-loved with the primitive, absorbing passion of the man who lives naturally and does not borrow his morals from his next-door neighbor. His code of ethics was his own, thought out by himself. Val hated her husband, and her husband did not seem to care much for her. They were tied together legally. And a mere legality could not hold back the emotions and the desires of Kent Burnett. With him, it was not a question of morals: it was a question of Val's feeling in the matter.

Val looked up at him, found something strange in his eyes, and immediately looked away again.

"Your eyes are always saying things I can't hear," she observed irrelevantly.

"Are they? Do you want me to act as interpreter?"

"No. I just want you to listen. Have you noticed anything different about me lately, Kent?" She tilted her head, while she passed judgment upon a cluster of speckled blossoms, odd but not particularly pretty.

"What do you mean, anyway? I'm liable to get off wrong if I tell you —"

"Oh, you're so horribly cautious! Have I seemed any more content-any happier lately?"

Kent picked a spray of flowers and puled them ruthlessly to pieces. "Maybe I've kinda hoped so," he said, almost in a whisper.

"Well, I've a new interest in life. I just discovered it by accident, almost —"

Kent lifted his head and looked keenly at her, and his face was a lighter shade of brown than it had been.

"It seems to change everything. Pal, I —I've been writing things."

Kent discovered he had been holding his breath, and let it go in a long sigh.

"Oh!" After a minute he smiled philosophically. "What kinda things?" he drawled.

"Well, verses, but mostly stories. You see," she explained impulsively, "I want to earn some money-of my own. I haven't said much, because I hate whining; but really, things are growing pretty bad-between Manley and me. I hope it isn't my fault. I have tried every way I know to keep my faith in him, and to-to help him. But he's not the same as he was. You know that. And I have a good deal of pride. I can't —oh, it's intolerable having to ask a man for money! Especially when he doesn't want to give you any," she added naively. "At first it wasn't necessary; I had a little of my own, and all my things were new. But one must eventually buy things-for the house, you know, and for one's personal needs-and he seems to resent it dreadfully. I never would have believed that Manley could be stingy-actually stingy; but he is, unfortunately. I hate to speak of his faults, even to you. But I've got to be honest with you. It isn't nice to say that I'm writing, not for any particularly burning desire to express my thoughts, nor for the sentiment of it, but to earn money. It's terribly sordid, isn't it?" She smiled wistfully up at him. "But there seems to be money in it, for those who succeed, and it's work that I can do here. I have oceans of time, and I'm not disturbed!" Her lips curved into bitter lines. "I do so much thinking, I might as well put my brain to some use." With one of her sudden changes of mood, she turned to Kent and clasped both hands upon his arm.

"Now you see, pal, how much our friendship means to me," she said softly. "I couldn't have told this to another living soul! It seems awfully treacherous, saying it even to you —I mean about him. But you're so good-you always understand, don't you, pal?"

"I guess so." Kent forced the words out naturally, and kept his breath even, and his arms from clasping her. He considered that he performed quite a feat of endurance.

"You're modest!" She gave his arm a little shake. "Of course you do. You know I'm not treacherous, really. You know I'd do anything I could for him. But this is something that doesn't concern him at all. He doesn't know it, but that is because he would only sneer. When I have really sold something, and received the money for it, then it won't matter to me who knows. But now it's a solemn secret, just between me and my pal." Her yellow-brown eyes dwelt upon his face.

Kent, stealing a glance at her from under his drooped lids, wondered if she had ever given any time to analyzing herself. He would have given much to know if, down deep in her heart, she really believed in this pal business; if she was really a friend, and no more. She puzzled him a good deal, sometimes.

"Well-if anybody can make good at that business, you sure ought to; you've got brains enough to write a dictionary." He permitted himself the indulgence of saying that much, and he was perfectly sincere. He honestly considered Val the cleverest woman in the world.

She laughed with gratification. "Your sublime confidence, while it is undoubtedly mistaken, is nevertheless appreciated," she told him primly, moving away with her hands full of flowers. "If you've got the nerve, come inside and read some of my stuff; I want to know if it's any good at all."

Presently he was seated upon the couch in the little, pathetically bright front room, and he was knitting his eyebrows over Val's beautifully regular handwriting, —pages and pages of it, so that there seemed no end to the task, —and was trying to give his mind to what he was reading instead of to the author, sitting near him with her hands folded demurely in her lap and her eyes fixed expectantly upon his face, trying to read his decision even as it was forming.

Some verses she had tried on him first. Kent, by using all his determination of character, read them all, every word of them.

"That's sure all right," he said, though, beyond a telling phrase or two, —one line in particular which would stick in his memory:

"Men live and love and die in that lonely land," —

he had no very clear idea of what it was all about. Certain lines seemed to go bumping along, and one had to mispronounce some of the final words to make them rhyme with others gone before, but it was all right-Val wrote it.

"I think I do better at stories," she ventured modestly. "I wrote one —a little story about university life-and sent it to a magazine. They wrote a lovely letter about it, but it seems that field is overdone, or something. The editor asked me why, living out here in the very heart of the West, I don't try Western stories. I think I shall-and that's why I said I should need your help. I thought we might work together, you know. You've lived here so long, and ought to have some splendid ideas-things that have happened, or that you've heard-and you could tell me, and I'd write them up. Wouldn't you like to collaborate —'go in cahoots' on it?"

"Sure." Kent regarded her thoughtfully. She really was looking brighter and happier, and her enthusiasm was not to be mistaken. Her world had changed. "Anything I can do to help, you know —"

"Of course I know, I think it's perfectly splendid, don't you? We'll divide the money-when there *is* any, and —"

"Will we?" His tone was noncommittal in the extreme.

"Of course. Now, don't let's quarrel about that till we come to it. I have a good idea of my own, I think, for the first story. A man comes out here and disappears, you know, and after a while his sister comes to find him. She gets into all kinds of trouble-is kidnapped by a gang of robbers, and kept in a cave. When the leader of the gang comes back-he has been away on some depredation-you see, I have only the bare outline of the story yet-and, well, it's her brother! He kills the one who kidnapped her, and she reforms him. Of course, there ought to be some love interest. I think, perhaps, one member of the gang ought to fall in love with her, don't you know? And after a while he wins her —"

"She'll reform him, too, I reckon."

"Oh, yes. She couldn't love a man she couldn't respect-no woman could."

"Oh!" Kent took a minute to apply that personally. It was of value to him, because it was an indication of Val's own code. "Maybe," he suggested tentatively, "she'd get busy and reform the whole bunch."

"Oh, say-that would be great! She's an awfully sweet little thing-perfectly lovely, you know-and they'd all be in love with her, so it wouldn't be improbable. Don't you remember, Kent, you told me once that a man would do *anything* for a woman, if he cared enough for her?"

"Sure. He would, too." Kent fought back a momentary temptation to prove the truth of it by his own acquiescence in this pal business. He was saved from disaster by a suspicion that Val would not be able to see it from his point of view, and by the fact that he would much rather be pals than nothing.

She would have gone on, talking and planning and discussing, indefinitely. But the sun slid lower and lower, and Kent was not his own master. The time came when he had to go, regardless of his own wishes, or hers.

When he came again, the story was finished, and Val was waiting, with extreme impatience, to read it to him and hear his opinion before she sent it away. Kent was not so impatient to hear it, but he did not tell her so. He had not seen her for a month, and he wanted to talk; not about anything in particular-just talk about little things, and see her eyes light up once in a while, and her lips purse primly when he said something daring, and maybe have her play something on the violin, while he smoked and watched her slim wrist bend and rise and fall with the movement of the bow. He could imagine no single thing more fascinating than that-that, and the way she cuddled the violin under her chin, in the hollow of her neck.

But Val would not play-she had been too busy to practice, all spring and summer; she scarcely ever touched the violin, she said. And she did not want to talk-or if she did, it was plain that she had only one theme. So Kent, perforce, listened to the story. Afterward, he assured her that it was "outa sight." As a matter of fact, half the time he had not heard a word of what she was reading; he had been too busy just looking at her and being glad he was there. He had, however, a dim impression that it was a story with people in it whom one does not try to imagine as ever being alive, and with a West which, beyond its evident scarcity of inhabitants, was not the West he knew anything about. One paragraph of description had caught his attention, because it seemed a fairly accurate picture of the bench land which surrounded Cold Spring Coulee; but it had not seemed to have anything to do with the story itself. Of course, it must be good-Val wrote it. He began to admire her intensely, quite apart from his own personal subjugation.

Val was pleased with his praise. For two solid hours she talked of nothing but that story, and she gave him some fresh chocolate cake and a pitcher of lemonade, and urged him to come again in about three weeks, when she expected to hear from the magazine she thought would be glad to take the story; the one whose editor had suggested that she write of the West.

In the fall, and in the winter, their discussions were frequently hampered by Manley's presence. But Val's enthusiasm, though nipped here and there by unappreciative editors, managed, somehow, to live; or perhaps it had developed into a dogged determination to succeed in spite of everything. She still wrote things, and she still read them to Kent when there was time and opportunity; sometimes he was bold enough to criticize the worst places, and to tell her how she might, in his opinion, remedy them. Occasionally Val would take his advice.

So the months passed. The winds blew and brought storm and heat and sunshine and cloud. Nothing, in that big land, appreciably changed, except the people; and they so imperceptibly that they failed to realize it until afterward.

# Chapter XVIII. Val's Discovery

With a blood-red sun at his back and a rosy tinge upon all the hills before him, Manley rode slowly down the western rim of Cold Spring Coulee, driving five rebellious calves that had escaped the branding iron in the spring. Though they were not easily driven in any given direction, he was singularly patient with them, and refrained from bellowing epithets and admonitions, as might have been expected. When he was almost down the hill, he saw Val standing in the kitchen door, shading her eyes with her hands that she might watch his approach.

"Open the corral gate!" he shouted to her, in the tone of command. "And stand back where you can head 'em off if they start up the coulee!"

Val replied by doing as she was told; she was not in the habit of wasting words upon Manley; they seemed always to precipitate an unpleasant discussion of some sort, as if he took it for granted she disapproved of all he did or said, and was always upon the defensive.

The calves came on, lumbering awkwardly in a half-hearted gallop, as if they had very little energy left. Their tongues protruded, their mouths dribbled a lathery foam, and their rough, sweaty hides told Val of the long chase-for she was wiser in the ways of the range land than she had been. She stood back, gently waving her ruffled white apron at them, and when they dodged into the corral, rolling eyes at her, she ran up and slammed the gate shut upon them, looped the chain around the post, and dropped the iron hook into a link to fasten it. Manley galloped up, threw himself off his panting horse, and began to unsaddle.

"Get some wood and start a fire, and put the iron in, Val," he told her brusquely.

Val looked at him quickly. "Now? Supper's all ready, Manley. There's no hurry about branding them, is there?" And she added: "Dear me! The round-up must have just skimmed the top off this range last spring. You've had to brand a lot of calves that were missed."

"What the devil is it to you?" he demanded roughly. "I want that fire, madam, and I want it *now*. I rather think I knew when I want to brand without asking your advice."

Val curved her lips scornfully, shrugged and obeyed She was used to that sort of thing, and she did not mind very much. He had brutalized by degrees, and by degrees she had hardened. He could rouse no feeling now but contempt.

"If you'll kindly wait until I put back the supper," she said coldly. "I suppose in your zeal one need not sacrifice your food; you're still rather particular about that. I observe."

Manley was leading his horse to the stable, and, though he answered something, the words were no more than a surly mumble.

"He's been drinking again," Val decided dispassionately, on the way to the house. "I suppose he carried a bottle in his pocket-and emptied it."

She was not long; there was a penalty of profane reproach attached to delay, however slight, when Manley was in that mood. She had the fire going and the VP iron heating by the time he had stabled and fed his horse, and had driven the calves into the smaller pen. He drove a big, line-backed heifer into a corner, roped and tied her down with surprising dexterity, and turned impatiently.

"Come! Isn't that iron ready yet?"

Val, on the other side of the fence, drew it out and inspected it indifferently.

"It is not, Mr. Fleetwood. If you are in a very great hurry, why not apply your temper to it-and a few choice remarks?"

"Oh, don't try to be sarcastic-it's too pathetic. Kick a little life into that fire."

"Yes, sir-thank you, sir." Val could be rather exasperating when she chose. She always could be sure of making Manley silently furious when she adopted that tone of respectful servility-as employed by butlers and footmen upon the stage. Her mimicry, be it said, was very good.

"'Ere it is, sir ——thank you, sir —'ope I 'aven't kept you wyting, sir," she announced, after he had fumed for two minutes inside the corral, and she had cynically hummed her way quite through the hymn which begins "Blest be the tie that binds." She passed the white-hot iron deftly through the rails to him, and fixed the fire for another heating.

Really, she was not thinking of Manley at all, nor of his mood, nor of his brutal coarseness. She was thinking of the rebuilt typewriter, advertised as being exactly as good as a new one, and scandalously cheap, for which she had sold her watch to Arline Hawley to get money to buy. She was counting mentally the days since she had sent the money order, and was thinking it should come that week surely.

She was also planning to seize upon the opportunity afforded by Manley's next absence for a day from the ranch, and drive to Hope on the chance of getting the machine. Only-she wished she could be sure whether Kent would be coming soon. She did not want to miss seeing him; she decided to sound Polycarp Jenks the next time he came. Polycarp would know, of course, whether the Wishbone outfit was in from round-up. Polycarp always knew everything that had been done, or was intended, among the neighbors.

Manley passed the ill-smelling iron back to her, and she put it in the fire, quite mechanically. It was not the first time, nor the second, that she had been called upon to help brand. She could heat an iron as quickly and evenly as most men, though Manley had never troubled to tell her so.

Five times she heated the iron, and heard, with an inward quiver of pity and disgust, the spasmodic blat of the calf in the pen when the VP went searing into the hide on its ribs. She did not see why they must be branded that evening, in particular, but it was as well to have it done with. Also, if Manley meant to wean them, she would have to see that they were fed and watered, she supposed. That would make her trip to town a hurried one, if she went at all; she would have to go and come the same day, and Arline Hawley would scold and beg her to stay, and call her a fool.

"Now, how about that supper?" asked Manley, when they were through, and the air was clearing a little from the smoke and the smell of burned hair.

"I really don't know—I smelled the potatoes burning some time ago. I'll see, however." She brushed her hands with her handkerchief, pushed back the lock of hair that was always falling across her temple, and, because she was really offended by Manley's attitude and tone, she sang softly all the way to the house, merely to conceal from him the fact that he could move her even to irritation. Her best weapon, she had discovered long ago, was absolute indifference-the indifference which overlooked his presence and was deaf to his recriminations.

She completed her preparations for his supper, made sure that nothing was lacking and that the tea was just right, placed his chair in position, filled the water glass beside his plate, set the tea-pot where he could reach it handily, and went into the living room and closed the door between. In the past year, filed as it had been with her literary ambitions and endeavors, she had neglected her music; but she took her violin from the box, hunted the cake of resin, tuned the strings, and, when she heard him come into the kitchen and sit down at the table, seated herself upon the front doorstep and began to play.

There was one bit of music which Manley thoroughly detested. That was the "Traumerei." Therefore, she played the "Traumerei" slowly-as it should, of course, be played-with full value given to all the pensive, long-drawn notes, and with a finale positively creepy in its dreamy wistfulness. Val, as has been stated, could be very exasperating when she chose.

In the kitchen there was the subdued rattle of dishes, unbroken and unhurried. Val went on playing, but she forgot that she had begun in a half-conscious desire to annoy her husband. She stared dreamily at the hill which shut out the world to the east, and yielded to a mood of loneliness; of longing, in the abstract, for all the pleasant things she was missing in this life which she had chosen in her ignorance.

When Manley flung open the inner door, she gave a stifled exclamation; she had forgotten all about Manley.

"By all the big and little gods of Greece!" he swore angrily. "Calves bawling their heads off in the corral, and you squalling that whiny stuff you call music in the house-home's sure a hell of a happy place! I'm going to town. You don't want to leave the place till I come back—I want those calves looked after." He seemed to consider something mentally, and then added:

"If I'm not back before they quit bawling, you can turn 'em down in the river field with the rest. You know when they're weaned and ready to settle down. Don't feed 'em too much hay, like you did that other bunch; just give 'em what they need; you don't have to pile the corral full. And don't keep 'em shut up an hour longer than necessary."

Val nodded her head to show that she heard, and went on playing. There was seldom any pretense of good feeling between them now. She tuned the violin to minor, and poised the bow over the strings, in some doubt as to her memory of a serenade she wanted to try next.

"Shall I have Polycarp take the team and haul up some wood from the river?" she asked carelessly. "We're nearly out again."

"Oh, *I* don't care-if he happens along." He turned and went out, his mind turning eagerly to the town and what it could give him in the way of pleasure.

Val, still sitting in the doorway, saw him ride away up the grade and disappear over the brow of the hill. The dusk was settling softly upon the land, so that his figure was but a vague shape. She was alone again; she rather liked being alone, now that she had no longer a blind, unreasoning terror of the empty land. She had her thoughts and her work; the presence of Manley was merely an unpleasant interruption to both.

Some time in the night she heard the lowing of a cow somewhere near. She wondered dreamily what it could be doing in the coulee, and went to sleep again. The five calves were all bawling in a chorus of complaint against their forced separation from their mothers, and the deeper, throaty tones of the cow mingled not inharmoniously with the sound.

Range cattle were not permitted in the coulee, and when by chance they found a broken panel in the fence and strayed down there, Val drove them out; afoot, usually, with shouts and badly aimed stones to accelerate their lumbering pace.

After she had eaten her breakfast in the morning she went out to investigate. Beyond the corral, her nose thrust close against the rails, a cow was bawling dismally. Inside, in much the same position, its tail waving a violent signal of its owner's distress, a calf was clamoring hysterically for its mother and its mother's milk.

Val sympathized with them both; but the cow did not belong in the coulee, and she gathered two or three small stones and went around where she could frighten her away from the fence without, however, exposing herself too recklessly to her uncertain temper. Cows at weaning time did sometimes object to being driven from their calves.

"Shoo! Go on away from there!" Val raised a stone and poised it threateningly.

The cow turned and regarded her, wild-eyed. It backed a step or two, evidently uncertain of its next move.

"Go on away!" Val was just on the point of throwing the rock, when she dropped it unheeded to the ground and stared. "Why, you-you-why-the *idea!*" She turned slowly white. Certain things must filter to the understanding through amazement and disbelief; it took Val a minute or two to grasp the significance of what she saw. By the time she did grasp it, her knees were beading weakly beneath the weight of her body. She put out a groping hand and caught at the corner of the corral to keep herself from falling. And she stared and stared.

"It-oh, surely not!" she whispered, protesting against her understanding. She gave a little sob that had no immediate relation to tears. "Surely —*surely* —not!" It was of no use; understanding came, and came clearly, pitilessly. Many things-trifles, all of them-to which she had given no thought at the time, or which she had forgotten immediately, came back to her of their own accord; things she tried *not* to remember.

The cow stared at her for a minute, and, when she made no hostile move, turned its attention back to its bereavement. Once again it thrust its moist muzzle between two rails, gave a preliminary, vibrant *mmm-mmmmm —m*, and then, with a spasmodic heaving of ribs and of flank, burst into a long-drawn *baww-aw-aw-aw*, which rose rapidly in a tremulous crescendo and died to a throaty rumbling.

Val started nervously, though her eyes were fixed upon the cow and she knew the sound was coming. It served, however, to release her from the spell of horror which had gripped her. She was still white, and when she moved she felt intolerably heavy, so that her feet dragged; but she was no longer dazed. She went slowly around to the gate, reached up wearily and undid the chain fastening, opened the gate slightly, and went in.

Four of the calves were huddled together for mutual comfort in a corner. They were blatting indefatigably. Val went over to where the fifth one still stood beside the fence, as near the cow as it could get, and threw a small stone, that bounced off the calf's rump. The calf jumped and ran aimlessly before her until it reached the half-open gate, when it dodged out, as if it could scarcely believe its own good fortune. Before Val could follow it outside, it was nuzzling rapturously its mother, and the cow was contorting her body so that she could caress her offspring with her tongue, while she rumbled her satisfaction.

Val closed and fastened the gate carefully, and went back to where the cow still lingered. With her lips drawn to a thin, colorless line, she drove her across the coulee and up the hill, the calf gamboling close alongside. When they had gone out of sight, up on the level, Val turned back and went slowly to the house. She stood for a minute staring stupidly at it and at the coulee, went in and gazed around her with that blankness which follows a great mental shock. After a minute she shivered, threw up her hands before her face, and dropped, a pitiful, sorrowing heap of quivering rebellion, upon the couch.

# Chapter XIX. Kent's Confession

Polycarp Jenks came ambling into the coulee, rapped perfunctorily upon the door-casing, and entered the kitchen as one who feels perfectly at home, and sure of his welcome; as was not unfitting, considering the fact that he had "chored around" for Val during the last year, and longer.

"Anybody to home?" he called, seeing the front door shut tight.

There was a stir within, and Val, still pale, and with an almost furtive expression in her eyes, opened the door and looked out.

"Oh, it's you, Polycarp," she said lifelessly. "Is there anything —"

"What's the matter? Sick? You look kinda peaked and frazzled out. I met Man las' night, and he told me you needed wood; I thought I'd ride over and see. By granny, you do look bad."

"Just a headache," Val evaded, shrinking back guiltily. "Just do whatever there is to do, Polycarp. I think —I don't believe the chickens have had anything to eat to-day —"

"Them headaches are sure a fright; they're might' nigh as bad as rheumatiz, when they hit you hard. You jest go back and lay down, and I'll look around and see what they is to do. Any idee when Man's comin' back?"

"No." Val brought the word out with an involuntary sharpness.

"No, I reckon not. I hear him and Fred De Garmo come might' near havin' a fight las' night. Blumenthall was tellin' me this mornin'. Fred's quit the Double Diamond, I hear. He's got himself appointed dep'ty stock inspector-and how he managed to git the job is more 'n I can figure out. They say he's all swelled up over it-got his headquarters in town, you know, and seems he got to lordin' it over Man las' night, and I guess if somebody hadn't stopped 'em they'd of been a mix-up, all right. Man wasn't in no shape to fight-he'd been drinkin' pretty —"

"Yes-well, just do whatever there is to do, Polycarp. The horses are in the upper pasture, I think-if you want to haul wood." She closed the door-gently, but with exceeding firmness, and, Polycarp took the hint.

"Women is queer," he muttered, as he left the house. "Now, she knows Man drinks like a fish-and she knows everybody else knows it-but if you so much as mention sech a thing, why —" He waggled his head disapprovingly and proceeded, in his habitually laborious manner, to take a chew of tobacco. "No matter how much they may know a thing is so, if it don't suit 'em you can't never git 'em to stand right up and face it out-seems like, by granny, it comes natural to 'em to make believe things is different. Now, she knows might' well she can't fool *me*. I've hearn Man swear at her like —"

He reached the corral, and his insatiable curiosity turned his thoughts into a different channel. He inspected the four calves gravely, wondered audibly where Man had found them, and how the round-up came to miss them, and criticized his application of the brand; in the opinion of Polycarp, Manley either burned too deep or not deep enough.

"Time that line-backed heifer scabs off, you can't tell what's on her," he asserted, expectorating solemnly before he turned away to his work.

Prom a window, Val watched him with cold terror. Would he suspect? Or was there anything to suspect? "It's silly-it's perfectly idiotic," she told herself impatiently; "but if he hangs around that corral another minute, I shall scream!" She watched until she saw him mount his horse and ride off toward the upper pasture. Then she went out and began apathetically picking seed pods off her sweet-peas, which the early frosts had spared.

"Head better?" called Polycarp, half an hour later, when he went rattling past the house with the wagon, bound for the river bottom where they got their supply of wood.

"A little," Val answered inattentively, without looking at him.

It was while Polycarp was after the wood, and while she was sitting upon the edge of the porch, listlessly arranging and rearranging a handful of long-stemmed blossoms, that Kent galloped down the hill and up to the gate. She saw him coming and set her teeth hard together. She did not want to see Kent just then; she did not want to see anybody.

Kent, however, wanted to see her. It seemed to him at least a month since he had had a glimpse of her, though it was no more than half that time. He watched her covertly while he came up the path. His mind, all the way over from the Wishbone, had been very clear and very decided. He had a certain thing to tell her, and a certain thing to do; he had thought it all out during the nights when he could not sleep and the days when men called him surly, and there was no going back, no reconsideration of the matter. He had been telling himself that, over and over, ever since the house came into view and he saw her sitting there on the porch. She would probably want to argue, and perhaps she would try to persuade him, but it would be absolutely useless; absolutely.

"Well, hello!" he cried, with more than his usual buoyancy of manner-because he knew he must hurt her later on. "Hello, Madam Authoress. Why this haughty air? This stuckupiness? Shall I get a ladder and climb up where you can hear me say howdy?" He took off his hat and slapped her gently upon the top of her head with it. "Come out of the fog!"

"Oh —I wish you wouldn't!" She glanced up at him so briefly that he caught only a flicker of her yellow-brown eyes, and went on fumbling her flowers. Kent stood and looked down at her for a moment.

"Mad?" he inquired cheerfully. "Say, you look awfully savage. On the dead, you do. What do *you* care if they sent it back? You had all the fun of writing it-and you know it's a dandy. Please smile. *Pretty* please!" he wheedled. It was not the first time he had discovered her in a despondent mood, nor the first time he had bantered and badgered her out of her gloom. Presently it dawned upon him that this was more serious; he had never seen her quite so colorless or so completely without spirit.

"Sick, pal?" he asked gently, sitting down beside her.

"No-o —I suppose not." Val bit her lips, as soon as she had spoken, to check their quivering.

"Well, what is it? I wish you'd tell me. I came over here full of something I had to tell you-but I can't, now; not while you're like this." He watched her yearningly.

"Oh, I can't tell you. It's nothing." Val jerked a sweet-pea viciously from its stem, pressed her hand against her mouth, and turned reluctantly toward him. "What was it you came to tell me?"

He watched her narrowly. "I'll gamble you're down in the mouth about something hubby has said or done. You needn't tell me-but I just want to ask you if you think it's worth while? You needn't tell me that, either. You know blamed well it ain't. He can't deal you any more misery than you let him hand out; you want to keep that in mind."

Another blossom was demolished. "What was it you came to tell me?" she repeated steadily, though she did not look at him.

"Oh, nothing much. I'm going to leave the country, is all."

"Kent!" After a minute she forced another word out. "Why?"

Kent regarded her somberly. "You better think twice before you ask me that," he warned; "because I ain't much good at beating all around the bush. If you ask me again, I'll tell you-and I'm liable to tell you without any frills." He drew a hard breath. "So I'd advise you not to ask," he finished, half challengingly.

Val placed a pale lavender blossom against a creamy white one, and held the two up for inspection.

"When are you going?" she asked evenly.

"I don't know exactly-in a day or so. Saturday, maybe."

She hesitated over the flowers in her lap, and selected a pink one, which she tried with the white and the lavender.

"And —*why* are you going?" she asked him deliberately.

Kent stared at her fixedly. A faint, pink flush was creeping into her cheeks. He watched it deepen, and knew that his silence was filling her with uneasiness. He wondered how much she guessed of what he was going to say, and how much it would mean to her.

"All right —I'll tell you why, fast enough." His tone was grim. "I'm going to leave the country because I can't stay any longer-not while you're in it."

"Why-Kent!" She seemed inexpressibly shocked.

"I don't know," he went on relentlessly, "what you think a man's made of, anyhow. And I don't know what *you* think of this pal business; I know what I think: It's a mighty good way to drive a man crazy. I've had about all of it I can stand, if you want to know."

"I'm sorry, if you don't —if you can't be friends any longer," she said, and he winced to see how her eyes filled with tears. "But, of course, if you can't —if it bores you —"

Kent seized her arm, a bit roughly, "Have I got to come right out and tell you, in plain English, that I —that it's because I'm so deep in love with you I can't. If you only knew what it's cost me this last year-to play the game and not play it too hard! What do you think a man's made of? Do you think a man can care for a woman, like I care for you, and-Do you think he wants to be just pals? And stand back and watch some drunken brute abuse her-and never-Here!" His voice grew testier. "Don't do that-don't! I didn't want to hurt you-God knows I didn't want to hurt you!" He threw his seem around her shoulders and pulled her toward him.

"Don't —pal, I'm a brute, I guess, like all the rest of the male humans. I don't mean to be-it's the way I'm made. When a woman means so much to me that I can't think of anything else, day or night, and get to counting days and scheming to see her-why-being friends-like we've been-is like giving a man a teaspoon of milk and water when he's starving to death, and thinking that oughta do. But I shouldn't have let it hurt you. I tried to stand for it, little woman. These were times when I just had to fight myself not to take you up in my arms and carry you of and keep you. You must admit," he argued, smiling rather wanly, "that, considering how I've felt about it, I've done pretty tolerable well up till now. You don't —you never will know how much it's cost. Why, my nerves are getting so raw I can't stand anything any more. That's why I'm going. I don't want to hang around till I do something-foolish."

He took his arm away from her shoulders and moved farther off; he was not sure how far he might trust himself.

"If I thought you cared-or if there was anything I could do for you," he ventured, after a moment, "why, it would be different. But —"

Val lifted her head and turned to him.

"There is something-or there was-or-oh, I can't think any more! I suppose" —doubtfully — "if you feel as you say you do, why-it would be-wicked to stay. But you don't; you must just imagine it."

"Oh, all right," Kent interpolated ironically.

"But if you go away —" She got up and stood before him, breathing unevenly, in little gasps. "Oh, you mustn't go away! Please don't go! I —there's something terrible happened-oh, Kent, I need you! I can't tell you what it is-it's the most horrible thing I ever heard of! You can't imagine anything more horrible, Kent!"

She twisted her fingers together nervously, and the blossoms dropped, one by one, on the ground. "If you go," she pleaded, "I won't have a friend in the country, not a real friend. And-and I never needed a friend as much as I do now, and you mustn't go. I —I can't let you go!" It was like her hysterical fear of being left alone after the fire.

Kent eyed her keenly. He knew there must have been something to put her into this state-something more than his own rebellion. He felt suddenly ashamed of his weakness in giving way-in telling her how it was with him. The faint, far-off chuckle of a wagon came to his ears. He turned impatiently toward the sound. Polycarp was driving up the coulee with a load of wood; already he was nearing the gate which opened into the lower field. Kent stood up, reached out, and caught Val by the hand.

"Come on into the house," he said peremptorily. "Polly's coming, and you don't want him goggling and listening. And I want you," he added, when he had led her inside and closed the door, "to tell me what all this is about. There's something, and I want to know what. If it concerns you, then it concerns me a whole lot, too. And what concerns me I'm going to find out about-what is it?"

Val sat down, got up immediately, and crossed the room aimlessly to sit in another chair. She pressed her palms tightly against both cheeks, drew in her breath as if she were going to speak, and, after all, said nothing. She looked out of the window, pushing back the errant strand of hair.

"I can't —I don't know how to tell you," she began desperately. "It's too horrible."

"Maybe it is —I don't know what you'd call too horrible; I kinda think it wouldn't be what I'd tack those words to. Anyway-what is it?" He went close, and he spoke insistently.

She took a long breath.

"Manley's a thief!" She jerked the words out like as automaton. They were not, evidently, the Words she had meant to speak, for she seemed frightened afterward.

"Oh, that's it!" Kent made a sound which was not far from a snort. "Well, what about it? What's he done? How did you find it out?"

Val straightened in the chair and gazed up at him. Once more her tawny eyes gave him a certain shock, as if he had never before noticed them.

"After all our neighbors have done for him," she cried bitterly; "after giving him hay, when his was burned and he couldn't buy any; after building stables, and corral, and-everything they did-the kindest, best neighbors a man ever had-oh, it's too shameful for utterance! I might forgive it —I might, only for that. The-the ingratitude! It's too despicable-too —"

Kent laid a steadying hand upon her arm.

"Yes-but what is it?" he interrupted.

Val shook off his hand unconsciously, impatient of any touch.

"Oh, the bare deed itself-well, it's rather petty, too-and cheap." Her voice became full of contempt. "It was the calves. He brought home five last night-five that hadn't been branded last spring. Where he found them *I* don't know —I didn't care enough about it to ask. He had been drinking, I think; I can usually tell-and he often carries a bottle in his pocket, as I happen to know.

"Well, he had me make a fire and heat the iron for him, and he branded them-last night; he was very touchy about it when I asked him what was his hurry. I think now it was a stupid thing for him to do. And-well, in the night, some time, I heard a cow bawling around close, and this morning I went out to drive her away; the fence is always down somewhere —I suppose she found a place to get through. So I went out to drive her away." Her eyes dropped, as if she were making a confession of her own misdeed. She clenched her hands tightly in her lap.

"Well-it was a Wishbone cow." After all, she said it very quietly.

"The devil it was!" Kent had been prepared for something of the sort; but, nevertheless, he started when he heard his own outfit mentioned.

"Yes. It was a Wishbone cow." Her voice was flat and monotonous. "He had stolen her calf. He had it in the corral, and he had branded it with his own brand-with a VP. *With my initials!*" she wailed suddenly, as if the thought had just struck her, and was intolerably bitter. "She had followed-had been hunting her calf; it was rather a little calf, smaller than the others. And it was crowded up against the fence, trying to get to her. There was no mistaking their relationship. I tried to think he had made a mistake; but it's of no use —I know he didn't. I know he *stole* that calf. And for all I know, the others, too. Oh, it's perfectly horrible to think of!"

Kent could easily guess her horror of it, and he was sorry for her. But his mind turned instantly to the practical side of it.

"Well-maybe it can be fixed up, if you feel so bad about it. Does Polycarp-did he see the cow hanging around?"

Val shook her head apathetically. "No-he didn't come till just a little while ago. That was this morning. And I drove her out of the coulee-her and her calf. They went off up over the hill."

Kent stood looking down at her rather stupidly.

"You —*what?* What was it you did?" It seemed to him that something-some vital point of the story-had eluded him.

"I drove them away. I didn't think they ought to be permitted to hang around here." Her lips quivered again. "I —I didn't want to see him-get-into any trouble."

"You drove them away? Both of them?" Kent was frowning at her now.

Val sprang up and faced him, all a-tremble with indignation. "Certainly, both! *I'm* not a thief, Kent Burnett! When I knew-when there was no possible doubt-why, what, in Heaven's name, *could* I do? It wasn't Manley's calf. I turned it loose to go back where it belonged."

"With a VP on its ribs!" Kent was staring at her curiously.

"Well, I don't care! Fifty VP's couldn't make the calf Manley's. If anybody came and saw that cow, why —" Val looked at him rafter pityingly, as if she could not quite understand how he could even question her upon that point. "And, after all," she added forlornly, "he's my husband. I couldn't —I had to do what I could to shield him-just for sake of the past, I suppose. Much as I despise him, I can't forget that-that I cared once. It's because I wanted your advice that I —"

"It's a pity you didn't get it sooner, then! Can't you see what you've done? Why, think a minute! A VP calf running with a Wishbone cow-why, it's —you couldn't advertise Man as a rustler any better if you tried. The first fellow that runs onto that cow and calf-well, he won't need to do any guessing-he'll *know*. It's a ticket to Deer Lodge-that VP calf. Now do you see?" He turned away to the window and stood looking absently at the brown hillside, his hands thrust deep into his pockets.

"And there's Fred De Garmo, with his new job, ranging around the country just aching to cinch somebody and show his authority. It's a matter of days almost. He'd like nothing better than to get a whack at Man, even if the Wishbone —"

Outside, they could hear Polycarp throwing the wood off the wagon; knowing him as they did, they knew, it would not be long before he found an excuse for coming into the house. He had more than once evinced a good deal of interest in Kent's visits there, and shown an unmistakable desire to know what they were talking about. They had never paid much attention to him; but now even Val felt a vague uneasiness lest he overhear. She had been sitting, her face buried in her arms, crushed beneath the knowledge of what she had done.

"Don't worry, little woman." Kent went over and passed his hand lightly over her hair. "You did what looked to you to be the right thing-the honest thing. And the chances are he'd get caught before long, anyhow. I don't reckon this is the first time he's done it."

"Oh-h —but to think-to think that *I* should do it-when I wanted to save him! He-Kent, I despise him-he has killed all the love I ever felt for him-killed it over and over-but if anybody finds that calf, and-and if they-Kent, I shall go crazy if I have to feel that *I* sent him-to-prison. To think of him-shut up there-and to know that I did it —I can't bear it!" She caught his arm. She pressed her forehead against it. "Kent, isn't there some way to get it back? If I should find it-and-and shoot it-and pay the Wishbone what it's worth-oh, *any* amount-or shoot the cow-or —" she raised her face imploringly to his —"tell me, pal-or I shall go stark, raving mad!"

Polycarp came into the kitchen, and, from the sound, he was trying to enter as unobtrusively as possible, even to the extent of walking on his toes.

"Go see what that darned old sneak wants," Kent commanded in an undertone. "Act as if nothing happened-if you can." He watched anxiously, while she drew a long breath, pressed her hands hard against her cheeks, closed her lips tightly, and then, with something like composure, went quietly to the door and threw it open. Polycarp was standing very close to it, on the other side. He drew back a step.

"I wondered if I better git another load, now I've got the team hooked up," he began in his rasping, nasal voice, his slitlike eyes peering inquisitively into the room. "Hello, Kenneth —I *thought* that was your horse standin' outside. Or would you rather I cut up a pile? I dunno but what I'll have to go t'town t'-morrerr or next day-mebby I better cut you some wood, hey? If Man ain't likely to be home, mebby —"

"I think, Polycarp, well have a storm soon. So it would be good policy to haul another load, don't you think? I can manage very well with what there is cut until Manley returns; and there are always small branches that I can break easily with the axe. I really think it would be safer to have another load hauled now while we can. Don't you think so?" Val even managed to smile at him. "If my head wasn't so bad," she added deceitfully, "I should be tempted to go along, just for a dose sight of the river. Mr. Burnett is going directly-perhaps I may walk down later on. But you had better not wait —I shouldn't want to keep you working till dark."

Polycarp, eying her and Kent, and the room in all its details, forced his hand into his trousers pocket, brought up his battered plug of tobacco and pried off a piece, which he rolled into his left cheek with his tongue.

"Jest as you say," he surrendered, though it was perfectly plain that he would much prefer to cut wood and so be able to see all that went on, even though he was denied the gratification of hearing what they said. He waited a moment, but Val turned away, and even had the audacity to close the door upon his unfinished reply. He listened for a moment, his head craned forward.

"Purty kinda goings-on!" he mumbled. "Time Man had a flea put in 'is ear, by granny, if he don't want to lose that yeller-eyed wife of hisn." To Polycarp, a closed door-when a man and woman were alone upon the other side-could mean nothing but surreptitious kisses and the like. He went stumbling out and drove away down the coulee, his head turning automatically so that his eyes were constantly upon the house; from his attitude, as Kent saw him through the window Polycarp expected an explosion, at the very least. His outraged virtue vested itself in one more sentence; "Purty blamed nervy, by granny-to go 'n' shut the door right in m' face!"

Inside the room, Val stood for a minute with her back against the door, as if she half feared Polycarp would break in and drag her secret from her. When she heard him leave the kitchen she drew a long breath, eloquent in itself: when the rattle of the wagon came to them there, she left the door and went slowly across the room until she stood close to Kent. The interruption had steadied them both. Her voice was a constrained calm when she spoke.

"Well-is there anything I can do? Because I suppose every minute is dangerous."

Kent kept his eyes upon the departing Polycarp.

"There's nothing you can do, no. Maybe I can do something; soon as that granny gossip is outa sight, I'll go and round up that cow and calf-if somebody hasn't beaten me to it."

Val looked at him with a certain timid helplessness.

"Oh! Will you-won't it be against the law if you-if you kill it?" She grew slightly excited again. "Kent, you shall not get into any trouble for-for his sake! If it comes to a choice, why-let him suffer for his crime. You shall not!"

Kent turned his head slowly and gazed down at her. "Don't run away with the idea I'm doing it for him," he told her distinctly. "I love Man Fleetwood like I love a wolf. But if that VP calf catches him up, you'd fight your head over it, God only knows how long. I know you! You'd think so much about the part you played that you'd wind up by forgetting everything else. You'd get to thinking of him as a martyr, maybe! No-it's for you. I kinda got you into this, you recollect? If I'd let you see Man drank, that day, you'd never have married him; I know that now. So I'm going to get you out of it. My side of the question can wait."

She stared up at him with a grave understanding.

"But you know what I said-you won't do anything that can make you trouble-won't you tell me, Kent, what you're going to do?"

He had already started to the door, but he stopped and smiled reassuringly.

"Nothing so fierce. If I can find 'em, I aim to bar out that VP. Sabe?"

# Chapter XX. A Blotched Brand

At the brow of the hill, which was the western rim of the coulee, Kent turned and waved a farewell to Val, watching him wistfully from the kitchen door. She had wanted to go along; she had almost cried to go and help, but Kent would not permit her-and beneath the unpleasantness of denying her anything, there had been a certain primitive joy in feeling himself master of the situation and of her actions; for that one time it was as if she belonged to him. At the last he had accepted the field glasses, which she insisted upon lending him, and now he was tempted to take them from their worn, leathern case and focus them upon her face, just for the meager satisfaction of one more look at her. But he rode on, oat of sight, for the necessity which drove him forth did not permit much loitering if he would succeed in what he had set out to do.

Personally he would have felt no compunctions whatever about letting the calf go, a walking advertisement of Manley's guilt. It seemed to him a sort of grim retribution, and no more than he deserved. He had not exaggerated his sentiments when he intimated plainly to her his hatred of Manley, and he agreed with her that the fellow was making a despicable return for the kindness his neighbors had always shown him. No doubt he had stolen from the Double Diamond as well as the Wishbone.

Once Kent pulled up, half minded to go back and let events shape themselves without any interference from him. But there was Val-women were so queer about such things. It seemed to Kent that, if any man had caused him as much misery as Manley had caused Val, he would not waste much time worrying over him, if he tangled himself up with his own misdeeds. However, Val wanted that bit of evidence covered up; so, while Kent did not approve, he went at the business with his customary thoroughness.

The field glasses were a great convenience. More than once they saved him the trouble of riding a mile or so to inspect a small bunch of stock. Nevertheless, he rode for several hours before, just at sundown, he discovered the cow feeding alone with her calf in a shallow depression near the rough country next the river. They were wild, and he ran them out of the hollow and up on high ground before he managed to drop his loop over the calf's head.

"You sure are a dandy-fine sign-post, all right," he observed, and grinned down at the staring VP brand.

"It's a pity you can't be left that way." He glanced cautiously around him at the great, empty prairie. A mile or two away, a lone horseman was loping leisurely along, evidently bound for the Double Diamond.

"Say-this is kinda public," Kent complained to the calf. "Let's you and me go down outa sight for a minute." He started off toward the hollow, dragging the calf, a protesting bundle of stiffened muscles pulling against the rope. The cow, shaking her head in a halfhearted defiance, followed. Kent kept an uneasy eye upon the horseman, and hoped fervently the fellow was absorbed in meditation and, would not glance in his direction. Once he was almost at the point of turning the calf loose; for barring out brands, even illegal brands, is justly looked upon with disfavor, to say the least.

Down in the hollow, which Kent reached with a sigh of relief, he dismounted and hastily started a little fire on a barren patch of ground beneath a jutting sandstone ledge. The calf, tied helpless, lay near by, and the cow hovered close, uneasy, but lacking courage for a rush.

Kent laid hand upon his saddle, hesitated, and shook his head; he might need it in a hurry, and cinch ring takes time both in the removal and the replacement-and is vitally important withal. His knife he had lost on the last round-up. He scowled at the necessity, lifted his heel, and took off a spur. "And if that darned ginny don't get too blamed curious and cone fogging over this way —" He spoke the phrase aloud, out of the middle of a mental arrangement of the chance he was taking.

To heat the spur red-hot, draw it across the fresh VP again and again, and finally drag it crisscross once or twice to make assurance an absolute certainty, did not take long. Kent was particular about not wasting any seconds. The calf stopped its dismal blatting, and when Kent released it and coiled his rope, it jumped up and ran for its life, the cows ambling solicitously at its heels. Kent kicked the dirt over the fire, eyed it sharply a moment to make sure it was perfectly harmless, mounted in haste, and rode up the sloping side down, which he had come. Just under the top of the slope, he peeked anxiously out over the prairie, ducked precipitately, and went clattering away down the hollow to the farther side; dodged around a spur of rocks, forced his horse down over a wicked jumble of boulders to level land below, and rode as if a hangman's noose were the penalty for delay.

When he reached the river-which he did after many windings and turnings-he got off and washed his spur, scrubbing it diligently with sand in an effort to remove the traces of fire. When the evidence was at least less conspicuous, he put it on his heel and jogged down the river bank quite innocently, inwardly thankful over his escape. He had certainly done nothing wrong; but one sometimes finds it rather awkward to be forced into an explanation of a perfectly righteous deed.

"If I'd been stealing that calf, I'd never have been crazy enough to take such a long chance," he mused, and laughed a little. "I'll bet Fred thought he was due to grab a rustler right in the act-only he was a little bit slow about making up his mind; deputy stock inspectors had oughta think quicker than that-he was just about five minutes too deliberate. I'll gamble he's scratching his head, right now, over that blotched brand, trying to *sabe* the play-which he won't, not in a thousand years!"

He gave the reins a twitch and began to climb through the dusk to the lighter hilltop, at a point just east of Cold Spring Coulee. At the top he put the spurs to his horse and headed straight as might be for the Wishbone ranch. He would like to have told Val of his success, but he was afraid Manley might be there, or Polycarp; it was wise always to avoid Polycarp Jenks, if one had anything to conceal from his fellows.

# Chapter XXI. Val Decides

It was the middle of the next forenoon when Manley came riding home, sullen from drink and a losing game of poker, which had kept him all night at the table, and at sunrise sent him forth in the mood which meets a grievance more than half-way. He did not stop at the house, though he saw Val through the open door; he did not trouble to speak to her, even, but rode on to the stable, stopping at the corral to look over the fence at the calves, still bawling sporadically between half-hearted nibblings at the hay which Polycarp had thrown in to them.

Just at first he did not notice anything wrong, but soon a vague disquiet seized him, and he frowned thoughtfully at the little group. Something puzzled him; but his brain, fogged with whisky and loss of sleep, and the reaction from hours of concentration upon the game, could not quite grasp the thing that troubled him. In a moment, however, he gave an inarticulate bellow, wheeled about, and rode back to the house. He threw himself from the horse almost before it stopped, and rushed into the kitchen. Val, ironing one of her ruffled white aprons, looked up quickly, turned rather pale, and then stiffened perceptibly for the conflict that was coming.

"There's only four calves in the corral-and I brought in five. Where's the other one?" He came up and stood quite close to her-so close that Val took a step backward. He did not speak loud, but there was something in his tone, in his look, that drove the little remaining color from her face.

"Manley," she said, with a catch of the breath, "why did you do that horrible thing? What devil possessed you? I —"

"I asked you 'where is that other calf'? Where is it? There's only four. I brought in five." His very calmness was terrifying.

Val threw back her head, and her eyes were-as they frequently became in moments of stress-yellow, inscrutable, like the eyes of a lion in a cage.

"Yes, you brought in five. One of the five, at least, you-stole. You put your brand, Manley Fleetwood, on a calf that did not belong to you; it belonged to the Wishbone, and you know it. I have learned many disagreeable things about you, Manley, in the past two years; yesterday morning I learned that you were a *thief*. Ah-h —I despise you! Stealing from the very men who helped you-the men to whom you owe nothing but gratitude and-and friendship! Have you no manhood whatever? Besides being weak and shiftless, are you a criminal as well? *How* can you be so utterly lacking in-in common decency, even?" She eyed him as she would look at some strange monster in a museum about which she was rather curious.

"I asked you where that other calf is-and you'd better tell me!" It was the tone which goes well with a knife thrust or a blow. But the contempt in Val's face did not change.

"Well, you'll have to hunt for it if you want it. The cow —a Wishbone cow, mind you! —came and claimed it; I let her have it. No stolen goods can remain on this ranch with my knowledge, Manley Fleetwood. Please remember —"

"Oh, you turned it out, did you? You turned it out?" He had her by the throat, shaking her as a puppy shakes a purloined shoe. "I could —*kill* you for that!"

"Manley! Ah-h-h —" It was not pleasant-that gurgling cry, as she straggled to get free.

He had the look of a maniac as he pressed his fingers into her throat and glared down into her purpling face.

With a sudden impulse he cast her limp form violently from him. She struck against a chair, fell from that to the floor, and lay a huddled heap, her crisp, ruffled skirt just giving a glimpse of tiny, half-worn slippers, her yellow hair fallen loose and hiding her face.

He stared down at her, but he felt no remorse-she had jeopardized his liberty, his standing among men. A cold horror caught him when he thought of the calf turned loose on the range, his brand on its ribs. He rushed in a panic from the kitchen, flung himself into the saddle, and went off across the coulee, whipping both sides of his horse. She had not told him-indeed, he had not asked her-which way the cow had gone, but instinctively he rode to the west, the direction from which he had driven the calves. One thought possessed him utterly; he must find that calf.

So he rode here and there, doubling and turning to search every feeding herd he glimpsed, fearing to face the possibility of failure and its inevitable consequence.

The cat with the white spots on its sides-Val called her Mary Arabella, for some whimsical reason-came into the kitchen, looked inquiringly at the huddled figure upon the floor, gave a faint mew, and went slowly up, purring and arching her back; she snuffed a moment at Val's hair, then settled herself in the hollow of Val's arm, and curled down for a nap. The sun, sliding up to midday, shone straight in upon them through the open door.

Polycarp Jenks, riding that way in obedience to some obscure impulse, lifted his hand to give his customary tap-tap before he walked in; saw Val lying there, and almost fell headlong into the room in his haste and perturbation. It looked very much as if he had at last stumbled upon the horrible tragedy which was his one daydream. To be an eyewitness of a murder, and to be able to tell the tale afterward with minute, horrifying detail-that, to Polycarp, would make life really worth living. He shuffled over to Val, pushed aside the mass of yellow hair, turned her head so that he could look into her face, saw at once the bruised marks upon her throat, and stood up very straight.

"Foul play has been done here!" he exclaimed melodramatically, eying the cat sternly. "Murder-that's what it is, by granny —a foul murder!"

The victim of the foul murder stirred slightly. Polycarp started and bent over her again, somewhat disconcerted, perhaps, but more humanly anxious.

"Mis' Fleetwood-Mis' Fleetwood! You hurt? It's Polycarp Jenks talkin' to you!" He hesitated, pushed the cat away, lifted Val with some difficulty, and carried her into the front room and deposited her on the couch. Then he hurried after some water.

"Come might' nigh bein' a murder, by granny-from the marks on 'er neck-come might' nigh, all right!"

He sprinkled water lavishly upon her face, bethought him of a possible whisky flask in the haystack, and ran every step of the way there and back. He found a discarded bottle with a very little left in it, and forced the liquor down her throat.

"That'll fetch ye if anything will —*he-he!*" he mumbled, tittering from sheer excitement. Beyond a very natural desire to do what he could for her, he was extremely anxious to bring her to her senses, so that he could hear what had happened, and how it had happened.

"Betche Man got jealous of her'n Kenneth-by granny, I betche that's how it come about-hey? Feelin' better, Mis' Fleetwood?"

Val had opened her eyes and was looking at him rather stupidly. There was a bruise upon her head, as well as upon her throat. She had been stunned, and her wits came back slowly. When she recognized Polycarp, she tried ineffectually to sit up.

"I —he-is-he-gone?" Her voice was husky, her speech labored.

"Man, you mean? He's gone, yes. Don't you be afeared-not whilst I'm here, by granny! How came it he done this to ye?"

Val was still staring at him bewilderedly. Polycarp repeated his question three times before the blank look left her eyes.

"I —turned the calf-out-the cow-came and-claimed it-Manley —" She lifted her hand as if it were very, very heavy, and fumbled at her throat. "Manley-when I told him-he was a —thief—" She dropped her hand wearily to her side and closed her eyes, as if the sight of Polycarp's face, so close to hers and so insatiably curious and eager and cunning, was more than she could bear.

"Go away," she commanded, after a minute or two. "I'm —all right. It's nothing. I fell. It was-the heat. Thank you-so much —" She opened her eyes and saw him there still. She looked at him gravely, speculatively. She waved her hand toward the bedroom. "Get me my hand glass-in there on the dresser," she said.

When he had tiptoed in and got it for her, she lifted it up slowly, with both hands, until she could see her throat. There were distinct, telltale marks upon the tender flesh-unmistakable finger prints. She shivered and dropped the glass to the floor. But she stared steadily up at Polycarp, and after a moment she spoke with a certain fierceness.

"Polycarp Jenks, don't ever tell-about those marks. I —I don't want any one to know. When-after a while —I want to think first-perhaps you can help me. Go away now-not away from the ranch, but-let me think. I'm all right-or I will be. Please go."

Polycarp recognized that tone, however it might be hoarsened by bruised muscles and the shock of what she had suffered. He recognized also that look in her eyes; he had always obeyed that look and that tone-he obeyed them now, though with visible reluctance. He sat down in the kitchen to wait, and while he waited he chewed tobacco incessantly, and ruminated upon the mystery which lay behind the few words Val had first spoken, before she realized just what it was she was saying.

After a long, long while-so long that even Polycarp's patience was feeling the strain-Val opened the door and stood leaning weakly against the casing. Her throat was swathed in a piece of white silk.

"I wish, Polycarp, you'd get the team and hitch it to the light rig," she said. "I want to go to town, and I don't feel able to drive. Can you take me in? Can you spare the time?"

"Why, certainly, I c'n take you in, Mis' Fleetwood. I was jest thinkn' it wa'n't safe for you out here —"

"It is perfectly safe," Val interrupted chillingly. "I am going because I Want to see Arline Hawley." She raised her hand to the bandage. "I have a sore throat," she stated, staring hard at him. Then, with one of her impulsive changes, she smiled wistfully.

"You'll be my friend, Polycarp, won't you?" she pleaded. "I can trust you, I know, with my-secret. It is a secret-it *must* be a secret! I'll tell you the truth, Polycarp. It was Manley-he had been drinking again. He-we had a quarrel-about something. He didn't know what he was doing-he didn't mean to hurt me. But I fell —I struck my head; see, there is a great lump there." She pushed back her hair to show him the place. "So it's a secret-just between you and me, Polycarp Jenks!"

"Why, certainly, Mis' Fleetwood; don't you be the least mite oneasy; I'm your friend —I always have been. A feller ain't to be held responsible when he's drinkin' —by granny, that's a fact, he ain't."

"No," Val agreed laconically, "I suppose not. Let us go, then, as soon as we can, please. I'll stay overnight with Mrs. Hawley, and you can bring me back to-morrow, can't you? And you'll remember not to mention-anything, won't you, Polycarp?"

Polycarp stood very straight and dignified.

"I hope, Mis' Fleetwood, you can always depend on Polycarp Jenks," he replied virtuously. "Your secret is safe with me."

Val smiled-somewhat doubtfully, it is true-and let him go. "Maybe it is —I hope so," she sighed, as she turned away to dress for the trip.

All through that long ride to town, Polycarp talked and talked and talked. He made surmises and waited openly to hear them confirmed or denied; he gave her advice; he told her everything he had ever heard about Manley, or had seen or knew from some other source; everything, that is, save what was good. The sums he had lost at poker, or had borrowed; the debts he owed to the merchants; the reputation he had for "talking big and doing little;" the trouble he had had with this man and that man; and what he did not know for a certainty he guessed at, and so kept the subject alive.

True, Val did not speak at all, except when he asked her how she felt. Then she would reply dully, "Pretty well, thank you, Polycarp." Invariably those were the words she used. Whenever he stole a furtive, sidelong glance at her, she was staring straight ahead at the great, undulating prairie with the brown ribbon, which was the trail, thrown carelessly across to the sky line.

Polycarp suspected that she did not see anything-she just stared with her eyes, while her thoughts were somewhere else. He was not even sure that she heard what he was saying. He thought she must be pretty sick, she was so pale, and she had such wide, purple rings under her eyes. Also, he rather resented her desire to keep her trouble a secret; he favored telling everybody, and organizing a party to go out and run Man Fleetwood out of the country, as the very mildest rebuke which the outraged community could give and remain self-respecting. He even fell silent daring the last three or four miles, while he dwelt longingly upon the keen pleasure there would be in leading such an expedition.

"You'll remember, Polycarp, not to speak of this?" Val urged abruptly when he drew up before the Hawley Hotel. "Not a hint, you know until-until I give you permission. You promised."

"Oh, certainly, Mis' Fleetwood. Certainly. Don't you be a mite oneasy." But the tone of Polycarp was dejected in the extreme.

"And please be ready to drive me back in the morning. I should like to be at the ranch by noon, at the latest." With that she left him and went into the hotel.

# Chapter XXII. A Friend in Need

"And so," Val finished, rather apathetically, pushing back the fallen lock of hair, "it has come to that. I can't remain here and keep any shred of self-respect. All my life I've been taught to believe divorce a terrible thing —a crime, almost; now I think it is sometimes a crime *not* to be divorced. For months I have been coming slowly to a decision, so this is really not as sudden as it may seem to you. It is humiliating to be compelled to borrow money-but I would much rather ask you than any of my own people. My pride is going to suffer enough when I meet them, as it is; I can't let them know just how miserable and sordid a failure —"

Arline gave an inarticulate snort, bent her scrawny body nearly double, and reached frankly into her stocking. She fumbled there a moment and straightened triumphantly, grasping a flat, buckskin bag.

"I'd feel like shakin' you if you went to anybody else but me," she declared, untying the bag. "I know what men is-Lord knows I see enough of 'em and their meanness-and if I can help a woman outa the clutches of one, I'm tickled to death to git the chancet. I ain't sayin' they're all of 'em bad —I c'n afford to give the devil his due and still say that men is the limit. The good ones is so durn scarce it ain't one woman in fifty lucky enough to git one. All I blame you for is stayin' with him as long as you have. I'd of quit long ago; I was beginnin' to think you never would come to your senses. But you had to fight that thing out for yourself; every woman has to.

"I'm glad you've woke up to the fact that Man Fleetwood didn't git a deed to you, body and soul, when he married you; you've been actin' as if you thought he had. And I'm glad you've got sense enough to pull outa the game when you know the best you can expect is the worst of it. There ain't no hope for Man Fleetwood; I seen that when he went back to drinkin' again after you was burnt out. I did think that would steady him down, but he ain't the kind that braces up when trouble hits him-he's the sort that stays down ruther than go to the trouble of gittin' up. He's hopeless now as a rotten egg, and has been for the last year. Here; you take the hull works, and if you need more, I can easy git it for you by sendin' in to the bank."

"Oh, but this is too much!" Val protested when she had counted the money. "You're so good-but really and truly, I won't need half—"

Arline pushed away the proffered money impatiently. "How'n time are you goin' to tell how much you'll need? Lemme tell you, Val Peyson —I ain't goin' to call you by his name no more, the dirty cur! —I've been packin' that money in my stockin' for six months, jest so'st to have it handy when you wanted it. Divorces cost more'n marriage licenses, as you'll find out when you git started. And —"

"You-why, the idea!" Val pursed her lips with something like her old spirit. "How could *you* know I'd need to borrow money? I didn't know it myself, even. I —"

"Well, I c'n see through a wall when there's a knothole in it," paraphrased Arline calmly. "You may not know it, but you've been gittin' your back-East notions knocked outa you pretty fast the last year or so. It was all a question of what kinda stuff you was made of underneath. You c'n put a polish on most anything, so I couldn't tell, right at first, what there was to you. But you're all right —I've seen that a long time back; and so I knowed durn well you'd be wantin' money to pull loose with. It takes money, though I know it ain't polite to say much about real dollars 'n' cents. You'll likely use every cent of that before you're through with the deal-and remember, there's a lot more growin' on the same bush, if you need it. It's only waitin' to be picked."

Val stared, found her eyes blurring so that she could not see, and with a sudden, impulsive movement leaned over and put her arms around Arline, unkempt, scrawny, and wholly unlovely though she was.

"Arline, you're an angel of goodness!" she cried brokenly. "You're the best friend I ever had in my life —I've had many who petted me and flattered me-but you-you *do* things! I'm ashamed-because I haven't loved you every minute since I first saw you. I judged you —I mean-oh, you're pure, shining gold inside, instead of—"

"Oh, git out!" Arline was compelled to gulp twice before she could say even that much. "I don't shine nowhere-inside er out. I know that well enough. I never had no chancet to shine. It's always been wore off with hard knocks. But I like shiny folks all right-when they're fine clear through, and —"

"Arline-dear, I do love you. I always shall. I —"

Arline loosened her clasp and jumped up precipitately.

"Git out!" she repeated bashfully. "If you git me to cryin', Val Peyson, I'll wish you was in Halifax. You go to bed, 'n' go to sleep, er I'll —" She almost ran from the room. Outside, she stopped in a darkened corner of the hallway and stood for some minutes with her checked gingham apron pressed tightly over her face, and several times she sniffed audibly. When she finally returned to the kitchen her nose was pink, her eyelids were pink, and she was extremely petulant when she caught Minnie eying her curiously.

Val had refused to eat any supper, and, beyond telling Arline that she had decided to leave Manley and return to her mother in Fern Hill, she had not explained anything very clearly-her colorless face, for instance, nor her tightly swathed throat, nor the very noticeable bruise upon her temple.

Arline had not asked a single question. Now, however, she spent some time fixing a tray with the daintiest food she knew and could procure, and took it upstairs with a certain diffidence in her manner and a rare tenderness in her faded, worldly-wise eyes.

"You got to eat, you know," she reminded Val gently. "You're bucking up ag'inst the hardest part of the trail, and grub's a necessity. Take it like you would medicine-unless your throat's too sore. I see you got it all tied up."

Val raised her hands in a swift alarm and clasped her throat as if she feared Arline would remove the bandages.

"Oh, it's not sore-that is, it is sore —I mean not very much," she stammered betrayingly.

Arline set down the tray upon the dresser and faced Val grimly.

"I never asked you any questions, did I?" she demanded. "But you act for all the world as if-do you want me to give a guess about that tied-up neck, and that black'n'blue lump on your forehead? I never asked any questions —I didn't need to. Man Fleetwood's been maulin' you abound. I was kinda afraid he'd git to that point some day when he got mad enough; he's just the brand to beat up a woman. But if it took a beatin' to bring you to the quitting point, I'm glad he done it. *Only*," she added darkly, "he better keep outa my reach; I'm jest in the humor to claw him up some if I should git close enough. And if I happened to forget I'm a lady, I'd sure bawl him out, and the bigger crowd heard me the better. Now, you eat this-and don't get the idee you can cover up any meanness of Man Fleetwood's; not from me, anyhow. I know men better'n you do; you couldn't tell me nothing about 'em that would su'prise me the least bit. I'm only thankful he didn't murder you in cold blood. Are you going to eat?"

"Not if you keep on reminding me of such h-horrid things," wailed Val, and sobbed into her pillow. "It's bad enough to-to have him ch-choke me without having you t-talk about it all the time!"

"Now, honey, don't you waste no tears on a brute like him-he ain't w-worth it!" Arline was on her bony knees beside the bed, crying with sympathy and self-reproach.

So, in truly feminine fashion, the two wept their way back to the solid ground of everyday living. Before they reached that desirable state of composure, however, Val told her every-thing-within certain limits set not by caution, but rather by her woman's instinct. She did not, for instance, say much about Kent, though she regretted openly that Polycarp knew so much about it.

"Hope never needed no newspaper so long as Polycarp lives here," Arline grumbled when Val was sitting up again and trying to eat Arline's toast, and jelly made of buffalo berries, and sipping the tea which had gone cold. "But if I can round him up in time, I'll try and git him to keep his mouth shet. I'll scare the liver outa him some way. But if he caught onto that calf deal —" She shook her head doubtfully. "The worst of it is, Fred's in town, and he's always pumpin' Polycarp dry, jest to find out all that's goin' on. You go to bed, and I'll see if I can find out whether they're together. If they are-but you needn't to worry none. I reckon I'm a match for the both of 'em. Why, I'd dope their coffee and send 'em both to sleep till Man got outa the country, if I had to!"

She stood with her hands upon her angular hips and glared at Val.

"I sure would do that, very thing-for *you*," she reiterated solemnly, "I don't purtend I'd do it for Man-but I would for you. But it's likely Kent has fixed things up so they can't git nothing on Man if they try. He would if he said he would; that there's *one* feller that's on the square. You go to bed now, whilst I go on a still hunt of my own. I'll come and tell you if there's anything to tell."

It was easy enough to make the promise, but keeping it was so difficult that she yielded to the temptation of going to bed and letting Val sleep in peace; which she could not have done if she had known that Polycarp Jenks and Fred De Garmo left town on horseback within an hour after Polycarp had entered it, and that they told no man their errand.

Over behind Brinberg's store, Polycarp had told Fred all he knew, all he suspected, and all he believed would come to pass. "Strictly on the quiet," of course-he reminded Fred of that, over and over, because he had promised Mrs. Fleetwood that he would not mention it.

"But, by granny," he apologized, "I didn't like the idee of keepin' *a* thing like that from *you*; it would kinda look as if I was standin' in on the deal, which I ain't. Nobody can't accuse me of rustlin', no matter what else I might do; you know that, Fred."

"Sure, I know you're honest, anyway," Fred responded quite sincerely.

"Well, I considered it my duty to tell you. I've kinda had my suspicions all fall, that there was somethin' scaly goin' on at Cold Spring. Looked to me like Man had too blamed many calves missed by spring round-up —for the size of his herd. I dunno, of course, jest where he gits 'em-you'll have to find that out. But he's brung twelve er fourteen to the ranch, two er three at a time. And what she said when she first come to-told me right out, by granny, 'at Man choked her because she called 'im a thief, and somethin' about a cow comin' an' claimin' her calf, and her turnin' it out. That oughta be might' nigh all the evidence you need, Fred, if you find it. She don't know she said it, but she wouldn't of told it, by granny, if it wasn't so-now would she?"

"And you say all this happened to-day?" Fred pondered for a minute. "That's queer, because I almost caught a fellow last night doing some funny work on a calf. A Wishbone cow it was, and her calf fresh burned —a barred-out brand, by thunder! If it was to-day, I'd, say Man found it and blotched the brand. I wish now I'd hazed them over to the Double Diamond and corralled 'em, like I had a mind to. But we can find them, easy enough. But that was last night, and you say this big setting came off to-day; you *sure*, Polly?"

"'Course I'm sure." Polycarp waggled his head solemnly. He was enjoying himself to the limit. He was the man on the inside, giving out information of the greatest importance, and an officer of the law was hanging anxiously upon his words. He spoke slowly, giving weight to every word. "I rode up to the house-Man's house somewhere close to noon, an' there she was, layin' on the kitchen floor. Didn't know nothin', an' had the marks of somebody's fingers on 'er throat; the rest of her neck's so white they showed up, by granny, like-like —" Polycarp never could think of a simile. He always expectorated in such an emergency, and left his sentence unfinished. He did so now, and Fred cut in unfeelingly.

"Never mind that-you've gone over it half a dozen times. You say it was to-day, at noon, or thereabouts. Man must have done it when he found out she'd turned the calf loose-he wouldn't unless he was pretty mad, and scared. He isn't cold-blooded enough to wait till he'd barred out the brand, and then go home and choke his wife. He didn't know about the calf till to-day, that's a cinch." He studied the matter with an air of grave importance.

"Polycarp," he said abruptly, "I'm going to need you. We've got to find that bunch of cattle-it ought to be easy enough, and haze 'em down into Man's field where his bunch of calves are-see? Any calf that's been weaned in the last three weeks will be pretty likely to claim its mother; and if he's got any calves branded that claim cows with some other brand-well —" He threw out his hands in a comprehensive gesture. "That's the quickest way I know to get him," he said. "I want a witness along, and some help. And you," he eyed Polycarp keenly, "ain't safe running around town loose. All your brains seem to leak out your mouth. So you come along with me."

"Well-any time after to-morrer," hedged Polycarp, offended by the implication that he talked too much. "I've got to drive the team home for Mis' Fleetwood to-morrer, I tol' her I would —"

"Well, you won't. You're going to hit the trail with me just as soon as I can find a horse for you to ride. We'll sleep at the Double Diamond, and start from there in the morning. And if I catch you letting a word outa you about this deal, I'll just about have to arrest you for —" He did not quite know what, but the very vagueness of the threat had its effect upon Polycarp.

He went without further argument, though first he went to the Hawley Hotel-with Fred close beside him as a precaution against imprudent gossip-and left word in the office that he would not be able to drive Mrs. Fleetwood home, the next morning, but would be back to take her out the day after that, if she did not mind staying in town. It was that message which Arline deliberately held back from Val until morning.

"You better stay here," she advised then. "Polycarp an' Fred's up to some devilment, that's a cinch; but whatever it is, you're better off right here with me. S'posen you should drive out there and run into Man-what then?"

Val shivered. "I —that's the only thing I can't bear," she admitted, as if the time for proud dignity and reserve had gone by. "If I could be sure I wouldn't need to meet him, I'd rather go alone; really and truly, I would. You know the horses are perfectly safe —I've driven them to town fifty times if I have once. I had to, out there alone so much of the time. I'd rather not have Polycarp spying around. I've got to pack up-there are so many things of no value to-to *him*, things I brought out here with me. And there are all my manuscripts; I can't leave them lying around, even if they aren't worth anything; especially since they aren't worth anything." She pushed back her hair with a weary movement. "If I could only be sure-if I knew where *he* is," she sighed.

"I'll lend you my gun," Arline offered in good faith. "If he comes around you and starts any funny business again, you can stand him off, even if you got some delicate feelin's about blowin' his brains out."

"Oh, I couldn't. I'm deadly afraid of guns." Val shuddered.

"Well, then you can't go atone. I'd go with you, if you could git packed up so as to come back to-day. I guess Min could make out to git two meals alone."

"Oh, no. Really and truly, Arline, I'd just as soon go alone. I would rather, dear."

Arline was not accustomed to being called "dear." She surrendered with some confusion and a blush.

"Well, you better wait," she admonished temporizingly. "Something may turn up."

Presently something did turn up. She rushed breathlessly into Val's room and caught her by the arm.

"Now's your chancet, Val," she hissed in a loud whisper. "Man jest now rode into town; he's over in Pop's place —I seen him go in. He's good for the day, sure. I'll have Hank hitch right up, an' you can go down to the stable and start from there, so'st he won't see you. An' I'll keep an eye out, 'n' if he leaves town I won't be fur behind, lemme tell you. He won't, though; there ain't one chancet in a hundred he'll leave that saloon till he's full-an' if he tries t' go then, I'll have somebody lock 'im up in the ice house till you git back. You want to hurry up that packin', an' git in here quick's you can."

She went to the stable with Val, her apron thrown over her head for want of a hat. "When Val was settling herself in the seat, Arline caught at the wheel.

"Say! How'n time you goin' to git your trunks loaded into the wagon?" she cried. "You can't do it alone." Val parsed her lips; she had not thought of that.

"But Polycarp will come, by the time I am ready," she decided. "You couldn't keep him away, Arline; he would be afraid he might miss something, because I suppose ours is the only ranch in the country where the wheels aren't turning smoothly. Polycarp and I can manage."

Hank, grinning under his ragged, brown mustache, handed her the lines. "I've got my orders," he told her briefly. "I'll watch out the trail's kept clear."

"Oh, thank you. I've so many good friends," Val answered, giving him a smile to stir his sluggish blood. "Good-bye, Arline. Don't worry about me, there's a dear. I shall not be back before to-morrow night, probably."

Both Arline and Hank stood where they were and watched her out of sight before they turned back to the sordid tasks which made up their lives.

"She'll make it-she's the proper stuff," Hank remarked, and lighted his pipe. Arline, for a wonder, sighed and said nothing.

After two nights and a day of torment unbearable, Kent bolted from his work, which would have taken him that day, as it had done the day before, in a direction opposite to that which his mind and his heart followed, and without apology or explanation to his foreman rode straight to Cold Spring Coulee. He had no very definite plan, except to see Val. He did not even know what he would say when he faced her.

Michael was steaming from nose to tail when he stopped at the yard gate, which shows how impatience had driven his master. Kent glanced quickly around the place as he walked up the narrow path to the house. Nothing was changed in the slightest particular, as far as he could see, and he realized then that he had been uneasy as well as anxious. Both doors were closed, so that he was obliged to knock before Val became visible. He had a fleeting impression of extreme caution in the way she opened the door and looked out, but he forgot it immediately in his joy at seeing her.

"Oh, it's you. Come in, and-you won't mind if I close the door? I'm afraid I'm the victim of nerves, to-day."

"Why?" Kent was instantly solicitous. "Has anything happened since I was here?"

Val shook her head, smiling faintly. "Nothing that need to worry *you*, pal. I don't want to talk about worries. I want to be cheered up; I haven't laughed, Kent, for so long I'm afraid my facial muscles are getting stiff. Say something funny, can't you?"

Kent pushed his hat far back on his head and sat down upon a corner of the table. "Such is life in the far West-and the farther West you go, the livelier —" he began to declaim dutifully.

"The livelier it gets. Yes, I've heard that a million tunes, I believe. I can't laugh at that; I never did think it funny." She sighed, and twitched her shoulders impatiently because of it. "I see you brought back the glasses," she remarked inanely. "You certainly weren't in any great hurry, were you?"

"Oh, they had us riding over east of the home ranch, hazing in some outa the hills. I'm supposed to be over there right now-but I ain't. I expect I'll get the can, all right —"

"If you're going away, what do you care?" she taunted.

"H'm —sure, what do I care?" He eyed her from under his brows while he bent to light a match upon the sole of his boot. Val had long ago settled his compunctions about smoking in her presence. "You seem to be all tore up, here," he observed irrelevantly. "Cleaning house?"

"Yes-cleaning house." Val smiled ambiguously.

"Hubby in town?"

"Yes-he went in yesterday, and hasn't come back yet."

Kent smoked for a moment meditatively. "I found that calf, all right," he informed her at last. "It was too late to ride around this way and tell you that night. So you needn't worry any more about that."

"I'm not worrying about that." Val stooped and picked up a hairpin from the floor, and twirled it absently in her fingers. "I don't think it matters, any more. Yesterday afternoon Fred De Garmo and Polycarp Jenks came into the coulee with a bunch of cattle, and turned all the calves out of the river field with them; and, after a little, they drove the whole lot of them away somewhere-over that way." She waved a slim hand to the west. "They let out the calves in the corral, too. I saw them from the window, but I didn't ask them any questions. I really didn't need to, did I?" She grazed him with a glance. "I thought perhaps you had failed to find that calf; I'm glad you did, though-so it wasn't that started them hunting around here-Polycarp and Fred I mean."

Kent looked at her queerly. Her voice was without any emotion whatever, as if the subject held no personal interest for her. He finished his cigarette and threw the stub out into the yard before either of them spoke another word. He closed the door again, stood there for a minute making up his mind, and went slowly over to where she was sitting listlessly in a chair, her hands folded loosely in her lap. He gripped with one hand the chairback and stared down at her high-piled, yellow hair.

"How long do you think I'm going to stand around and let you be dragged into trouble like this?" he began abruptly. "You know what I told you the other day—I could say the same thing over again, and a lot more; and I'd mean more than I could find words for. Maybe you can stand this sort of thing—I can't. I'm not going to try. If you're bound to stick to that-that gentleman, I'm going to get outa the country where I can't see you killed by inches. Every time I come, you're a little bit whiter, and a little bigger-eyed—I can't stand it, I tell you!

"You weren't made for a hell like you're living. You were meant to be happy-and I was meant to make you happy. Every morning when I open my eyes-do you know what I think? I think it's another day we oughta be happy in, you and me." He took her suddenly by the shoulder and brought her up, facing him, where he could look into her eyes.

"We've only got just one life to live, Val!" he pleaded. "And we could be happy together—I'd stake my life on that. I can't go on forever just being friends, and eating my heart out for you, and seeing you abused-and what for? Just because a preacher mumbled some words over you two! Only for that, you wouldn't stay with him over-night, and you know it! Is *that* what ought to tie two human beings together-without love, or even friendship? You hate him; you can't look me in the eyes and say you don't. And he's tired of you. Some other woman would please him better. And I could make you happy!"

Val broke away from his grasp, and retreated until the table was between them. Her listlessness was a thing forgotten. She was panting with the quick beating of her heart.

"Kent-don't, pal! You mustn't say those things-it's wicked."

"It's true," he cried hotly. "Can you look at me and say it ain't the truth?"

"You've spoiled our friendship, Kent!" she accused, while she evaded his question. "It meant so much to me-just your dear, good friendship."

"My love could mean a whole lot more," he declared sturdily.

"But you mustn't say those things-you mustn't feel that way, Kent!"

"Oh!" He laughed grimly. "Mustn't I? How are you going to stop me?" He stared hard at her, his face growing slowly rigid. "There's just one way to stop me from saying such wicked things," he told her. "You can tell me you don't care anything about me, and never could, not even if that down-east conscience of yours didn't butt into the game. You can tell me that, and swear it's the truth, and I'll leave the country. I'll go so far you'll newer see me again, so I'll never bother you any more. I can't promise I'll stop loving you-but for my own sake I'll sure try hard enough." He set his teeth hard together and stood quiet, watching her.

Val tied to answer him. Evidently she could not manage her voice, for he saw her begin softly beating her lips with her fist, fighting to get back her self-control. Once or twice he had seen her do that, when, womanlike, the tears would come in spite of her.

"I don't want you to go a away," she articulated at last, with a hint of stubbornness.

"Well, what *do* you want? I can't stay, unless—" He did not attempt to finish the sentence. He knew there was no need; she understood well enough the alternative.

For long minutes she did not speak, because she could not. Like many women, she fought desperately against the tears which seemed a badge of her femininity. She sat down in a chair, dropped her face upon her folded arms, and bit her lips until they were sore. Kent took a step toward her, reconsidered, and went over to the window, where he stood staring moodily out until she began speaking. Even then, he did not turn immediately toward her.

"You needn't go, Kent," she said with some semblance of calm. "Because I'm going. I didn't tell you-but I'm going home. I'm going to get free, by the same law that tied me to him. You are right—I have a 'down-east' conscience. I think I was born with it. It demands that I get my freedom honestly; I can't steal it-pal. I couldn't be happy if I did that, no matter how hard I might try-or you."

He turned eagerly toward her then, but she stopped him with a gesture.

"No-stay where you are. I want to solve my problem and-and leave you out of it; you're a complication, pal-when you talk like-like you've just been talking. It makes my conscience wonder whether I'm honest with myself. I've got to leave you out, don't you see? And so, leaving you out, I don't feel that any woman should be expected to go on like I'm doing. You don't know —I couldn't tell you just how-impossible-this marriage of mine has become. The day after-well, yesterday-no, the day before yesterday-he came home and found out-what I'd done. He —I couldn't stay here, after that, so —"

"What did he do?" Kent demanded sharply. "He didn't dare to lay his hands on you-did he? By —"

"Don't swear, Kent —I hear so much of that from him!" Val smiled curiously. "He-he swore at me. I couldn't stay with him, after that-could I, dear?" Whether she really meant to speak that last word or not, it set Kent's blood dancing so that he forgot to urge his question farther. He took two eager steps toward her, and she retreated again behind the table.

"Kent, don't! How can I tell you anything, if you won't be good?" She waited until he was standing rather sulkily by the window again. "Anyway, it doesn't matter now what he has done. I am going to leave him. I'm going to get a divorce. Not even the strictest 'down-east' conscience could demand that I stay. I'm perfectly at ease upon that point. About this last trouble-with the calves-if I could help him, I would, of course. But all I could say would only make matters worse-and I'm a wretched failure at lying. I can help him more, I think, by going away. I feel certain there's going to be trouble over those calves. Fred De Garmo never would have come down here and driven them all away, would he, unless there was going to be trouble?"

"If he came in here and got the calves, it looks as if he meant business, all right." Kent frowned absently at the white window curtain. "I've seen the time," he added reflectively, "when I'd be all broke up to have Man get into trouble. We used to be pretty good friends!"

"A year ago it would have broken my heart," Val sighed. "We do change so! I can't quite understand Why I should feel so indifferent about it now; even the other day it was terrible. But when I felt his fingers —" she stopped guiltily. "He seems a stranger to me now. I don't even hate him so very much. I don't want to meet him, though."

"Neither do I." But there was a different meaning in Kent's tone. "So you're going to quit?" He looked at her thoughtfully —"You'll leave your address, I hope!"

"Oh, yes." Val's voice betrayed some inward trepidation. "I'm not running away; I'm just going."

"I see." He sighed, impatient at the restraint she had put upon him. "That don't mean you won't ever come back, does it? Or that the trains are going to quit carrying passengers to your town? Because you can't *always* keep me outa your 'problem,' let me tell you. Is it against the rules to ask when you're going-and how?"

"Just as soon as I can get my trunks packed, and Polycarp-or somebody-comes to help me load them into the spring wagon. I promised Arline Hawley I would be in town to-night. I don't know, though —I don't seem to be making much progress with my packing." She smiled at him more brightly. "Let's wade ashore, pal, and get to work instead of talking about things better left alone. I know just exactly what you're thinking-and I'm going to let you help me instead of Polycarp. I'm frightfully angry with him, anyway. He promised me, on his word of honor, that he wouldn't mention a thing-and he must have actually hunted for a chance to tell! He didn't have the nerve to come to the house yesterday, when he was here with Fred-perhaps he won't come to-day, after all. So you'll have to help me make my getaway, pal."

Kent wavered. "You're the limit, all right," he told her after a period of hesitation. "You just wait, old girl, till you get that conscience of yours squared! What shall I do? I can pack a war-bag in one minute and three-quarters, and a horse in five minutes-provided he don't get gay and pitch the pack off a time or two, and somebody's around to help throw the hitch. Just tell me where to start in, and you won't be able to see me for dust!"

"You seem in a frightful hurry to have me go," Val complained, laughing nevertheless with the nervous reaction. "Packing a trunk takes time, and care, and intelligence."

"Now isn't that awful?" Kent's eyes flared with mirth, all the more pronounced because it was entirely superficial. "Well, you take the time and care, Mrs. Goodpacker, and I'll cheerfully furnish the intelligence, This goes, I reckon?" He squeezed a pink cushion into as small a space as possible, and held it out at arm's length.

"That goes-to Arline. *Don't* put it in there!" Val's laughter was not far from hysteria. Kent was pretending to stuff the pink cushion into her hand bag.

"Better take it; you'll —"

The front door was pushed violently open and Manley almost fell into the room. Val gave a little, inarticulate cry and shrank back against the wall before she could recover herself. They had for the moment forgotten Manley, and all he stood for in the way of heartbreak.

A strange-looking Manley he was, with his white face and staring, bloodshot eyes, and the cruel, animal lines around his mouth. Hardly recognizable to one who had not seen him since three or four years before, he would have been. He stopped short just over the threshold, and glanced suspiciously from one to the other before he came farther into the room.

"Dig up some grub, Val-in a bag, so I can carry it on horseback," he commanded. "And a blanket-where did you put those rifle cartridges?" He hurried across the room to where his rifle and belt hung upon the wall, just over the little, homemade bookcase. "I had a couple of boxes-where are they?" He snatched down the rifle, took the belt, and began buckling it around him with fumbling fingers.

Mechanically Val reached upon a higher shelf and got him the two boxes of shells. Her eyes were fixed curiously upon his face.

"What has happened?" she asked him as he tore open a box and began pushing the shells, one by one, into his belt.

"Fred De Garmo-he tried to arrest me-in town —I shot him dead," He glanced furtively at Kent. "Can I take your horse, Kent? I want to get across the river before —"

"You shot-Fred —" Val was staring at him stupidly. He whirled savagely toward her.

"Yes, and I'd shoot any man that walked up and tried to take me. He was a fool if he thought all he had to do was crook his finger and say 'Come along.' It was over those calves-and I'd say you had a hand in it, if I hadn't found that calf, and saw how you burned out the brand before you turned it loose. You might have told me —I wouldn't have —" He shifted his gaze toward Kent. "The hell of it is, the sheriff happened to be in town for something; he's back a couple of miles-for God's sake, move! And get that flour and bacon, and some matches. I've got to get across the river. I can shake 'em off, on the other side. Hurry, Val!"

She went out into the kitchen, and they heard her moving about, collecting the things he needed.

"I'll have to take your horse, Kent." Manley turned to him with a certain wheedling tone, infinitely disgusting to the other. "Mine's all in —I rode him down, getting this far. I've got to get across the river, and into the hills the other side —I can dodge 'em over there. You can have my horse-he's good as yours, anyway." He seemed to fed a slight discomfort at Kent's silence. "You've always stood by me-anyway, it wasn't so much my fault-he came at me unawares, and says 'Man Fleetwood, you're my prisoner!' Why, the very tone of him was an insult-and I won't stand for being arrested —I pulled my gun and got him through the lungs-heard 'em yelling he was dead-Hurry up with that grub! I can't wait here till —"

"I ought to tell you Michael's no good for water," Kent forced himself to say. "He's liable to turn back on you; he's scared of it."

"He won't turn back with *me* —not with old Jake Bondy at my heels!" Manley snatched the bag of provisions from Val when she appeared, and started for the door.

"You better leave off some of that hardware, then," Kent advised perfunctorily. "You're liable to have to swim."

"I don't care how I get across, just so —" A panic seemed to seize him then. Without a word of thanks or farewell he rushed out, threw himself into Kent's saddle without taking time to tie on his bundle of bacon and flour, or remembering the blanket he had asked for. Holding his provisions under his arm, his rifle in one hand, and his reins clutched in the other, he struck the spurs home and raced down the coulee toward the river. Fred and Polycarp had not troubled to put up the wire gate after emptying the river field, so he had a straight run of it to the very river bank. The two stood together at the window and watched him go.

# Chapter XXIV. Retribution

"He thought it was I burned out that, brand; did you notice what he said?" Val, as frequently happens in times of stress, spoke first of a trivial matter, before her mind would grasp the greater issues.

"He'll never make it," said Kent, speaking involuntarily his thought. "There comes old Jake Bondy, now, down the hill. Still, I dunno-if Michael takes to the water all right —"

"If the sheriff comes here, what shall we tell him? Shall we —"

"He won't. He's turning off, don't you see? He must have got a sight of Man from the top of the hill. Michael's tolerably fresh, and Jake's horse isn't; that makes a big difference."

Val weakened unexpectedly, as the full meaning of it all swept through her mind.

"Oh, it's horrible!" she whispered. "Kent, what can we do?"

"Not a thing, only keep our heads, and don't give way to nerves," he hinted. "It's something out of our reach; let's not go all to pieces over it, pal."

She steadied under his calm voice.

"I'm always acting foolish just at the wrong time-but to think he could —"

"Don't think! You'll have enough of that to do, managing your own affairs. All this doesn't change a thing for you. It makes you feel bad-and for that I could kill him, almost!" So much flashed out, and then he brought himself in hand again. "You've still got to pack your trunks, and take the train home, just the same as if this hadn't happened. I didn't like the idea at first, but now I see it's the best thing you can do, for the present. After awhile-we'll see about it. Don't look out, if it upsets you, Val. You can't do any good, and you've got to save your nerves. Let pull down the shade —"

"Oh, I've got to see!" Perversely, she caught up the field glasses from the table, drew them from their case, and, letting down the upper window sash with a slam, focused the glasses upon the river. "He usually crosses right at the mouth of the coulee —" She swung the glasses slowly about. "Oh, there he is-just on the bank. The river looks rather high-oh, your horse doesn't want to go in, Kent. He whirls on his hind feet, and tried to bolt when Manley started in —"

Kent had been watching her face jealously. "Here, let me take a look, will you? I can tell —" She yielded reluctantly, and in a moment he had caught the focus.

"Tell me what you see, Kent-everything," she begged, looking anxiously from his face to the river.

"Well, old Jake is fogging along down the coulee-but he ain't to the river yet, not by a long shot! Ah-h! Man's riding back to take a run in. That's the stuff-got Michael's feet wet that time, the old freak! They came near going clean outa sight."

"The sheriff-is he close enough —" Val began fearfully. "Oh, we're too far away to do a thing!"

Kent kept his eyes to the glasses. "We couldn't do a thing if we were right there. Man's in swimming water already. Jake ain't riding in-from the motions he's ordering Man back."

"Oh, please let me look a minute! I won't get excited, Kent, and I'll tell you everything I see —please!" Val's teeth were fairly chattering with excitement, so that Kent hesitated before he gave up the glasses. But it seemed boorish to refuse. She snatched at them as he took them from his eyes, and placed them nervously to her own.

"Oh, I see them both!" she cried, after a second or two. "The sheriff's got his rifle in his hands-Kent, do you suppose he'd —"

"Just a bluff, pal. They all do it. What —"

Val gave a start. "Oh, he shot, Kent! I saw him take aim-it looked as if he pointed it straight at Manley, and the smoke —" She moved the glasses slowly, searching the river.

"Well, he'd have to be a dandy, to hit anything on the water, and with the sun in his eyes, too," Kent assured her, hardly taking his eyes from her face with its varying expression. Almost he could see what was taking place at the river, just by watching her.

"Oh, there's Manley, away out! Why, your Michael is swimming beautifully, Kent! His head is high out of the water, and the water is churning like-Oh, Manley's holding his rifle up over his head-he's looking back toward shore. I wonder," she added softly, "what he's thinking about! Manley! you're my husband-and once I—"

"Draw a bead on that gazabo on shore," Kent interrupted her faint faring up of sentiment toward the man she had once loved and loved no more.

Val drew a long breath and turned the glasses reluctantly from the fugitive. "I don't see him-oh, yes! He's down beside a rock, on one knee, and he's taking a rest across the rock, and is squinting along-oh, he can't hit him at that distance, can he, Kent? Would he dare-why, it would be murder, wouldn't it? Oh-h —*he shot again!*"

Kent reached up a hand and took the glasses from her eyes with a masterful gesture. "You let me look," he said laconically. "I'm steadier than you."

Val crept closer to him, and looked up into his face. She could read nothing there; his mouth was shut tight so that it was a stern, straight line, but that told her nothing. He always looked so when he was intent upon something, or thinking deeply. She turned her eyes toward the river, flowing smoothly across the mouth of the coulee. Between, the land lay sleeping lazily in the hazy sunlight of mid-autumn. The grass was brown, the rocky outcroppings of the coulee wall yellow and gray and red-and the river was so blue, and so quiet! Surely that sleepy coulee and that placid river could not be witnessing a tragedy. She turned her head, irritated by its very calmness. Her eyes dwelt wistfully upon Kent's half-concealed face.

"What are they doing now, Kent?" Her tone was hushed.

"I can't—exactly—" He mumbled absently, his mind a mile away. She waited a moment.

"Can you see-Manley?"

This time he did not answer at all; he seemed terribly far off, as if only his shell of a body remained with her in the room.

"Why don't you talk?" she wailed. She waited until she could endure no more, then reached up and snatched the glasses from his eyes.

"I can't help it —I shall go crazy standing here. I've just got to see!" she panted.

For a moment he clung to the glasses and stared down at her. "You better not, sweetheart," he urged gently, but when she still held fast he let them go. She raised them hurriedly to her eyes, and turned to the river with a shrinking impatience to know the worst and have it over with.

"E-everything j-joggles so," she whimpered complainingly, trying vainly to steady the glasses. He slipped his arms around her, and let her lean against him; she did not even seem to realize it. Just then she had caught sight of something, and her intense interest steadied her so that she stood perfectly still.

"Why, your horse —" she gasped. "Michael-he's got his feet straight up in the air-oh, Kent, he's rolling over sad over! I can't see —" She held her breath.

The glasses sagged as if they had grown all at once too heavy to hold. "I —I thought I saw —" She shivered and hid her face upon one upflung arm.

Kent caught up the glasses and looked long at the river, unmindful of the girl sobbing wildly beside him. Finally he turned to her, hesitated, and then gathered her close in his arms. The glasses slid unheeded to the floor.

"Don't cry-it's better this way, though it's hard enough, God knows." His voice was very gentle. "Think how awful it would have been, Val, if the law had got him. Don't cry like that! Such things are happening every day, somewhere —" He realized suddenly that this was no way to comfort her, and stopped. He patted her shoulder with a sense of blank helplessness. He could make love-but this was not the time for love-making; and since he was denied that outlet for his feelings, he did not know what to do, except that he led her to the couch, and settled her among the cushions so that she would be physically comfortable, at least. He turned restlessly to the window, looked; out, and then went to the couch and bent over her.

"I'm going out to the gate —I want to see Jake Bondy. He's coming up the coulee," he said. "I won't be far. Poor little girl-poor little pal, I wish I could help you." He touched his lips to her hair, so lightly she could not feel it, and left her.

At the gate he met, not the sheriff, who was riding slowly, and had just passed through the field gate, but Arline and Hank, rattling up in the Hawley buck-board.

"Thank the good Lord!" he exclaimed when he helped her from the rig. "I never was so glad to see anybody in my life. Go on in-she's in there crying her heart out. Man's dead-the sheriff shot him in the river-oh, there's been hell to pay out here!"

"My heavens above!" Arline stared up at him while she grasped the significance of his words. "I knowed he'd hit for here —I followed right out as quick as Hank could hitch up the team. Did you hear about Fred —"

"Yes, yes, yes, I know all about it!" Kent was guilty of pulling her through the gate, and then pushing her toward the house. "You go and do something for that poor girl. Pack her up and take her to town as quick as God'll let you. There's been misery enough for her out here to kill a dozen women."

He watched until she had reached the porch, and then swung back to Hank, sitting calmly in the buckboard, with the lines gripped between his knees while he filled his pipe.

"I can take care of the man's side of this business, fast enough," Kent confessed whimsically, "but there's some things it takes a woman to handle." He glanced again over his shoulder, gave a huge sigh of relief when he glimpsed Arline's thin face as she passed the window and knelt beside the couch, and turned with a lighter heart to meet the sheriff.

# The Uphill Climb

"Hell-o, Ford, where the blazes did you drop down from?" a welcoming voice yelled.

## Chapter I. "Married! and I Don't Know Her Name!"

Ford lifted his arms above his head to yawn as does a man who has slept too heavily, found his biceps stiffened and sore, and massaged them gingerly with his finger-tips. His eyes took on the vacancy of memory straining at the leash of forgetfulness. He sighed largely, swung his head slowly from left to right in mute admission of failure to grasp what lay just behind his slumber, and thereby discovered other muscles that protested against sudden movement. He felt his neck with a careful, rubbing gesture. One hand strayed to his left cheekbone, hovered there tentatively, wandered to the bridge of his nose, and from there dropped inertly to the bed.

"Lordy me! I must have been drunk last night," he said aloud, mechanically taking the straight line of logic from effect to cause, as much experience had taught him to do.

"You was—and then some," replied an unemotional voice from somewhere behind him.

"Oh! That you, Sandy?" Ford lay quiet, trying to remember. His finger-tips explored the right side of his face; now and then he winced under their touch, light as it was.

"I must have carried an awful load," he decided, again unerringly taking the backward trail from effect to cause. Later, logic carried him farther. "Who'd I lick, Sandy?"

"Several." The unseen Sandy gave one the impression of a man smoking and speaking between puffs. "Can't say just who—you did start in on. You wound up on—the preacher."

"Preacher?" Ford's tone matched the flicker of interest in his eyes.

"Uhn-hunh."

Ford meditated a moment. "I don't recollect ever licking a preacher before," he observed curiously.

Life, stale and drab since his eyes opened, gathered to itself the pale glow of awakening interest. Ford rose painfully, inch by inch, until he was sitting upon the side of the bed, got from there to his feet, looked down and saw that he was clothed to his boots, and crossed slowly to where a cheap, flyspecked looking-glass hung awry upon the wall. His self-inspection was grave and minute. His eyes held the philosophic calm of accustomedness.

"Who put this head on me, Sandy?" he inquired apathetically. "The preacher?"

"I d' know. You had it when you come up outa the heap. You licked the preacher afterwards, I think."

Sandy was reading a ragged-backed novel while he smoked; his interest in Ford and Ford's battered countenance was plainly perfunctory.

Outside, the rain fell aslant in the wind and drummed dismally upon the little window beside Sandy. It beat upon the door and trickled underneath in a thin rivulet to a shallow puddle, formed where the floor was sunken. A dank warmth and the smell of wet wood heating to the blazing point pervaded the room and mingled with the coarse aroma of cheap, warmed-over coffee.

"Sandy!"

"Hunh?"

"Did anybody get married last night?" The leash of forgetfulness was snapping, strand by strand. Troubled remembrance peered out from behind the philosophic calm in Ford's eyes.

"Unh-hunh." Sandy turned a leaf and at the same time flicked the ashes from his cigarette with a mechanical finger movement. "You did." He looked briefly up from the page. "That's why you licked the preacher," he assisted, and went back to his reading.

A subdued rumble of mid-autumn thunder jarred sullenly overhead. Ford ceased caressing the purple half-moon which inclosed his left eye and began moodily straightening his tie.

"Now what'n hell did I do that for?" he inquired complainingly.

"Search *me*," mumbled Sandy over his book. He read half a page farther. "Do what for?" he asked, with belated attention.

Ford swore and went over and lifted the coffeepot from the stove, shook it, looked in, and made a grimace of disgust as the steam smote him in the face. "Paugh!" He set down the pot and turned upon Sandy.

"Get your nose out of that book a minute and talk!" he commanded in a tone beseeching for all its surly growl. "You say I got married. I kinda recollect something of the kind. What I want to know is who's the lady? And what did I do it for?" He sat down, leaned his bruised head upon his palms, and spat morosely into the stove-hearth. "Lordy me," he grumbled. "I don't know any lady well enough to marry her-and I sure can't think of any female lady that would marry me-not even by proxy!"

Sandy closed the book upon a forefinger and regarded Ford with that blend of pity, amusement, and tolerance which is so absolutely unbearable to one who has behaved foolishly and knows it. Ford would not have borne the look if he had seen it; but he was caressing a bruise on the point of his jaw and staring dejectedly into the meager blaze which rimmed the lower edge of the stove's front door, and so remained unconscious of his companion's impertinence.

"Who was the lady, Sandy?" he begged dispiritedly, after a silence.

"Search *me*" Sandy replied again succinctly. "Some stranger that blew in here with a license and the preacher and said you was her fee-ancy." (Sandy read romances, mostly, and permitted his vocabulary to profit thereby.) "You never denied it, even when she said your name was a nomdy gair; and you let her marry you, all right."

"Are you sure of that?" Ford looked up from under lowering eyebrows.

"Unh-hunh —that's what you done, all right." Sandy's voice was dishearteningly positive.

"Lordy me!" gasped Ford under his breath.

There was a silence which slid Sandy's interest back into his book. He turned a leaf and was half-way down the page before he was interrupted by more questions.

"Say! Where's she at now?" Ford spoke with a certain furtive lowering of his voice.

"I d' know." Sandy read a line with greedy interest. "She took the 'leven-twenty," he added then. Another mental lapse. "You seen her to the train yourself."

"The hell I did!" Ford's good eye glared incredulity, but Sandy was again following hungrily the love-tangle of an unpronounceable count in the depths of the Black Forest, and he remained perfectly unconscious of the look and the mental distress which caused it. Ford went back to studying the meager blaze and trying to remember. He might be able to extract the whole truth from Sandy, but that would involve taking his novel away from him-by force, probably; and the loss of the book would be very likely to turn Sandy so sullen that he would refuse to answer, or to tell the truth, at any rate; and Ford's muscles were very, very sore. He did not feel equal to a scuffle with Sandy, just then. He repeated something which sounded like an impromptu litany and had to do with the ultimate disposal of his own soul.

"Hunh?" asked Sandy.

Whereupon Ford, being harassed mentally and in great physical discomfort as well, specifically disposed of Sandy's immortal soul also.

Sandy merely grinned at him. "You don't want to take it to heart like that," he remonstrated cheerfully.

Ford, by way of reply, painstakingly analyzed the chief deficiencies of Sandy's immediate relatives, and was beginning upon his grandparents when Sandy reached barren ground in the shape of three long paragraphs of snow, cold, and sunrise artistically blended with prismatic adjectives. He waded through the first paragraph and well into the second before he mired in a hopeless jumble of unfamiliar polysyllables. Sandy was not the skipping kind; he threw the book upon a bench and gave his attention wholly to his companion in time to save his great-grandfather from utter condemnation.

"What's eating you, Ford?" he began pacifically-for Sandy was a weakling. "You might be a lot worse off. You're married, all right enough, from all I c'n hear-but she's left town. It ain't as if you had to live with her."

Ford looked at him a minute and groaned dismally.

"Oh, I ain't meaning anything against the lady herself," Sandy hastened to assure him. "Far as I know, she's all right —"

"What I want to know," Ford broke in, impatient of condolence when he needed facts, "is, who *is* she? And what did I go and marry her for?"

"Well, you'll have to ask somebody that knows. I never seen her, myself, except when you was leadin' her down to the depot, and you and her talked it over private like-the way I heard it. I was gittin' a hair-cut and shampoo at the time. First I heard, you was married. I should think you'd remember it yourself." Sandy looked at Ford curiously.

"I kinda remember standing up and holding hands with some woman and somebody saying: 'I now pronounce you man and wife,'" Ford confessed miserably, his face in his hands again. "I guess I must have done it, all right."

Sandy was kind enough when not otherwise engaged. He got up and put a basin of water on the stove to warm, that Ford might bathe his hurts, and he made him a very creditable drink with lemon and whisky and not too much water.

"The way I heard it," he explained further, "this lady come to town looking for Frank Ford Cameron, and seen you, and said you was him. So —"

"I ain't," Ford interrupted indignantly. "My name's Ford Campbell and I'll lick any darned son-of-a-gun —"

"Likely she made a mistake," Sandy soothed. "Frank Ford Cameron, she had you down for, and you went ahead and married her willing enough. Seems like there was some hurry-up reason that she explained to you private. She had the license all made out and brought a preacher down from Garbin. Bill Wright said he overheard you tellin' her you'd do anything to oblige a lady —"

"That's the worst of it; I'm always too damned polite when I'm drunk!" grumbled Ford.

Sandy, looking upon his bruised and distorted countenance and recalling, perhaps, the process by which Ford reached that lamentable condition, made a sound like a diplomatically disguised laugh. "Not always," he qualified mildly.

"Anyway," he went on, "you sure married her. That's straight goods. Bill Wright and Rock was the witnesses. And if you don't know why you done it —" Sandy waved his hands to indicate his inability to enlighten Ford. "Right afterwards you went out to the bar and had another drink-all this takin' place in the hotel dining-room, and Mother McGrew down with neuralagy and not bein' present-and one drink leads to another, you know. I come in then, and the bunch was drinkin' luck to you fast as Sam could push the bottles along. Then you went back to the lady-and if you don't know what took place you can search me-and pretty soon Bill said you'd took her and her grip to the depot. Anyway, when you come back, you wasn't troubled with no attack of politeness!

"You went in the air with Bill, first," continued Sandy, testing with his finger the temperature of the water in the basin, "and bawled him out something fierce for standing by and seeing you make a break like that without doing something. You licked him-and then Rock bought in because some of your remarks kinda included him too. I d' know," said Sandy, scratching his unshaven jaw reflectively, "just how the fight did go between you 'n' Rock. You was both using the whole room, I know. Near as I could make out, you-or maybe it was Rock-tromped on Big Jim's bunion. This cold spell's hard on bunions-and Big Jim went after you both with blood in his eye.

"After that" —Sandy spread his arms largely —"it was go-as-you-please. Sam and me was the only ones that kept out, near as I can recollect, and when it thinned up a bit, you had Aleck down and was pounding the liver outa him, and Big Jim was whanging away at you, and Rock was clawin' Jim in the back of the neck, and you was all kickin' like bay steers in brandin' time. I reached in under the pile and dragged you out by one leg and left the rest of 'em fighting. They never seemed to miss you none." He grinned. "Jim commenced to bump Aleck's head up and down on the floor instead of you-and I knew he didn't have nothing against Aleck."

"Bill —"

"Bill, he'd quit right in the start." Sandy's grin became a laugh. "Seems like pore old Bill always gits in bad when you commence on your third pint. You wasn't through, though, seems like. You was going to start in at the beginning and en-core the whole performance, and you started out after Bill. Bill, he was lookin' for a hole big enough to crawl into by that time. But you run into the preacher. And you licked him to a fare-you-well and had him crying real tears before I or anybody else could stop you."

"What'd I lick him for?" Ford inquired in a tone of deep discouragement.

Sandy's indeterminate, blue-gray eyes rounded with puzzlement.

"Search me," he repeated automatically. But later he inadvertently shed enlightenment. He laughed, bending double, and slapping his thigh at the irresistible urge of a mental picture.

"Thought I'd die," he gasped. "Me and Sam was watching from the door. You had the preacher by the collar, shakin' him, and once in awhile liftin' him clean off the ground on the toe of your boot; and you kept saying: 'A sober man, and a preacher-and you'd marry that girl to a fellow like me!' And then biff! And he'd let out a squawk. 'A drinkin', fightin', gamblin' son-of-a-gun like me, you swine!' you'd tell him. And when we finally pulled you loose, he picked up his hat and made a run for it."

Ford meditated gloomily. "I'll lick him again, and lick him when I'm sober, by thunder!" he promised grimly. "Who was he, do you know?"

"No, I don't. Little, dried-up geezer with a nose like a kit-fox's and a whine to his voice. He won't come around here no more."

The door opened gustily and a big fellow with a skinned nose and a whimsical pair of eyes looked in, hesitated while he stared hard at Ford, and then entered and shut the door by the simple method of throwing his shoulders back against it.

"Hello, old sport-how you comin'?" he cried cheerfully. "Kinda wet for makin' calls, but when a man's loaded down with a guilty conscience —" He sighed somewhat ostentatiously and pulled forward a chair rejuvenated with baling-wire braces between the legs, and a cowhide seat. "What's that cookin' —coffee, or sheep-dip?" he inquired facetiously of Sandy, though his eyes dwelt solicitously upon Ford's bowed head. He leaned forward and slapped Ford in friendly fashion upon the shoulder.

"Buck up —'the worst is yet to come,'" he shouted, and laughed with an exaggeration of cheerfulness. "You can't ever tell when death or matrimony's goin' to get a man. By hokey, seems like there's no dodgin' either one."

Ford lifted a bloodshot eye to the other. "And I always counted you for a friend, Bill," he reproached heavily. "Sandy says I licked you good and plenty. Well, looks to me like you had it coming, all right."

"Well —I got it, didn't I?" snorted Bill, his hand lifting involuntarily to his nose. "And I ain't bellering, am I?" His mouth took an abused, downward droop. "I ain't holdin' any grudge, am I? Why, Sandy here can tell you that I held one side of you up whilst he was leadin' the other side of you home! And I am sorry I stood there and seen you get married off and never lifted a finger; I'm darned sorry. I shoulda hollered misdeal, all right. I know it now." He pulled remorsefully at his wet mustache, which very much resembled a worn-out sharing brush.

Ford straightened up, dropped a hand upon his thigh, and thereby discovered another sore spot, which he caressed gently with his palm.

"Say, Bill, you were there, and you saw her. On the square now-what's she like? And what made me marry her?"

Bill pulled so hard upon his mustache that his teeth showed; his breath became unpleasantly audible with the stress of emotion. "So help me, I can't tell you what she's like, Ford," he confessed. "I don't remember nothing about her looks, except she looked good to me, and I never seen her before, and her hair wasn't red —I always remember red hair when I see it, drunk or sober. You see," he added as an extenuation, "I was pretty well jagged myself. I musta been. I recollect I was real put out because my name wasn't Frank Ford-By hokey!" He laid an impressive forefinger upon Ford's knee and tapped several times. "I never knew your name was rightly Frank Ford Cameron. I always —"

"It ain't." Ford winced and drew away from the tapping process, as if his knee also was sensitive that morning.

"You told her it was. I mind that perfectly, because I was so su'prised I swore right out loud and was so damned ashamed I couldn't apologize. And say! She musta been a real lady or I wouldn't uh felt that way about it!" Bill glanced triumphantly from one to the other. "Take it from me, you married a lady, Ford. Drunk or sober, I always make it a point to speak proper before the ladies —t'other kind don't count-and when I make a break, you betcher life I remember it. She's a real lady—I'd swear to that on a stack uh bibles ten feet high!" He settled back and unbuttoned his steaming coat with the air of a man who has established beyond question the vital point of an argument.

"Did I tell her so myself, or did I just let it go that way?" Ford, as his brain cleared, stuck close to his groping for the essential facts.

"Well, now —I ain't dead sure as to that. Maybe Rock'll remember. Kinda seems to me now, that she asked you if you was really Frank Ford Cameron, and you said: 'I sure am,' or something like that. The preacher'd know, maybe. He musta been the only sober one in the bunch-except the girl. But you done chased him off, so —"

"Sandy, I wish you'd go hunt Rock up and tell him I want to see him." Ford spoke with more of his natural spirit than he had shown since waking.

"Rock's gone on out to Riley's camp," volunteered Bill. "Left this morning, before the rain started in."

"What was her name-do you know?" Ford went back to the mystery.

"Ida-or was it Jenny? Some darned name —I heard it, when the preacher was marrying you." Bill was floundering hopelessly in mental fog, but he persisted. "And I seen it wrote in the paper I signed my name to. I mind she rolled up the paper afterwards and put it-well, I dunno where, but she took it away with her, and says to you: 'That's safe, now' —or 'You're safe,' or 'I'm safe,'—anyway, some darned thing was safe. And I was goin' to kiss the bride-mebbe I did kiss her-only I'd likely remember it if I had, drunk or sober! And-oh, now I got it!" Bill's voice was full of elation. "You was goin' to kiss the bride-that was it, it was you goin' to kiss her, and she slap-no, by hokey, she didn't slap you, she just-or was it Rock, now?" Doubt filled his eyes distressfully. "Darn my everlastin' hide," he finished lamely, "there was some kissin' somew'ere in the deal, and I mind her cryin' afterwards, but whether it was about that, or-Say, Sandy, what was it Ford was lickin' the preacher for? Wasn't it for kissin' the bride?"

"It was for marrying him to her," Sandy informed him sententiously.

Ford got up and went to the little window and looked out. Presently he came back to the stove and stood staring disgustedly down upon the effusively friendly Bill, leering up at him pacifically.

"If I didn't feel so rotten," he said glumly, "I'd give you another licking right now, Bill-you boozing old devil. I'd like to lick every darned galoot that stood back and let me in for this. You'd ought to have stopped me. You'd oughta pounded the face off me before you let me do such a fool thing. That," he said bitterly, "shows how much a man can bank on his friends!"

"It shows," snorted Bill indignantly, "how much he can bank on himself!"

"On whisky, to let him in for all kinds uh trouble," revised Sandy virtuously. Sandy had a stomach which invariably rebelled at the second glass and therefore, remaining always sober perforce, he took to himself great credit for his morality.

"Married! —and I don't so much as know her name!" gritted Ford, and went over and laid himself down upon the bed, and sulked for the rest of that day of rain and gloom.

## Chapter II. Wanted: Information

Sulking never yet solved a mystery nor will it accomplish much toward bettering an unpleasant situation. After a day of unmitigated gloom and a night of uneasy dreams, Ford awoke to a white, shifting world of the season's first blizzard, and to something like his normal outlook upon life.

That outlook had ever been cheerful, with the cheerfulness which comes of taking life in twenty-four-hour doses only, and of looking not too far ahead and backward not at all. Plenty of persons live after that fashion and thereby attain middle life with smooth foreheads and cheeks unlined by thought; and Ford was therefore not much different from his fellows. Never before had he found himself with anything worse than bodily bruises to sour life for him after a tumultuous night or two in town, and the sensation of a discomfort which had not sprung from some well-defined physical sense was therefore sufficiently novel to claim all his attention.

It was not the first time he had fought and forgotten it afterwards. Nor was it a new experience for him to seek information from his friends after a night full of incident. Sandy he had always found tolerably reliable, because Sandy, being of that inquisitive nature so common to small persons, made it a point to see everything there was to be seen; and his peculiar digestive organs might be counted upon to keep him sober. It was a real grievance to Ford that Sandy should have chosen the hour he did for indulging in such trivialities as hair-cuts and shampoos, while events of real importance were permitted to transpire unseen and unrecorded. Ford, when the grievance thrust itself keenly upon him, roused the recreant Sandy by pitilessly thrusting an elbow against his diaphragm.

Sandy grunted at the impact and sat bolt upright in bed before he was fairly awake. He glanced reproachfully down at Ford, who stared back at him from a badly crumpled pillow.

"Get up," growled Ford, "and start a fire going, darn you. You kept me awake half the night, snoring. I want a beefsteak with mushrooms, devilled kidneys, waffles with honey, and four banana fritters for breakfast. I'll take it in bed; and while I'm waiting, you can bring me the morning paper and a package of Egyptian Houris."

Sandy grunted again, slid reluctantly out into the bitterly cold room, and crept shivering into his clothes. He never quite understood Ford's sense of humor, at such times, but he had learned that it is more comfortable to crawl out of bed than to be kicked out, and that vituperation is a mere waste of time when matched against sheer heartlessness and a superior muscular development.

"Y' ought to make your wife build the fires," he taunted, when he was clothed and at a safe distance from the bed. He ducked instinctively afterwards, but Ford was merely placing a match by itself on the bench close by.

"That's one," Ford remarked calmly. "I'm going to thrash every misguided humorist who mentions that subject to me in anything but a helpful spirit of pure friendship. I'm going to give him a separate licking for every alleged joke. I'll want two steaks, Sandy. I'll likely have to give you about seven distinct wallopings. Hand me some more matches to keep tally with. I don't want to cheat you out of your just dues."

Sandy eyed him doubtfully while he scraped the ashes from the grate.

"You may want a dozen steaks, but that ain't saying you're going to git 'em," he retorted, with a feeble show of aggression. "And 's far as licking me goes —" He stopped to blow warmth upon his fingers, which were numbed with their grasp of the poker. "As for licking me, I guess you'll have to do that on the strength uh bacon and sour-dough biscuits; if you do it at all, which I claim the privilege uh doubting a whole lot."

Ford laughed a little at the covert challenge, made ridiculous by Sandy's diminutive stature, pulled the blankets up to his eyes, and dozed off luxuriously; and although it is extremely tiresome to be told in detail just what a man dreams upon certain occasions, he did dream, and it was something about being married. At any rate, when the sizzling of bacon frying invaded even his slumber and woke him, he felt a distinct pang of disappointment that it was Sandy's carroty head bent over the frying-pan, instead of a wife with blond hair which waved becomingly upon her temples.

"Wonder what color her hair is, anyway," he observed inadvertently, before he was wide enough awake to put the seal of silence on his musings.

"Hunh?"

"I asked when those banana fritters are coming up," lied Ford, getting out of bed and yawning so that his swollen jaw hurt him, and relapsed into his usual taciturnity, which was his wall of defense against Sandy's inquisitiveness.

He ate his breakfast almost in silence, astonishing Sandy somewhat by not complaining of the excess of soda in the biscuits. Ford was inclined toward fastidiousness when he was sober —a trait which caused men to suspect him of descending from an upper stratum of society; though just when, or just where, or how great that descent had been, they had no means of finding out. Ford, so far as his speech upon the subject was concerned, had no existence previous to his appearance in Montana, five or six years before; but he bore certain earmarks of a higher civilization which, in Sandy's mind, rather concentrated upon a pronounced distaste for soda-yellowed bread, warmed-over coffee, and scorched bacon. That he swallowed all these things and seemed not to notice them, struck Sandy as being almost as remarkable as his matrimonial adventure.

When he had eaten, Ford buttoned himself into his overcoat, pulled his moleskin cap well down, and went out into the storm without a word to Sandy, which was also unusual; it was Ford's custom to wash the dishes, because he objected to Sandy's economy of clean, hot water. Sandy flattened his nose against the window, saw that Ford, leaning well forward against the drive of the wind, was battling his way toward the hotel, and guessed shrewdly that he would see him no more that day.

"He better keep sober till his knuckles git well, anyway," he mumbled disapprovingly. "If he goes to fighting, the shape he's in now —"

Ford had no intention of fighting. He went straight up to the bar, it is true, but that was because he saw that Sam was at that moment unoccupied, save with a large lump of gum. Being at the bar, he drank a glass of whisky; not of deliberate intent, but merely from force of habit. Once down, however, the familiar glow of it through his being was exceedingly grateful, and he took another for good measure.

"H'lo, Ford," Sam bethought him to say, after he had gravely taken mental note of each separate scar of battle, and had shifted his cud to the other side of his mouth, and had squeezed it meditatively between his teeth. "Feel as rocky as you look?"

"Possibly." Ford's eyes forbade further personalities. "I'm out after information, Sam, and if you've got any you aren't using, I'd advise you to pass it over; I can use a lot, this morning. Were you sober, night before last?"

Sam chewed solemnly while he considered. "Tolerable sober, yes," he decided at last. "Sober enough to tend to business; why?"

With his empty glass Ford wrote invisible scrolls upon the bar. "I —did you happen to see-my-the lady I married?" He had been embarrassed at first, but when he finished he was glaring a challenge which shifted the disquiet to Sam's manner.

"No. I was tendin' bar all evenin' —and she didn't come in here."

Ford glanced behind him at the sound of the door opening, saw that it was only Bill, and leaned over the bar for greater secrecy, lowering his voice as well.

"Did you happen to hear who she was?"

Sam stared and shook his head.

"Don't you know anything about her at all-where she came from-and why, and where she went?"

Sam backed involuntarily. Ford's tone made it a crime either to know these things or to be guilty of ignorance; which, Sam could not determine. Sam was of the sleek, oily-haired type of young men, with pimples and pale eyes and a predilection for gum and gossip. He was afraid of Ford and he showed it.

"That's just what (no offense, Ford—I ain't responsible) that's what everybody's wondering. Nobody seems to know. They kinda hoped you'd explain—"

"Sure!" Ford's tone was growing extremely ominous. "I'll explain a lot of things-if I hear any gabbling going on about my affairs." He was seized then with an uncomfortable feeling that the words were mere puerile blustering and turned away from the bar in disgust.

In disgust he pulled open the door, flinched before the blast of wind and snow which smote him full in the face and blinded him, and went out again into the storm. The hotel porch was a bleak place, with snow six inches deep and icy boards upon which a man might easily slip and break a bone or two, and with a whine overhead as the wind sucked under the roof. Ford stood there so long that his feet began to tingle. He was not thinking; he was merely feeling the feeble struggles of a newborn desire to be something and do something worth while —a desire which manifested itself chiefly in bitterness against himself as he was, and in a mental nausea against the life he had been content to live.

The mystery of his marriage was growing from a mere untoward incident of a night's carouse into a baffling thing which hung over him like an impending doom. He was not the sort of man who marries easily. It seemed incredible that he could really have done it; more incredible that he could have done it and then have wiped the slate of his memory clean; with the crowning impossibility that a strange young woman could come into town, marry him, and afterward depart and no man know who she was, whence she had come, or where she had gone. Ford stepped suddenly off the porch and bored his way through the blizzard toward the depot. The station agent would be able to answer the last question, at any rate.

The agent, however, proved disappointingly ignorant of the matter. He reminded Ford that there had not been time to buy a ticket, and that the girl had been compelled to run down the platform to reach the train before it started, and that the wheels began to turn before she was up the steps of the day coach.

"And don't you remember turning around and saying to me: 'I'm a poor married man, but you can't notice the scar,' or something like that?" The agent was plainly interested and desirous of rendering any assistance possible, and also rather diffident about discussing so delicate a matter with a man like Ford.

Ford drummed his fingers impatiently upon the shelf outside the ticket window. "I don't remember a darned thing about it," he confessed glumly. "I can't say I enjoy running all around town trying to find out who it was I married, and why I married her, and where she went afterwards, but that's just the kinda fix I'm in, Lew. I don't suppose she came here and did it just for fun-and I can't figure out any other reason, unless she was plumb loco. From all I can gather, she was a nice girl, and it seems she thought I was Frank Ford Cameron-which I am not!" He laughed, as a man will laugh sometimes when he is neither pleased nor amused.

"I might ask McCreery-he's conductor on Fourteen. He might remember where she wanted to go," the agent suggested hesitatingly. "And say! What's the matter with going up to Garbin and looking up the record? She had to get the license there, and they'd have her name, age, place of residence, and-and whether she's white or black." The agent smiled uncertainly over his feeble attempt at a joke. "I got a license for a friend once," he explained hastily, when he saw that Ford's face did not relax a muscle. "There's a train up in forty minutes—"

"Sure, I'll do that." Ford brightened. "That must be what I've been trying to think of and couldn't. I knew there was some way of finding out. Throw me a round-trip ticket, Lew. Lordy me! I can't afford to let a real, live wife slip the halter like this and leave me stranded and not knowing a thing about her. How much is it?"

The agent slid a dark red card into the mouth of his office stamp, jerked down the lever, and swung his head quickly toward the sounder chattering hysterically behind him. His jaw slackened as he listened, and he turned his eyes vacantly upon Ford for a moment before he looked back at the instrument.

"Well, what do you know about that?" he queried, under his breath, released the ticket from the grip of the stamp, and flipped it into the drawer beneath the shelf as if it were so much waste paper.

"That's my ticket," Ford reminded him levelly.

"You don't want it now, do you?" The agent grinned at him. "Oh, I forgot you couldn't read that." He tilted his head back toward the instrument. "A wire just went through-the court-house at Garbin caught fire in the basement-something about the furnace, they think-and she's going up in smoke. Hydrants are froze up so they can't get water on it. That fixes your looking up the record, Ford."

Ford stared hard at him. "Well, I might hunt up the preacher and ask him," he said, his tone dropping again to dull discouragement.

The agent chuckled. "From all I hear," he observed rashly, "you've made that same preacher mighty hard to catch!"

Ford drummed upon the shelf and scowled at the smoke-blackened window, beyond which the snow was sweeping aslant. Upon his own side of the ticket window, the agent pared his nails with his pocket-knife and watched him furtively.

"Oh, hell! What do I care, anyway?" Revulsion seized Ford harshly. "I guess I can stand it if she can. She came here and married me-it isn't my funeral any more than it is hers. If she wants to be so darned mysterious about it, she can go plumb-to-New York!" There were a few decent traits in Ford Campbell; one was his respect for women, a respect which would not permit him to swear about this wife of his, however exasperating her behavior.

"That's the sensible way to look at it, of course," assented the agent, who made it a point to agree always with a man of Ford's size and caliber, on the theory that amiability means popularity, and that placation is better than plasters. "You sure ought to let her do the hunting-and the worrying, too. You aren't to blame if she married you unawares. She did it all on her own hook-and she must have known what she was up against."

"No, she didn't," flared Ford unexpectedly. "She made a mistake, and I wanted to point it out to her and help her out of it if I could. She took me for some one else, and I was just drunk enough to think it was a joke, I suppose, and let it go that way. I don't believe she found out she tied up to the wrong man. It's entirely my fault, for being drunk."

"Well, putting it that way, you're right about it," agreed the adaptable Lew. "Of course, if you hadn't been —"

"If whisky's going to let a fellow in for things like this, it's time to cut it out altogether." Ford was looking at the agent attentively.

"That's right," assented the other unsuspectingly. "Whisky is sure giving you the worst of it all around. You ought to climb on the water-wagon, Ford, and that's a fact. Whisky's the worst enemy you've got."

"Sure. And I'm going to punish all of it I can get my hands on!" He turned toward the door. "And when I'm good and full of it," he added as an afterthought, "I'm liable to come over here and lick you, Lew, just for being such an agreeable cuss. You better leave your mother's address handy." He laughed a little to himself as he pulled the door shut behind him. "I bet he'll keep the frost thawed off the window to-day, just to see who comes up the platform," he chuckled.

He would have been more amused if he had seen how the agent ducked anxiously forward to peer through the ticket window whenever the door of the waiting room opened, and how he started whenever the snow outside creaked under the tread of a heavy step; and he would have been convulsed with mirth if he had caught sight of the formidable billet of wood which Lew kept beside his chair all that day, and had guessed its purpose, and that it was a mute witness to the reputation which one Ford Campbell bore among his fellows. Lew was too wise to consider for a moment the revolver meant to protect the contents of the safe. Even the unintelligent know better than to throw a lighted match into a keg of gunpowder.

Ford leaned backward against the push of the storm and was swept up to the hotel. He could not remember when he had felt so completely baffled; the incident of the girl and the ceremony was growing to something very like a calamity, and the mystery which surrounded it began to fret him intolerably; and the very unusualness of a trouble he could not settle with his fists whipped his temper to the point of explosion. He caught himself wavering, nevertheless, before the wind-swept porch of the hotel "office." That, too, was strange. Ford was not wont to hesitate before entering a saloon; more often he hesitated about leaving.

"What's the matter with me, anyway?" he questioned himself impatiently. "I'm acting like I hadn't a right to go in and take a drink when I feel like it! If just a slight touch of matrimony acts like that with a man, what can the real thing be like? I always heard it made a fool of a fellow." To prove to himself that he was still untrammeled and at liberty to follow his own desire, he stamped across the porch, threw open the door, and entered with a certain defiance of manner.

Behind the bar, Sam was laughing with his mouth wide open so that his gum showed shamelessly. Bill and Aleck and Big Jim were leaning heavily upon the bar, laughing also.

"I'll bet she's a Heart-and-Hander, tryin' a new scheme to git a man. Think uh nabbing a man when he's drunk. That's a new one," Sam brought his lips close enough together to declare, and chewed vigorously upon the idea, —until he glanced up and saw Ford standing by the door. He turned abruptly, caught up a towel, and began polishing the bar with the frenzy of industry which never imposes upon one in the slightest degree.

Bill glanced behind him and nudged Aleck into caution, and in the silence which followed, the popping of a piece of slate-veined coal in the stove sounded like a volley of small-caliber pistol shots.

## Chapter III. One Way to Drown Sorrow

Ford walked up to the bar, with a smile upon his face which Sam misunderstood and so met with a conciliatory grin and a hand extended toward a certain round, ribbed bottle with a blue-and-silver label. Ford waved away the bottle and leaned, not on the bar but across it, and clutching Sam by the necktie, slapped him first upon one ear and next upon the other, until he was forced by the tingling of his own fingers to desist. By that time Sam's green necktie was pulled tight just under his nose, and he had swallowed his gum-which, considering the size of the lump, was likely to be the death of him.

Ford did not say a word. He permitted Sam to jerk loose and back into a corner, and he watched the swift crimsoning of his ears with a keen interest. Since Sam's face had the pasty pallor of the badly scared, the ears appeared much redder by contrast than they really were. Next, Ford turned his attention to the man beside him, who happened to be Bill. For one long minute the grim spirit of war hovered just over the two.

"Aw, forget it, Ford," Bill urged ingratiatingly at last. "You don't want to lick anybody-least of all old Bill! Look at them knuckles! You couldn't thump a feather bed. Anyway, you got the guilty party when you done slapped Sam up to a peak and then knocked the peak off. Made him swaller his cud, too, by hokey! Say, Sam, my old dad used to feed a cow on bacon-rinds when she done lost her cud. You try it, Sam. Mebby it might help them ears! Shove that there trouble-killer over this way, Sammy, and don't look so fierce at your uncle Bill; he's liable to turn you across his knee and dust your pants proper." He turned again to Ford, scowling at the group and at life in general, while the snow melted upon his broad shoulders and trickled in little, hurrying drops down to the nearest jumping-off place. "Come, drownd your sorrer," Bill advised amiably. "Nobody said nothing but Sammy, and I'll gamble he wishes he hadn't, now." If his counsel was vicious, his smile was engaging-which does not, in this instance, mean that it was beautiful.

Ford's fingers closed upon the bottle, and with reprehensible thoroughness he proceeded to drown what sorrows he then possessed. Unfortunately he straightway produced a fresh supply, after his usual method. In two hours he was flushed and argumentative. In three he had whipped Bill-cause unknown to the chronicler, and somewhat hazy to Ford also after it was all over. By mid-afternoon he had Sammy entrenched in the tiny stronghold where barreled liquors were kept, and scared to the babbling stage. Aleck had been put to bed with a gash over his right eye where Ford had pointed his argument with a beer glass, and Big Jim had succumbed to a billiard cue directed first at his most sensitive bunion and later at his head. Ford was not using his fists, that day, because even in his whisky-brewed rage he remembered, oddly enough, his skinned knuckles.

Others had come-in fact, the entire male population of Sunset was hovering in the immediate vicinity of the hotel-but none had conquered. There had been considerable ducking to avoid painful contact with flying glasses from the bar, and a few had retreated in search of bandages and liniment; the luckier ones remained as near the storm-center as was safe and expostulated. To those Ford had but one reply, which developed into a sort of war-chant, discouraging to the peace-loving listeners.

"I'm a rooting, tooting, shooting, fighting son-of-a-gun —*and a good one!*" Ford would declaim, and with deadly intent aim a lump of coal, billiard ball, or glass at some unfortunate individual in his audience. "Hit the nigger and get a cigar! You're just hanging around out there till I drink myself to sleep-but I'm fooling you a few! I'm watching the clock with one eye, and I take my dose regular and not too frequent. I'm going to kill off a few of these smart boys that have been talking about me and my wife. She's a lady, my wife is, and I'll kill the first man that says she isn't." (One cannot, you will understand, be too explicit in a case like this; not one thousandth part as explicit as Ford was.)

"I'm going to begin on Sam, pretty quick," he called through the open door. "I've got him right where I want him." And he stated, with terrible exactness, his immediate intentions towards the bartender.

Behind his barricade of barrels, Sam heard and shivered like a gun-shy collie at a turkey shoot; shivered until human nerves could bear no more, and like the collie he left the storeroom and fled with a yelp of sheer terror. Ford turned just as Sam shot through the doorway into the dining-room, and splintered a beer bottle against the casing; glanced solemnly up at the barroom clock and, retreating to the nearly denuded bar, gravely poured himself another drink; held up the glass to the dusk-filmed window, squinted through it, decided that he needed a little more than that, and added another teaspoonful. Then he poured the contents of the glass down his throat as if it were so much water, wiped his lips upon a bar towel, picked a handful of coal from the depleted coal-hod, went to the door, and shouted to those outside to produce Sam, that he might be killed in an extremely unpleasant manner.

The group outside withdrew across the street to grapple with the problem before them. It was obviously impossible for civilized men to sacrifice Sam, even if they could catch him-which they could not. Sam had bolted through the dining-room, upset the Chinaman in the kitchen, and fallen over a bucket of ashes in the coal-shed in his flight for freedom. He had not stopped at that, but had scurried off up the railroad track. The general opinion among the spectators was that he had, by this time, reached the next station and was hiding in a cellar there.

Bill Wright hysterically insisted that it was up to Tom Aldershot, who was a deputy town marshal. Tom, however, was working on the house he hoped to have ready for his prospective bride by Thanksgiving, and hated to be interrupted for the sake of a few broken heads only.

"He ain't shooting up nobody," he argued from the platform, where he was doing "inside work" on his dining-room while the storm lasted. "He never does cut loose with his gun when he's drunk. If I arrested him, I'd have to take him clear up to Garbin-and I ain't got time. And it wouldn't be nothin' but a charge uh disturbin' the peace, when I got him there. Y'oughta have a jail in Sunset, like I've been telling yuh right along. Can't expect a man to stop his work just to take a man to jail-not for anything less than murder, anyhow."

Some member of the deputation hinted a doubt of his courage, and Tom flushed.

"I ain't scared of him," he snorted indignantly. "I should say not! I'll go over and make him behave-as a man and a citizen. But I ain't going to arrest him as an officer, when there ain't no place to put him." Tom reluctantly threw down his hammer, grumbling because they would not wait till it was too dark to drive nails, but must cut short his working day, and went over to the hotel to quell Ford.

Ingress by way of the front door was obviously impracticable; the marshal ducked around the corner just in time to avoid a painful meeting with a billiard ball. Mother McGrew had piled two tables against the dining-room door and braced them with the mop, and stubbornly refused to let Tom touch the barricade either as man or officer of the law.

"Well, if I can't get in, I can't do nothing," stated Tom, with philosophic calm.

"He's tearing up the whole place, and he musta found all them extra billiard balls Mike had under the bar, and is throwin' 'em away," wailed Mrs. McGrew, "and he's drinkin' and not payin'. The damage that man is doin' it would take a year's profits to make up. You gotta do something, Tom Aldershot-you that calls yourself a marshal, swore to pertect the citizens uh Sunset! No, sir —I ain't a-goin' to open this door, neither. I'm tryin' to save the dishes, if you want to know. I ain't goin' to let my cups and plates foller the glasses in there. A town full uh men-and you stand back and let one crazy —"

Tom had heard Mrs. McGrew voice her opinion of the male population of Sunset on certain previous occasions. He left her at that point, and went back to the group across the street.

At length Sandy, whose imagination had been developed somewhat beyond the elementary stage by his reading of romantic fiction, suggested luring Ford into the liquor room by the simple method of pretending an assault upon him by way of the storeroom window, which could be barred from without by heavy planks. Secure in his belief in Ford's friendship for him, Sandy even volunteered to slam the door shut upon Ford and lock it with the padlock which guarded the room from robbery. Tom took a chew of tobacco, decided that the ruse might work, and donated the planks for the window.

It did work, up to a certain point. Ford heard a noise in the storeroom and went to investigate, caught a glimpse of Tom Aldershot apparently about to climb through the little window, and hurled a hammer and considerable vituperation at the opening. Whereupon Sandy scuttled in and slammed the door, according to his own plan, and locked it. There was a season of frenzied hammering outside, and after that Sunset breathed freer, and discussed the evils of strong drink, and washed down their arguments by copious draughts of the stuff they maligned.

Later, they had to take him out of the storeroom, because he insisted upon knocking the bungs out of all the barrels and letting the liquor flood the floor, and Mike McGrew's wife objected to the waste, on the ground that whisky costs money. They fell upon him in a body, bundled him up, hustled him over to the ice-house, and shut him in; and within ten minutes he kicked three boards off one side and emerged breathing fire and brimstone like the dragons of old. He had forgotten about wanting to kill Sam; he was willing-nay, anxious-to murder every male human in Sunset.

They did not know what to do with him after that. They liked Ford when he was sober, and so they hated to shoot him, though that seemed the only way in which they might dampen his enthusiasm for blood. Tom said that, if he failed to improve in temper by the next day, he would try and land him in jail, though it did seem rigorous treatment for so common a fault as getting drunk. Meanwhile they kept out of his way as well as they could, and dodged missiles and swore. Even that was becoming more and more difficult-except the swearing-because Ford developed a perfectly diabolic tendency to empty every store that contained a man, so that it became no uncommon sight to see a back door belching forth hurrying figures at the most unseasonable times. No man could lift a full glass, that night, and feel sure of drinking the contents undisturbed; whereat Sunset grumbled while it dodged.

It may have been nine o'clock before the sporadic talk of a jail crystallized into a definite project which, it was unanimously agreed, could not too soon be made a reality.

They built the jail that night, by the light of bonfires which the slightly wounded kept blazing in the intervals of standing guard over the workers; ready to give warning in case Ford appeared as a war-cloud on their horizon. There were fifteen able-bodied men, and they worked fast, with Ford's war-chant in the saloon down the street as an incentive to speed. They erected it close to Tom Aldershot's house, because the town borrowed lumber from him and they wanted to save carrying, and because it was Tom's duty to look after the prisoner, and he wanted the jail handy, so that he need not lose any time from his house-building.

They built it strong, and they built it tight, without any window save a narrow slit near the ceiling; they heated it by setting a stove outside under a shelter, where Tom could keep up the fire without the risk of going inside, and ran pipe and a borrowed "drum" through the jail high enough so that Ford could not kick it. And to discourage any thought of suicide by hanging, they ceiled the place tightly with Tom's matched flooring of Oregon pine. Tom did not like that, and said so; but the citizens of Sunset nailed it on and turned a deaf ear to his complaints.

Chill dawn spread over the town, dulling the light of the fires and bringing into relief the sodden tramplings in the snow around the jail, with the sharply defined paths leading to Tom Aldershot's lumber-pile. The watchers had long before sneaked off to their beds, for not a sign of Ford had they seen since midnight. The storm had ceased early in the evening and all the sky was glowing crimson with the coming glory of the sun. The jail was almost finished. Up on the roof three crouching figures were nailing down strips of brick-red building paper as a fair substitute for shingles, and on the side nearest town the marshal and another were holding a yard-wide piece flat against the wall with fingers that tingled in the cold, while Bill Wright fastened it into place with shingle nails driven through tin disks the size of a half-dollar.

Ford, partly sober after a sleep on the billiard table in the hotel barroom, heard the hammering, wondered what industrious soul was up and doing carpenter work at that unseemly hour, and after helping himself to a generous "eye-opener" at the deserted bar, found his cap and went over to investigate. He was much surprised to see Bill Wright working, and smiled to himself as he walked quietly up to him through the soft, step-muffling snow.

"What you doing, Bill-building a chicken house?" he asked, a quirk of amusement at the corner of his lips.

Bill jumped and came near swallowing a nail; so near that his eyes bulged at the feel of it next his palate. Tom Aldershot dropped his end of the strip of paper, which tore with a dull sound of ripping, and remarked that he would be damned. Necks craned, up on the roof, and startled eyes peered down like chipmunks from a tree. Some one up there dropped a hammer which hit Bill on the head, but no one said a word.

"You act like you were nervous, this morning," Ford observed, in the tone which indicates a conscious effort at good-humored ignorance. "Working on a bet, or what?"

"What!" snarled Bill sarcastically. "I wisht, Ford, next time you bowl up, you'd pick on somebody that ain't too good a friend to fight back! I'm gittin' tired, by hokey—"

"What-did I lick you again, Bill?" Ford's smile was sympathetic to a degree. "That's too bad, now. Next time you want to hunt a hole and crawl into it, Bill. I don't want to hurt you-but seems like I've kinda got the habit. You'll have to excuse me." He hunched his shoulders at the chill of the morning and walked around the jail, inspecting it with half-hearted interest.

"What is this, anyway?" he inquired of Tom. "Smoke-house?"

"It's a jail," snapped Tom. "To put you into if you don't watch your dodgers. What 'n thunder you want to carry on like you did last night, for? And then go and sober up just when we've got a jail built to put you into! That ain't no way for a man to do—I'll leave it to Bill if it is! I've a darned good mind to swear out a warrant, anyway, Ford, and pinch you for disturbin' the peace! That's what I ought to do, all right." Tom beat his hands about his body and glared at Ford with his ultra-official scowl.

"All right, if you want to do it." Ford's tone embellished the reply with a you-take-the-consequences sort of indifference. "Only, I'd advise you never to turn me loose again if you do lock me up in this coop once."

"I know I wouldn't uh worked all night on the thing if I'd knowed you was goin' to sleep it off," Bill complained, with deep reproach in his watery eyes. "I made sure you was due to keep things agitated around here for a couple uh days, at the very least, or I never woulda drove a nail, by hokey!"

"It is a darned shame, to have a nice, new jail and nobody to use it on," sympathized Ford, his eyes half-closed and steely. "I'd like to help you out, all right. Maybe I'd better kill you, Bill; they *might* stretch a point and call it manslaughter-and I could use the bounty to help pay a lawyer, if it ever come to a head as a trial."

Whereat Bill almost wept.

Ford pushed his hands deep into his pockets and walked away, sneering openly at Bill, the marshal, the jail, and the town which owned it, and at wives and matrimony and the world which held all these vexations.

He went straight to the shack, drank a cup of coffee, and packed everything he could find that belonged to him and was not too large for easy carrying on horseback; and when Sandy, hovering uneasily around him, asked questions, he told him briefly to go off in a corner and lie down; which advice Sandy understood as an invitation to mind his own affairs.

Like Bill, Sandy could have wept at the ingratitude of this man. But he asked no more questions and he made no more objections. He picked up the story of the unpronounceable count who owned the castle in the Black Forest and had much tribulation and no joy until the last chapter, and when Ford went out, with his battered, sole-leather suitcase and his rifle in its pigskin case, he kept his pale eyes upon his book and refused even a grunt in response to Ford's grudging: "So long, Sandy."

# Chapter IV. Reaction

Even when a man consistently takes Life in twenty-four-hour doses and likes those doses full-flavored with the joys of this earth, there are intervals when the soul of him is sick, and Life becomes a nauseous progression of bleak futility. He may, in his revulsion against it, attempt to end it all; he may, in sheer disgust of it, take his doses stronger than ever before, as if he would once for all choke to death that part of him which is fine enough to rebel against it; he may even forswear, in melancholy penitence, that which has served to give it flavor, and vow him vows of abstemiousness at which the grosser part of him chuckles ironically; or, he may blindly follow the first errant impulse for change of environment, in the half-formed hope that new scenes may, without further effort on his part, serve to make of him a new man —a man for whom he can feel some respect.

Ford did none of these things, however. The soul-sick incentive was there, and if he had been a little less of a reasoning animal and a little less sophisticated, he would probably have forsworn strong drink just as he forswore all responsibility for his inadvertent marriage. His reason and his experience saved him from cluttering his conscience with broken vows, although he did yield to the impulse of change to the extent of leaving Sunset while yet the inhabitants were fortifying themselves for the ardors of the day with breakfast and some wild prophecies concerning Ford's next outbreak.

Apprehension over Bill's immediate future was popular amongst his friends, Ford's sardonic reference to manslaughter and bounty being repeated often enough in Bill's presence to keep that peace-loving gentleman in a state of trepidation which he sought to hide behind vague warnings.

"He better think twicet before he comes bothering around me, by hokey!" Bill would mutter darkly. "I've stood a hull lot from Ford; I like 'im, when he's himself. But I've stood about as much as a man can be expected to stand. And he better look out! That's all I got to say-he better look out!" Bill himself, it may be observed incidentally, spent the greater portion of that day in "looking out." He was careful not to sit down with his back to a door, for instance, and was keenly interested when a knob turned beneath unseen fingers, and plainly relieved when another than Ford entered his presence. Bill's mustache was nearly pulled from its roots, that day-but that is not important to the story, which has to do with Ford Campbell, sometime the possessor of a neat legacy in coin, later a rider of the cattle ranges, last presiding genius over the poker table in Scotty's back room in Sunset, always an important factor-and too often a disturbing element-in any community upon which he chose to bestow his dynamic presence.

Scotty hoped that Ford would show up for business when the lamps were lighted, that night. There had been some delicacy on the part of Ford's acquaintances that day in the matter of calling upon him at the shack. They believed-and hoped-that Ford was "sleeping it off," and there was a unanimous reluctance to disturb his slumbers. Sandy, indulging himself in the matter of undisturbed spinal tremors over "The Haunted Chamber," had not left shelter, save when the more insistent shiverings of chilled flesh recalled him from his pleasurable nerve-crimplings and drove him forth to the woodpile. So that it was not until evening was well advanced that Sunset learned that Ford was no longer a potential menace within its meager boundaries. Bill took a long breath, observed meaningly that "He'd *better* go-whilst his credit's good, by hokey!" and for the first time that day sat down with his back toward an outer door.

Ford was not worrying about Sunset half as much as Sunset was worrying about him. He was at that moment playing pinochle half-heartedly with a hospitable sheep-herder, under the impression that, since his host had frankly and profanely professed a revulsion against solitaire and a corresponding hunger for pinochle, his duty as a guest lay in satisfying that hunger. He played apathetically, overlooked several melts he might have made, and so lost three games in succession to the gleeful herder, who had needed the diversion almost as much as he needed a hair-cut.

His sense of social responsibility being eased thereby, Ford took his headache and his dull disgust with life to the wall side of the herder's frowsy bunk, and straightway forgot both in heavy slumber, leaving to the morrow any definite plan for the near future-the far future being as little considered as death and what is said to lie beyond.

That day had done for him all he asked of it. It had put him thirty miles and more from Sunset, against which he felt a resentment which it little deserved; of a truth it was as inoffensive a hamlet as any in that region, and its sudden, overweening desire for a jail was but a legitimate impulse toward self-preservation. The fault was Ford's, in harassing the men of Sunset into action. But several times that day, and again while he was pulling the stale-odored blankets snugly about his ears, Ford anathematized the place as "a damned, rotten hole," and was as nearly thankful as his mood would permit, when he remembered that it lay far behind him and was likely to be farther before his journeyings were done.

Sleep held him until daylight seeped in through the one dingy window. Ford awoke to the acrid smell of scorched bacon, thought at first that Sandy was once more demonstrating his inefficiency as a cook, and when he remembered that Sandy's name was printed smudgily upon that page of his life which he had lately turned down as a blotted, unlearned lesson is pushed behind an unwilling schoolboy, he began to consider seriously his next step.

Outside, the sheep were blatting stridently their demand for breakfast. The herder bolted coffee and coarse food until he was filled, and went away to his dreary day's work, telling Ford to make himself at home, and flinging back a hope of further triumphs in pinochle, that night.

Ford washed the dishes, straightened the blankets in the bunk, swept the grimy floor as well as he could with the stub of broom he found, filled the wood-box and then, being face to face with his day and the problem it held, rolled a cigarette, and smoked it in deep meditation.

He wanted to get away from town, and poker games, and whisky, and the tumult it brewed. Something within him hungered for clean, wind-swept reaches and the sane laughter of men, and Ford was accustomed to doing, or at least trying to do, the thing he wanted to do. He was not getting into the wilderness because of any inward struggle toward right living, but because he was sick of town and the sordid life he had lived there.

Somewhere, back toward the rim of mountains which showed a faint violet against the sky to the east, he owned a friend; and that friend owned a stock ranch which, Ford judged, must be of goodly extent; two weeks before, hearing somehow that Ford Campbell was running a poker game in Sunset, the friend had written and asked him to come and take charge of his "outfit," on the plea that, his foreman having died, he was burdened with many cares and in urgent need of help.

Ford, giving the herder's frying-pan a last wipe with the dish-cloth, laughed at the thought of taking the responsibility offered him in that letter. It occurred to him, however, that the Double Cross (which was the brand-name of Mason's ranch) might be a pleasant place to visit. It was long since he had seen Ches-and there had been a time when one bed held the two of them through many a long, weary night; when one frying-pan cooked the scanty food they shared between them. And there had been a season of grinding days and anxious, black nights between, when the one problem, to Ford, consisted of getting Ches Mason out of the wild land where they wandered, and getting him out alive. The problem Ford solved and at the solution men wondered. Afterward they had drifted apart, but the memory of those months would hold them together with a bond which not even time could break —a bond which would pull taut whenever they met.

Ford set down the frying-pan and went to the door and looked out. A chinook had blown up in the night, and although the wind was chill, the snow had disappeared, save where drifts clung to the hollows, shrinking and turning black beneath the sweeping gusts; sodden masses which gave to the prairie a dreary aspect of bleak discomfort. But Ford was well pleased at the sight of the brown, beaten grasses. Impulse was hardening to decision while he stared across the empty land toward the violet rim of hills; a decision to ride over to the Double Cross, and tell Ches Mason to his face that he was a chump, and have a smoke with the old Turk, anyway.

Ches had married, since that vividly remembered time when adventure changed to hardship and hazard and walked hand in hand with them through the wild places. Ford wondered fleetingly if matrimony had changed old Ches; probably not-at least, not in those essential man-traits which appeal to men. Ford suddenly hungered for the man's hearty voice, where kindly humor lurked always, and for a grip of his hand.

It was like him to forget all about the herder and the promise of pinochle that night. He went eagerly to the decrepit little shed which housed Rambler, his long-legged, flea-bitten gray; saddled him purposefully and rode away toward the violet hills at the trail-trot which eats up the miles with the least effort.

That night, although he slept in a hamlet which called itself a town, his purpose kept firm hold of him, and he rode away at a decent hour the next morning, —and he rode sober. He kept his face toward the hills, and he did not trouble himself with any useless analysis of his unusual temperateness. He was going to blow in to the Double Cross some time before he slept that night, and have a talk with Ches. He had a pint of fairly good whisky in his pocket, in case he felt the need of a little on the way, and beyond those two satisfactory certainties he did not attempt to reason. They were significant, in a way, to a man with a tendency toward introspection; but Ford was interested in actualities and never stopped to wonder why he bought a pint, rather than a quart, or why, with Ches Mason in his mind, he declined to "set in" to the poker game which was running to tempting jackpots, the night before; or why he took one glass of wine before he mounted Rambler and let it go at that. He never once dreamed that the memory of cheerful, steady-going Ches influenced him toward starting on his friendly pilgrimage the Ford Campbell whom Mason had known eight years before; a very different Ford Campbell, be it said, from the one who had caused a whole town to breathe freer for his absence.

Of his wife Ford had thought less often and less uncomfortably since he left the town wherein had occurred the untoward incident of his marriage. He was not unaccustomed to doing foolish things when he was drunk, and as a rule he made it a point to ignore them afterwards. His mysterious, matrimonial accident was beginning to seem less of a real catastrophe than before, and the anticipation of meeting Ches Mason was rapidly taking precedence of all else in his mind.

So, with almost his normal degree of careless equanimity, he faced again the rim of hills-nearer they were now, with a deeper tinge that was almost purple where the shadows lined them here and there. Somewhere out that way lay the Double Cross ranch. Forty miles, one man told him it was; another, forty-three. At best it was far enough for the shortened daylight of one fall day to cover the journey. Ford threw away the stub of his after-breakfast cigarette and swung into the trail at a lope.

Ford's range-trained vision told him, while yet afar off, that the lone horse feeding upon a side hill was saddled and bridled, with reins dragging; the telltale, upward toss of its head when it started on to find a sweeter morsel was evidence enough of the impeding bridle, even before he was near enough to distinguish the saddle.

Your true range man owns blood-relationship with the original Good Samaritan; Ford swung out of the trail and untied his rope as a matter of course. The master of the animal might have turned him loose to feed, but if that were the case, he had strayed farther than was ever intended; the chances, since no human being was in sight, were all against design and in favor of accident. At any rate Ford did not hesitate. It is not good to let a horse run loose upon the range with a saddle cinched upon its back, as every one knows.

Ford was riding along the sheer edge of a water-worn gully, seeking a place where he might safely jump it-or better, a spot where the banks sloped so that he might ride down into it and climb the bank beyond-when he saw a head and pair of shoulders moving slowly along, just over the brow of the hill where fed the stray. He watched, and when the figure topped the ridge and started down the slope which faced him, his eyes widened a trifle in surprise.

Skirts to the tops of her shoes betrayed her a woman. She limped painfully, so that Ford immediately pictured to himself puckered eyebrows and lips pressed tightly together. "And I'll bet she's crying, too," he summed up aloud. While he was speaking, she stumbled and fell headlong.

When he saw that she made no attempt to rise, but lay still just as she had fallen, Ford looked no longer for an easy crossing. He glanced up and down the washout, saw no more promising point than where he was, wheeled and rode back twenty yards or so, turned and drove deep his spurs.

It was a nasty jump, and he knew it all along. When Rambler rose gamely to it, with tensed muscles and forefeet flung forward to catch the bank beyond, he knew it better. And when, after a sickening minute of frenzied scrambling at the crumbling edge, they slid helplessly to the bottom, he cursed his idiocy for ever attempting it.

Rambler got up with a pronounced limp, but Ford had thrown himself from the saddle and escaped with nothing worse than a skinned elbow. They were penned, however, in a box-like gully ten feet deep, and there was nothing to do but follow it to where they might climb out. Ford was worried about the girl, and made a futile attempt to stand in the saddle and from there climb up to the level. But Rambler, lame as he was, plunged so that Ford finally gave it up and started down the gulch, leading Rambler by the reins.

There were many sharp turns and temper-trying windings, and though it narrowed in many places so that there was barely room for them to pass, it never grew shallower; indeed, it grew always deeper; and then, without any warning, it stopped abruptly upon a coulée's rim, with jumbled rocks and between them a sheer descent to the slope below. Ford guessed then that he was boxed up in one of the main waterways of the foot-hills he had been skirting for the past hour or so, and that he should have ridden up the gulch instead of down it.

He turned, though the place was so narrow that Rambler's four feet almost touched one another and his rump scraped the bank, as Ford pulled him round, and retraced his steps. It was too rough for riding, even if he had not wanted to save the horse, and he had no idea how far he must go before he could get out. Ford, at that time, was not particularly cheerful.

He must have gone a mile and more before he reached the point where, by hard scrambling, he attained level ground upon the same side as the girl. Ten minutes he spent in urging Rambler up the bank, and when the horse stood breathing heavily beside him, Ford knew that, for all the good there was in him at present, he might as well have left him at the bottom. He walked around him, rubbing leg and shoulder muscles until he located the hurt, and shook his head when all was done. Then he started on slowly, with Rambler hobbling painfully after him. Ford knew that every rod would aggravate that strained shoulder and that a stop would probably make it impossible for the horse to go on at all.

He was not quite sure, after all those windings where he could not see, just where it was he had seen the girl, but he recognized at last the undulating outline of the ridge over which she had appeared, and made what haste he could up the slope. The grazing horse was no longer in sight, though he knew it might be feeding in a hollow near by.

He had almost given up hope of finding her, when he turned his head and saw her off to one side, lying half concealed by a clump of low rose bushes. She was not unconscious, as he had thought, but was crying silently, with her face upon her folded arms and her hat askew over one ear. He stooped and touched her upon the shoulder.

She lifted her head and looked at him, and drew away with a faint, withdrawing gesture, which was very slight in itself but none the less eloquent and unmistakable. Ford backed a step when he saw it and closed his lips without speaking the words he had meant to say.

She lifted her head and looked at him, and drew away.

"Well, what do you want?" the girl asked ungraciously, after a minute spent in fumbling unseen hairpins and in straightening her hat. "I don't know why you're standing there like that, staring at me. I don't need any help."

"Appearances are deceitful, then," Ford retorted. "I saw you limping over the hill, after your horse, and I saw you fall down and stay down. I had an idea that a little help would be acceptable, but of course —"

"That was an hour ago," she interrupted accusingly, with a measuring glance at the sun, which was settling toward the sky-line.

"I had trouble getting across that washout down there. I don't know this part of the country, and I went down it instead of up. What are you crying about-if you don't need any help?"

She eyed him askance, and chewed upon a corner of her lip, and flipped the upturned hem of her riding skirt down over one spurred foot with a truly feminine instinct, before she answered him. She seemed to be thinking hard and fast, and she hesitated even while she spoke. Ford wondered at the latent antagonism in her manner.

"I was crying because my foot hurts so and because I don't see how I'm going to get back to the ranch. I suppose they'll hunt me up if I stay away long enough-but it's getting toward night, and —I'm scared to death of coyotes, if you must know!"

Ford laughed-at her defiance, in the face of her absolute helplessness, more than at what she said. "And you tell me you don't need any help?" he bantered.

"I might borrow your horse," she suggested coldly, as if she grudged yielding even that much to circumstance. "Or you might catch mine for me, I suppose."

"Sure. But you needn't hate me because you're in trouble," he hinted irrelevantly. "I'm not to blame, you know."

"I —I hate to ask help from —a stranger," she said, watching him from under her lashes. "And I can't help showing what I feel. I hate to feel under an obligation —"

"If that's all, forget it," he assured her calmly. "It's a law of the open-to help a fellow out in a pinch. When I headed for here, I thought it was a man had been set afoot."

She eyed him curiously. "Then you didn't know —"

"I thought you were a man," he repeated. "I didn't come just because I saw it was a girl. You needn't feel under any obligation whatever. I'm a stranger in the country and a stranger to you. I'm perfectly willing to stay that way, if you prefer. I'm not trying to scrape acquaintance on the strength of your being in trouble; but you surely don't expect a man to ride on and leave a woman out here on the bald prairie-do you? Especially when she's confessed she's afraid of the dark-and coyotes!"

She was staring at him while he spoke, and she continued to stare after he had finished; the introspective look which sees without seeing, it became at last, and Ford gave a shrug at her apparent obstinacy and turned away to where Rambler stood with his head drooped and his eyes half closed. He picked up the reins and chirped to him, and the horse hesitated, swung his left foot painfully forward, hobbled a step, and looked at Ford reproachfully.

"Your horse is crippled as badly as I am, it would seem," the girl observed, from where she sat watching them.

"I strained his shoulder, trying to make him jump that washout. That was when I first got sight of you over here. We went to the bottom and it took me quite a while to find a way out. That's why I was so long getting here." Ford explained indifferently, with his back to her, while he rubbed commiseratingly the swelling shoulder.

"Oh." The girl waited. "It seems to me you need help yourself. I don't see how you expect to help any one else, with your horse in that condition," she added. And when he still did not speak, she asked: "Do you know how far it is to the nearest ranch?"

"No. I told you I'm a stranger in this country. I was heading for the Double Cross, but I don't know just —"

"We're eight miles, straight across, from there; ten, the way we would have to go to get there. There are other washouts in this country-which it is unwise to attempt jumping, Mr. —"

"Campbell," Ford supplied shortly.

"I beg your pardon? You mumbled—"

"Campbell!" Ford was tempted to shout it but contented himself with a tart distinctness. A late, untoward incident had made him somewhat touchy over his name, and he had not mumbled.

"Oh. Did you skin your face and blacken your eye, Mr. Campbell, when you tried to jump that washout?"

"No." Ford did not offer any explanation. He remembered the scars of battle which were still plainly visible upon his countenance, and he turned red while he bent over the fore ankles of Rambler, trying to discover other sprains. He felt that he was going to dislike this girl very much before he succeeded in getting her to shelter. He could not remember ever meeting before a woman under forty with so unpleasant a manner and with such a talent for disagreeable utterances.

"Then you must have been fighting a wildcat," she hazarded.

"Pardon me; is this a Methodist experience meeting?" he retorted, looking full at her with lowering brows. "It seems to me the only subject which concerns us mutually is the problem of getting to a ranch before dark."

"You'll have to solve it yourself. I never attempt puzzles." The girl, somewhat to his surprise, showed no resentment at his rebuff. Indeed, he began to suspect her of being secretly amused. He began also mentally to accuse her of not being too badly hurt to walk, if she wanted to; indeed, his skepticism went so far as to accuse her of deliberately baiting him-though why, he did not try to conjecture. Women were queer. Witness his own late experience with one.

Being thus in a finely soured mood, Ford suggested that, as she no doubt knew the shortest way to the nearest ranch, they at least make a start in that direction.

"How?" asked the girl, staring up at him from where she sat beside the rose bushes.

"By walking, I suppose-unless you expect me to carry you." Ford's tone was not in any degree affable.

"I fancy it would be asking too great a favor to suggest that you catch my horse for me?"

Ford dropped Rambler's reins and turned to her, irritated to the point where he felt a distinct desire to shake her.

"I'd far rather catch your horse, even if I had to haze him all over the country, than carry you," he stated bluntly.

"Yes. I suspected that much." She had plucked a red seed-ball off the bush nearest her and was nibbling daintily the sweet pulp off the outside.

"Where is the horse?" Ford was holding himself rigidly hack from an outburst of temper.

"Oh, I don't know, I'm sure." She picked another seed-ball and began upon it. "He should be somewhere around, unless he has taken a notion to go home."

Ford said something under his breath and untied his rope from the saddle. He knew about where the horse had been feeding when he saw him, and he judged that it would naturally graze in the direction of home-which would probably be somewhere off to the southeast, since the trail ran more or less in that direction. Without a word to the girl, or a glance toward her, he started up the hill, hoping to get his bearings and a sight of the horse from the top. He could not remember when he had been so angry with a woman. "If she was a man," he gritted as he climbed, "I'd give her a thrashing or leave her out there, just as she deserves. That's the worst of dealing with a woman-she can always hand it to you, and you've got to give her a grin and thank-you, because she ain't a man."

He glanced back, then, and saw her sitting with her head dropped forward upon her hands. There was something infinitely pitiful and lonely in her attitude, and he knitted his brows over the contrast between it and her manner when he left her. "I don't suppose a woman knows, herself, what she means, half the time," he hazarded impatiently. "She certainly didn't have any excuse for throwing it into me the way she did; maybe she's sorry for it now."

After that his anger cooled imperceptibly, and he hurried a little faster because the day was waning with the chill haste of mid-autumn, and he recalled what she had said at first about being afraid of coyotes. And, although the storm of three days ago had been swept into mere memory by that sudden chinook wind, and the days were once more invitingly warm and hazily tranquil, night came shiveringly upon the land and the unhoused thought longingly of hot suppers and the glow of a fire.

The girl's horse was, he believed, just disappearing into a deep depression half a mile farther on; but when he reached the place where he had seen it, there was nothing in sight save a few head of cattle and a coyote trotting leisurely up the farther slope. He went farther down the shallow coulée, then up to the high level beyond, his rope coiled loosely over one arm with the end dragging a foot behind him. But there was nothing to be seen from up there, except that the sun was just a red disk upon the far-off hills, and that the night was going to be uncomfortably cool if that wind kept blowing from the northwest.

He began to feel slightly uneasy about the girl, and to regret wasting any time over her horse, and to fear that he might not be able to get close enough to rope the beast, even if he did see him.

He turned back then and walked swiftly through the dusk toward the ridge, beyond which she and Rambler were waiting. But it was a long way-much farther than he had realized until he came to retrace his steps-and the wind blew up a thin rift of clouds which made the darkness come quickly. He found it difficult to tell exactly at which point he had crossed the ridge, coming over; and although experience in the open develops in a man a certain animal instinct for directions handed down by our primitive ancestry, Ford went wide in his anxiety to take the shortest way back to his unwilling protégée. The westering slope was lighter, however, and five minutes of wandering along the ridge showed him a dim bulk which he knew was Rambler. He hurried to the place, and the horse whinnied shrilly as he approached.

"I looked as long as I could see, almost, but I couldn't locate your horse," Ford remarked to the dark shadow of the rose bushes. "I'll put you on mine. It will be slow going, of course-lame as he is-but I guess we can manage to get somewhere."

He waited for the chill, impersonal reply. When she did not speak, he leaned and peered at the spot where he knew she must be. "If you want to try it, we'd better be starting," he urged sharply. "It's going to be pretty cold here on this side-hill."

When there was silence still-and he gave her plenty of time for reply-Ford stooped and felt gropingly for her, thinking she must be asleep. He glanced back at Rambler; unless the horse had moved, she should have been just there, under his hands; or, he thought, she may have moved to some other spot, and be waiting in the dark to see what he would do. His palms touched the pressed grasses where she had been, but he did not say a word. He would not give her that satisfaction; and he told himself grimly that he had his opinion of a girl who would waste time in foolery, out here in the cold-with a sprained ankle, to boot.

He pulled a handful of the long grass which grows best among bushes. It was dead now, and dry. He twisted it into a makeshift torch, lighted and held it high, so that its blaze made a great disk of brightness all around him. While it burned he looked for her, and when it grew to black cinders and was near to scorching his hand, he made another and looked farther. He laid aside his dignity and called, and while his voice went booming full-lunged through the whispering silence of that empty land, he twisted the third torch, and stamped the embers of the second into the earth that it might not fire the prairie.

There was no dodging the fact; the girl was gone. When Ford was perfectly sure of it, he stamped the third torch to death with vicious heels, went back to the horse, and urged him to limp up the hill. He did not say anything then or think anything much; at least, he did not think coherently. He was so full of a wordless rage against the girl, that he did not at first feel the need of expression. She had made a fool of him.

He remembered once shooting a big, beautiful, blacktail doe. She had dropped limply in her tracks and lain there, and he had sauntered up and stood looking at her stretched before him. He was out of meat, and the doe meant all that hot venison steaks and rich, brown gravy can mean to a man meat-hungry. While he unsheathed his hunting knife, he gloated over the feast he would have, that night. And just when he had laid his rifle against a rock and knelt to bleed her, the deer leaped from under his hand and bounded away over the hill. He had not said a word on that occasion, either.

This night, although the case was altogether different and the disappearance of the girl was in no sense a disaster-rather a relief, if anything-he felt that same wordless rage, the same sense of utter chagrin. She had made a fool of him. After awhile he felt his jaws aching with the vicelike pressure of his teeth together.

They topped the ridge, Rambler hobbling stiffly. Ford had in mind a sheltering rim of sandstone at the nearest point of the coulée he had crossed in searching for the girl's horse, and made for it. He had noticed a spring there, and while the water might not be good, the shelter would be welcome, at any rate.

He had the saddle off Rambler, the shoulder bathed with cold water from the spring, and was warming his wet hands over a little fire when the first gleam of humor struck through his anger and lighted for a moment the situation.

"Lordy me! I must be a hoodoo, where women are concerned," he said, kicking the smoking stub of a bush into the blaze. "Soon as one crosses my trail, she goes and disappears off the face of the earth!" He fumbled for his tobacco and papers. It was a "dry camp" he was making that night, and a smoke would have to serve for a supper. He held his book of papers absently while he stared hard at the fire.

"It ain't such a bad hoodoo," he mused. "I can spare this particular girl just as easy as not; and the other one, too, for that matter."

After a minute spent in blowing apart the thin leaves and selecting a paper:

"Queer where she got to-and it's a darned mean trick to play on a man that was just trying to help her out of a fix. Why, I wouldn't treat a stray dog that way! Darn these women!"

# Chapter VI. The Problem of Getting Somewhere

Dawn came tardily after a long, cheerless night, during which the wind whined over the prairie and the stars showed dimly through a shifting veil of low-sweeping clouds. Ford had not slept much, for hunger and cold make poor bedfellows, and all the brush he could glean on that barren hillside, with the added warmth of his saddle-blanket wrapped about him, could no more make him comfortable than could cigarettes still the gnawing of his hunger.

When he could see across the coulée, he rose from where he had been sitting with his back to the ledge and his feet to the meager fire, brooding over all the unpleasant elements in his life thus far, particularly the feminine element. He folded the saddle-blanket along its original creases and went over to where Rambler stood dispiritedly with his back humped to the cold, creeping wind and his tail whipping between his legs when a sudden gust played with it. Ford shivered, and beat his gloved hands about his body, and looked up at the sky to see whether the sun would presently shine and send a little warmth to this bleak land where he wandered. He blamed the girl for all of this discomfort, and he told himself that the next time a woman appeared within his range of vision he would ride way around her. They invariably brought trouble; of various sorts and degrees, it is true, but trouble always. It was perfectly safe, he decided, to bank on that. And he wished, more than ever, that he had not improvidently given that pint of whisky to a disconsolate-looking sheep-herder he had met the day before on his way out from town; or that he had put two flasks in his pocket instead of one. In his opinion a good, big jolt right now would make a new man of him.

Rambler, as he had half expected, was obliged to do his walking with three legs only; which is awkward for a horse accustomed to four exceedingly limber ones, and does not make for speed, however great one's hurry. Ford walked around him twice, scooped water in his hands, and once more bathed the shoulder-not that he had any great faith in cold water as a liniment, but because there was nothing else that he could do, and his anxiety and his pity impelled service of some sort. He rubbed until his fingers were numb and his arm aching, tried him again, and gave up all hope of leading the horse to a ranch. A mile he might manage, if he had to but ten! He rubbed Rambler's nose commiseratingly, straightened his forelock, told him over and over that it was a darned shame, anyway, and finally turned to pick up his saddle. He could not leave that lying on the prairie for inquisitive kit-foxes to chew into shoestrings, however much he might dread the forty-pound burden of it on his shoulders. He was stooping to pick it up when he saw a bit of paper twisted and tied to the saddle-horn with a red ribbon.

"Lordy me!" he ejaculated ironically. "The lady left a note on my pillow-and I never received it in time! Now, ain't that a darned shame?" He plucked the knot loose, and held up the ribbon and the note, and laughed.

"'When this reaches you, I shall be far away, though it breaks my heart to go and this missive is mussed up scandalous with my bitter tears. Forgive me if you can, and forget me if you have to. It is better thus, for it couldn't otherwise was,'" he improvised mockingly, while his chilled fingers fumbled to release the paper, which was evidently a leaf torn from a man's memorandum book. "Lordy me, a letter from a lady! Ain't that sweet!"

When he read it, however, the smile vanished with a click of the teeth which betrayed his returning anger. One cold, curt sentence bidding him wait until help came-that was all. His eye measured accusingly the wide margin left blank under the words; she had not omitted apology or explanation for lack of space, at any rate. His face grew cynically amused again.

"Oh, certainly! I'd roost on this side-hill for a month, if a lady told me to," he sneered, speaking aloud as he frequently did in the solitude of the range land. He glanced from ribbon to note, ended his indecision by stuffing the note carelessly into his coat pocket and letting the ribbon drop to the ground, and with a curl of the lips which betrayed his mental attitude toward all women and particularly toward that woman, picked up his saddle.

"I can't seem to recollect asking that lady for help, anyway," he summed up before he dismissed the subject from his mind altogether. "I was trying to help her; it sure takes a woman to twist things around so they point backwards!"

He turned and glanced pityingly at Rambler, watching him with ears perked forward inquiringly. "And I crippled a damned good horse trying to help a blamed poor specimen of a woman!" he gritted. "And didn't get so much as a pleasant word for it. I'll sure remember that!"

Rambler whinnied after him wistfully, and Ford set his teeth hard together and walked the faster, his shoulders slightly bent under the weight of the saddle. His own physical discomfort was nothing, beside the hurt of leaving his horse out there practically helpless; for a moment his fingers rested upon the butt of his six-shooter, while he considered going back and putting an end to life and misery for Rambler. But for all the hardness men had found in Ford Campbell, he was woman-weak where his horse was concerned. With cold reason urging him, he laid the saddle on the ground and went back, his hand clutching grimly the gun at his hip. Rambler's nicker of welcome stopped him half-way and held him there, hot with guilt.

"Oh, damn it, I can't!" he muttered savagely, and retraced his steps to where the saddle lay. After that he almost trotted down the coulée, and he would not look back again until it struck him as odd that the nickerings of the horse did not grow perceptibly fainter. With a queer gripping of the muscles in his throat he did turn, then, and saw Rambler's head over the little ridge he had just crossed. The horse was making shift to follow him rather than be left alone in that strange country. Ford waited, his lashes glistening in the first rays of the new-risen sun, until the horse came hobbling stiffly up to him.

"You old devil!" he murmured then, his contrite tone contrasting oddly with the words he used. "You contrary, ornery, old devil, you!" he repeated softly, rubbing the speckled nose with more affection than he had ever shown a woman. "You'd tag along, if-if you didn't have but one leg to carry you! And I was going to —" He could not bring himself to confess his meditated deed of mercy; it seemed black-hearted treachery, now, and he stood ashamed and humbled before the dumb brute that nuzzled him with such implicit faith.

It was slow journeying, after that. Ford carried the saddle on his own back rather than burden the horse with it, and hungry as he was, he stopped often and long, and massaged the sprained shoulder faithfully while Rambler rested it, with all his weight on his other legs and his nose rooting gently at Ford's bowed head.

A stray rider assured him that he was on the right trail, but it was past noon when he thankfully reached the Double Cross, threw his saddle down beside the stable door, and gave Rambler a chance at the hay in the corral.

# Chapter VII. The Foreman of the Double Cross

"Hell-o, Ford, where the blazes did you drop down from?" a welcoming voice yelled, when he was closing the gate of the corral behind him and thinking that it was like Ches Mason to have a fine, strong corral and gate, and then slur the details by using a piece of baling wire to fasten it. The last ounce of disgust with life slid from his mind when he heard the greeting, and he turned and gripped hard the gloved hand thrust toward him. Ches Mason it was-the same old Ches, with the same humorous wrinkles around his eyes and mouth, the same kindliness, the same hearty faith in the world as he knew it and in his fellowmen as he found them-the unquestioning faith that takes it for granted that the other fellow is as square as himself. Ford held his hand while he permitted himself a swift, reckoning glance which took in these familiar landmarks of the other's personality.

"Don't seem to have hurt you much-matrimony," he observed whimsically, as he dropped the hand. "You look just like you always did-with your hat on." In the West, not to say in every other locality, there is a time-honored joke about matrimony, for certain strenuous reasons, producing premature baldness.

Ches grinned and removed his hat. Eight years had heightened his forehead perceptibly and thinned the hair on his temples. "You see what it's done to me," he pointed out lugubriously. "You ain't married yourself, I suppose? You look like you'd met up with some kinda misfortune." Mason was regarding Ford's scarred face with some solicitude.

"Just got tangled up a little with my fellow-citizens, in Sunset," Ford explained drily. "I tried to see how much of the real stuff I could get outside of, and then how many I could lick." He shrugged his shoulders a little. "I did quite a lot of both," he added, as an afterthought.

Mason was rubbing his jaw reflectively and staring hard at Ford. "The wife's strong on the temperance dope," he said hesitatingly. "I reckon you'll want to bunk down with the boys till you grow some hide on your face-there's lady company up at the house, and —"

"The bunk-house for mine, then," Ford cut in hastily. "No lady can get within gunshot of me; not if I see her coming in time!" Though he smiled when he said it, there was meaning behind the mirth.

Mason pulled a splinter from a corral rail and began to snap off little bits with his fingers. "Kate will go straight up in the air with me if she knows you're here and won't come to the house, though," he considered uneasily. "She's kept a big package of gratitude tucked away with your name on it, ever since that Alaska deal. And lemme tell you, Ford, when a woman as good as Kate goes and gets grateful to a man-gosh! Had your dinner?"

"Not lately, I haven't," Ford declared. "I kinda remember eating, some time in the past; it was a long time ago, though."

Mason laughed and tagged the answer as being the natural exaggeration of a hungry man. "Well, come along and eat, then-if you haven't forgotten how to make your jaws go. I've got Mose Freeman cooking for me; you know Mose, don't you? Hired him the day after the Fourth; the Mitten outfit fired him for getting soused and trying to clean out the camp, and I nabbed him before they had time to forgive him. Way they had of disciplining him-when he'd go on a big tear they'd fire him for a few days and then take him back. But they can't git him now-not if I can help it. A better cook never throwed dishwater over a guy-rope than that same old Mose, but —" He stopped and looked at Ford hesitantly. "Say! I hate like the deuce to tie a string on you as soon as you hit the ranch, Ford, but-if you've got anything along, you won't spring it on Mose, will you? A fellow's got to watch him pretty close, or —"

"I haven't got a drop." Ford's tone was reprehensibly regretful.

"You do look as if you'd put it all under your belt," Mason retorted dryly. "Left anything behind?"

"Some spoiled beauties, and a nice new jail that was built by my admiring townspeople, with my name carved over the door. I didn't stay for the dedication services. Sunset was getting all fussed up over me and I thought I'd give them a chance to settle their nerves; loss of sleep sure plays hell with folks when their nerves are getting frazzly." He smiled disarmingly at Mason.

"I'd kinda lost track of you, Ches, till I got your letter. I've been traveling pretty swift, and that's no lie. I meant to write, but-you know how a man gets to putting things off. And then I took a notion to ride over this way, and sample your grub for a day or so, and abuse you a little to your face, you old highbinder!"

"Sure. I've been kinda looking for you, too. But —I wish you hadn't quite so big an assortment of battle-signs, Ford. Kate's got ideals and prejudices-and she don't know all your little personal traits. She's heard a lot about you, of course. We was married right after we came outa the North, you know, and of course-Well, you know how a woman sops up adventure stories; and seeing you was the star performer —"

"And that's a lie," Ford put in modestly, albeit a trifle bluntly.

"No, it ain't. She got the truth. And she's so darned grateful," he added lugubriously, "that I don't know how to square your record with that face! Unless we can rig up some yarn about a holdup —" He paused just outside the mess-house door and eyed Ford questioningly. "We might —"

"No, you don't. If you've gone and lied to her, and made me out a little tin angel, you deserve what's coming. Anyway, I won't stay long, and I'll stop down here with the boys. Call me Jack Jones and let it go at that. Honest, Ches, I don't want to get mixed up with no more females. I'm plumb scared of 'em. Lordy me, that coffee sure does smell good to me!"

Mason looked at him doubtfully, saw that Ford was, for the time being, absolutely devoid of anything remotely approaching penitence for his sins, or compunction over his appearance, or uneasiness over "Kate's" opinion of him. He was hungry. And since it is next to impossible to whip up the conscience of a man whose thoughts are concentrated upon his physical needs, Mason was wise enough to wait, though the one point which he considered of vital importance to them both-the question of Ford's acceptance or refusal of the foremanship of the Double Cross-had not yet been touched upon.

While Ford ate with a controlled voraciousness which spoke eloquently of his twenty-four hours of fasting and exposure, Mason gossiped inattentively and studied the man.

Eight years leave their impress of mental growth or deterioration upon a man. Outwardly Ford was not much changed since Mason had come with him out of Alaska and lost sight of him afterwards. There was the maturity which the man of thirty possessed and which the virile young fellow of twenty-one had lacked. There was the same straight glance, the same atmosphere of squareness and mental poise. Those were qualities which Mason set down as valuable factors in his estimate of the man. Besides, there were other signs which did not make so pleasant a reading.

Eight years-and a few of them, at least, had been spent wastefully in tearing down what the other years had built; Mason had heard that Ford was "going to the dogs," and that by the short trail men blazed for themselves centuries ago and which those who came after have made a highway-the whisky trail. Mason had heard, now and then, of ten thousand dollars coming to Ford upon the death of his father and going almost as suddenly as it had come. That, at least, had been the rumor. Also he had heard, just lately, that Ford had taken to gambling as a profession and to terrorizing Sunset periodically as a pastime. And Mason remembered the Ford Campbell who had carried him on his back out of a wild place in Alaska, and had nearly starved himself that the sick man's strength might not fail him utterly. He had remembered-had Ches Mason; and, being one of those tenacious souls who cling to friendship and to a resilient faith in the good that is in the worst of us, he had thrown out a tentative life-line, as it were, and hoped that Ford might clutch it before he became quite submerged in the sodden morass of inebriety.

Ford may or may not have grasped eagerly at the line. At any rate he was there in the mess-house of the Double Cross, and he was not quite so sodden as Mason had feared to find him-provided he found him at all. So much, at least, was encouraging, and for the rest, Mason was content to wait.

Mose, recognizing Ford at once, had asked him, with a comical attempt at secrecy, if he had anything to drink. When Ford shook his head, Mose stifled a sigh and went back to his dishwashing, not more than half convinced and inclined toward resentfulness. That a "booze-fighter" like Ford Campbell should come only a day's ride from town and not be fairly well supplied with whisky was too remarkable to be altogether plausible. He eyed the two sourly while they talked, and he did not bring forth one of the fresh pies he had baked, as he had meant to do.

It was not until Ford was ready to light his after-dinner cigarette that Mason led the way into the next room, which held the bunks and general belongings of the men, and closed the door so that they might talk in confidence without fear of Mose's loose tongue. Ford immediately pulled off his boots, laid himself down upon one of the bunks, doubled a pillow under his head, and began to eye Mason quizzically. Then he said:

"Say, you kinda played your hand face down, didn't you, Ches, when you wrote and asked me to come out here and take charge? Eight years is a long time to expect a man to stay right where he was when you saw him last. You've lost a whole lot of horse sense since I knew you."

"Well, what about it? You came, I notice." Mason grinned and would not help Ford otherwise to an understanding.

"I didn't come to hog-tie that foreman job, you chump. I just merely want to tell you that you'll get into all kinds of trouble, some day, if you go laying yourself wide open like that. Why, it's plumb crazy to offer a job like that to a fellow you haven't seen for as long as you have me. And if you heard anything about me, it's a cinch it wasn't what would recommend me to any Sunday-school as a teacher of their Bible class! How did you know I wouldn't take it? And let you in for —"

"Well, you're here, and I've seen you. The job's still waiting for you. You can start right in, to-morrow morning." Ches got out his pipe and began to fill it as calmly and with as much attention to the small details as if he were not mentally tensed for the struggle he knew was coming; a struggle which struck much deeper than the position he was offering Ford.

Ford almost dropped his cigarette in his astonishment. "Well, you damn' fool!" he ejaculated pityingly.

"Why? I thought you knew enough-you punched cows for the Circle for four or five years, didn't you? Nelson told me you were his top hand while you stayed with him, and that you ran the outfit one whole summer, when —"

"That ain't the point." A hot look had crept into Ford's face —a tinge which was not a flush- and a glow into his eyes. "I know the cow-business, far as that goes. It's me; you can't —why, Lordy me! You ought to be sent to Sulphur Springs and get your think-tank hoed out. Any man that will offer a foreman's job to a —a —"

"'A rooting, tooting, shooting, fighting son-of-a-gun, and a good one!'" assisted Mason equably. "'The only original go-getter —' Sure. That's all right."

The flush came slowly and darkened Ford's cheeks and brow and throat. He threw his half-smoked cigarette savagely at the hearth of the rusty box-stove, and scowled at the place where it fell. "Well, ain't that reason enough?" he demanded harshly, after a minute.

Mason had been studying that flush. He nodded assent to some question he had put to himself, and crowded tobacco into his pipe. "No reason at all, one way or the other. I need a foreman-one I can depend on. I've got to make a trip out to the Coast, this fall, and I've got to leave somebody here I can trust."

Ford shot him a quick, questioning glance, and bit his lip. "That," he said more calmly, "is just what I'm driving at. You can't trust me. You can't depend on me, Ches."

"Oh, yes I can," Mason contradicted blandly. "It's just because I can that I want you."

"You can't. You know damn' well you can't! Why, you-don't you know I've got the name of being a drunkard, and a —a bad actor all around? I'm not like I was eight years ago, remember. I've traveled a hard old trail since we bucked the snow together, Ches-and it's been mostly down grade. I was all right for awhile, and then I got ten thousand dollars, and it seemed a lot of money. I bought a fellow out-he had a ranch and a few head of horses-so he could take his wife back East to her mother. She was sick. I didn't want the darned ranch. And so help me, Ches, that's the only thing I've done in the last four years that I hadn't ought to be ashamed of. The rest of the money I just simply blew. I —well, you see me; you didn't want to take me up to the house to meet your wife, and I don't blame you. You'd be a chump if you did. And this is nothing out of the ordinary. I've got my face bunged up half the time, seems like." He thumped the pillow into a different position, settled his head against it, and looked at Mason with his old, whimsical smile. "So when you talk about that foreman job, and depending on me, you're-plumb delirious. I was going to write and tell you so, but I kept putting it off. And then I took a notion I'd hunt you up and give you some good advice. You're a good fellow, Ches, but the court ought to appoint a guardian for you."

"I'll stick around for three or four weeks," Mason observed, in the casual tone of one who is merely discussing the details of an everyday affair, "till the calves are all gathered. We're a little late this year, on account of old Slow dying right in round-up time. We got most of the beef shipped-all I care about gathering, this fall. I've got most all young stock, and it won't hurt to let 'em run another season; there ain't many. I'll let you take the wagons out, and I'll go with you till you get kinda harness-broke. And —"

"I told you I don't want the job." Ford's mouth was set grimly.

"You tried to tell me what I want and what I don't want," Mason corrected amiably. "Now I've got my own ideas on that subject. This here outfit belongs to me. I like to pick my men to suit myself; and if I want a certain man for foreman, I guess I've got a right to hire him-if he'll let himself be hired. I've picked my man. It don't make any difference to me how many times he played hookey when he was a kid, or how many men he's licked since he growed up. I've hired him to help run the Double Cross, and run it right; and I ain't a bit afraid but what he'll make good." He smiled and knocked the ashes gently from his pipe into the palm of his hand, because the pipe was a meerschaum just getting a fine, fawn coloring around the base of the bowl, and was dear to the heart of him. "Down to the last, white chip," he added slowly, "he'll make good. He ain't the kind of a man that will lay down on his job." He got up and yawned, elaborately casual in his manner.

"You lay around and take it easy this afternoon," he said. "I've got to jog over to the river field; the boys are over there, working a little bunch we threw in yesterday. To-morrow we can ride around a little, and kinda get the lay of the land. You better go by-low, right now-you look as if it wouldn't do you any harm!" Whereupon he wisely took himself off and left Ford alone.

The door he pulled shut after him closed upon a mental battle-ground. Ford did not go "by-low." Instead, he rolled over and lay with his face upon his folded arms, alive to the finger-tips; alive and fighting. For there are times when the soul of a man awakes and demands a reckoning, and reviews pitilessly the past and faces the future with the veil of illusion torn quite away-and does it whether the man will or no.

# Chapter VIII. "I Wish You'd Quit Believing in Me!"

A distant screaming roused Ford from his bitter mood of introspection. He raised his head and listened, his heavy-lidded eyes staring blankly at the wall opposite, before he sprang off the bunk, pulled on his boots, and rushed from the room. Outside, he hesitated long enough to discover which direction he must take to reach the woman who was screaming inarticulately, her voice vibrant with sheer terror. The sound came from the little, brown cottage that seemed trying modestly to hide behind a dispirited row of young cottonwoods across a deep, narrow gully, and he ran headlong toward it. He crossed the plank footbridge in a couple of long leaps, vaulted over the gate which barred his way, and so reached the house just as a woman whom he knew must be Mason's "Kate," jerked open the door and screamed "Chester!" almost in his face. Behind her rolled a puff of slaty blue smoke.

Ford pushed past her in the doorway without speaking; the smoke told its own urgent tale and made words superfluous. She turned and followed him, choking over the pungent smoke.

"Oh, where's Chester?" she wailed. "The whole garret's on fire-and I can't carry Phenie-and she's asleep and can't walk anyway!" She rushed half across the room and stopped, pointing toward a closed door, with Ford at her heels.

"She's in there!" she cried tragically. "Save her, quick-and I'll find Chester. You'd think, with all the men there are on this ranch, there'd be some one around-oh, and my new piano!"

She ran out of the house, scolding hysterically because the men were gone, and Ford laughed a little as he went to the door she had indicated. When his fingers touched the knob, it turned fumblingly under another hand than his own; the door opened, and he confronted the girl whom he had tried to befriend the day before. She had evidently just gotten out of bed, and into a flimsy blue kimono, which she was holding together at the throat with one hand, while with the other she steadied herself against the wall. She stared blankly into his eyes, and her face was very white indeed, with her hair falling thickly upon either side in two braids which reached to her hips.

Ford gave her one quick, startled glance, said "Come on," quite brusquely, and gathered her into his arms with as little sentiment as he would have bestowed upon the piano. His eyes smarted with the smoke, which blinded him so that he bumped into chairs on his way to the door. Outside he stopped, and looked down at the girl, wondering what he should do with her. Since Kate had stated emphatically that she could not walk, it seemed scarcely merciful to deposit her on the ground and leave her to her own devices. She had closed her eyes, and she looked unpleasantly like a corpse; and there was an insistent crackling up in the roof, which warned Ford that there was little time for the weighing of fine points. He was about to lay her on the bare ground, for want of a better place, when he glimpsed Mose running heavily across the bridge, and went hurriedly to meet him.

"Here! You take her down and put her in one of the bunks, Mose," he commanded, when Mose confronted him, panting a good deal because of his two hundred and fifty pounds of excess fat and a pair of down-at-the-heel slippers which hampered his movements appreciably. Mose looked at the girl and then at his two hands.

"I can't take her," he lamented. "I got m'hands full of aigs!"

Ford's reply was a sweep of the girl's inert figure against Mose's outstretched hands, which freed them effectually of their burden of eggs. "You darned chump, what's eggs in a case like this?" he cried sharply, and forced the girl into his arms. "You take her and put her on a bunk. I've got to put out that fire!"

So Mose, a reluctant knight and an awkward one, carried the girl to the bunk-house, and left Ford free to save the house if he could. Fortunately the fire had started in a barrel of old clothing which had stood too close to the stovepipe, and while the smoke was stifling, the flames were as yet purely local. And, more fortunately still, that day happened to be Mrs. Mason's wash-day and two tubs of water stood in the kitchen, close to the narrow stairway which led into the loft. Three or four pails of water and some quick work in running up and down the stairs was all that was needed. Ford, standing in the low, unfinished loft, looked at the rafter which was burnt half through, and wiped his perspiring face with his coat sleeve.

"Lordy me!" he observed aloud, "I sure didn't come any too soon!"

"Oh, it's all out! I don't know how I ever shall thank you in this world! With Phenie in bed with a sprained ankle so she couldn't walk, and the men all gone, I was just wild! I —why —" Kate, standing upon the stairs so that she could look into the loft, stopped suddenly and stared at Ford with some astonishment. Plainly, she had but then discovered that he was a stranger- and it was quite as plain that she was taking stock of his blackened eyes and other bruises, and that with the sheltered woman's usual tendency to exaggerate the disfigurements.

"That's all right; I don't need any thanks." Ford, seeing no other way of escape, approached her steadily, the empty bucket swinging in his hand. "The fire's all out, so there's nothing more I can do here, I guess."

"Oh, but you'll have to bring Josephine back!" Kate's eyes met his straightforward glance reluctantly, and not without reason; for Ford had dark, greenish purple areas in the region of his eyes, a skinned cheek, and a swollen lip; his chin was scratched and there was a bruise on his forehead where, on the night of his marriage, he had hit the floor violently under the impact of two or three struggling male humans. Although they were five days old-six, some of them-these divers battle-signs were perfectly visible, not to say conspicuous; so that Kate Mason was perhaps justified in her perfectly apparent diffidence in looking at him. So do we turn our eyes self-consciously away from a cripple, lest we give offense by gazing upon his misfortune.

"*I* can't carry her, and she can't walk-her ankle is sprained dreadfully. So if you'll bring her back to the house, I'll be ever so much —"

"Certainly; I'll bring her back right away." Ford came down the stairs so swiftly that she retreated in haste before him, and once down he did not linger; indeed, he almost ran from the house and from her embarrassed gratitude. On the way to the bunk-house it occurred to him that it might be no easy matter, now, for Mason to conceal Ford's identity and his sins. From the way in which she had stared wincingly at his battered countenance, he realized that she did, indeed, have ideals. Ford grinned to himself, wondering if Ches didn't have to do his smoking altogether in the bunk-house; he judged her to be just the woman to wage a war on tobacco, and swearing, and muddy boots, and drinking out of one's saucer, and all other weaknesses peculiar to the male of our species. He was inclined to pity Ches, in spite of his mental acknowledgment that she was a very nice woman indeed; and he was half inclined to tell Mason when he saw him that he'd have to look further for a foreman.

He found the girl lying upon a bunk just inside the door, still with closed eyes and that corpse-like look in her face. He was guilty of hoping that she would remain in that oblivious state for at least five minutes longer, but the hope was short-lived; for when he lifted her carefully in his arms, her eyes flew open and stared up at him intently.

Ford shut his lips grimly and tried not to mind that unwinking gaze while he carried her out and up the path, across the little bridge and on to the house, and deposited her gently upon her own bed. He had not spoken a word, nor had she. So he left her thankfully to Kate's tearful ministrations and hurried from the room.

"Lordy me!" he sighed, as he closed the door upon them and went back to the bunk-house, which he entered with a sigh of relief. One tribute he paid her, and one only: the tribute of feeling perturbed over her presence, and of going hot all over at the memory of her steady stare into his face. She was a queer girl, he told himself; but then, so far as he had discovered, all women were queer; the only difference being that some women were more so than others.

He sat down on the bunk where she had lain, and speedily forgot the girl and the incident in facing the problem of that foremanship. He could not get away from the conviction that he was not to be trusted. He did not trust himself, and there was no reason why any man who knew him at all should trust him. Ches Mason was a good fellow; he meant well, Ford decided, but he simply did not realize what he was up against. He meant, therefore, to enlighten him further, and go his way. He was almost sorry that he had come.

Mason, when Ford confronted him later at the corral and bluntly stated his view of the matter, heard him through without a word, and did not laugh the issue out of the way, as he had been inclined to do before.

"I'll be all right for a month, maybe," Ford finished, "and that's as long as I can bank on myself. I tell you straight, Ches, it won't work. You may think you're hiring the same fellow that came out of the North with you-but you aren't. Why, damn it, there ain't a man I know that wouldn't give you the laugh if they knew the offer you've made me! They would, that's a fact. They'd laugh at you. You're all right, Ches, but I won't stand for a deal like that. I can't make good."

Mason waited until he was through. Then he came closer and put both hands on Ford's shoulders, so that they stood face to face, and he looked straight into Ford's discolored eyes with his own shining a little behind their encircling wrinkles.

"You can make good!" he said calmly. "I know it. All you need is a chance to pull up. Seeing you won't give yourself one, I'm giving it to you. You'll do for me what you won't do for yourself, Ford-and if there's a yellow streak in you, I never got a glimpse of it; and the yellow will sure come to the surface of a man when he's bucking a proposition like you and me bucked for two months. You didn't lay down on that job, and you were just a kid, you might say. Gosh, Ford, I'd bank on you any old time-put you on your mettle, and I would! You can make good here-and damn it, you will!"

"I wish I was as sure of that as you seem to be," Ford muttered uneasily, and turned away. Mason's easy chuckle followed him, and Ford swung about and faced him again.

"I haven't made any cast-iron promise —"

"Did I ask you to make any?" Mason's voice sharpened.

"But-Lordy me, Ches! How do you know I —"

"I know. That's enough."

"But-maybe I don't want the darned job. I never said —"

Mason was studying him, as a man studies the moods of an untamed horse. "I didn't think you'd dodge," he drawled, and the blood surged answeringly to Ford's cheeks. "You do want it."

"If I should happen to get jagged up in good shape, about the first thing I'd do would be to lick the stuffing out of you for being such a simple-minded cuss," Ford prophesied grimly, as one who knows well whereof he speaks.

"Ye-es —but you won't get jagged."

"Oh, Lord! I wish you'd quit believing in me! You used to have some sense," Ford grumbled. But he reached out and clenched his fingers upon Mason's arm so tight that Mason set his teeth, and he looked at him long, as if there was much that he would like to put into words and could not. "Say! You're white clear down to your toes, Ches," he said finally, and walked away hurriedly with his hat jerked low over his eyes.

Mason looked after him as long as he was in sight, and afterwards took off his hat, and wiped beads of perspiration from his forehead. "Gosh!" he whispered fervently. "That was nip and tuck-but I got him, thank the Lord!" Whereupon he blew his nose violently, and went up to his supper with his hands in his pockets and his humorous lips pursed into a whistle.

Before long he was back, chuckling to himself as he bore down upon Ford in the corral, where he was industriously rubbing Rambler's sprained shoulder with liniment.

"The wife says you've got to come up to the house," he announced gleefully. "You've gone and done the heroic again, and she wants to do something to show her gratitude."

"You go back and tell your wife that I'm a bold, bad man and I won't come." Ford, to prove his sincerity, sat down upon the stout manger there, and crossed his legs with an air of finality.

"I did tell her," Mason confessed sheepishly. "She wanted to know who you was, and I told her before I thought. And she wanted to know what was the matter with your face, 'poor fellow,' and I told her that, too-as near as I knew it. I told her," he stated sweepingly, "that you'd been on a big jamboree and had licked fourteen men hand-running. There ain't," he confided with a twinkle, "any use at all in trying to keep a secret from your wife; not," he qualified, "from a wife like Kate! So she knows the whole darned thing, and she's sore as the deuce because I didn't bring you up to the house right away when you came. She thinks you're sufferin' from them wounds and she's going to doctor 'em. That's the way with a woman-you never can tell what angle she's going to look at a thing from. You're the man that packed me down out of the Wrangel mountains on your back, and that's enough for her-dang it, Kate thinks a lot of me! Besides, you done the heroic this afternoon. You've got to come."

"There ain't anything heroic in sloshing a few buckets of water on a barrel of burning rags," Ford belittled, seeking in his pockets for his cigarette papers.

"How about rescuing a lady?" Mason twitted. "You come along. I want you up there myself. Gosh! I want somebody I can talk to about something besides dresses and the proper way to cure sprained ankles, and whether the grocer sent out the right brand of canned peaches. Women are all right-but a man wants some one around to talk to. You ain't married!"

"Oh. Ain't I?" Ford snorted. "And what if I ain't?"

"Say, there's a mighty nice girl staying with us; the one you rescued. She's laid up now-got bucked off, or fell off, or something yesterday, and hurt her foot-but she's a peach, all right. You'll —"

"I know the lady," Ford cut in dryly. "I met her yesterday, and we commenced hating each other as soon as we got in talking distance. She sent me to catch her horse, and then she pulled out before I got back. She's a peach, all right!"

"Oh. You're the fellow!" Mason regarded him attentively. "Now, I don't believe she said a word to Kate about that, and she must have known who it was packed her out of the house. I wonder why she didn't say anything about it to Kate! But she wasn't to blame for leaving you out there, honest she wasn't. I went out to hunt her up-Kate got kinda worried about her-and she told me about you, and we did wait a little while. But it was getting cold, and she was hurt pretty bad and getting kinda wobbly, so I put her on my horse and brought her home. But she left a note for you, and I sent a man back after you with a horse. He come back and said he couldn't locate you. So we thought you'd gone to some other ranch." He stopped and looked quizzically at Ford. "So you're the man! And you're both here for the winter-at least, Kate says she's going to keep her all winter. Gosh! This is getting romantic!"

"Don't you believe it!" Ford urged emphatically. "I don't want to bump into her again; a little of her company will last me a long while!"

"Oh, you won't meet Jo to-night; Josephine, her name is. She's in bed, and will be for a week or so, most likely. You've just got to come, Ford. Kate'll be down here after you herself, if I go back without you-and she'll give me the dickens into the bargain. I want you to get acquainted with my kid-Buddy. He's down in the river field with the boys, but he'll be back directly. Greatest kid you ever saw, Ford! Only seven, and he can ride like a son-of-a-gun, and wears chaps and spurs, and can sling a loop pretty good, for a little kid! Come on!"

"Wel-ll, all right-but Lordy me! I do hate to, Ches, and that's a fact. Women I'm plumb scared of. I never met one in my life that didn't hand me a package of trouble so big I couldn't see around it. Why —" He shut his teeth upon the impulse to confide to Mason his matrimonial mischance.

"These two won't. My wife's the real goods, once you get to know her; a little fussy, maybe, over some things-most all women are. But she's all right, you bet. And Josephine's the proper stuff too. A little abrupt, maybe —"

"Abrupt!" Ford echoed, and laughed over the word. "Yes, she is what you might call a lit-tle-abrupt!"

# Chapter IX. Impressions

Josephine waited languidly while Kate chose a second-best cushion from the couch and, lifting the bandaged foot as gently as might be, placed it, with many little pats and pulls, under the afflicted member. Josephine screwed her lips into a soundless expression of pain, smiled afterwards when Kate glanced at her commiseratingly, and pulled a long, dark-brown braid forward over her chest.

"Do you want tea, Phenie? —or would you rather have chocolate to-day? I can make chocolate just as easy as not; I think I shall, anyway. Buddy is so fond of it and —"

"Is that man here yet?" Josephine's tone carried the full weight of her dislike of him.

"I don't know why you call him 'that man,' the way you do," Kate complained, turning her mind from the momentous decision between tea and chocolate. "Ford's simply fine! Chester thinks there's no one like him; and Buddy just tags him around everywhere. You can always," asserted Kate, with the positiveness of the person who accepts unquestioningly the beliefs of others, living by faith rather than reason, "depend upon the likes and dislikes of children and dogs, you know."

"Has the swelling gone out of his eyes?" Josephine inquired pointedly, with the irrelevance which seemed habitual to her and Kate when they conversed.

"Phenie, I don't think it's kind of you to harp on that. Yes, it has, if you want to know. He's positively handsome-or will be when the-when his nose heals perfectly. And I don't think that's anything one should hold against Ford; it seems narrow, dear."

"The skinned place?" Josephine's tone was perfectly innocent, and her fingers were busy with the wide, black bow which becomingly tied the end of the braid.

"Phenie! If you hadn't a sprained ankle, and weren't such a dear in every other respect, I'd shake you! It isn't fair. Because Ford was pounced upon by a lot of men-sixteen, Chester told me —"

"I suppose he counted the dead after the battle, and told Ches truthfully —"

"Phenie, that sounds catty! When you get down on a man, you're perfectly unmerciful, and Ford doesn't deserve it. You shouldn't judge men by the narrow, Eastern standards. I know it's awful for a man to drink and fight. But Ford wasn't altogether to blame. They got him to drinking and," she went on with her voice lowered to the pitch at which women are wont to relate horrid, immoral things, " —I wouldn't be surprised if they put something in it! Such things are done; I've heard of men being drugged and robbed and all sorts of things. And I'm just as much of an advocate for temperance as you are, Phenie-and I think Ford was just right to fight those men. There are," she declared wisely, "circumstances where it's perfectly just and right for a man to fight. I can imagine circumstances under which Chester would be justified in fighting —"

"In case sixteen men should hold his nose and pour drugged whisky down his throat?" Phenie inquired mildly, curling the end of her braid over a slim forefinger.

Mrs. Kate made an inarticulate sound which might almost be termed a snort, and walked from the room with her head well up and a manner which silently made plain to the onlooker that she might say many things which would effectually crush her opponent, but was magnanimously refraining from doing so.

Josephine did not even pay her the tribute of looking at her; she had at that moment heard a step upon the porch, and she was leaning to one side so that she might see who was coming into the dining-room. As it happened, it was Mason himself. Miss Josephine immediately lost interest in the arrival and took to tracing with her finger the outline of a Japanese lady with a startling coiffure and an immense bow upon her spine, who was simpering at a lotus bed on Josephine's kimono. She did not look up until some one stepped upon the porch again.

This time it was Ford, and he stopped and painstakingly removed the last bit of soil from his boot-soles upon the iron scraper which was attached to one end of the top step; when that duty had been performed, he paid further tribute to the immaculate house he was about to enter, by wiping his feet upon a mat placed with mathematical precision upon the porch, at the head of the steps. Josephine watched the ceremonial, and studied Ford's profile, and did not lay her head back upon the cushion behind her until he disappeared into the dining-room. Then she stared at a colored-crayon portrait of Buddy which hung on the wall opposite, and her eyes were the eyes of one who sees into the past.

Buddy, when he opened the door and projected himself into the room, startled her into a little exclamation.

"Dad says he'll carry you out to the table and you can have a whole side to yourself," he announced without preface. "They'll just pick up your chair, and pack chair and all in, and set you down as ee-asy—do you want to eat out there with us?"

Josephine hesitated for two seconds. "All right," she consented then, in a supremely indifferent tone which was of course quite wasted on Buddy, who immediately disappeared with a whoop.

"Come on, dad-she says yes, all right, she'll come," he announced gleefully. Buddy was Josephine's devoted admirer, at this point in their rather brief acquaintance; which, according to his mother's well-known theory, was convincing proof of her intrinsic worth-Mrs. Kate having frequently strengthened her championship of Ford to his detractor, Miss Josephine, by pointing out that Buddy was fond of him.

Josephine spent the brief interval in tucking back locks of hair and in rearranging the folds of her long, Japanese kimono, and managed to fall into a languidly indifferent attitude by the time Chester opened the door. Behind him came Ford; Miss Josephine moved her lips and tilted her head in a perfunctory greeting, and afterward gave him no more attention than if he had been a Pullman porter assisting with her suitcases. For the matter of that, she gave quite as much attention as she received from him-and Mason's lips twitched betrayingly at the spectacle.

Through dinner they seemed mutually agreed upon ignoring each other as much as was politely possible, which caused Mason to watch them with amusement, and afterwards relieve his feelings by talking about them to Kate in the kitchen.

"Gosh! Jo and Ford are sure putting up a good bluff," he chuckled, while he selected the freshest dish towel from the rack behind the pantry door. "They'd be sticking out their tongues at each other if they was twenty years younger; pity they ain't, too; it would be a relief to 'em both!"

"Phenie provokes me almost past endurance!" Mrs. Kate complained, burying two plump forearms in a dishpan of sudsy hot water, and bringing up a handful of silver. "It's because Ford had been fighting when he came here, and she knows he has been slightly addicted to liquor. She looks down on him, and I don't think it's fair. If a man wants to reform, I believe in helping him instead of pushing him father down." (Mrs. Kate had certain little peculiarities of speech; one was an italicized delivery, and another was the omission of an r now and then. She always said "father" when she really meant "farther.") "There's a lot that one can do to help. I believe in showing trust and confidence in a man, when he's trying to live down past mistakes. I think it was just fine of you to make him foreman here! If Phenie would only be nice to him, instead of turning up her nose the way she does! You see yourself how she treats Ford, and I just think it's a shame! I think he's just splendid!"

"She don't treat him any worse than he does her," observed Mason, just to the core. "Seems to me, if I was single, and a girl as pretty as Jo—"

"Well, I'm glad Ford has got spunk enough not to care," Mrs. Kate interposed hastily. "Phenie's pretty, of course-but it takes more than that to attract a man like Ford. You can't expect him to like her when she won't look at him, hardly; it makes me feel terribly, because he's sure to think it's because he—I've tried to make her see that it isn't right to condemn a man because he has made one mistake. He ought to be encouraged, instead of being made to feel that he is a—an outcast, practically. And—"

"Jo don't like Ford, because she's stuck on Dick," stated a shrill, positive young voice behind them, and Mrs. Kate turned sharply upon her offspring. "They was waving hands to each other just now, through the window. I seen 'em," Buddy finished complacently. "Dick was down fixing the bridge, and —"

"Buddy, you run right out and play! You must not listen to older people and try to talk about some-thing you don't understand."

"Aw, I understand them two being stuck on each other," Buddy maintained loftily. "And I seen Dick —"

"Chase yourself outdoors, like your mother said; and don't butt in on —"

"Chester!" reproved Mrs. Kate, waving Buddy out of the kitchen. "How can you expect the child to learn good English, when you talk to him like that? Run along, Buddy, and play like a good boy." She gave him a little cake to accelerate his departure and to turn his mind from further argument, and after he was gone she swung the discussion to Buddy and his growing tendency toward grappling with problems beyond his seven years. Also, she pointed out the necessity for choosing one's language carefully in his presence.

Mason, therefore, finished wiping the dishes almost in silence, and left the house as soon as he was through, with the feeling that women were not by nature intended to be really companionable. He had, for instance, been struck with the humorous side of Ford and Josephine's perfectly ridiculous antipathy, and had lingered in the kitchen because of a half-conscious impulse to enjoy the joke with some one. And Mrs. Kate had not taken the view-point which appealed to him, but had been self-consciously virtuous in her determination to lend Ford a helping hand, and resentful because Josephine failed to feel also the urge of uplifting mankind.

Mason, poor man, was vaguely nettled; he did not see that Ford needed any settlement-worker encouragement. If he was let alone, and his moral regeneration forgotten, and he himself treated just like any other man, Mason felt that Ford would thereby have all the encouragement he needed. Ford was once more plainly content with life, and was taking it in twenty-four-hour doses again; healthful doses, these, and different in every respect from those days spent in the sordid round of ill-living in town; nor did he flay his soul with doubts lest he should disappoint this man who trusted him so rashly and so implicitly. Ford was busy at work which appealed to the best of him. He was thrown into companionship with men who perforce lived cleanly and naturally, and with Ches Mason, who was his friend. At meals he sometimes gave thought to Mrs. Kate, and frequently to Josephine. The first he admired impersonally for her housewifely skill, and smiled at secretly for her purely feminine outlook upon life and her positive views upon subjects of which she knew not half the alphabet. He had discovered that Mason did indeed refrain from smoking in the house because she discountenanced tobacco; and since she had a talent for making a man uncomfortably aware of her disapproval by certain wordless manifestations of scorn for his weaknesses, Ford also took to throwing away his cigarette before he crossed the bridge on his way to her domain. He did not, however, go so far as Ches, who kept his tobacco, pipe, and cigarette papers in the stable, and was always borrowing "the makings" from his men.

Ford also followed Mason's example in sterilizing his vocabulary whenever he crossed that boundary between the masculine and feminine element on the ranch, the bridge. Mrs. Kate did not approve of slang. Ford found himself carefully eliminating from his speech certain grammatical inaccuracies in her presence, and would not so much as split an infinitive if he remembered in time. It was trying, to be sure. Ford thanked God that he still retained a smattering of the rules he had reluctantly memorized in school, and that he was not married (at least, not uncomfortably so), and that he was not compelled to do more than eat his meals in the house. Mrs. Kate was a nice woman; Ford would tell any man so in perfect sincerity. He even considered her nice looking, with her smooth, brown hair which was never disordered, her fine, clear skin, her white teeth, her clear blue eyes, and her immaculate shirt-waists. But she was not a comfortable woman to be with; an ordinary human wearied of adjusting his speech, his manners, and his morals to her standard of propriety. Ford, quietly studying matrimony from the well-ordered example before him, began to congratulate himself upon not being able to locate his own wife-since accident had afflicted him with one. When he stopped, during these first busy days at the Double Cross, to think deeply or seriously upon the mysterious entanglement he had fallen into, he was inclined to the opinion that he had had a narrow escape. The woman might have remained in Sunset—and Ford flinched at the thought.

As to Josephine, Ford's thoughts dwelt with her oftener than they did with Mrs. Kate. The thought of her roused a certain resentment which bordered closely upon dislike. Still, she piqued his interest; for a week she was invisible to him, yet her presence in the house created a tangible atmosphere which he felt but could not explain. His first sight of her—beyond a fleeting glimpse once or twice through the window—had been that day when he had helped Mason carry her and her big chair into the dining-room. The brief contact had left with him a vision of the delicate parting in her soft, brown hair, and of long, thick lashes which curled daintily up from the shadow they made on her cheeks. He did not remember ever having seen a woman with such eyelashes. They impelled him to glance at her oftener than he would otherwise have done, and to wonder, now and then, if they did not make her eyes seem darker than they really were. He thought it strange that he had not noticed her lashes that day when he carried her from the house and back again—until he remembered that at first his haste had been extreme, and that when he took her from the bunk-house she had stared at him so that he would not look at her.

He did not know that Ches Mason was observant of his rather frequent glances at her during the meal, and he would have resented Mason's diagnosis of that particular symptom of interest. Ford would, if put to the question, have maintained quite sincerely that he was perfectly indifferent to Josephine, but that she did have remarkable eyelashes, and a man couldn't help looking at them.

After all, Ford's interest was centered chiefly upon his work. They were going to start the wagons out again to gather the calves for weaning, and he was absorbed in the endless details which fall upon the shoulders of the foreman. Even the fascination of a woman's beauty did not follow him much beyond the bridge.

Mason, hurrying from the feminine atmosphere at the house, found him seriously discussing with Buddy the diet and general care of Rambler, who had been moved into a roomy box stall for shelter. Buddy was to have the privilege of filling the manger with hay every morning after breakfast, and every evening just before supper. Upon Buddy also devolved the duty of keeping his drinking tub filled with clean water; and Buddy was making himself as tall as possible during the conference, and was crossing his heart solemnly while he promised, wide-eyed, to keep away from Rambler's heels.

"I never knew him to kick, or offer to; but you stay out of the stall, anyway. You can fill his tub through that hole in the wall. And you let Walt rub him down good every day—you see that he does it, Bud! And when he gets well, I'll let you ride him, maybe. Anyway, I leave him in your care, old-timer. And it's a privilege I wouldn't give every man. I think a heap of this horse." He turned at the sound of footsteps, and lowered an eyelid slowly for Mason's benefit. "Bud's going to have charge of Rambler while we're gone," he explained seriously. "I want to be sure he's in good hands."

The two men watched Buddy's departure for the house, and grinned over the manifest struggle between his haste to tell his mother and Jo, and his sense of importance over the trust.

"A kid of your own makes up for a whole lot," Mason observed abstractedly, reaching up to the narrow shelf where he kept his tobacco. "I wish I had two or three more; they give a man something to work for, and look ahead and plan for."

Ford, studying his face with narrowed eyelids, was more than ever thankful that he was not hampered by matrimony.

## Chapter X. In Which the Demon Opens an Eye and Yawns

A storm held the Double Cross wagons in a sheltered place in the hills, ten miles from the little town where Ford had spent a night on his way to the ranch a month before. Mason, taking the inaction as an excuse, rode home to his family and left Ford to his own devices with no compunctions whatever. He should, perhaps, have known better; but he was acting upon his belief that nothing so braces a man as the absolute confidence of his friends, and to have stayed in camp on Ford's account would, according to Mason's code, have been an affront to Ford's manifest determination to "make good."

It is true that neither had mentioned the matter since the day of Ford's arrival at the ranch; men do not, as a rule, harp upon the deeper issues within their lives. For that month, it had been as though the subject of intemperance concerned them as little as the political unrest of a hot-tempered people beyond the equator. They had argued the matter to a more or less satisfactory conclusion, and had let it rest there.

Ford had ridden with him a part of the way, and when they came to a certain fork in the trail, he had sent a whimsically solemn message to Buddy, had pulled the collar of his coat closer together under his chin, and had faced the wind with a clean conscience, and with bowed head and hat pulled low over his brows. There were at least three perfectly valid reasons why Ford should ride into town that day. He wanted heavier socks and a new pair of gloves; he was almost out of tobacco, and wanted to see if he could "pick up" another man so that the hours of night-guarding might not fall so heavily upon the crew. Ford had been standing the last guard himself, for the last week, to relieve the burden a little, and Mason had been urgent on the subject of another man-or two, he suggested, would be better. Ford did his simple shopping, therefore, and then rode up to the first saloon on the one little street, and dismounted with a mind at ease. If idle men were to be found in that town, he would have to look for them in a saloon; a fact which every one took for granted, like the shortening of the days as winter approached.

Perhaps he over-estimated his powers of endurance, or under-estimated the strength of his enemy. Certain it is that he had no intention of drinking whisky when he closed the door upon the chill wind; and yet, he involuntarily walked straight up to the bar. There he stuck. The bartender waited expectantly. When Ford, with a sudden lift of his head, turned away to the stove, the man looked after him curiously.

At the stove Ford debated with himself while he drew off his gloves and held his fingers to the welcome heat which emanated from a red glow where the fire burned hottest within. He had not made any promise to himself or any one else, he remembered. He had simply resolved that he would make good, if it were humanly possible to do so. That, he told himself, did not necessarily mean that he should turn a teetotaler out and out. Taking a drink, when a man was cold and felt the need of it, was not —

At that point in the argument two of his own men entered, stamping noisily upon the threshold. They were laughing, from pure animal satisfaction over the comforts within, rather than at any tangible cause for mirth, and they called to Ford with easy comradeship. Dick Thomas-the Dick whom Buddy had mentioned in connection with Josephine-waved his hand hospitably toward the bar.

"Come on, Campbell," he invited. He may have seen the hesitancy in Ford's face, for he laughed. "I believe in starting on the inside and driving the frost out," he said.

The two poured generously from the bottle which the bartender pushed within easy reach, and Ford watched them. There was a peculiar lift to Dick's upper lip-the lift which comes when scorn is the lever. Ford's eyes hardened a little; he walked over and stood beside Dick, and he took a drink as unemotionally as if it had been water. He ordered another round, threw a coin upon the bar, and walked out. He had rather liked Dick, in an impersonal sort of way, but that half-sneer clung disagreeably to his memory. A man likes to be held the master-be the slave circumstance, danger, an opposing human, or his own appetite; and although Ford was not the type of man who troubles himself much about the opinions of his fellows, it irked him much that Dick or any other man should sneer at him for a weakling.

He went to another saloon, found and hired a cow-puncher strayed up from Valley County, and when Dick came in, a half-hour later, Ford went to the bar and deliberately "called up the house." He had been minded to choose a mineral water then, but he caught Dick's mocking eye upon him, and instead took whisky straight, and stared challengingly at the other over the glass tilted against his lips.

After that, the liquor itself waged relentless war against his good resolutions, so that it did not need the urge of Dick's fancied derision to send him down the trail which the past had made familiar. He sat in to a poker game that was creating a small zone of subdued excitement at the far end of the room, and while he was arranging his stacks of red, white, and blue chips neatly before him, he was unpleasantly conscious of Dick's supercilious smile. Never mind-he was not the first foreman who ever played poker; they all did, when the mood seized them. Ford straightened his shoulders instinctively, in defiance of certain inner misgivings, and pushed forward his ante of two white chips.

Jim Felton came up and stood at his shoulder, watching the game in silence; and although he did not once open his lips except to let an occasional thin ribbon of cigarette smoke drift out and away to mingle with the blue cloud which hung under the ceiling, Ford sensed a certain good-will in his nearness, just as intangibly and yet as surely as he sensed Dick's sardonic amusement at his apparent lapse.

With every bet he made and won he felt that silent approbation behind him; insensibly it steadied Ford and sharpened his instinct for reading the faces of the other players, so that the miniature towers of red chips and blue grew higher until they threatened to topple-whereupon other little towers began to grow up around them. And the men in the saloon began to feel the fascination of his success, so that they grouped themselves about his chair and peered down over his shoulder at the game.

Ford gave them no thought, except a vague satisfaction, now and then, that Jim Felton stuck to his post. Later, when he caught the dealer, a slit-eyed, sallow-skinned fellow with fingers all too nimble, slipping a card from the bottom of the deck, and gave him a resounding slap which sent him and his cards sprawling all over that locality, he should have been more than ever glad that Jim was present.

Jim kept back the gambler's partner and the crowd and gave Ford elbow-room and some moral support, which did its part, in that it prevented any interference with the chastisement Ford was administering.

It was not a fight, properly speaking. The gambler, once Ford had finished cuffing him and stating his opinion of cheating the while, backed away and muttered vague threats and maledictions. Ford gathered together what chips he felt certain were his, and cashed them in with a certain grim insistence of manner which brooked no argument. After that he left the saloon, with Jim close behind him.

"If you're going back to camp now, I reckon I'll ride along," said Jim, at his elbow. "There's just nice time to get there for supper-and I sure don't want to miss flopping my lip over Mose's beefsteak; that yearling we beefed this morning is going to make some fine eating, if you ask me." His tone was absolutely devoid of anything approaching persuasion; it simply took a certain improbable thing as a commonplace fact, and it tilted the balance of Ford's intentions.

He did not go on to the next saloon, as he had started to do, but instead he followed Jim to the livery stable and got his horse, without realizing that Jim had anything to do with the change of impulse. So Ford went to camp, instead of spending the night riotously in town as he would otherwise have done, and contented himself with cursing the game, the gambler who would have given a "crooked deal," the town, and all it contained. A mile out, he would have returned for a bottle of whisky; but Jim said he had enough for two, and put his horse into a lope. Ford, swayed by a blind instinct to stay with the man who seemed friendly, followed the pace he set and so was unconsciously led out of the way of further temptation. And so artfully was he led, that he never once suspected that he did not go of his own accord.

Neither did he suspect that Jim's stumbling and immediate spasm of regretful profanity at the bed-wagon where they unsaddled, was the result of two miles of deep cogitation, and calculated to account plausibly for not being able to produce a full flask upon demand. Jim swore volubly and said he had "busted the bottle" by falling against the wagon wheel; and Ford, for a wonder, believed and did not ask for proof. He muddled around camp for a few indecisive minutes, then rolled himself up like a giant cocoon in his blankets, and slept heavily through the night.

He awoke at daylight, found himself fully clothed and with a craving for whisky which he knew of old, and tried to remember just what had occurred the night before; when he could not recall anything very distinctly, he felt the first twinge of fear that he had known for years.

"Lordy me! I wonder what kinda fool I made of myself, anyway!" he thought distressfully. Later, when he discovered more money in his pockets than his salary would account for, and remembered playing poker, and having an argument of some sort with some one, his distress grew upon him. In reality he had not done anything disgraceful, according to the easy judgment of his fellows; but Ford did not know that, and he flayed himself unmercifully for a spineless, drunken idiot whom no man could respect or trust. It seemed to him that the men eyed him askance; though they were merely envious over his winnings and inclined to admire the manner in which he had shown his disapproval of the dealer's attempt at cheating.

He dreaded Mason's return, and yet he was anxious to see him and tell him, once for all, that he was not to be trusted. He held aloof from Jim and he was scantily civil to Dick Thomas, whose friendship rang false. He pushed the work ahead while the air was still alive with swirls of mote-like snowflakes, and himself bore the brunt of it just to dull that gnawing self-disgust which made his waking hours a mental torment.

Before, when disgust had seized upon him in Sunset, it had been an abstract rebellion against the futility of life as he was living it. This was different: This was a definite, concrete sense of failure to keep faith with himself and with Mason; the sickening consciousness of a swinish return to the wallow; a distrust of himself that was beyond any emotion he had ever felt in his life.

So, for a week of hard work and harder thinking. Mason sent word by a migratory cowboy, who had stopped all night at the ranch and whom he had hired and sent on to camp, that he would not return to the round-up, and that Ford was to go ahead as they had planned. That balked Ford's determination to turn the work over to Mason and leave the country, and, after the first day of inner rebellion, he settled down insensibly to the task before him and let his own peculiar moral problem wait upon his leisure. He did not dream that the cowboy had witnessed his chastisement of the gambler and had gleefully, and in perfect innocence, recounted the incident at the Double Cross ranch, and that Mason had deliberately thrown Ford upon his own resources in obedience to his theory that nothing so braces a man as responsibility.

Ford went about his business with grim industry and a sureness of judgment born of his thorough knowledge of range work. There was the winnowing process which left the bigger, stronger calves in charge of two men, at a line camp known locally as Ten Mile, and took the younger ones on to the home ranch, where hay and shelter were more plentiful and the loss would be correspondingly less.

Not until the last cow of the herd was safe inside the big corral beyond the stables, did Ford relax his vigilance and ride over to where Ches Mason and Buddy were standing in the shelter of the stable, waiting to greet him.

"Good boy!" cried Mason, when Ford dismounted and flung the stirrup up over the saddle, that he might loosen the latigo and free his steaming horse of its burden. "I didn't look for you before to-morrow night, at the earliest. But I'm mighty glad you're here, let me tell you. That leaves me free to hit the trail to-morrow. I've got to make a trip home; the old man's down with inflammatory rheumatism, and they want me to go-haven't been home for six years, so I guess they've got a license to put in a bid for a month or two of my time, huh? I didn't want to pull out, though, till you showed up. I'm kinda leery about leaving the women alone, with just a couple of sow-egians on the ranch. Bud, you go get a pan of oats for old Schley. Supper's about ready, Ford. Have the boys shovel some hay into the corral, and we'll leave the bunch there till morning. Say, the wagons didn't beat you much; they never pulled in till after three. Mose says the going's bad, on them dobe patches."

Not much of an opening, that, for saying what Ford felt he was in duty bound to say. He was constrained to wait until a better opportunity presented itself-and, as is the way with opportunity, it did not seem as if it would ever come of its own accord. There was Buddy, full of exciting anecdotes about Rambler, and how he had rubbed the liniment on, all alone, and Rambler never kicked or did a thing; and how he and Josephine rode clear over to Jenson's and got caught in the storm and almost got lost-only Buddy's horse knew the way home. And, later, there was Mrs. Kate's excellent supper and gracious welcome, and an evening devoted to four-handed cribbage-with Josephine and Mason as implacable adversaries-and a steady undercurrent of latent hostility between him and the girl, which prevented his thinking much about himself and his duty to Mason. There was everything, in fact, to thwart a man's resolution to discharge honorably a disagreeable duty, and to distract his attention.

Ford went to bed with the baffled sense of being placed in a false position against his will; and, man-like, he speedily gave over thinking of that, and permitted his thoughts to dwell upon a certain face which owned a perfectly amazing pair of lashes, and upon a manner tantalizingly aloof, with glimpses now and then of fascinating possibilities in the way of comradeship, when the girl inadvertently lowered her guard in the excitement of close playing.

# Chapter XI. "It's Going to Be an Uphill Climb!"

Ford was no moral weakling except, perhaps, when whisky and he came to hand-grips. He had made up his mind that Mason must be told of his backsliding, and protected from the risk of leaving a drunkard in charge of his ranch. And when he saw that the opportunity for opening the subject easily did not show any sign of presenting itself, he grimly interrupted Mason in the middle of a funny story about Josephine and Buddy and Kate, involving themselves in a three-cornered argument to the complete discomfiture of the women.

"I tell you, Ford, that kid's a corker! Kate's got all kinds of book theories about raising children, but they don't none of 'em work, with Bud. He gets the best of her right along when she starts to reason with him. Gosh! You can't reason with a kid like Bud; you've got to take him on an equal footing, and when he goes too far, just set down on him and no argument about it. Kate's going to have her hands full while I'm gone, if—"

"She sure will, Ches, unless you get somebody here you can depend on," was the way in which Ford made his opportunity. "You've got the idea, somehow, that cutting out whisky is like getting rid of a mean horse. It's something you don't—"

"Oh, don't go worrying over that, no more," Mason expostulated hastily. "Forget it. That's the quickest cure; try Christian Science dope on it. The more you worry about it, the more—"

"But wait till I tell you! That day I went to town, and you came on home, I got drunk as a fool, Ches. I don't know what all I did, but I know—"

"Well, I know-more about it than you do, I reckon," Mason cut in dryly. "I was told five different times, by one stranger and four of these here trouble-peddlin' friends that clutter the country. That's all right, Ford. A little slip like that—" He held out his hand for Ford's sack of tobacco.

"I ain't the least bit uneasy over that, old man. I'm just as sure as I stand here that you're going to pull up, all right."

"I know you are, Ches." Ford's voice was humble. "That's the hell of it. You're more sure than sensible-but-But look at it like I was a stranger, Ches. Just forget you ever knew me when I was kinda half-way decent. You ain't a fool, even if you do act like one. You know what I'm up against. I'm going to put up the damnedest fight I've got in me, but I don't want you to take any gamble on it. Maybe I'll win, and then again maybe I won't. Maybe I'll go down and out. I don't know—I don't feel half as sure of myself as I did before I made that bobble in town. Before that, I did kinda have an idea that all there was to it was to quit. I thought, once I made up my mind, that would settle it. But that's just the commencement; you've got to fight something inside of you that's as husky a fighter as you are. You've got to—"

"There!" Mason reached out and tapped him impressively on the arm with a match he was about to light. "Now you've got the bull right by the horns! You ain't so darned sure of yourself now-and so I'm dead willing to gamble on you. I ain't a bit afraid to go off and let you have full swing."

"Well, I hope you won't feel like kicking me all over the ranch when you get back," Ford said, after a long pause, during which Mason's whole attention seemed centered upon his cigarette. "It's going to be an uphill climb, old-timer—and a blamed long hill at that. And it's going to be pretty darned slippery, in places."

"I sabe that, all right," grinned Mason. "But I sabe you pretty well, too. You'll dig in your toes and hang on by your eye-winkers if you have to. But you'll get up, all right; I'll bank on that.

"Speaking of booze-fighters," he went on, without giving Ford a chance to contradict him, "I wish you'd keep an eye on old Mose. Now, there's a man that'll drink whisky as long as it's made, if he can get it. I wouldn't trust that old devil as far as I can throw him, and that's a fact. I have to watch pretty close, to keep it off the ranch, and him on. It's the only way to get along with him-he's apt to run amuck, if he gets full enough; and good cooks are as scarce as good foremen." A heartening smile went with the last sentence.

"If he does make connections with the booze, don't can him, Ford, if you can help it. Just shut him up somewhere till he gets over it. There's nothing holds good men with an outfit like the right kind of grub-and Mose sure can cook. The rest of the men you can handle to suit yourself. Slim and Johnnie are all right over at Ten Mile-you made a good stab when you picked them two out-and you will want a couple of fellows here besides Walt, to feed them calves. When the cows are throwed back on the range and the fences gone over careful —I ought to have tended to that before, but I got to putting it off-you can pay off what men you don't need or want."

There was no combating the friendship of a man like that. Ford mentally squared his shoulders and set his feet upon the uphill trail.

He realized to the full the tribute Mason paid to his innate trustworthiness by leaving him there, master of the ranch and guardian of his household god-and goddess, to say nothing of Josephine, whom Mason openly admired and looked upon as one of the family.

Of a truth, it would seem that she had really become so. Ford had gathered, bit by bit, the information that she was quite alone in the world, so far as immediate relatives were concerned, and that she was Kate's cousin, and that Kate insisted that this was to be her home, from now on. Josephine's ankle was well enough now so that she was often to be met in unexpected places about the ranch, he discovered. And though she was not friendly, she was less openly antagonistic than she had been-and when all was said and done, eminently able to take care of herself.

So also was Kate, for that matter. No sooner was her beloved Chester out of sight over the hill a mile away, than Mrs. Kate dried her wifely tears and laid hold of her scepter with a firmness that amused Ford exceedingly. She ordered Dick up to work in the depressed-looking area before the house, which she called her flower garden, a task which Dick seemed perfectly willing to perform, by the way-although his assistance would have been more than welcome at other work than tying scraggly rose bushes and protecting them from the winter already at hand.

As to Buddy, he surely would have resented, more keenly than the women, the implication that he needed any one to take care of him. Buddy's allegiance to Ford was wavering, at that time. Dick had gone to some trouble to alter an old pair of chaps so that Buddy could wear them, and his star was in the ascendant; a pair of chaps with fringes were, in Buddy's estimation, a surer pledge of friendship and favor than the privilege of feeding a lame horse.

Buddy was rather terrible, sometimes. He had a way of standing back unnoticed, and of listening when he was believed to be engrossed in his play. Afterward he was apt to say the things which should not be said; in other words, he was the average child of seven, living without playmates, and so forced by his environment to interest himself in the endless drama played by the grown-ups around him. Buddy, therefore, was not unusually startling, one day at dinner, when he looked up from spatting his potato into a flat cake on his plate.

"What hill you going to climb, Ford?" was his manner of exploding his bomb. "Bald pinnacle? I can climb that hill myself."

"I don't know as I'm going to climb any hills at all," Ford said indulgently, accepting another helping of potato salad from Mrs. Kate.

"You told dad before he went to gran'ma's house you was going to climb a big, long hill, and he was more sure than sensible." He giggled and showed where two front teeth were missing from among their fellows. "Dad told him he'd make it, but he'd have to dig in his toes and hang on by his eye-winkers," he added to the two women. "Gee! I'd like to see Ford hang onto a hill by his eye-winkers. Jo could do it-she's got winkers six feet long."

Miss Josephine had been looking at Ford's face going red, as enlightenment came to him, but when she caught a quick glance leveled at her lashes, she drooped them immediately so that they almost touched her cheeks. Bud gave a squeal and pointed to her with his fork.

"Jo's blushing! I guess she's ashamed because she's got such long winkers, and Ford keeps looking at 'em all the time. Why don't you shave 'em off with dad's razor? Then Ford would like you, maybe. He don't now. He told dad —"

"Robert Chester Mason, do you want me to get the hairbrush?" This, it need not be explained, from Mrs. Kate, in a voice that portended grave disaster.

"I guess we can get along without it, mamma," Buddy answered her, with an ingratiating smile. Even in the first seven years of one's life, one learns the elementary principles of diplomacy. He did not retire from the conversation, but he prudently changed the subject to what he considered a more pleasant channel.

"Dick likes you anyway, Jo," he informed her soothingly. "He likes you, winkers and all. I can tell, all right. When you go out for a ride he gives me nickels if I tell him where —"

"Robert Ches —"

"Oh, all right." Buddy's tone was wearily tolerant. "A man never knows what to talk about to women, anyway. I'd hate to be married to 'em-wouldn't you, Ford?"

"A little boy like you —" began his mother, somewhat pinker of cheeks than usual.

"I guess I'm pretty near a man, now." He turned his eyes to Ford, consciously ignoring the feminine members of his family. "If I had a wife," he stated calmly, "I'd snub her up to a post and then I'd talk to her about anything I damn pleased!"

Mrs. Kate rose up then in all the terrifying dignity of outraged motherhood, grasped Buddy by the wrist, and led him away, in the direction of the hairbrush, if one would judge by Buddy's reluctance to go.

"So you are going to climb the-Big Hill, are you?" Miss Josephine observed, when the two were quite alone. "It is to be hoped, Mr. Campbell, that you won't find it as steep as it looks-from the bottom."

Ford was not an adept at reading what lies underneath the speech of a woman. To himself he accented the last three words, so that they overshadowed all the rest and made her appear to remind him where he stood-at the bottom.

"I suppose a hollow does look pretty high, to a man down a well," he retorted, glancing into his teacup because he felt and was resisting an impulse to look at her.

"One can always keep climbing," she murmured, "and never give up —" Miss Josephine, also, was tilting her teacup and looking studiously into it as if she would read her fortune in the specks of tea leaves there.

"Like the frog in the well-that climbed one jump and fell back two!" he interrupted, but she paid no attention, and went on.

"And the reward for reaching the top —"

"Is there supposed to be a reward?" Ford could not tell why he asked her that, nor why he glanced stealthily at her from under his eyebrows as he awaited her reply.

"There-might-there usually is a reward for any great achievement-and —" Miss Josephine was plainly floundering where she had hoped to float airily upon the surface.

"What's the reward for-climbing hills, for instance?" He looked at her full, now, and his lips were ready to smile.

Miss Josephine looked uneasily at the door. "I —really, I never-investigated the matter at all." She gave a twitch of shoulders and met his eyes steadily. "The inner satisfaction of having climbed the hill, I suppose," she said, in the tone of one who has at last reached firm ground. "Will you have more tea, Mr. Campbell?"

Her final words were chilly and impersonal, but Ford left the table, smiling to himself. At the door he met Dick, whom Buddy had mentioned with disaster to himself. Dick saw the smile, and within the room he saw Miss Josephine sitting alone, her chin resting in her two palms and her eyes fixed upon vacancy.

"Hello," Ford greeted somewhat inattentively. "Do you want me for anything, Dick?"

"Can't say I do," drawled Dick, brushing past Ford in the doorway.

Ford hesitated long enough to give him a second glance-an attentive enough glance this time-and went his way; without the smile, however.

"Lordy me!" he said to himself, when his foot touched the bridge, but he did not add anything to the exclamation. He was wondering when it was that he had begun to dislike Dick

Thomas; a long while, it seemed to him, though he had never till just now quite realized it, beyond resenting his covert sneer that day in town. He had once or twice since suspected Dick of a certain disappointment that he himself was not foreman of the Double Cross, and once he had asked Mason why he hadn't given the place to Dick.

"Didn't want to," Mason had replied succinctly, and let it go at that.

If Dick cherished any animosity, however, he had not made it manifest in actual hostility. On the contrary, he had shown a distinct inclination to be friendly; a friendliness which led the two to pair off frequently when they were riding, and to talk over past range experiences more or less intimately. Looking back over the six weeks just behind him, Ford could not remember a single incident —a sentence, even-that had been unpleasant, unless he clung to his belief in Dick's contempt, and that he had since set down to his own super-sensitiveness. And yet —

"He's got bad eyes," he concluded. "That's what it is; I never did like eyes the color of polished steel; nickel-plated eyes, I call 'em; all shine and no color. Still, a man ain't to blame for his eyes."

Then Dick overtook him with Buddy trailing, red-eyed, at his heels, and Ford forgot, in the work to be done that day, all about his speculations. He involved himself in a fruitless argument with Buddy, upon the subject of what a seven-year-old can stand in the way of riding, and yielded finally before the quiver of Buddy's lips. They were only going over on Long Ridge, anyway, and the day was fine, and Buddy had frequently ridden as far, according to Dick. Indeed, it was Dick's easy-natured, "Ah, let the kid go, why don't you?" which gave Ford an excuse for reconsidering.

And Buddy repaid him after his usual fashion. At the supper table he looked up, round-eyed, from his plate.

"Gee, but I'm hungry!" he sighed. "I eat and eat, just like a horse eating hay, and I just can't fill up the hole in me."

"There, never mind, honey," Mrs. Kate interposed hastily, fearing worse. "Do you want more bread and butter?"

"Yes-you always use bread for stuffing, don't you? I want to be stuffed. All the way home my b —my stomerch was a-flopping against my backbone, just like Dick's. Only Dick said —"

"Never mind what Dick said." Mrs. Kate thrust the bread toward him, half buttered.

"Dick's mad, I guess. He's mad at Ford, too."

Buddy regarded his mother gravely over the slice of bread.

"First I've heard of it," Ford remarked lightly. "I think you must be mistaken, old-timer."

But Buddy never considered himself mistaken about anything, and he did not like being told that he was, even when the pill was sweetened with the term "old-timer." He rolled his eyes at Ford resentfully.

"Dick is mad! He got mad when you galloped over where Jo's red ribbon was hanging onto a bush. I saw him a-scowling when you rolled it up and put it in your shirt pocket. Dick wanted that ribbon for his bridle; and you better give it to him. Jo ain't your girl. She's Dick's girl. And you have to tie the ribbon of your bestest girl on your bridle. That's why," he added, with belated gallantry, "I tie my own mamma's ribbons on mine. And," he returned with terrible directness to the real issue, "Jo's Dick's girl, 'cause he said so. I heard him tell Jim Felton she's his steady, all right-and you are his girl, ain't you, Jo?"

His mother had tried at first to stop him, had given up in despair, and was now sitting in a rather tragic calm, waiting for what might come of his speech.

Josephine might have saved herself some anxious moments, if she had been so minded; perhaps she would have been minded, if she had not caught Ford's eyes fixed rather intently upon her, and sensed the expectancy in them. She bit her lip, and then she laughed.

"A man shouldn't make an assertion of that sort," she said quizzically, in the direction of Buddy-though her meaning went straight across the table to another —"unless he has some reason for feeling very sure."

Buddy tried to appear quite clear as to her meaning. "Well, if you are Dick's girl, then you better make Ford give that ribbon —"

"I have plenty of ribbons, Buddy," Josephine interrupted, smiling at him still. "Don't you want one?"

"I tie my own mamma's ribbons on my bridle," Buddy rebuffed. "My mamma is my girl-you ain't. You can give your ribbons to Dick."

"Mamma won't be your girl if you don't stop talking so much at the table-and elsewhere," Mrs. Kate informed him sternly, with a glance of trepidation at the others. "A little boy mustn't talk about grown-ups, and what they do or say."

"What can I talk about, then? The boys talk about their girls all the time —"

"I wish to goodness I had let you go with your dad. I shall not let you eat with us, anyway, if you don't keep quiet. You're getting perfectly impossible." Which even Buddy understood as a protest which was not to be taken seriously.

Ford stayed long enough to finish drinking his tea, and then he left the house with what he privately considered a perfectly casual manner. As a matter of fact, he was extremely self-conscious about it, so that Mrs. Kate felt justified in mentioning it, and in asking Josephine a question or two-when she had prudently made an errand elsewhere for Buddy.

Josephine, having promptly disclaimed all knowledge or interest pertaining to the affair, Mrs. Kate spoke her mind plainly.

"If Ford's going to fall in love with you, Phenie," she said, "I think you're foolish to encourage Dick. I believe Ford is falling in love with you. I never thought he even liked you till to-night, but what Buddy said about that ribbon —"

"I don't suppose Bud knows what he's talking about-any more than you do," snapped Josephine. "If you're determined that I shall have a love affair on this ranch, I'm going home." She planted her chin in her two palms, just as she had done at dinner, and stared into vacancy.

"Where?" asked Mrs. Kate pointedly, and then atoned for it whole-heartedly. "There, I didn't mean that-only-this is your home. It's got to be; I won't let it be anywhere else. And you needn't have any love affair, Phene-you know that. Only you shan't hurt Ford. I think he's perfectly splendid! What he did for Chester —I —I can't think of that without getting a lump in my throat, Phene. Think of it! Going without food himself, because there wasn't enough for two, and-and-well, he just simply threw away his own chance of getting through, to give Chester a better one. It was the bravest thing I ever heard of! And the way he has conquered —?"

"How do you know he has conquered? Rumor says he hasn't. And lots of men save other men's lives; it's being done every day, and no one hears much about it. You think it was something extraordinary, just because it happened to be Chester that was saved. Anybody will do all he can for a sick partner, when they're away out in the wilds. I haven't a doubt Dick would have done the very same thing, when it comes to that." Josephine got up from the table then, and went haughtily into her own room.

Mrs. Kate retired quite as haughtily into the kitchen, and there was a distinct coolness between them for the rest of the day, and a part of the next. The chill of it affected Ford sufficiently to keep him away from the house as much as possible, and unusually silent and unlike himself when he was with the men.

But, unlike many another, he did not know that his recurrent dissatisfaction with life was directly traceable to the apparent intimacy between Josephine and Dick. Ford, if he had tried to put his gloomy unrest into words, would have transposed his trouble and would have mistaken effect for cause. In other words, he would have ignored Josephine and Dick entirely, and would have said that he wanted whisky-and wanted it as the damned are said to want water.

## Chapter XII. At Hand-Grips with the Demon

Mose was mad. He was flinging tinware about the kitchen with a fine disregard of the din or the dents, and whenever the blue cat ventured out from under the stove, he kicked at it viciously. He was mad at Ford; and when a man gets mad at his foreman-without knowing that the foreman has been instructed to bear with his faults and keep him on the pay-roll at any price-he must, if he be the cook, have recourse to kicking cats and banging dishes about, since he dare not kick the foreman. For in late November "jobs" are not at all plentiful in the range land, and even an angry cook must keep his job or face the world-old economic problem of food, clothing, and shelter.

But if he dared not speak his mind plainly to Ford, he was not averse to pouring his woes into the first sympathetic ear that came his way. It happened that upon this occasion the ear arrived speedily upon the head of Dick Thomas.

"Matter, Mose?" he queried, sidestepping the cat, which gave a long leap straight for the door, when it opened. "Cat been licking the butter again?"

Mose grunted and slammed three pie tins into a cupboard with such force that two of them bounced out and rolled across the floor. One came within reach of his foot, and he kicked it into the wood-box, and swore at it while it was on the way. "And I wisht it was Ford Campbell himself, the snoopin', stingy, kitchen-grannying, booze-fightin', son-of-a-sour-dough bannock!" he finished prayerfully.

"He surely hasn't tried to mix in here, and meddle with you?" Dick asked, helping himself to a piece of pie. You know the tone; it had just that inflection of surprised sympathy which makes you tell your troubles without that reservation which a more neutral listener would unconsciously impel.

I am not going to give Mose's version, because he warped the story to make it fit his own indignation, and did not do Ford justice. This, then, is the exact truth:

Ford chanced to be walking up along the edge of the gully which ran past the bunk-house, and into which empty cans and other garbage were thrown. Sometimes a can fell short, so that all the gully edge was liberally decorated with a gay assortment of canners' labels. Just as he had come up, Mose had opened the kitchen door and thrown out a cream can, which had fallen in front of Ford and trickled a white stream upon the frozen ground. Ford had stooped and picked up the can, had shaken it, and heard the slosh which told of waste. He had investigated further, and decided that throwing out a cream can before it was quite empty was not an accident with Mose, but might be termed a habit. He had taken Exhibit A to the kitchen, but had laughed while he spoke of it. And these were his exact words:

"Lordy me, Mose! Somebody's liable to come here and get rich off us, if we don't look out. He'll gather up the cream cans you throw into the discard and start a dairy on the leavings." Then he had set the can down on the water bench beside the door and gone away.

"I've been cookin' for cow-camps ever since I got my knee stiffened up so's't I couldn't ride and that's sixteen year ago last Fourth-and it's the first time I ever had any darned foreman go snoopin' around my back door to see if I scrape out the cans clean!" Mose seated himself upon a corner of the table with the stiff leg for a brace and the good one swinging free, and folded his bare arms upon his heaving chest.

"And that ain't all, Dick," he went on aggrievedly. "He went and cut down the order I give him for grub. That's something Ches never done-not with me, anyway. Asked me-asked me, what I wanted with so much choc'late. And I wanted boiled cider for m' mince-meat, and never got it. And brandy, too-only I didn't put that down on the list; I knowed better than to write it out. But I give Jim money-out uh my own pocket! —to git some with, and he never done it. Said Ford told him p'tic'ler not to bring out nothin' any nearer drinkable than lemon extract! I've got a darned good mind," he added somberly, "to fire the hull works into the gully. He don't belong on no cow ranch. Where he'd oughta be is runnin' the W.C.T.U. So darned afraid of a pint uh brandy —"

"If I was dead sure your brains wouldn't get to leaking out your mouth," Dick began guardedly, "I might put you wise to something." He took a drink of water, opened the door that he might throw out what remained in the dipper, and made sure that no one was near the bunk-house before he closed the door again. Mose watched him interestedly.

"You know me, Dick—I never do tell all I know," he hinted heavily.

"Well," Dick stood with his hand upon the door-knob and a sly grin upon his face, "I ain't saying a word about anything. Only-if you might happen to want some-eggs-for your mince pies, you might look good under the southeast corner of the third haystack, counting from the big corral. I believe there's a —nest-there."

"The deuce!" Mose brightened understandingly and drummed with his fingers upon his bare, dough-caked forearm. "Do yuh know who-er-what hen laid 'em there?"

"I do," said Dick with a rising inflection. "The head he-hen uh the flock. But if I was going to hunt eggs, I'd take down a chiny egg and leave it in the nest, Mose."

"But I ain't got —" Mose caught Dick's pale glance resting with what might be considered some significance upon the vinegar jug, and he stopped short. "That wouldn't work," he commented vaguely.

"Well, I've got to be going. Boss might can me if he caught me loafing around here, eating pie when I ought to be working. Ford's a fine fellow, don't you think?" He grinned and went out, and immediately returned, complaining that he never could stand socks with a hole in the toe, and he guessed he'd have to hunt through his war-bag for a good pair.

Mose, as need scarcely be explained, went immediately to the stable to hunt eggs; and Dick, in the next room, smiled to himself when he heard the door slam behind him. Dick did not change his socks just then; he went first into the kitchen and busied himself there, and he continued to smile to himself. Later he went out and met Ford, who was riding moodily up from the river field.

"Say, I'm going to be an interfering kind of a cuss, and put you next to something," he began, with just the right degree of hesitation in his manner. "It ain't any of my business, but —" He stopped and lighted a cigarette. "If you'll come up to the bunk-house, I'll show you something funny!"

Ford dismounted in silence, led his horse into the stable, and without waiting to unsaddle, followed Dick.

"We've got to hurry, before Mose gets back from hunting eggs," Dick remarked, by way of explaining the long strides he took. "And of course I'm taking it for granted, Ford, that you won't say anything. I kinda thought you ought to know, maybe-but I'd never say a word if I didn't feel pretty sure you'd keep it behind your teeth."

"Well—I'm waiting to see what it is," Ford replied non-committally.

Dick opened the kitchen door, and led Ford through that into the bunk-room. "You wait here —I'm afraid Mose might come back," he said, and went into the kitchen. When he returned he had a gallon jug in his hand. He was still smiling.

"I went to mix me up some soda-water for heartburn," he said, "and when I picked up this jug, Mose took it out of my hand and said it was boiled cider, that he'd got for mince-meat. So when he went out, I took a taste. Here: You sample it yourself, Ford. If that's boiled cider, I wouldn't mind having a barrel!"

Ford took the jug, pulled the cork, and sniffed at the opening. He did not say anything, but he looked up at Dick significantly.

"Taste it once!" urged Dick innocently. "I'd just like to have you see the brand of slow poison a fool like Mose will pour down him."

Ford hesitated, sniffed, started to set down the jug, then lifted it and took a swallow.

"That isn't as bad as some I've seen," he pronounced evenly, shoving in the cork. "Nor as good," he added conservatively. "I wonder where he got it."

"Search me-oh, by jiminy, here he comes! I'm going to take a scoot, Ford. Don't give me away, will you? And if I was you, I wouldn't say anything to Mose —I know that old devil pretty well. He'll keep mighty quiet about it himself-unless you jump him about it. Then he'll roar around to everybody he sees, and claim it was a plant."

He slid stealthily through the outer door, and Ford saw him run down into the gully and disappear, while Mose was yet half-way from the stable.

Ford sat on the edge of a bunk and looked at the jug beside him. If Dick had deliberately planned to tempt him, he had chosen the time well; and if he had not done it deliberately, there must have been a malignant spirit abroad that day.

For twenty-four hours Ford had been more than usually restless and moody. Even Buddy had noticed that, and complained that Ford was cross and wouldn't talk to him; whereupon Mrs. Kate had scolded Josephine and accused her of being responsible for his gloom and silence. Since Josephine's conscience sustained the charge, she resented the accusation and proceeded deliberately to add to its justice; which did not make Ford any the happier, you may be sure. For when a man reaches that mental state which causes him to carry a girl's ribbon folded carefully into the most secret compartment of his pocketbook, and to avoid the girl herself and yet feel like committing assault and battery with intent to kill, because some other man occasionally rides with her for an hour or two, he is extremely sensitive to averted glances and chilly tones and monosyllabic conversation.

Since the day before, when she had ridden as far as the stage road with Dick, when he went to the line-camp, Ford had been fighting the desire to saddle a horse and ride to town; and the thing that lured him townward confronted him now in that gray stone jug with the brown neck and handle.

He lifted the jug, shook it tentatively, pulled out the cork with a jerk that was savage, and looked around the room for some place where he might empty the contents and have done with temptation; but there was no receptacle but the stove, so he started to the door with it, meaning to pour it on the ground. Mose just then shambled past the window, and Ford sat down to wait until the cook was safe in the kitchen. And all the while the cork was out of that jug, so that the fumes of the whisky rose maddeningly to his nostrils, and the little that he had swallowed whipped the thirst-devil to a fury of desire.

In the kitchen, Mose rattled pans and hummed a raucous tune under his breath, and presently he started again for the stable. Dick, desultorily bracing a leaning post of one of the corrals, saw him coming and grinned. He glanced toward the bunk-house, where Ford still lingered, and the grin grew broader. After that he went all around the corral with his hammer and bucket of nails, tightening poles and braces and, incidentally, keeping an eye upon the bunk-house; and while he worked, he whistled and smiled by turns. Dick was in an unusually cheerful mood that day.

Mose came shuffling up behind him and stood with his stiff leg thrust forward and his hands rolled up in his apron. Dick could see that he had something clasped tightly under the wrappings.

"Say, that he-lien  she laid twice in the same place!" Mose announced confidentially. "Got 'em both-for m'mince pies!" He waggled his head, winked twice with his left eye, and went back to the bunk-house.

Still Ford did not appear. Josephine came, however, in riding skirt and gray hat and gauntlets, treading lightly down the path that lay all in a yellow glow which was not so much sunlight as that mellow haze which we call Indian Summer. She looked in at the stable, and then came straight over to Dick. There was, when Josephine was her natural self, something very direct and honest about all her movements, as if she disdained all feminine subterfuges and took always the straight, open trail to her object.

"Do you know where Mr. Campbell is, Dick?" she asked him, and added no explanation of her desire to know.

"I do," said Dick, with the rising inflection which was his habit, when the words were used for a bait to catch another question.

"Well, where is he, then?"

Dick straightened up and smiled down upon her queerly. "Count ten before you ask me that again," he parried, "because maybe you'd rather not know."

Josephine lifted her chin and gave him that straight, measuring stare which had so annoyed Ford the first time he had seen her. "I have counted," she said calmly after a pause. "Where is Mr. Campbell, please?"—and the "please" pushed Dick to the very edge of her favor, it was so coldly formal.

"Well, if you're sure you counted straight, the last time I saw him he was in the bunk-house."

"Well?" The tone of her demanded more.

"He was in the bunk-house —sitting close up to a gallon jug of whisky." His eyelids flickered. "He's there yet-but I wouldn't swear to the gallon —"

"Thank you very much." This time her tone pushed him over the edge and into the depths of her disapproval. "I was sure I could depend upon you-to tell!"

"What else could I do, when you asked?"

But she had her back to him, and was walking away up the path, and if she heard, she did not trouble to answer. But in spite of her manner, Dick smiled, and brought the hammer down against a post with such force that he splintered the handle.

"Something's going to drop on this ranch, pretty quick," he prophesied, looking down at the useless tool in his hand. "And if I wanted to name it, I'd call it Ford." He glanced up the path to where Josephine was walking straight to the west door of the bunk-house, and laughed sourly. "Well, she needn't take my word for it if she don't want to, I guess," he muttered. "Nothing like heading off a critter-or a woman-in time!"

Josephine did not hesitate upon the doorstep. She opened the door and went in, and shut the door behind her before the echo of her step had died. Ford was lying as he had lain once before, upon a bunk, with his face hidden in his folded arms. He did not hear her-at any rate he did not know who it was, for he did not lift his head or stir.

Josephine looked at the jug upon the floor beside him, bent and lifted it very gently from the floor; tilted it to the window so that she could look into it, tilted her nose at the odor, and very, very gently put it back where she had found it. Then she stood and looked down at Ford with her eyebrows pinched together.

She did not move, after that, and she certainly did not speak, but her presence for all that became manifest to him. He lifted his head and stared at her over an elbow; and his eyes were heavy with trouble, and his mouth was set in lines of bitterness.

"Did you want me for something?" he asked, when he saw that she was not going to speak first.

She shook her head. "Is it-pretty steep?" she ventured after a moment, and glanced down at the jug.

He looked puzzled at first, but when his own glance followed hers, he understood. He stared up at her somberly before he let his head drop back upon his arms, so that his face was once more hidden.

"You've never been in bell, I suppose," he told her, and his voice was dull and tired. After a minute he looked up at her impatiently. "Is it fun to stand and watch a man-What do you want, anyway? It doesn't matter-to you."

"Are you sure?" she retorted sharply. "And-suppose it doesn't. I have Kate to think of, at least."

He gave a little laugh that came nearer being a snort. "Oh, if that's all, you needn't worry. I'm not quite that far gone, thank you!"

"I was thinking of the ranch, and of her ideals, and her blind trust in you, and of the effect on the cmen," she explained impatiently.

He was silent a moment. "I'm thinking of myself!" he told her grimly then.

"And-don't you ever-think of me?" She set her teeth sharply together after the words were out, and watched him, breathing quickly.

Ford sprang up from the bunk and faced her with stern questioning in his eyes, but she only flushed a little under his scrutiny. Her eyes, he noticed, were clear and steady, and they had in them something of that courage which fears but will not flinch.

"I don't want to think of you!" he said, lowering his voice unconsciously. "For the last month I've tried mighty hard not to think of you. And if you want to know why—I'm married!"

She leaned back against the door and stared up at him with widening pupils. Ford looked down and struck the jug with his toe. "That thing," he said slowly, "I've got to fight alone. I don't know which is going to come out winner, me or the booze. I—don't—know." He lifted his head and looked at her. "What did you come in here for?" he asked bluntly.

She caught her breath, but she would not dodge. Ford loved her for that. "Dick told me-and I was—I wanted to-well, help. I thought I might-sometimes when the climb is too steep, a hand will keep one from-slipping."

"What made you want to help? You don't even like me." His tone was flat and unemotional, but she did not seem able to meet his eyes. So she looked down at the jug.

"Dick said-but the jug is full practically. I don't understand how—"

"It isn't as full as it ought to be; it lacks one swallow." He eyed it queerly. "I wish I knew how much it would lack by dark," he said.

She threw out an impulsive hand. "Oh, but you must make up your mind! You mustn't temporize like that, or wonder-or —"

"This," he interrupted rather flippantly, "is something little girls can't understand. They'd better not try. This isn't a woman's problem, to be solved by argument. It's a man's fight!"

"But if you would just make up your mind, you could win."

"Could I?" His tone was amusedly skeptical, but his eyes were still somber.

"Even a woman," she said impatiently, "knows that is not the way to win a fight-to send for the enemy and give him all your weapons, and a plan of the fortifications, and the password; when you know there's no mercy to be hoped for!"

He smiled at her simile, and at her earnestness also, perhaps; but that black gloom remained, looking out of his eyes.

"What made you send for it? A whole gallon!"

"I didn't send for it. That jug belongs to Mose," he told her simply. "Dick told me Mose had it; rather, Dick went into the kitchen and got it, and turned it over to me." In spite of the words, he did not give one the impression that he was defending himself; he was merely offering an explanation because she seemed to demand one.

"Dick got it and turned it over to you!" Her forehead wrinkled again into vertical lines. She studied him frowningly. "Will you give it to me?" she asked directly.

Ford folded his arms and scowled down at the jug. "No," he refused at last, "I won't. If booze is going to be the boss of me I want to know it. And I can't know it too quick."

"But-you're only human, Ford!"

"Sure. But I'm kinda hoping I'm a man, too." His eyes lightened a little while they rested upon her.

"But you've got the poison of it-it's like a traitor in your fort, ready to open the door. You can't do it! I —oh, you'll never understand why, but I can't let you risk it. You've got to let me help; give it to me, Ford!"

"No, You go on to the house, and don't bother about me. You can't help-nobody can. It's up to me."

She struck her hands together in a nervous rage. "You want to keep it because you want to drink it! If you didn't want it, you'd hate to be near it. You'd want some one to take it away. You just want to get drunk, and be a beast. You-you-oh-you don't know what you're doing, or how much it means! You don't know!" Her hands went up suddenly and covered her face.

Ford walked the length of the room away from her, turned and came back until he faced her where she stood leaning against the door, with her face still hidden behind her palms. He reached out his arms to her, hesitated, and drew them back.

"I wish you'd go," he said. "There are some things harder to fight than whisky. You only make it worse."

"I'll go when you give me that." She flung a hand out toward the jug.

"You'll go anyway!" He took her by the arm, quietly pulled her away from the door, opened it, and then closed it while, for just a breath or two, he held her tightly clasped in his arms. Very gently, after that, he pushed her out upon the doorstep and shut the door behind her. The lock clicked a hint which she could not fail to hear and understand. He waited until he heard her walk away, sat down with the air of a man who is very, very weary, rested his elbows upon his knees, and with his hands clasped loosely together, he glowered at the jug on the floor. Then the soul of Ford Campbell went deep down into the pit where all the devils dwell.

# Chapter XIII. A Plan Gone Wrong

It was Mose crashing headlong into the old messbox where he kept rattly basins, empty lard pails, and such, that roused Ford. He got up and went into the kitchen, and when he saw what was, the matter, extricated Mose by the simple method of grabbing his shoulders and pulling hard; then he set the cook upon his feet, and got full in his face the unmistakable fumes of whisky.

"What? You got another jug?" he asked, with some disgust, steadying Mose against the wall.

"Ah —I ain't got any jug uh nothin'," Mose protested, rather thickly. "And I never took them bottles outa the stack; that musta been Dick done that. Get after him about it; he's the one told me where yuh hid 'em-but I never touched 'em, honest I never. If they're gone, you get after Dick. Don't yuh go 'n' lay it on me, now!" He was whimpering with maudlin pathos before he finished. Ford scowled at him thoughtfully.

"Dick told you about the bottles in the haystack, did he?" he asked. "Which stack was it? And how many bottles?"

Mose gave him a bleary stare. "Aw, you know. You hid 'em there yourself! Dick said so. I ain't goin' to say which stack, or how many bottles-or-any other-darn thing about it." He punctuated his phrases by prodding a finger against Ford's chest, and he wagged his head with all the self-consciousness of spurious virtue. "Promised Dick I wouldn't, and I won't. Not a — darn-word about it. Wanted some-for m' mince-meat, but I never took any outa the haystack." Whereupon he began to show a pronounced limpness in his good leg, and a tendency to slide down upon the floor.

Ford piloted him to a chair, eased him into it, and stood over him in frowning meditation. Mose was drunk; absolutely, undeniably drunk. It could not have been the jug, for the jug was full. Till then the oddity of a full jug of whisky in Mose's kitchen after at least twenty-four hours must have elapsed since its arrival, had not occurred to him. He had been too preoccupied with his own fight to think much about Mose.

"Shay, I never took them bottles outa the stack," Mose looked up to protest solemnly. "Dick never told me about 'em, neither. Dick tol' me —" tapping Ford's arm with his finger for every word, " —'at there was aigs down there, for m' mince-meat." He stopped suddenly and goggled up at Ford. "Shay, yuh don't put aigs in-mince-meat," he informed him earnestly. "Not a darn aig! That's what Dick tol' me-aigs for m' mince-meat. Oh, I knowed right off what he meant, all right," he explained proudly. "He didn't wanta come right out 'n' shay what it was-an' I —got-the-aigs!"

"Yes-how many-eggs?" Ford held himself rigidly quiet.

"Two quart-aigs!" Mose laughed at the joke. "I wisht," he added pensively, "the hens'd all lay them kinda aigs. I'd buy up all the shickens in-the whole worl'." He gazed raptly upon the vision the words conjured. "Gee! Quart aigs —'n' all the shickens in the worl' layin' reg'lar!"

"Have you got any left?"

"No-honest. Used 'em all up-for m' mince-meat!"

Ford knew he was lying. His eyes searched the untidy tables and the corners filled with bags and boxes. Mose was a good cook, but his ideas of order were vague, and his system of housekeeping was the simple one of leaving everything where he had last been using it, so that it might be handy when he wanted it again. A dozen bottles might be concealed there, like the faces in a picture-puzzle, and it would take a housecleaning to disclose them all. But Ford, when he knew that no bottle had been left in sight, began turning over the bags and looking behind the boxes.

He must have been "growing warm" when he stood wondering whether it was worth while to look into the flour-bin, for Mose gave an inarticulate snarl and pounced on him from behind. The weight of him sent Ford down on all fours and kept him there for a space, and even after he was up he found himself quite busy. Mose was a husky individual, with no infirmity of the arms and fists, even if he did have a stiff leg, and drunkenness frequently flares and fades in a man like a candle guttering in the wind. Besides, Mose was fighting to save his whisky.

Still, Ford had not sent all of Sunset into its cellars, figuratively speaking, for nothing; and while a man may feel more enthusiasm for fighting when under the influence of the stuff that cheers sometimes and never fails to inebriate, the added incentive does not necessarily mean also added muscular development or more weight behind the punch. Ford, fighting as he had always fought, be he drunk or sober, came speedily to the point where he could inspect a skinned knuckle and afterwards gaze in peace upon his antagonist.

He was occupied with both diversions when the door was pushed open as by a man in great haste. He looked up from the knuckle into the expectant eyes of Jim Felton, and over the shoulder of Jim he saw a gloating certainty writ large upon the face of Dick Thomas. They had been running; he could tell that by their uneven breathing, and it occurred to him that they must have heard the clamor when he pitched Mose head first into the dish cupboard. There had been considerable noise about that time, he remembered; they must also have heard the howl Mose gave at the instant of contact. Ford glanced involuntarily at that side of the room where stood the cupboard, and mentally admitted that it looked like there had been a slight disagreement, or else a severe seismic disturbance; and Montana is not what one calls an earthquake country. His eyes left the generous sprinkle of broken dishes on the floor, with Mose sprawled inertly in their midst, looking not unlike a broken platter himself-or one badly nicked-and rested again upon the grinning face behind the shoulder of Jim Felton.

Ford was ever a man of not many words, even when he had a grievance. He made straight for Dick, and when he had pushed Jim out of the way, he reached him violently. Dick tottered upon the step and went off backward, and Ford landed upon him fairly and with full knowledge and intent.

Dick tottered upon the step and went off backward.

Jim Felton was a wise young man. He stood back and let them fight it out, and when it was over he said never a word until Dick had picked himself up and walked off, holding to his nose a handkerchief that reddened rapidly.

"Say, you are a son-of-a-gun to fight," he observed admiringly then to Ford. "Don't you know Dick's supposed to be abso-lute-ly unlickable?"

"May be so-but he sure shows all the symptoms of being licked right at present." Ford moved a thumb joint gently to see whether it was really dislocated or merely felt that way.

"He's going up to the house now, to tell the missus," remarked Jim, craning his neck from the doorway.

"If he does that," Ford replied calmly, "I'll half kill him next time. What I gave him just now is only a sample package left on the doorstep to try." He sat down upon a corner of the table and began to make himself a smoke. "Is he going up to the house-honest?" He would not yield to the impulse to look and see for himself.

"We-el, the trail he's taking has no other logical destination," drawled Jim. "He's across the bridge." When Ford showed no disposition to say anything to that, Jim came in and closed the door. "Say, what laid old Mose out so nice?" he asked, with an indolent sort of curiosity. "Booze? Or just bumps?"

"A little of both," said Ford indifferently, between puffs. He was thinking of the tale Dick would tell at the house, and he was thinking of the probable effect upon one listener; the other didn't worry him, though he liked Mrs. Kate very much.

Jim went over and investigated; discovering that Mose was close to snoring, he sat upon a corner of the other table, swung a spurred boot, and regarded Ford interestedly over his own cigarette building. "Say, for a man that's supposed to be soused," he began, after a silence, "you act and talk remarkably lucid. I wish I could carry booze like that," he added regretfully. "But I can't; my tongue and my legs always betray the guilty secret. Have you got any particular system, or is it just a gift?"

"No" —Ford shook his head —"nothing like that. I just don't happen to be drunk." He eyed Jim sharply while he considered within himself. "It looks to me," he began, after a moment, "as if our friend Dick had framed up a nice little plant. One way and another I got wise to the whole thing; but for the life of me, I can't see what made him do it. Lordy me! I never kicked him on any bunion!" He grinned, as memory flashed a brief, mental picture of Sunset and certain incidents which occurred there. But memory never lets well enough alone, and one is lucky to escape without seeing a picture that leaves a sting; Ford's smile ended in a scowl.

"Jealousy, old man," Jim pronounced without hesitation. "Of course, I don't know the details, but-details be darned. If he has tried to hand you a package, take it from me, jealousy's the string he tied it with. I don't mind saying that Dick told me when I first rode up to the corral that you and Mose were both boozing up to beat the band; and right after that we heard a deuce of a racket up here, and it did look—" He waved an apologetic hand at Mose and the fragments of pottery which framed like a "still life" picture on the floor, and let it go at that. "I'm strong for you, Ford," he added, and his smile was frank and friendly. "Double Cross is the name of this outfit, but I'm all in favor of running that brand on the cow-critters and keeping it out of the bunk-house. If you should happen to feel like elucidating—" he hinted delicately.

Ford had always liked Jim Felton; now he warmed to him as a real friend, and certain things he told him. As much about the jug with the brown neck and handle as concerned Dick, and all he knew of the bottles in the haystack, while Jim smoked, and swung the foot which did not rest upon the floor, and listened.

"Sounds like Dick, all right," he passed judgment, when Ford had finished. "He counted on your falling for the jug-and oh, my! It was a beautiful plant. I'd sure hate to have anybody sing 'Yield not to temptation' at me, if a gallon jug of the real stuff fell into my arms and nobody was looking." He eyed Ford queerly. "You've got quite a reputation—" he ventured.

"Well, I earned it," Ford observed laconically.

"Dick banked on it —I'd stake my whole stack of blues on that. And after you'd torn up the ranch, and pitched the fragments into the gulch, he'd hold the last trump, with all high cards to keep the lead. Whee!" He meditated admiringly upon the strategy. "But what I can't seem to understand," he said frankly, "is why the deuce it didn't work! Is your swallower out of kilter? If you don't mind my asking!"

"I never noticed that it was paralyzed," Ford answered grimly. He got up, lifted a lid of the stove, and threw in the cigarette stub mechanically. Then he bethought him of his interrupted search, and prodded a long-handled spoon into the flour bin, struck something smooth and hard, and drew out a befloured, quart bottle half full of whisky. He wiped the bottle carefully, inspected it briefly, and pitched it into the gully, where it smashed odorously upon a rock. Jim, watching him, knew that he was thinking all the while of something else. When Ford spoke, he proved it.

"Are you any good at all in the kitchen, Jim?" he asked, turning to him as if he had decided just how he would meet the situation.

"Well, I hate to brag, but I've known of men eating my grub and going right on living as if nothing had happened," Jim admitted modestly.

"Well, you turn yourself loose in here, will you? The boys will be good and empty when they come-it's dinner time right now. I'll help you carry Mose out of the way before I go."

Jim looked as if he would like to ask what Ford meant to do, but he refrained. There was something besides preoccupation in Ford's face, and it did not make for easy questioning. Jim did yield to his curiosity to the extent of watching through a window, when Ford went out, to see where he was going; and when he saw Ford had the jug, and that he took the path which led across the little bridge and so to the house, he drew back and said "Whee-e-e!" under his breath. Then he remarked to the recumbent Mose, who was not in a condition either to hear or understand: "I'll bet you Dick's got all he wants, right now, without any postscript." After which Jim hunted up a clean apron and proceeded, with his spurs on his heels, his hat on the back of his head, and a smile upon his lips, to sweep out the broken dishes so that he might walk without hearing them crunch unpleasantly under his boots. "I'll take wildcats in mine, please," he remarked once irrelevantly aloud, and smiled again.

# Chapter XIV. The Feminine Point of View

When Ford stepped upon the porch with the jug in his hand, he gave every indication of having definitely made up his mind. When he glimpsed Josephine's worried face behind the lace curtain in the window, he dropped the jug lower and held it against his leg in such a way as to indicate that he hoped she could not see it, but otherwise he gave no sign of perturbation. He walked along the porch to the door of his own room, went in, locked the door after him, and put the jug down on a chair. He could hear faint sounds of dishes being placed upon the table in the dining-room, which was next to his own, and he knew that dinner was half an hour late; which was unusual in Mrs. Kate's orderly domain. Mrs. Kate was one of those excellent women whose house is always immaculate, whose meals are ever placed before one when the clock points to a certain hour, and whose table never lacks a salad and a dessert-though how those feats are accomplished upon a cattle ranch must ever remain a mystery. Ford was therefore justified in taking the second look at his watch and in holding it up to his ear, and also in lifting his eyebrows when all was done. Fifteen minutes by the watch it was before he heard the silvery tinkle of the tea bell, which was one of the ties which bound Mrs. Kate to civilization, and which announced that he might enter the dining-room.

He went in as clean and fresh and straight-backed and quiet as ever he had done, and when he saw that the room was empty save for Buddy, perched upon his long-legged chair with his heels hooked over the top round and a napkin tucked expectantly inside the collar of his blue blouse, he took in the situation and sat down without waiting for the women. The very first glance told him that Mrs. Kate had never prepared that meal. It was, putting it bluntly, a scrappy affair hastily gathered from various shelves in the pantry and hurriedly arranged haphazard upon the table.

Buddy gazed upon the sprinkle of dishes with undisguised dissatisfaction. "There ain't any potatoes," he announced gloomily. "My own mamma always cooks potatoes. Josephine's the limit! I been working to-day. I almost dug out a badger, over by the bluff. I got where I could hear him scratching to get away, and then it was all rocks, so I couldn't dig any more. Gee, it was hard digging! And I'm just about starved, if you want to know. And there ain't any potatoes."

"Bread and butter is fine when you're hungry," Ford suggested, and spread a slice for Buddy, somewhat inattentively, because he was also keeping an eye upon the kitchen door, where he had caught a fleeting glimpse of Josephine looking in at him.

"You're putting the butter all in one place," Buddy criticised, with his usual frankness. "I guess you're drunk, all right. If you're too drunk to spread butter, let me do it."

"What makes you think I'm drunk?" Ford questioned, lowering his voice because of the person he suspected was in the kitchen.

"Mamma and Jo was quarreling about it; that's why. And my own mamma cried, and shut the door, and wouldn't let me go in. And Jo pretty near cried too, all right. I guess she did, only not when any one was looking. Her eyes are awful red, anyway." Buddy took great, ravenous bites of the bread and butter and eyed Ford unwinkingly.

"What's disslepointed?" he demanded abruptly, after he had given himself a white mustache with his glass of milk.

"Why do you want to know?"

"That's what my own mamma is, and that's what Jo is. Only my own mamma is it about you, and Jo's it about mamma. Say, did you lick Dick? Jo told my own mamma she wisht you'd killed him. Jo's awful mad to-day. I guess she's mad at Dick, because he ain't very much of a fighter. Did you lick him easy? Did you paste him one in the jaw?"

Josephine entered then with Ford's belated tea. Her eyelids were pink, as Buddy had told him, and she did not look at him while she filled his cup.

"Kate has a sick headache," she explained primly, "and I did the best I could with lunch. I hope it's —"

"It is," Ford interrupted reassuringly. "Everything is fine and dandy."

"You didn't cook any potatoes!" Buddy charged mercilessly. "And Ford's too drunk to put the butter on right. I'm going to tell my dad that next time he goes to Oregon I'm going along. This outfit will sure go to the devil if he stays much longer!"

"Where did you hear that, Bud?" Josephine asked, still carefully avoiding a glance at Ford.

"Well, Dick said it would go to the devil. I guess," he added on his own account, with an eloquent look at the table, "it's on the trail right now."

Ford looked at Josephine, opened his lips to say that it might still be headed off, and decided not to speak. There was a stubborn streak in Ford Campbell. She had said some bitter things, in her anger. Perhaps she had not entirely believed them herself, and perhaps Mrs. Kate had not been accurately quoted by her precocious young son; she may not have said that she was disappointed in Ford. They might not have believed whatever it was Dick told them, and they might still have full confidence in him, Ford Campbell. Still, there was the stubborn streak which would not explain or defend. So he left the table, and went into his own room without any word save a muttered excuse; and that in spite of the fact that Josephine looked full at him, at last, and with a wistfulness that moved him almost to the point of taking her in his arms and kissing away the worry-if he could.

He went up to the table where stood the jug, looked at it, lifted it, and set it down again. Then he lifted it again and pulled the cork out with a jerk, wondering if the sound of it had reached through the thin partition to the ears of Josephine; he was guilty of hoping so. He put back the cork-this time carefully-walked to the outer door, turned the key, opened the door, and closed it again with a slam. Then, with a grim set of the lips, he walked softly into the closet and pulled the door nearly shut.

He knew there was a chance that Josephine, if she were interested in his movements, would go immediately into the sitting-room, where she could see the path, and would know that he had not really left the house. But she did not, evidently. She sat long enough in the dining-room for Ford to call himself a name or two and to feel exceedingly foolish over the trick, and to decide that it was a very childish one for a grown man to play upon a woman. Then she pushed back her chair, came straight toward his room, opened the door, and looked in; Ford knew, for he saw her through the crack he had left in the closet doorway. She stood there looking at the jug on the table, then went up and lifted it, much as Ford had done, and pulled the cork with a certain angry defiance. Perhaps, he guessed shrewdly, Josephine also felt rather foolish at what she was doing-and he smiled over the thought.

Josephine turned the jug to the light, shut one eye into an adorable squint, and peered in. Then she set the jug down and pushed the cork slowly into place; and her face was puzzled. Ford could have laughed aloud when he saw it, but instead he held his breath for fear she should discover him. She stood very still for a minute or two, staring at nothing at all; moved the jug into the exact place where it had stood before, and went out of the room on her toes.

So did Ford, for that matter, and he was in a cold terror lest she should look out and see him walking down the path where he should logically have walked more than five minutes before. He did not dare to turn and look-until he was outside the gate; then inspiration came to aid him and he went back boldly, stepped upon the porch with no effort at silence, opened his door, and went in as one who has a right there.

He heard the click of dishes which told that she was clearing the table, and he breathed freer. He walked across the room, waited a space, and walked back again, and then went out with his heart in its proper position in his chest; Ford was unused to feeling his heart rise to his palate, and the sensation was more novel than agreeable. When he went again down the path, there was a certain exhilaration in his step. His thoughts arranged themselves in clear-cut sentences, as if he were speaking, instead of those vague, almost wordless impressions which fill the brain ordinarily.

"She's keeping cases on that jug. She must care, or she wouldn't do that. She's worried a whole lot; I could see that, all along. Down at the bunk-house she called me Ford twice-and she said it meant a lot to her, whether I make good or not. I wonder-Lordy me! A man could make good, all right, and do it easy, if she cared! She doesn't know what to think-that jug staying right up to high-water mark, like that!" He laughed then, silently, and dwelt upon the picture she had made while she had stood there before the table.

"Lord! she'd want to kill me if she knew I hid in that closet, but I just had a hunch-that is, if she cared anything about it. I wonder if she did really say she wished I'd killed Dick?

"Anyway, I can fight it now, with her keeping cases on the quiet. I know I can fight it. Lordy me, I've got to fight it! I've got to make good; that's all there is about it. Wonder what she'll think when she sees that jug don't go down any? Wonder-oh, hell! She'd never care anything about me. If she did —" His thoughts went hazy with vague speculation, then clarified suddenly into one hard fact, like a rock thrusting up through the lazy sweep of a windless tide. "If she did care, I couldn't do anything. I'm married!"

His step lost a little of its spring, then, and he went into the bunk-house with much the same expression on his face as when he had left it an hour or so before.

He did not see Dick that day. The other boys watched him covertly, it seemed to him, and showed a disposition to talk among themselves. Jim was whistling cheerfully in the kitchen. He turned his head and laughed when Ford went in.

"I found a dead soldier behind the sack of spuds," Jim announced, and produced an empty bottle, mate to the one Ford had thrown into the gully. "And Dick didn't seem to have any appetite at all, and Mose is still in Sleepytown. I guess that's all the news at this end of the line. Er-hope everything is all right at the house?"

"Far as I could see, it was," Ford replied, with an inner sense of evasion. "I guess we'll just let her go as she looks, Jim. Did you say anything to the boys?"

Jim reddened under his tan, but he laughed disarmingly. "I cannot tell a lie," he confessed honestly, "and it was too good to keep to myself. I'm the most generous fellow you ever saw, when it comes to passing along a good story that won't hurt anybody's digestion. You don't care, do you? The joke ain't on you."

"If you'd asked me about it, I'd have said keep it under your hat. But —"

"And that would have been a sin and a shame," argued Jim, licking a finger he had just scorched on a hot kettle-handle. "The fellows all like a good story-and it don't sound any worse because it's on Dick. And say! I kinda got a clue to where he connected with that whisky. Walt says he come back from the line-camp with his overcoat rolled up and tied behind the saddle-and it wasn't what you could call a hot night, either. He musta had that jug wrapped up in it. I'll bet he sent in by Peterson, the other day, for it. He was over there, I know. He's sure a deliberate kind of a cuss, isn't he? Must have had this thing all figured out a week ago. The boys are all tickled to death at the way he got it in the neck; they know Dick pretty well. But if you'd told me not to say anything, I'd have said he stubbed his toe on his shadow and fell all over himself, and let it go at that."

"Lordy me! Jim, you needn't worry about it; you ought to know you can't keep a thing like this quiet, on a ranch. It doesn't matter much how he got that whisky here, either; I know well enough you didn't haul it out. I'd figured it out about as Walt says.

"Say, it looks as if you'll have to wrastle with the pots and pans till to-morrow. The lower fence I'll ride, this afternoon; did you get clear around the Pinnacle field?"

"I sure did-and she's tight as a drum. Say, Mose is a good cook, but he's a mighty punk housekeeper, if you ask me. I'm thinking of getting to work here with a hoe!"

So life, which had of late loomed big and bitter before the soul of Ford, slipped back into the groove of daily routine.

# Chapter XV. The Climb

Into its groove of routine slipped life at the Double Cross, but it did not move quite as smoothly as before. It was as if the "hill" which Ford was climbing suffered small landslides here and there, which threatened to block the trail below. Sometimes-still keeping to the simile-it was but a pebble or two kicked loose by Ford's heel; sometimes a bowlder which one must dodge.

Dick, for instance, must have likened Mose to a real landslide when he came at him the next day, with a roar of rage and the rolling-pin. Mose had sobered to the point where he wondered how it had all happened, and wanted to get his hands in the wool of the "nigger" said to lurk in woodpiles. He asked Jim, with various embellishments of speech, what it was all about, and Jim told him and told him truly.

"He was trying to queer you with the outfit, Mose, and that's a fact," he finished; which was the only exaggeration Jim was guilty of, for Dick had probably thought very little of Mose and his ultimate standing with the Double Cross. "And he was trying to queer Ford-but you can search me for the reason why he didn't make good, there."

Mose, like many of us, was a self-centered individual. He wasted a minute, perhaps, thinking of the trick upon Ford; but he spent all of that forenoon and well into the afternoon in deep meditation upon the affair as it concerned himself. And the first time Dick entered the presence of the cook, he got the result of Mose's reasoning.

"Tried to git me in bad, did yuh? Thought you'd git me fired, hey?" he shouted, as a sort of punctuation to the belaboring.

A rolling pin is considered a more or less fearsome weapon in the hands of a woman, I believe; when wielded by an incensed man who stands close to six feet and weighs a solid two hundred pounds, and who has the headache which follows inevitably in the wake of three pints of whisky administered internally in the short space of three hours or so, a rolling-pin should justly be classed with deadly weapons.

Jim said afterward that he never had believed it possible to act out the rough stuff of the silly supplements in the Sunday papers, but after seeing Mose perform with that rolling-pin, he was willing to call every edition of the "funny papers" realistic to a degree. Since it was Jim who helped pull Mose off, naturally he felt qualified to judge. Jim told Ford about the affair with sober face and eyes that laughed.

"And where's Dick?" Ford asked him, without committing himself upon the justice of the chastisement.

"Gone to bed, I believe. He didn't come out with anything worse than bumps, I guess-but what I saw of them are sure peaches; or maybe Italian prunes would hit them off closer; they're a fine purple shade. I ladled Three H all over him."

"I thought Dick was a fighter from Fighterville," grinned Ford, trying hard to remain non-committal and making a poor job of it.

"Well, he is, when he can stand up and box according to rule, or hit a man when he isn't looking. But my, oh! This wasn't a fight, Ford; this was like the pictures you see of an old woman lambasting her son-in-law with an umbrella. Dick never got a chance to begin. Whee-ee! Mose sure can handle a rolling-pin some!"

Ford laughed and went up to the house to his supper, and to the constrained atmosphere which was telling on his nerves more severely than did the gallon jug in his closet, and the moral effort it cost to keep that jug full to the neck.

He went in quietly, threw his hat on the bed, and sat down with an air of discouragement. It was not yet six o'clock, and he knew that Mrs. Kate would not have supper ready; but he wanted a quiet place in which to think, and he was closer to Josephine; though he would never have admitted to himself that her nearness was any comfort to him. He did admit, however, that the jug with the brown neck and handle pulled him to the room many times in spite of himself. He would take it from the corner of the closet and let his fingers close over the cork, but so far he had never yielded beyond that point. Always he had been able to set the jug back unopened.

He was getting circles under his eyes, two new creases had appeared on each side of his whimsical lips, and a permanent line was forming between his eyebrows; but he had not opened the jug, and it had been in his possession thirty-six hours. Thirty-six hours is not long, to be sure, when life runs smoothly with slight incidents to emphasize the figures on the dial, but it may seem long to the poor devil on the rack.

Just now Ford was trying to forget that a gallon of whisky stood in the right-hand corner of his closet, behind a pair of half-worn riding-boots that pinched his instep so that he seldom wore them, and that he had only to take the jug out from behind the boots, pull the cork, and lift the jug to his lips —

He caught himself leaning forward and staring at the closet door until his eyes ached with the strain. He drew back and passed his hand over his forehead; it ached, and he wanted to think about what he ought to do with Dick. He did not like to discharge him without first consulting Mrs. Kate, for he knew that Ches Mason was in the habit of talking things over with her, and since Mason was gone, she had assumed an air of latent authority. But Mrs. Kate had looked at him with such reproachful eyes, that day at dinner, and her voice had sounded so squeezed and unnatural, that he had felt too far removed from her for any discussion whatever to take place between them.

Besides, he knew he could prove absolutely nothing against Dick, if Dick were disposed to-ward flat denial. He might suspect-but the facts showed Ford the aggressor, and Mose also. What if Mrs. Kate declined to believe that Dick had put that jug of whisky in the kitchen, and had afterward given it to Ford? Ford had no means of knowing just what tale Dick had told her, but he did know that Mrs. Kate eyed him doubtfully, and that her conversation was forced and her manner constrained.

And Josephine was worse. Josephine had not spoken to him all that day. At breakfast she had not been present, and at dinner she had kept her eyes upon her plate and had nothing to say to any one.

He wished Mason was home, so that he could leave. It wouldn't matter then, he tried to be-lieve, what he did. He even dwelt upon the desire of Mason's return to the extent of calculating, with his eyes upon the fancy calendar on the wall opposite, the exact time of his absence. Ten days-there was no hope of release for another month, at least, and Ford sighed unconsciously when he thought of it; for although a month is not long, there was Josephine refusing to look at him, and there was Dick-and there was the jug in the closet.

As to Josephine, there was no help for it; he could not avoid her without making the avoidance plain to all observers, and Ford was proud. As to Dick, he would not send him off without some proof that he had broken an unwritten law of the Double Cross and brought whisky to the ranch; and of that he had no proof. As to his suspicions-well, he considered that Dick had almost paid the penalty for having roused them, and the matter would have to rest where it was; for Ford was just. As to the jug, he could empty it upon the ground and be done with that particular form of torture. But he felt sure that Josephine was secretly "keeping cases" on the jug; and Ford was stubborn.

That night Ford did not respond to the tinkle of the tea bell. His head ached abominably, and he did not want to see Josephine's averted face opposite him at the table. He lay still upon the bed where he had finally thrown himself, and let the bell tinkle until it was tired.

They sent Buddy in to see why he did not come. Buddy looked at him with the round, curious eyes of precocious childhood and went back and reported that Ford wasn't asleep, but was just lying there mad. Ford heard the shrill little voice innocently maligning him, and swore to himself; but, he did not move for all that. He lay thinking and fighting discouragement and thirst, while little table sounds came through the partition and made a clicking accompaniment to his thoughts.

If he were free, he was wondering between spells of temptation, would it do any good? Would Josephine care? There was no answer to that, or if there was he did not know what it was.

After awhile the two women began talking; he judged that Buddy had left them, because it was sheer madness to speak so freely before him. At first he paid no attention to what they were saying, beyond a grudging joy in the sound of Josephine's voice. It had come to that, with Ford! But when he heard his name spoken, and by her, he lifted shamelessly to an elbow and listened, glad that the walls were so thin, and that those who dwell in thin-partitioned houses are prone to forget that the other rooms may not be quite empty. They two spent most of their waking hours alone together, and habit breeds carelessness always.

"Do you suppose he's drunk?" Mrs. Kate asked, and her voice was full of uneasiness. "Chester says he's terrible when he gets started. I was sure he was perfectly safe! I just can't stand it to have him like this. Dick told me he's drinking a little all the time, and there's no telling when he'll break out, and-Oh, I think it's perfectly terrible!"

"Hsh-sh," warned Josephine.

"He went out, quite a while ago. I heard him," said Mrs. Kate, with rash certainty. "He hasn't been like himself since that day he fought Dick. He must be —"

"But how could he?" Josephine's voice interrupted sharply. "That jug he's got is full yet."

Ford could imagine Mrs. Kate shaking her head with the wisdom born of matrimony.

"Don't you suppose he could keep putting in water?" she asked pityingly. Ford almost choked when he heard that!

"I don't believe he would." Josephine's tone was dubious. "It doesn't seem to me that a man would do that; he'd think he was just spoiling what was left. That," she declared with a flash of inspiration, "is what a woman would do. And a man always does something different!" There was a pathetic note in the last sentence, which struck Ford oddly.

"Don't think you know men, my dear, until you've been married to one for eight years or so," said Mrs. Kate patronizingly. "When you've been —"

"Oh, for mercy's sake, do you think they're all alike?" Josephine's voice was tart and impatient. "I know enough about men to know they're all different. You can't judge one by another. And I don't believe that Ford is drinking at all. He's just —"

"Just what? —since you know so well!" Mrs. Kate was growing ironical.

"He's trying not to-and worrying." Her voice lowered until it took love to hear it. Ford did hear, and his breath came fast. He did not catch Mrs. Kate's reply; he was not in love with Mrs. Kate, and he was engaged in letting the words of Josephine sink into his very soul, and in telling himself over and over that she understood. It seemed to him a miracle of intuition, that she should sense the fight he was making; and since he felt that way about it, it was just as well he did not know that Jim Felton sensed it quite as keenly as Josephine-and with a far greater understanding of how bitter a fight it was, and for that reason a deeper sympathy.

"I wish Chester was here!" wailed Mrs. Kate, across the glow of his exultant thoughts. "I'm afraid to say anything to him myself, he's so morose. It's a shame, because he's so splendid when he's —himself."

"He's as much himself now as ever he was," Josephine defended hotly. "When he's drinking he's altogether —"

"You never saw him drunk," Mrs. Kate pointed to the weak spot in Josephine's defense of him. "Dick says —"

"Oh, do you believe everything Dick says? A week ago you were bitter against Dick and all enthusiasm for Ford."

"You were flirting with Dick then, and you'd hardly treat Ford decently. And Ford hadn't gone to drink —"

"Will you hush?" There were tears of anger in Josephine's voice. "He isn't, I tell you!"

"What does he keep that jug in the closet for? And every few hours he comes up to the house and goes into his room-and he never did that before. And have you noticed his eyes? He'll scarcely talk any more, and he just pretends to eat. At dinner to-day he scarcely touched a thing! It's a sure sign, Phenie."

Ford was growing tired of that sort of thing. It dimmed the radiance of Josephine's belief in him, to have Mrs. Kate so sure of his weakness. He got up from the bed as quietly as he could and left the house. He was even more thoughtful, after that, but not quite so gloomy-if one cared enough for his moods to make a fine distinction.

Have you ever observed the fact that many of life's grimmest battles and deepest tragedies scarce ripple the surface of trivial things? We are always rubbing elbows with the big issues and never knowing anything about it. Certainly no one at the Double Cross guessed what was always in the mind of the foreman. Jim thought he was "sore" because of Dick. Dick thought Ford was jealous of him, and trying to think of some scheme to "play even," without coming to open war. Mrs. Kate was positive, in her purely feminine mind-which was a very good mind, understand, but somewhat inadequate when brought to bear upon the big problems of life-that Ford was tippling in secret. Josephine thought-just what she said, probably, upon the chill day when she calmly asked Ford at the breakfast table if he would let her go with him.

Ford had casually remarked, in answer to a diffident question from Mrs. Kate, that he was going to ride out on Long Ridge and see if any stock was drifting back toward the ranch. He hadn't sent any one over that way for several days. Ford, be it said, had announced his intention deliberately, moved by a vague, unreasoning impulse.

"Can I go?" teased Buddy, from sheer force of habit; no one ever mentioned going anywhere, but Buddy shot that question into the conversation.

"No, you can't. You can't, with that cold," his mother vetoed promptly, and Buddy, whimpering over his hot cakes, knew well the futility of argument, when Mrs. Kate used that tone of finality.

"Will you let me go?" Josephine asked unexpectedly, and looked straight at Ford. But though her glance was direct, it was unreadable, and Ford mentally threw up his hands after one good look at her, and tried not to betray the fact that this was what he had wanted, but had not hoped for.

"Sure, you can go," he said, with deceitful brevity. Josephine had not spoken to him all the day before, except to say good-morning when he came in to his breakfast. Ford made no attempt to understand her, any more. He was carefully giving her the lead, as he would have explained it, and was merely following suit until he got a chance to trump; but he was beginning to have a discouraged feeling that the game was hers, and that he might as well lay down his hand and be done with it. Which, when he brought the simile back to practical affairs, meant that he was thinking seriously of leaving the ranch and the country just as soon as Mason returned.

He was thinking of trying the Argentine Republic for awhile, if he could sell the land which he had rashly bought while he was getting rid of his inheritance.

She did not offer any excuse for the request, as most women would have done. Neither did she thank him, with lips or with eyes, for his ready consent. She seemed distrait-preoccupied, as if she, also, were considering some weighty question.

Ford pushed back his chair, watching her furtively. She rose with Kate, and glanced toward the window.

"I suppose I shall need my heaviest sweater," she remarked practically, and as if the whole affair were too commonplace for discussion. "It does look threatening. How soon will you want to start?" This without looking toward Ford at all.

"Right away, if that suits you." Ford was still watchful, as if he had not quite given up hope of reading her meaning.

She told him she would be ready by the time he had saddled, and she appeared in the stable door while he was cinching the saddle on the horse he meant to ride.

"I hope you haven't given me Dude," she said unemotionally. "He's supposed to be gentle-but he bucked me off that day I sprained my ankle, and all the excuse he had was that a rabbit jumped out from a bush almost under his nose. I've lost faith in him since. Oh-it's Hooligan, is it? I'm glad of that; Hooligan's a dear-and he has the easiest gallop of any horse on the ranch. Have you tried him yet, Ford?"

The heart of Ford lifted in his chest at her tone and her words, along toward the last. He forgot the chill of her voice in the beginning, and he dwelt greedily upon the fact that once more she had called him Ford. But his joy died suddenly when he led his horse out and discovered that Dick and Jim Felton were coming down the path, within easy hearing of her. Ford did not know women very well, but most men are born with a rudimentary understanding of them. He suspected that her intimacy of tone was meant for Dick's benefit; and when they had ridden three or four miles and her share of the conversation during that time had consisted of "yes" twice, "no" three times, and one "indeed," he was sure of it.

So Ford began to wonder why she came at all-unless that, also, was meant to discipline Dick-and his own mood became a silent one. He did not, he told himself indignantly, much relish being used as a club to beat some other man into good behavior.

They rode almost to Long Ridge before Ford discovered that Josephine was stealing glances at his face whenever she thought he was not looking, and that the glances were questioning, and might almost be called timid. He waited until he was sure he was not mistaken, and then turned his head unexpectedly, and smiled into her startled eyes.

"What is it?" he asked, still smiling at her. "I won't bite. Say it, why don't you?"

She bit her lips and looked away.

"I wanted to ask something-ask you to do something," she said, after a minute. And then hurriedly, as if she feared her courage might ebb and leave her stranded, "I wish you'd give me that-jug!"

Sheer surprise held Ford silent, staring at her.

"I don't ask many favors —I wish you'd grant just that one. I wouldn't ask another."

"What do you want of it?"

"Oh —" she stopped, then plunged on recklessly. "It's getting on my nerves so! And if you gave it to me, you wouldn't have to fight the temptation —"

"Why wouldn't I? There's plenty more where that came from," he reminded her.

"But it wouldn't be right where you could get it any time the craving came. Won't you let me take it?" He had never before heard that tone from her; but he fought down the thrill of it and held himself rigidly calm.

"Oh, I don't know-the jug's doing all right, where it is," he evaded; what he wanted most was to get at her real object, and, man-like, to know beyond doubt whether she really cared.

"But you don't —you never touch it," she urged. "I know, because-well, because every day I look into it! I suppose you'll say I have no right, that it's spying, or something. But I don't care for that. And I can see that it's worrying you dreadfully. And if you don't drink any of it, why won't you let me have it?"

"If I don't drink it; what difference does it make who has it?" he countered.

"I'm afraid there'll be a time when you'll yield, just because you are blue and discouraged-or something; whatever mood it is that makes the temptation hardest to resist. I know myself that things are harder to endure some days than they are others." She stopped and looked at him in that enigmatical way she had. "You may not know it-but I've been staying here just to see whether you fail or succeed. I thought I understood a little of why you came, and I —I stayed." She leaned and twisted a wisp of Hooligan's mane nervously, and Ford noticed how the color came and went in the cheek nearest him.

"I —oh, it's awfully hard to say what I want to say, and not have it sound different," she began again, without looking at him. "But if you don't understand what I mean —" Her teeth clicked suggestively.

Ford leaned to her. "Say it anyway and take a chance," he urged, and his voice was like a kiss, whether he knew it or not. He did know that she caught her breath at the words or the tone, and that the color flamed a deeper tint in her cheek and then faded to a faint glow.

"What I mean is that I appreciate the way you have acted all along. I —it wasn't an easy situation to meet, and you have met it like a man-and a gentleman. I was afraid of you at first, and I misunderstood you completely. I'm ashamed to confess it, but it's true. And I want to see you make good in this thing you have attempted; and if there's anything on earth that I can do to help you, I want you to let me do it. You will, won't you?" She looked at him then with clear, honest eyes. "It's my way of wanting to thank you for-for not taking any advantage, or trying to, of-your-position that night."

Ford's own cheeks went hot. "I thought you knew all along that I wasn't a cur, at least," he said harshly. "I never knew before that you had any reason to be afraid of me, that night. If I'd known that-but I thought you just didn't like me, and let it go at that. And what I said I meant. You needn't feel that you have anything to thank me for; I haven't done a thing that deserves thanks-or fear either, for that matter."

"I thought you understood, when I left —"

"I didn't worry much about it, one way or the other," he cut in. "I hunted around for you, of course, and when I saw you'd pulled out for good, I went over the hill and camped. I didn't get the note till next morning; and I don't know," he added, with a brief smile, "as that did much toward making me understand. You just said to wait till some one came after me. Well, I didn't wait." He laughed and leaned toward her again. "Now there seems a chance of our being-pretty good friends," he said, in the caressing tone he had used before, and of which he was utterly unconscious, "we won't quarrel about that night, will we? You got home all right, and so did I. We'll forget all about it. Won't we?" He laid a hand on the horn of her saddle so that they rode close together, and tried futilely to read what was in her face, since she did not speak.

Josephine stared blankly at the brown slope before them. Her lips were set firmly together, and her brows were contracted also, and her gloved fingers gripped the reins tightly. She paid not the slightest attention to Ford's hand upon her saddle horn, nor at the steady gaze of his eyes. Later, when Ford observed the rigidity of her whole pose and sensed that mental withdrawing which needs no speech to push one off from the more intimate ground of companionship, he wondered a little. Without in the least knowing why he felt rebuffed, he took away his hand, and swung his horse slightly away from her; his own back stiffened a little in response to the chilled atmosphere.

"Yes," she said at last, "we'll forget all about it, Mr. Campbell."

"You called me Ford, a while ago," he hinted.

"Did I? One forms the habit of picking up a man's given name, out here in the West, I find. I'm sorry —"

"I don't want you to be sorry. I want you to do it again. All the time," he added boldly.

He caught the gleam of her eyes under her heavy lashes, as she glanced at him sidelong.

"If you go looking at me out of the corner of your eyes," he threatened recklessly, kicking his horse closer, "I'm liable to kiss you!"

And he did, before she could draw away.

"I've been kinda thinking maybe I'm in love with you, Josephine," he murmured, holding her close. "And now I'm dead sure of it. And if you won't love me back why-there'll be something doing, that's all!"

"Yes? And what would you do, please?" Her tone was icy, but he somehow felt that the ice was very, very thin, and that her heart beat warm beneath. She drew herself free, and he let her go.

"I dunno," he confessed whimsically. "But Lordy me! I'd sure do something!"

"Look for comfort in that jug, I suppose you mean?"

"No, I don't mean that." He stopped and considered, his forehead creased as if he were half angry at the imputation. "I'm pretty sure of where I stand, on that subject. I've done a lot of thinking, since I hit the Double Cross-and I've cut out whisky for good.

"I know what you thought, and what Mrs. Kate thinks yet; and I'll admit it was mighty tough scratching for a couple of days after I got hold of that jug. But I found out which was master-and it wasn't the booze!" He looked at her with eyes that shone. "Josie, girl, I took a long chance-but I put it up to myself this way, when the jug seemed to be on top. I told myself it was whisky or you; not that exactly, either. It's hard to say just what I do mean. Not you, maybe-but what you stand for. What I could get out of life, if I was straight and lived clean, and had a little woman like you. It may not be you at all; that's as you —"

He stopped as if some one had laid a hand over his mouth. It was not as she said. It might have been, only for that drunken marriage of his. Never before had he hated whisky as bitterly as he did then, when he remembered what it had done for him that night in Sunset, and what it was doing now. It closed his lips upon what he would have given much to be able to say; for he was a man with all the instincts of chivalry and honor-and he loved the girl. It was, he realized bitterly, just because he did love her so well, that he could not say more. He had said too much already; but her nearness had gone to his head, and he had forgotten that he was not free to say what he felt.

Perhaps Josephine mistook his sudden silence for trepidation, or humility. At any rate she reined impulsively close, and reached out and caught the hand hanging idly at his side.

"Ford, I'm no coquette," she said straightforwardly, with a blush for maiden-modesty's sake. "I believe you; absolutely and utterly I believe you. If you had been different at first-if you had made any overtures whatever toward-toward lovemaking, I should have despised you. I never would have loved you in this world! But you didn't. You kept at such a distance that I —I couldn't help thinking about you and studying you. And lately-when I knew you were fighting the-the habit —I loved you for the way you did fight. I was afraid, too. I used to slip into your room every time you left it, and look-and I just ached to help you! But I knew I couldn't do a thing; and that was the hardest part. All I could do was stand back-clear back out of sight, and hope. And-and love you, too, Ford. I'm proud of you! I'm proud to think that I —I love a man that is a man; that doesn't sit down and whine because a fight is hard, or give up and say it's no use. I do despise a moral weakling, Ford. I don't mind what you have been; it's what you are, that counts with me. And you're a man, every inch of you. I'm not a bit afraid you'll weaken. Only," she added half apologetically, "I did want you to give me the-the jug, because I couldn't bear to see you look so worried." She gave his fingers an adorable little squeeze, and flung his hand away from her, and laughed in a way to set his heart pounding heavily in his chest. "Now you know where I stand, Mr. Man," she cried lightly, "so let's say no more about it. I bet I can beat you across this flat!" She laughed again, wrinkled her nose at him impertinently, and was off in a run.

"Ford, I'm no coquette," she said straightforwardly.

If she had waited, Ford would have told her. If she had given him a chance, he would have told her afterward; but she did not. She was extremely careful not to let their talk become intimate, after that. She laughed, she raced Hooligan almost to the point of abuse, she chattered about everything under the sun that came into her mind, except their own personal affairs or anything that could possibly lead up to the subject.

Ford, for a time, watched for an opening honestly; saw at last the impossibility of telling her-unless indeed he shouted, "Say, I'm a married man!" to her without preface or extenuating explanation-and yielded finally to the reprieve the fates sent him.

Ford spent the rest of that day and all of the night that followed, in thinking what would be the best and the easiest method of gaining the point he wished to reach. All along he had been uncomfortably aware of his matrimonial entanglement and had meant, as soon as he conveniently could, to try and discover who was his wife, and how best to free himself and her. He had half expected that she herself would do something to clear the mystery. She had precipitated the marriage, he constantly reminded himself, and it was reasonable to expect that she would do something; though what, Ford could only conjecture.

When he faced Josephine across the breakfast table the next morning, and caught the shy glance she gave him when Mrs. Kate was not looking, a plan he had half formed crystallized into a determination. He would not tell her anything about it until he knew just what he was up against, and how long it was going to take him to free himself. And since he could not do anything about it while he rode and planned and gave orders at the Double Cross, he swallowed his breakfast rather hurriedly and went out to find Jim Felton.

"Say, Jim," he began, when he ran that individual to earth in the stable, where, with a pair of sheep shears, he was roaching the mane of a shaggy old cow pony to please Buddy, who wanted to make him look like a circus horse, even if there was no hope of his ever acting like one. "I'm going to hand you the lines and let you drive, for a few days. I've got to scout around on business of my own, and I don't know just how long it's going to take me. I'm going right away-to-day."

"Yeah?" Jim poised the shears in air and regarded him quizzically over the pony's neck. "Going to pass me foreman's privilege-to hire and fire?" he grinned. "Because I may as well tell you that if you do, Dick won't be far behind you on the trail."

"Oh, darn Dick. I'll fire him myself, maybe, before I leave. Yes," he added, thinking swiftly of Josephine as the object of Dick's desires, "that's what I'll do. Maybe it'll save a lot of trouble while I'm gone. He's a tricky son-of-a-gun."

"You're dead right; he is," Jim agreed. And then, dryly: "Grandmother just died?"

"Oh, shut up. This ain't an excuse-it's business. I've just got to go, and that's all there is to it. I'll fix things with the missus, and tell her you're in charge. Anyway, I won't be gone any longer than I can help."

"I believe that, too," said Jim softly, and busied himself with the shears.

Ford looked at him sharply, in doubt as to just how much or how little Jim meant by that. He finally shrugged his shoulders and went away to tell Mrs. Kate, and found that a matter which required more diplomacy than he ever suspected he possessed. But he did tell her, and he hoped that she believed the reason he gave for going, and also had some faith in his assurance that he would be back, probably, in a couple of days-or as soon afterwards as might be.

"There's nothing but chores to do now around the ranch, and Jack will ride fence," he explained unnecessarily, to cover his discomfort at her coldness. "Jim can look after things just as well as I can. There won't be any need to start feeding the calves, unless it storms; and if it does, Jim and Jack will go ahead, all right. I'm going to let Dick and Curly go. We don't need more than two men besides Walt, from now on."

"I wish Chester was here," said Mrs. Kate ambiguously.

Ford did not ask her why she wished that. He told her good-by as hastily as if he had to run to catch a train, and left her. He hoped he would be lucky enough to see Josephine-and then he hoped quite as sincerely that he would not see her, after all. It would be easier to go without her clear eyes asking him why.

What he meant to do first was to find Rock, and see if he had been sober enough that night in Sunset to remember what happened at the marriage ceremony, and could give him some clue as to the woman's identity and whereabouts. If he failed there, he intended to hunt up the preacher. That, also, presented certain difficulties, but Ford was in the mood to overcome obstacles. Once he discovered who the woman was, it seemed to him that there should be no great amount of trouble in getting free. As he understood it, he was not the man she had intended to marry; and not being the man she wanted, she certainly could not be over-anxious to cling to him.

While he galloped down the trail to town, he went over the whole thing again in his mind, to see if there might be some simpler plan than the one he had formed in the night.

"No, sir-it's Rock I've got to see first," he concluded. "But Lord only knows where I'll find him; Rock never does camp twice in the same place. Never knew him to stay more than a month with one outfit. But I'll find him, all right!"

And by one of those odd twists of circumstances which sets men to wondering if there is such a thing as telepathy and a specifically guiding hand and the like, it was Rock and none other whom he met fairly in the trail before he had gone another mile.

"Well, I'll be gol darned!" Ford whispered incredulously to himself, and pulled up short in the trail to wait for him.

Rock came loping up with elbows flapping loosely, as was his ungainly habit. His grin was wide and golden as of yore, his hat at the same angle over his right eyebrow.

"Gawd bless you, brother! May peace ride behind your cantle!" he declaimed unctuously, for Rock was a character, in his way, and in his speech was not in the least like other men. "Whither wendest thou?"

"My wending is all over for the present," said Ford, wheeling his horse short around, that he might ride alongside the other. "I started out to hunt you up, you old devil. How are you, anyway?"

"It is well with me, and well with my soul-what little I've got-but it ain't so well with my winter grub-stake. I'm just as tickled to see you as you ever dare be to meet up with me, and that's no lie. I heard you've got a stand-in with the Double Cross, and seeing they ain't on to my little peculiarities, I thought I'd ride out and see if I couldn't work you for a soft snap. Got any ducks out there you want led to water?"

"Maybe —I dunno. I just canned two men this morning, before I left." Ford was debating with himself how best to approach the subject to him most important.

"Good ee-nough! I can take the place of those two men; eat their share of grub, do their share of snoring, and shirk their share of work, and drink their share of booze-oh, lovely! But, in the words of the dead, immortal Shakespeare, 'What's eating you?' You look to me as if you hadn't enjoyed the delights of a good, stiff jag since —" He waved a hand vaguely. "Ain't a scar on you, so help me!" He regarded Ford with frank curiosity.

"Oh, yes there is. I've got the hide peeled off two knuckles, and one of my thumbs is just getting so it will move without being greased," Ford assured him, and then went straight at what was on his mind.

"Say, Rock, I was told that you had a hand in my getting married, back in Sunset that night."

Rock made his horse back until it nearly fell over a rock; his face showed exaggerated symptoms of terror.

"I couldn't help it," he wailed. "Spare muh-for muh poor mother's sake, oh spare muh life!" Whereat Ford laughed, just as Rock meant that he should do. "You licked Bill twice for that, they tell me," Rock went on, quitting his foolery and coming up close again. "And you licked the preacher that night, and-so the tale runneth-like to have put the whole town on the jinks. Is there anything in particular you'd like to do to me?"

"I just want you to tell me who I married-if you can." Ford reddened as the other stared, but he did not stop. "I was so darned full that night I let the whole business ooze out of my memory, and I haven't been able to —"

Rock was leaning over the saddle horn, howling and watery-eyed. Ford looked at him with a dawning suspicion.

"It did strike me, once or twice," he said grimly, "that the whole thing was a put-up job. If you fellows rigged up a josh like that, and let it go as far as this, may the Lord have mercy on your souls, for I won't!"

But Rock could only wave him off weakly; so Ford waited until he had recovered. Even then, it took some talking to convince Rock that the affair was truly serious and not to be treated any longer as a joke.

"Why, damn it, man, I'm in love with a girl and I want to marry her if I can get rid of this other darned, mysterious, Tom-fool of a woman," Ford gritted at last, in sheer desperation. "Or if it's just a josh, by this and by that I mean to find it out."

Rock sobered then. "It ain't any josh," he said, with convincing earnestness. "You got married, all right enough. And if it's as you say, Ford, I sure am sorry for it. I don't know the girl's name. I'd know her quick enough if I should see her, but I can't tell you who she was."

Ford swore, of course. And Rock listened sympathetically until he was done.

"That's the stuff; get it out of your system, Ford, and then you'll feel better. Then we can put our heads together and see if there isn't some way to beat this combination."

"Could you spot the preacher, do you reckon?" asked Ford more calmly.

"I could-if he didn't see us coming," Rock admitted guardedly. "Name of Sanderson, I believe. I've seen him around Garbin. He could tell-he must have some record of it; but would he?"

"Don't you know, even, why she came and glommed onto me like that?" Ford's face was as anxious as his tone.

"Only what you told me, confidentially, in a corner afterwards," said Rock regretfully. "Maybe you told it straight, and maybe you didn't; there's no banking on a man's imagination when he's soused. But the way you told it to me was this:

"You said the girl told you that she was working for some queer old party-an old lady with lots of dough; and she made her will and give her money all to some institution-hospital or some darned thing, I forget just what, or else you didn't say. Only, if this girl would marry her son within a certain time, he could have the wad. Seems the son was something of a high-roller, and the old lady knew he'd blow it in, if it was turned over to him without any ballast, like; and the girl was supposed to be the ballast, to hold him steady. So the old lady, or else it was the girl, writes to this fellow, and he agrees to hook up with the lady and take the money and behave himself. Near as I could make it out, the time was just about up before the girl took matters into her own hand, and come out on a hunt for this Frank Cameron. How she happened to sink her rope on you instead, and take her turns before she found out her mistake, you'll have to ask her-if you ever see her again.

"But this much you told me-and I think you got it straight. The girl was willing to marry you-or Frank Cameron-so he could get what belonged to him. She wasn't going to do any more, though, and you told me" —Rock's manner became very impressive here —"that you promised her, as a man and a gentleman, that you wouldn't ever bother her, and that she was to travel her own trail, and she didn't want the money. She just wanted to dodge that fool will, seems like. Strikes me I'd a let the fellow go plumb to Guinea, if I was in her place, but women get queer notions of duty, and the like of that, sometimes. Looks to me like a fool thing for a woman to do, anyway."

Though they talked a good while about it, that was all the real information which Ford could gain. He would have to find the minister and persuade him to show the record of the marriage, and after that he would have to find the girl.

Before they reached that definite conclusion, the storm which had been brewing for several days swooped down upon them, and drove Ford to the alternative of riding in the teeth of it to town, which was not only unpleasant but dangerous, if it grew any worse, or retracing his steps to the Double Cross and waiting there until it was over. So that is what he did, with Rock to bear him willing company.

They met Dick and Curly on the way, and though Ford stopped them and suggested that they turn back also, neither would do so. Curly intimated plainly that the joys of town were calling to him from afar, and that facing a storm was merely calculated to make his destination more alluring by contrast. "Turn back with two months' wages burning up my inside pocket?

Oh, no!" he laughed, and rode on. Dick did not say why, but he rode on also. Ford turned in the saddle and looked after them, as they disappeared in a swirl of fine snow.

"That's what I ought to do," he said, "but I'm not going to do it, all the same."

"Which only goes to prove," bantered Rock, "that the Double Cross pulls harder than all the preacher could tell you. I wonder if there isn't a girl at the Double Cross, now!"

"There is," Ford confessed, with a grin of embarrassment. "And you shut up."

"I just had a hunch there was," Rock permitted himself to say meekly, before he dropped the subject.

It was ten minutes before Ford spoke again.

"I'll take you up to the house and introduce you to her, Rock, if you'll behave yourself," he offered then, with a shyness in his manner that nearly set Rock off in one of his convulsions of mirth. "But the missus isn't wise-so watch out. And if you don't behave yourself," he added darkly, "I'll knock your block off."

"Sure. But my block is going to remain right where it's at," Rock assured him, which was a tacit promise of as perfect behavior as he could attain.

They looked like snow men when they unsaddled, with the powdery snow beaten into the very fabric of their clothing, and Ford suggested that they go first to the bunk-house to thaw out. "I'd sure hate to pack all this snow into Mrs. Kate's parlor," he added whimsically. "She's the kind of housekeeper that grabs the broom the minute you're gone, to sweep your tracks off the carpet. Awful nice little woman, but —"

"But not The One," chuckled Rock, treading close upon Ford's heels. "And I'll bet fifteen cents," he offered rashly, looking up, "that the person hitting the high places for the bunk-house is The One."

"How do you know?" Ford demanded, while his eyes gladdened at sight of Josephine, with a Navajo blanket flung over her head, running down the path through the blizzard to the bunk-house kitchen.

"'Cause she shied when she saw you coming. Came pretty near breaking back on you, too," Rock explained shrewdly.

They reached the kitchen together, and Ford threw open the door, and held it for her to pass.

"I came after some of Mose's mince-meat," she explained hastily. "It's a terrible storm, isn't it? I'm glad it didn't strike yesterday. I thought you were going to be gone for several days."

Ford, with embarrassed haste to match her own, presented Rock in the same breath with wishing that Rock was elsewhere; for Mose was not in the kitchen, and he had not had more than a few words with her for twenty-four hours. He was perilously close to forgetting his legal halter when he looked at her.

She was, he thought, about as sweet a picture of a woman as a man need ever look upon, as she stood there with the red Navajo blanket falling back from her dark hair, and with her wide, honest eyes fixed upon Rock. She was blushing, as if she, too, wished Rock elsewhere. She turned impulsively, set down the basin she had been holding in her arm, and pulled the blanket up so that it framed her face bewitchingly.

"Mose can bring up the mince-meat when he comes-since he isn't here," she said hurriedly. "We weren't looking for you back, but dinner will be ready in half an hour or so, I think." She pulled open the door and went out into the storm.

Rock stared at the door, still quivering with the slam she had given it. Then he looked at Ford, and afterward sat down weakly upon a stool, and began dazedly pulling the icicles from his mustache.

"Well —I'll-be-cremated!" he said in a whisper.

"And what's eating you, Rock?" Ford quizzed gayly. He had seen something in the eyes of Josephine, when he met her, that had set his blood jumping again. "Did Miss Melby —"

"Miss Melby my granny!" grunted Rock, in deep disgust. "That there is your wife!"

Ford backed up against the wall and stared at him blankly. Afterward he took a deep breath and went out as though the place was on fire.

Ford Campbell was essentially a man of action; he did not waste ten seconds in trying to deduce the whys and hows of the amazing fact; he would have a whole lifetime in which to study them. He started for the house, and the tracks he made in the loose, shifting snow were considerably more than a yard apart. He even forgot to stamp off the clinging snow and scour his boot-soles upon the porch rug, and when he went striding in, he pushed the door only half shut behind him, so that it swung in the wind and let a small drift collect upon the parlor carpet, until Mrs. Kate, feeling a draught, discovered it, and was shocked beyond words at the sacrilege.

Ford went into the dining-room, crossed it in just three strides, and ran his quarry to earth in the kitchen, where she was distraitly setting out biscuit materials. He started toward her, realized suddenly that the all-observing Buddy was at his very heels, and delayed the reckoning while he led that terrible man-child to his mother.

"I wish you'd close-herd this kid for about four hours," he told Mrs. Kate bluntly, and left her looking scared and unconsciously posing as protective motherhood, her arm around the outraged Robert Chester Mason. Mrs. Kate was absolutely convinced that Ford was at last really drunk and "on the rampage," and she had a terrible vision of slain girlhood in the kitchen, so that she was torn between mother-love and her desire to protect Phenie. But Ford had looked so threateningly at her and Buddy that she could not bring herself to attract his attention to the child or herself. Phenie had plenty of spirit; she could run down to the bunk-house —Mrs. Kate heard a door slam then, and shuddered. Phenie, she judged swiftly, had locked herself into the pantry.

Phenie had. Or, to be exact, she had run in and slammed the door shut in Ford's very face, and she was leaning her weight against it. Mrs. Kate, pressing the struggling Buddy closer to her, heard voices, a slight commotion, and then silence. She could bear no more. She threw a shawl over her head, grasped Buddy firmly by the arm, and fled in terror to the bunk-house.

The voices were a brief altercation between Ford and Josephine, on the subject of opening the door, before it was removed violently from its hinges. The commotion was when Josephine, between tears and laughter, failed to hold the door against the pressure of a strong man upon the other side, and, suddenly giving over the attempt, was launched against a shelf and dislodged three tin pans, which she barely saved from falling with a great clatter to the floor. The silence- the silence should explain itself; but since humanity is afflicted with curiosity, and demands details, this is what occurred immediately after Josephine had been kissed four times for her stubbornness, and the pans had been restored to their proper place.

"Say! Are you my wife?" was the abrupt question which Ford asked, and kissed her again while he waited for an answer.

"Why, yes-what makes you ask that? Of course I am; that is —" Josephine twisted in his arms, so that she could look into his face. She did not laugh at him, however. She was staring at him with that keen, measuring look which had so incensed him, when he had first met her. "I don't understand you at all, Ford," she said at last, with a frown of puzzlement. "I never have, for that matter. I'd think I was beginning to, and then you would say or do something that would put me all at sea. What do you mean, anyway?"

Ford told her what he meant; told her humbly, truthfully, with never an excuse for himself. And it speaks well for the good sense of Josephine that she heard him through with neither tears, laughter, nor anger to mar his trust in her.

"Of course, I knew you had been drinking, that night," she said, when his story was done, and his face was pressed lightly against the white parting in her soft, brown hair. "I saw it, after-after the ceremony. You-you were going to kiss me, and I caught the odor of liquor, and I felt that you wouldn't have done that if you had been yourself; it frightened me, a little. But you talked perfectly straight, and I never knew you weren't the man-Frank Cameron-until you came here. Then I saw you couldn't be he. Chester had known you when Frank was at home with his mother —I compared dates and was sure of that-and he called you Ford Campbell. So then I saw what a horrible blunder I'd made, and I was worried nearly to death! But I couldn't see what I could do about it, and you didn't —"

"Say, what about this Frank Cameron, anyway?" Ford demanded, with true male jealousy. "What did you want to marry him for? You couldn't have known him, or —"

"Oh, you wouldn't understand —" Josephine gave a little, impatient turn of the head, "unless you knew his mother. I did know Frank, a long time ago, when I was twelve or thirteen, and when I saw you, I thought he'd changed a lot. But it was his mother; she was the dearest thing, but-queer. Sort of childish, you know. And she just worshiped Frank, and used to watch for the postman-oh, it was too pitiful! Sometimes I'd write a letter myself, and pretend it was from him, and read it to her; her eyes were bad, so it was easy —"

"Where was this Frank?" Ford interrupted.

"Oh, I don't know! I never did know. Somewhere out West, we thought. I used to make believe the letters came from Helena, or Butte, because that was where she heard from him last. He was always promising to come home-in the letters. That used to make her so much better," she explained naïvely. "And sometimes she'd be able to go out in the yard and fuss with her flowers, after one like that. But he never came, and so she got the notion that he was wild and a spendthrift. I suppose he was, or he'd have written, or something. She had lots and lots of money and property, you know.

"Well," Josephine took one of Ford's hand and patted it reassuringly, "she got the notion that I must marry Frank, when he came home. I tried to reason her out of that, and it only made her worse. It grew on her, and I got so I couldn't bear to write any more letters, and that made it worse still. She made a will that I must marry Frank within a year after she died, or he wouldn't get anything but a hundred dollars-and she was worth thousands and thousands." Josephine snuggled closer. "She was shrewd, too. I was not to get anything except a few trinkets. And if we didn't marry, the money would all go to an old ladies' home.

"So, when she died, I felt as if I ought to do something, you see. It didn't seem right to let him lose the property, even if he wouldn't write to his mother. So I had the lawyers try to find him. I thought I could marry him, and let him get the property, and then-well, I counted on getting a divorce." She looked up quickly into Ford's face.

"And you know you did promise not to bother me-just to desert me, you see, so I could get a divorce in a year. I thought I'd come and live with Kate till the year was up, and then get a divorce, and go back home to work. My father left me enough to squeak along on, you see, if I lived in the country. Aunt Ida-that's Frank's mother-paid me a salary for staying with her and looking after her house and her rents and things. And then, when you followed me out here, I was furious! Just simply furious!" She bent her head and set her teeth gently into the fleshy part of Ford's thumb, and Ford flinched. It happened to be the sore one.

"Well, but that doesn't explain how you got your loop on me, girlie-though I sure am glad that you did!"

"Why, don't you see, the time was almost up, just for all the world like a play. 'Only one day more-and I must save the pa-apers!' So the lawyer Aunt Ida had for years, heard that Frank was-or had been-at Garbin. I rushed out here, and heard that there was a Cameron (only they must have meant Campbell) at Sunset. So I got a license, and the Reverend Sanderson, and took the evening train down there. At the hotel I asked for Mr. Cameron, and they sent you in. And you know the rest, you-you old fraud! How you palmed yourself off on me —"

"I never did! I must have just been in one of my obliging moods; and a man would have to be mighty rude and unkind not to say yes to a pretty girl when —"

That is as far as the discussion went, with anything like continuity or coherence even. Later, however, Josephine did protest somewhat muffledly: "But, Ford, I married you under the name of Frank Cameron, so I don't believe-and anyway —I'd like a real wedding-and a ring!"

Mrs. Kate, having been solemnly assured by Rock that Ford was sober and as nearly in his right mind as a man violently in love can be (Rock made it plain, by implication at least, that he did not consider that very near), ventured into the kitchen just then. She still looked scared and uncertain, until, through the half-open door of the pantry, she heard soft, whispery sounds like kissing-when the kissing is a rapture rather than a ceremony. Mrs. Kate had only been married eight years or so, and she had a good memory. She backed from the kitchen on her toes, and pulled the door shut with the caution of a thief. She did more; she permitted dinner to be an hour late, rather than disturb those two in the pantry.

---

The uphill climb was no climb at all, after that. For when a man has found the one woman in the world, and with her that elusive thing we call happiness, even the demon must perforce sheathe his claws and retire, discomfited, to the pit whence he came.

There was a period of impatient waiting, because Josephine and Mrs. Kate both stoutly maintained that the "real wedding" could not take place until Chester came back. After that, there was a Mrs. foreman at the Double Cross until spring. And after that, there was a new ranch and a new house and a new home where happiness came and dwelt unhindered.

**THE END**

www.ingramcontent.com/pod-product-compliance
Lightning Source LLC
Chambersburg PA
CBHW060352310726

48976CB00003B/798